BESIDE STILL WATERS

Robert Burslem

Cherrytree Publications
Dublin, Ireland

FORWARD

It's a sad truth that tragedy and misery attract our attention but more often than not acts of love and goodness go unnoticed. Unfortunately the only news is bad news for most of the Western media. This is most probably the reason why people who do not know Africa find it a confusing place that they can only associate with human hardship, brutality and want. It is also most probably the reason why people, who become familiar with African people and their diverse cultures are smitten and come to find the place irresistibly attractive. Africa is full of contradictions; it abounds with both good and bad in possibly equal proportions.

Africa is also a place where strange things happen. If an author had come up with a plot involving a single white man lost 'somewhere' on the continent of Africa, another white man setting off on foot to find him and both bumping into each other on the shore of a remote unknown lake it would undoubtedly have been dismissed as unrealistic and too far-fetched a story.

Yet in the 1860's, when technology was relatively primitive and the vast interior of the African continent was unknown, a single white man, lost for years, was found by HM Stanley and the words "*Dr Livingstone I presume*," became indelibly etched on the minds of millions. However improbable, the incident did happen. This demonstrates a dilemma for writers of historical novels. Their works needs to have believable plots but in reality quite unbelievable things happen, particularly in Africa.

In '*Beside Still Waters*' I have taken and described true incidents and tried to weld them together into a believable story. To make the story feel '*credible*' I have had to exercise care in my descriptions so as not to lose the faith of my readers.

Cabinda, where most of the story is set, is a very real place. The political history and geography I have described is pretty accurate (allowing for different interpretations). Most of the incidents described did actually occur. The characters are fictional but they are parodies of real people, many of whom are personally known to me.

This book has been more difficult to write than the first two books in the series: '*The Valley of the Shadow*' and '*Fear No Evil*'. It's been like a naughty child that has grown into an adult that I now love and respect. I hope it is both informative and entertaining. I'm sure people will let me know.

ACKNOWLEDGEMENTS

I am totally indebted to my Partner and best friend **Maureen Gutkin**. This book would not have been finished if it wasn't for her constant support and encouragement. For several months I didn't work on the manuscript at all, my thoughts just dried up. Thankfully she carefully put me back on track. In addition to that she has acted as my editor in chief, sounding board and critic. I have lost count of the hours she has spent correcting my poor English and providing ideas for plot improvement. Simply saying thank you feels decidedly inadequate.

A special thanks to my friend **Joe Mullane** who carried out the final proof read. His attention to detail is second to none and his honest comments are truly valued.

Finally thanks (and apologies) to all my family and friends who have had to put up with what must have been, from their perspective, my boring single mindedness.

LEGAL DISCLAIMER

The characters in this book are fictional. Any similarity to any person, living or dead is purely coincidental.

Robert Burslem
28th April 2014

BOOK ONE

Beside Still Waters

Chapter 1
August 8th 1979
Kimongo Province, Zaire / Angolan Border

She died trying to keep her entrails in the cavity with her own hands. She had lasted several hours. When the spark of life was finally extinguished she was left naked lying stretched, staring and contorted on the ground. There was surprisingly little blood and what there was had soaked into the mud floor around her.

Execution by disembowelling is not new, it was practiced by the ancients. Two types of people employ the method: the mad and the sane. Psychotic sadists, insane men, often fuelled by alcohol and drugs, carry out the execution in a crazed frenzy and draw some kind of weird personal satisfaction from watching the victim slowly die with terror in their eyes. These people have lost sight of moral boundaries. Compassion has been eradicated from their minds.

Intelligent sane people know what the moral boundaries are and they also know the value of transgressing them. They methodically harness the power of terror as a means of control, a way to assert their authority and domination. They know that disembowelling a single victim can bring a whole community under control. They draw no personal satisfaction from the process and may even feel sympathy for the victim.

People from more civilized societies think that atrocities are mainly carried out by madmen. Those who have experienced the worst of Africa know the opposite is true.

There are two important criteria to be met if the process is to achieve its full effect: the victim must be alive and conscious and there must be witnesses, if not to the actual event then at least to the result. The process is quite simple. The victim is restrained, an incision is made in the torso centre line with a sharp blade from just below the sternum to just above the pubis, the cut just deep enough to pierce the skin and the membrane that contains the victim's guts. The victim is then released and must use their own hands to keep their entrails within the bowel cavity. Death is inevitable.

Thirty-six hours had elapsed by the time they were approaching the hut. It was still early morning and the sun was low in the sky allowing the jungle canopy to cast shadows over the tiny clearing. As they got close to the mud hut with its elephant grass thatch they heard the steady buzz, a buzz that in suburbia could have been an electrical transformer but this was not suburbia and there wasn't any electricity.

The African guide ducked and entered the hut first; they followed. The buzz was louder but it was the stench, the stench of death, which made them reel. With hands over their nose and mouth they waited for their eyes to become accustomed to the darkness.

As the sight materialised in front of their eyes it looked, at first, like the victims entrails were moving, somehow squirming with life. But then it became clearer and they saw the mass of flies that were in the midst of a feeding frenzy, so thick on the wounds that no flesh was visible. Now it was obvious where the buzz was coming from. The flies were not just feeding; they were also laying their eggs. In a day or two the corpse would be maggot-ridden. Shortly after that it would become unrecognisable as human.

The final terror had distorted her facial features; her eyes were wide open, the whites bulging and pupils in a fixed stare. She was ugly now but once she had been pretty.

The man raised his camera and began shooting. Looking at the scene through a lens helped him keep an emotional distance. He clicked away with his Nikon whilst his female companion turned and vomited on to the floor.

"This is the worst one," said their African guide. "The soldiers most probably raped her before doing this. Most of the other villagers were just massacred; some shot others hacked with pangas."

The photographer stopped shooting and lowered his camera, his complexion turning ashen as the sight became more real to him. "How many?" he asked.

"More than thirty, mainly old people and children," answered the guide. "The rest of the villagers fled into the jungle. It will be some time before they come back. The soldiers did their work well."

It had started the previous afternoon. Simon and Melanie had been sitting on what passed for the veranda of the rough wooden chalet that was euphemistically referred to as the guest lodge. Simon was cleaning and checking his photographic equipment in preparation for the next morning's planned shoot, the last structured event of their fourteen day programme. Melanie was going through the detailed brief from their commissioning agent. It was their first solo African trip; it could turn out to be a career maker, or if they got it wrong, a career breaker. Success would be

3

Simon's pictures and her article featured in National Geographic. A lesser publication would most probably signify failure.

Dusk was approaching but even when the sun had disappeared they knew there would be no respite from the heavy humid heat. All that darkness held in store for them was a plague of the ubiquitous mosquitoes. They were not enjoying the climate of equatorial Africa but took solace in the fact that their programme had little time to run.

Melanie lifted her head from the papers on her lap and watched as one of the mission servants worked his way around the courtyard, lighting the oil lamps that hung from the wooden posts dotted around the compound, the lamps that provided the only outside light after sunset. There was a small generator at the mission but the Jesuits used it sparingly; if it broke it would be hard to get it fixed and in any event petrol was an exorbitant price.

"Right I'm done," said Simon as he put the final bits of his kit into their aluminium carrying cases.

The first Jesuits had arrived at Kimongo in the 1880's. It hadn't been either an altruistic or spontaneous decision by the hierarchy of the Society of Jesus to establish a mission close to the Congo delta. It had been a reaction to events. In the late nineteenth century explorers like Livingstone and Stanley had opened up the African interior for the three C's: commerce, civilisation and Christianity. But the church that those pioneers represented was the non-conformist and Reformed variety of Christianity, an anathema to the Church of Rome. Rome had decreed that they too must be represented on the Dark Continent and so their finest had been despatched.

From when the Jesuits arrived at the village of Kimongo the relationship with their non-conformist fellow Christians had been strained, at times even hostile but at least it had never descended into the outright '*Christian War*' similar to that which had erupted between Protestant and Catholic in the land that was to become Uganda. Over time the relationship had settled into a state of what could only be described as benign ambivalence.

During the first decades of the twentieth century the Jesuit mission had developed from a single native hut to a large walled compound surrounding several single storey buildings which included a dormitory, a refectory and administration house, store and a church. Also within the compound was a lone guest house for visitors, for it lay within the obligations of Jesuits to offer sanctuary. The guest house was little more than a hut, not an

African rondavel but a rickety wooden construction in the European style with a pitched corrugated iron roof and shuttered windows. Outside of the compound was the main reason for the Jesuit's presence, a school where African children could, whilst learning about spiritual salvation, glean the basics of reading and writing.

Simon and Melanie waited for the summons to join the monks in the refectory for the evening meal. The food would be taken in silence but then, for a single hour, the monks would talk freely. It was their only recreation period of the day. At all other times 'general' communication with Simon and Melanie was frowned upon.

It was then, in that quiet moment as the light began to fade, that the bell had rung. Somebody outside the high solid wooden gates was frantically pulling on the rope. The urgency of the ringing itself betrayed a panic in the ringer. Brother Bruno, a Swiss born Jesuit of Germanic stature, hurried towards the gates, his oatmeal coloured cassock struggling to keep up with him. He opened a tiny hatch and spoke with the unseen visitor. After a while the monk opened the Judas door, his movement without urgency, as if reluctant to let the caller in.

Despite the heat Banda Sitole wore a heavy but threadbare dark grey suit, something that had been bequeathed to him in the distant past. A black shirt and loose fitting dog collar hung around his neck announcing an ecclesiastical vocation. Simon and Melanie watched the two men, unable to make out the spoken words. But they could clearly see that the visitor was agitated; shifting from foot to foot, arms gesticulating; Father Bruno stood impassively shaking his head slowly from side to side as if unperturbed by the visitor's message.

Without warning Banda turned and broke away from the monk and hurried in the direction of the guest house. Father Bruno reached out and tried to stop him with a hand on his shoulder but the caller shrugged off the restraint easily. He arrived in front of the veranda a few steps ahead of the monk.

"You are the journalists?" He didn't wait for a reply. "My name is Banda; I had heard you were here. I have something important for you to see." Banda made no attempt to disguise the urgency in his voice.

Before either Simon or Melanie could answer Father Bruno interrupted. "I am sorry for the intrusion. If this man doesn't leave I will have him removed."

5

"Please listen to me," said Banda. "It is an important matter. I have a news story for you. If only for that, even if you are not moved by human compassion, you will be interested."

"You are mistaken Mr Banda," said Simon unsure how to react. "We are not journalists – not in the sense you think. We are here only to write about nature for a magazine. We do not represent a newspaper."

"Banda is my Christian name and I don't care if you are the wrong type of journalist. In the name of humanity what has happened needs to be recorded and shown to the world. Only when the world knows will this torture stop. Please I ask you with Christian humility to help me. In the name of God somebody must help."

"This man asks the impossible," interjected Brother Bruno again.

Melanie spoke, her question directed at Brother Bruno. "This man is a priest isn't he, a fellow Christian? Don't you work together?"

"He's no priest," responded Bruno a little too sharply, a flash of unchristian anger in his eyes. "He's a Protestant, a so called Methodist. He calls himself a Reverend. He is not part of my Church."

"In my country we are taught that all Christianity is good." It was a reflex response.

Bruno's rebuke was just as instinctive. "This is not your country. It is unwise to meddle in what you don't understand."

Simon broke in to protect his wife. "Melanie and I would like to hear what this man has to say. It is us he wants to speak to and it does not appear to be an unreasonable request."

Banda Sitole didn't wait for approval; he took the opportunity presented. "I come from the province of Cabinda, from a small village just on the on the other side of the river. Yesterday afternoon a group of military men, Angolan soldiers, arrived at a neighbouring village. They came quietly, with stealth. Not all the people had time to run and hide in the jungle. The old and the young, mothers with children had no time to escape. The soldiers gathered the people together. They accused them of helping the CLA and said that they had to pay for their treachery."

"What is the CLA?" asked Simon.

"It is the Cabinda Liberation Army. They fight for the independence of Cabinda. The villagers protested that they had not helped the CLA but the soldiers would not listen. Some of the soldiers found the village stock of cassava beer and began to

6

drink. Soon they were all drunk. When some of the villagers tried to run away they were hacked down with pangas. It was the signal, the soldiers went wild, the officer just watched. They killed the old and young and attacked the women. From the maelstrom one child escaped, but only after he had seen what had been done. He came to me. I went back with the boy. We hid in the jungle, listening, watching and praying. We were powerless to help. In the morning the soldiers left. As soon as we thought it was safe we went into the village and saw what remained.

I had heard that there were journalists here so I decided to come here with the boy and tell you. Perhaps we could show you what is happening to us. I am sure if the people in the West knew of these attacks they would make them stop. I cannot believe that Christian nations would allow these atrocities to continue. So I ask you, come with me and let me show you what has happened?"

"You cannot cross the river," said Brother Bruno. "It is too dangerous on the other side."

"Too dangerous for you to visit but safe enough for us to live," responded Banda. "You are our only hope, please help."

"Where is the boy? The one that warned you?" asked Melanie.

Banda's eyes saddened and voice faltered. "I failed him. I persuaded the boy to come with me but halfway across the river something happened in his mind. He stood up in the canoe. He said it was hopeless asking white people to help us; they had caused all the problems in the first place. Then he jumped into the river. He disappeared under the water. I don't know for sure but the crocodiles most likely finished him. It is improbable that he survived. I was too slow to stop him. I should not have tried to bring him here, not after what he'd witnessed. He was only seven years old."

Banda lifted his head and the tracks of his tears marked his dusty cheeks.

The next morning Banda Sithole led Melanie and Simon down to the river bank and the waiting canoe.

"Now that you have seen what I said is true and you have taken your photographs let me take you back to the mission. Then you can go and tell the world," said Banda.

Simon moved towards the door of the hut, ducking his head to get through. "Come on Melanie, there is nothing we can do here. She is beyond our help."

"Wait," said Melanie. "There is something about the way she is lying; it's as if she's looking at something."

Melanie walked over to the pile of clothes that lay by the hut wall and pulled at the bundle. There was movement. Cautiously she bent down and rummaged deeper. Then she stood and turned to face Simon, a tiny naked baby in her arms.

"She's still alive Simon!"

"Oh by the Grace of God let something good come from this." He hurried over to join his wife.

"We have to take her with us, she will die if we leave her," said Banda Sithole. Simon began poking around the hut.

"What are you doing?" asked Melanie.

"Looking for something to identify the child," he replied.

As the two men rummaged Melanie steeled herself and went to take a closer look at the mother's body. Her eyes fixed on a single item. It was primitive, but even in this macabre situation there was a certain beauty in the colourful stones strung on a cord to make a pretty necklace. "Should we take this?" asked Melanie.

The room was more than simple, it was sparse; spotless white painted walls, polished terracotta floor tiles. Brother Padraig sat at the wooden desk that faced the door, behind him, to the left stood Brother Bruno. A large wooden crucifix, fastened to the wall, looked down on the two men. The only colour in the room was from a four-foot painted statue of the Madonna. With tilted head she gently smiled, resplendent in a royal blue hooded cloak. The louvered shutters were fully open to allow what air there was to drift in. From the ceiling hung a large fan, dormant and now merely a reminder of a past time when electricity was more plentiful.

"Please sit," said Brother Padraig, offering his open hands to the two wooden chairs that stood in front of his desk. Simon and Melanie took the seats. The Reverend Banda Sitole remained standing. Melanie nursed the baby in her arms, the blackness of the face emphasized by the white sheet that was wrapped around the infant.

"*Father forgive them for they know not what they do,*" Brother Padraig spoke with lowered eyes and clasped hands, as if in prayer. The gentle Irish brogue was in stark contrast to the harsh Germanic words that had been uttered by Brother Bruno, but the message was to offer little more comfort.

8

Brother Padraig raised his gaze but not his voice. "Your actions have not been thought through; you have put many in the path of danger. No good will come of this."

"We've saved the life of a child," replied Melanie.

"And we've witnessed something terrible that the world needs to know about. I find it shocking that you appear to be so unconcerned," added Simon.

Padraig sighed. "I know it is difficult for you to understand. In this place the normal rules of human civilisation do not apply. What you witnessed is but a single bad deed inspired by the devil. Deeds like this are commonplace here. What to you seems astounding is normal in this part of the world. We have long since learnt that there is nothing we can do but try and teach the right road and offer our prayers to God."

"I think your Order has been here for nearly a hundred years. How can this type of thing still be going on? It's obvious that prayer alone is doing no good," responded Simon.

"God works in his own way. It is not our place to question His will and neither is it our place to exacerbate the situation, to make it worse than it already is, something I fear you may have done.

The river you crossed marks the border of the Congo and the Angolan province of Cabinda. A great struggle is taking place there and it is all we can do to stop the trouble spreading to this settlement. The fighters in Cabinda have little respect for international boundaries. If they feel we are interfering they will cross the river and wreak their revenge on the people here. It is more than possible they will see your visit as interference. We will have difficulties explaining away your actions and it would be better if you leave this place immediately for your own sakes as well as ours."

"Can't you even take any consolation in the life that we have saved?" asked Melanie. "Surely that was achieved by the grace of God."

Brother Padraig shook his head. "I do not expect you to understand but some things are worse than death. It would most probably have been better if you had left the child to her own fate. You have merely extended her agony."

Melanie's voice rose. "How could you say that? Just look at this child, she's beautiful and isn't she too a child of God.......?"

Simon put his hand on Melanie's arm to quieten her. "What do you mean?" he asked.

"There is no place for her here, no orphanage or good person willing to take the child. Girls are of little value in this society.

9

Infanticide is common. Nobody wants the burden of a girl let alone a girl from a different tribe. Only the unscrupulous will take her and her future will be nothing more than that of a slave at best and then only if she survives infancy."

"You mean you won't help her?"

"We are a teaching order. We do not have the capability."

Melanie struggled to conceal her shock. She turned to Banda Sitole. "There must be something that can be done."

"This is indeed a harsh place. Her only hope is that you take her with you."

"That's a big ask," said Simon shaking his head, "to take a child that doesn't even have a name."

"Oh you have a name," replied Banda. "Your own words were that she came by the grace of God. I think you named her Grace and by the grace of that God you will give her a life and I will pray that something good comes from this time."

Chapter 2
12th June 1994
Windhoek, South West Africa (Namibia)

Freifrau von Swartzstein fussed around her husband, doing her duty, picking at flecks of dust and smoothing the fabric of his suit jacket, seeking perfection. He stood statuesque in front of the full length mirror in the dressing room adjacent to their bedroom on the first floor of the great villa. He liked what he saw. For a fifty year old he looked remarkably well; perfect weight, straight back, high Germanic brow, square chin and his own immaculately groomed hair.

At last the Baroness stood back, satisfied with her efforts. "*Alles ist richtig meine Liebe,*" she said coming to attention, waiting for his approval.

Von Swartzstein once more looked closely at his reflection in the mirror before uttering the words, "*Ja gut.*"

With precision he turned, left the dressing room and descended the middle of the sweeping Italian marble staircase to the reception hall. The morning African sun sent shafts of coloured light through the stained glass of the atrium roof. He walked down the short hallway to the doors of the conference room. An African footman in morning dress opened the double doors ahead of von Swartzstein.

"*Freiherr Artur von Swartzstein kommt!*" he announced.

The eight men who were already assembled and seated inside came to their feet, seven of them in unison. They stood silently as their leader the Baron made his way to the head of the polished mahogany conference table.

"*Guten Morgen meine Herren. Bitte setzen Sie.*" Von Swartzstein avoided eye contact with any particular individual.

Nobody moved till the footman had pushed the chair forward and von Swartzstein had taken his place. Then, replicating a class of disciplined school children, they replied "*Guten Morgen Freiherr von Swartzstein,*" before retaking their seats.

There was silence as the footman withdrew from the room. For a brief moment eyes darted from von Swartzstein to others around the table. Like poker players seven of them looked for evidence of the Baron's mood or indication of his predisposition towards any individual. Belying the outward neutral composure of the assembled men there was an underlying rivalry and jealousy for the attention of their Chief. All but one of the eight was infatuated by their leader. A glance, the glimmer of a smile or

11

worse the downward curl of a lip, was what they were looking for – with both hope and trepidation.

He had several names. Sometimes in private he was simply referred to as the Chief, but never to his face; such informality was not permitted. Almost as a concession he would accept being called Baron von Swartzstein, or simply the Baron, but his full title was Freiherr Artur von Swartzstein of Brandenburg. He insisted on being addressed in *'Hochdeutsch'* or High German. The use of the formal *'Sie'* was compulsory, even an accidental slip to the informal *'du'* was enough to attract a disapproving scowl. All things had to be meticulously correct; it was not just part of his psyche, it was as if it were in his DNA. Informality and worse still improvisation were an anathema to him. His whole life was controlled by rules, etiquette and protocols but most of all by principles – his principles, principles that were not necessarily shared but that had been inherited from a blood line that had remained unbroken for almost a millennium.

He could trace his lineage back to the Second Crusade and the foundation of the Teutonic Knights, that band of Christian zealots that had settled in North-eastern Europe once their duties in the Holy Land had been fulfilled.

The hereditary title of Knight had passed down the generations from father to son, establishing a military dynasty with unshakable loyalty to the Holy Roman Empire and Pope until the Reformation. In the 14th century land in the East had been granted to the family in perpetuity. With it came elevation to the aristocracy and the title *"Freiherr"* or Baron. Over the centuries they had unwaveringly sprung to the defence of their land and had become a reliable ally to the monarchy and an integral part of the military machine that was the Prussian State. But the last hundred years had seen the Prussian Establishment shaken to the core.

In the 1850's the Swartzsteins had nailed their flag to the mast of Otto von Bismarck, the creator of modern Germany, the man who'd united the disparate Germanic principalities into a singal Nation and created the Second Reich and inflicted military defeats on the Austro-Hungarian Empire and most importantly, France. Under his tutelage Germany had come of age as the pre-eminent military power in Europe, and the Swartzsteins were in the vanguard.

When Bismarck died, a hapless Kaiser, blinded with an irrational belief in his own invincibility, led his country into the Great War, which he lost.

The terms of peace dictated by the allies saw the abolition of the monarchy and disbandment of the aristocracy. The 1919 treaties allowed the Swartzsteins to keep their titles and land; all that had been lost was hereditary political power.

Initially reluctant to become involved with Adolf Hitler and the new political elite in the 1930's, the family moved slowly but eventually came around, following the lead of the Hindenburgs and the promise of military glory. This martial lust led to further military defeat. The Russians had overrun the land and confiscated the Swartzstein Estates. The family, now dispossessed of their lands had turned to industry to rejuvenate their prosperity. They had benefited from the economic miracle that was Germany's recovery.

Throughout the Swartzstein family remained united and clung to the principles that they had held for nearly a thousand years. They demanded loyalty from their followers but knew that loyalty was a two-way process and that they must stand by the people that had been loyal to them – even if times were difficult. So it had fallen to Freiherr Artur von Swartzstein of Brandenburg to look after the survivors of the armies that had fought under their leadership. Not the rabble, the Nazis or dreaded SS, but the Wehrmacht, ordinary German soldiers who had only obeyed orders and had, for their troubles, been left dispossessed and pension-less by military defeat. It was a heavy burden, a financial burden far in excess of the Swartzstein family fortune.

The Nazi '*rats*' that fled Germany in the spring of 1945 had fled to South America. This destination was not for the Swartzsteins. Field Marshal Karl von Swartzstein, Artur's father, had chosen the former German colony of South West Africa for his exile. In 1946 it was simply the Protectorate of South West Africa. It had been a good choice; that country provided a safe haven for the Swartzsteins. But now that haven was threatened by the tide of Black Nationalism that was sweeping over the continent. The challenge was for the Baron to hold the dynasty together for the next generation and that time in the future when the Black Eagle of Germany once more soared above the world. The Fourth Reich!

The beginning of the meeting was as dry as the air pumped out by the air-conditioning unit that hummed away in the background. Each person in turn read out their pre-prepared report without emotion; facts and figures were in profusion, expounded without tonal deviation making it difficult for the listener to differentiate between the relevant and irrelevant, the important and unimportant. Nobody asked questions or offered comment. That would come later.

Udo Hueber was the last to present his report on the grim financial situation. He was worried; nobody liked to bring bad news to the chief. Despite the emotionless delivery it would have been difficult for anybody not to pick up on the fact that the situation was indeed serious. When he finished reading he placed his papers flat on the table and waited.

The Baron was purposefully silent for a few moments, as though deliberately awaiting the build up of tension. Eventually he spoke.

"Coffee!" He rose and led the way through double glass doors on to the veranda. Cups of strong German coffee and bites of buttered pretzels were offered by the footman and a black maid. The men talked: not chit-chat but carefully chosen words and comment, almost like a game of verbal chess. Seven out of the eight tried to outmanoeuvre one another with the twin objectives of minimising damage to themselves whilst exploiting chinks in their rival's armour.

The Baron had read all the reports the previous night but it was the first time the others had heard their colleagues' reports. The coffee break gave them a short time to sort out contradictions and conflicts and prepare their answers for the possible questions that might come.

After less than thirty minutes the Baron moved back inside. The others followed and took their seats. Now, sitting in the corner at a small table, was Baroness von Swartzstein with pencils and a shorthand notebook at the ready. This part of the meeting would be minuted and from the minutes would flow the list of written orders that would dictate the next three months of the attendee's lives.

"The problem that faces us is severe," began von Swartzstein. "Hueber has given us the bad news that our main investment is lost and our source of income severely reduced.

For clarity of mind let us look at the problem from a historical perspective. In 1946 our organisation was established here in Africa. Many officers of the Wehrmacht, the German Army, my father taking the lead, took great risks in the last days of the Second World War to get wealth out of Germany: gold, art works and even cash in the form of US dollars. That wealth was to be invested and the income used to secure the future of retired ordinary German soldiers and their families that had been treated unjustly by history for the crime of obeying orders.

Fate appeared to have smiled on us here. To the north is the Portuguese colony of Angola; perhaps not the best managed colony in the world but at least the Portuguese junta was tolerant and sympathetic towards us. It was a place we could do business without too many questions being asked. Then in 1955 the Portuguese discovered oil in the sea just off the coast of Cabinda at the mouth of the Congo River, an enclave of Angola. But they lacked the cash to exploit the discovery just at the same time as we were looking for investment opportunities. The deal was clear. We would supply the cash for developing the oil fields and the Portuguese would give us a guaranteed return which would fund our liabilities. All went well for nearly twenty years.

Then in 1974 the fascist regime in Lisbon collapsed overnight. Portugal hurried to divest itself of its colonies, including Angola. War broke out in that country as rival factions fought for power. The MPLA faction looked like they were losing the struggle until Cuban soldiers, sent by the Russians, arrived. The Cubans did not rush to crush the rival factions; instead their first priority was to secure the oil fields in Cabinda. They said they needed the revenue to fight the war but we really know their motive was to secure an oil supply for themselves in Cuba. In the beginning the Angolans continued paying royalties but two years ago they set up a national oil company, Sonangol. Our secure bonds were exchanged for share certificates and we were promised our income would go up. But in two years no dividend has been paid and there is no prospect of a dividend in the future. Our investment has been stolen." The Baron paused for effect.

"Is this a fair summary?"

Seven of the eight men silently nodded.

"So what is our current financial situation?" asked von Swartzstein looking directly at Hueber.

The object of the comment shifted uncomfortably in his seat. "Angola was not our only investment. We have smaller investments in gold and diamond mines in South Africa and also a holding in copper deposits in Zambia. They still bring us some income but each month we are eating into our reserves."

"How long can we last?"

"As we are," continued Hueber, "maybe two or three years at most."

"Has anybody any suggestions as to what we should do?" asked the Baron looking around the table.

15

His gaze landed on one man. It was the event seven out of the eight men dreaded. Being put on the spot was to be avoided at all costs. "Claus, what do you suggest?"

Claus shifted in his seat and stared straight ahead. "Possibly we could reduce our payments, accept no new claimants and see where savings could be made. If we restrict our outgoings perhaps we can go on a little longer."

"Claus you disappoint me." They were the words that Claus didn't want to hear but words that brought relief to the others - Claus was the whipping dog for the day. The Baron rarely focused his disdain on more than one person during a meeting.

"The very reason for our existence is to settle a debt of honour. There can be no price put on that honour. What our old soldiers, or their dependants, need they should have. Our difficulties should not be of concern to them; they should not even know of them. If we were looking after your children Claus would you be happy if I sent one of them a letter saying they could not attend university this semester because I am a little short? No! Your child should never have to worry; he should be assured that he is receiving what you have earned. Is that not correct? Honour before money."

Claus capitulated. "That is correct Freiherr von Swartzstein. I am sorry for my misinterpretation of the situation."

To resist would have been futile.

Having completed the ritual humiliation of one of the group the Baron turned to the one person in the group that remained unruffled.

"Gunter, what do you have to say?"

Gunter Siegburg was different from the others, not just in appearance although that was marked enough in itself. At thirty-five he was a big framed man, not fat but stocky with a huge heaving chest gained through years of physical exercise. Regardless of effort he could never match the clean cut businesslike appearance of the others that sat at the table. His round face was dominated by an unkempt blond walrus moustache; it always looked like he needed a shave and his hair, despite constant attention, never looked anything but un-groomed. He'd never owned a suit that fitted properly although in the past he'd spent a lot of money hoping to achieve that objective. With a final resignation that he would never fit into the formal establishment ensconced in his mind, he'd learnt to feel comfortable with and even to relish, his reputation as a flamboyant, if somewhat scruffy, eccentric.

There was something warm and welcoming about his smile, like the laughing uncle that every child wants. But it would be a mistake to underestimate the man. His working class origins and upbringing on a bleak Saxony farm that had been swept by frost laden Siberian winds in winter months had made him tough and resolute. The army had straightened him out to some extent, instilling the virtues of obedience and loyalty, but had been unable to remove the rough edges from his personality. He'd been a good soldier, a tough fearless fighter, calm under fire and never afraid to take the initiative. Leadership in the field came naturally and was noted. He'd never have survived the etiquette requirements of the officer corps but that did not mean his qualities had gone unrecognised.

Gunter Siegburg spoke his mind. There was never any discrepancy between his thoughts and the words that came from his lips; political intrigue and manoeuvring were alien concepts to this man. On occasion words came a little too easily and so Gunter didn't make many friends. Fortunately for him Freiherr Artur von Swartzstein could be considered as one of his friends. He tolerated Gunter's extrovert tendencies. From the beginning the Baron had seen something that most others had missed. Behind the narrow slits, almost hidden, lay piercing ice blue eyes portraying a concealed cold determination and a hint of callousness. Gunter knew the Chief had seen this and also knew he could get away with more than most – so long as von Swartzstein believed he remained true and loyal.

"So what do you say Gunter?" prompted the Baron for a second time.

"We take back what has been taken from us?"

"And how would we go about doing that?"

"There is a way to do everything. We only have to find it."

"Do you think you could find that way?"

"Given time and resources, yes."

"We have little time and few resources."

"I will make the time and find the resources." His words were calm and assured. Nobody in the room doubted Gunter.

Chapter 3
3rd December 1994
Stirling Farm, Okavango Delta, Botswana

They were all shaken but it had affected James more than anybody else. The sixteen year old had gone quietly to his bedroom and sobbed like a baby, unable to accept any words of comfort. The bottom had fallen out of his world. The only coherent words that he uttered were a request that Gus should be buried high on the kopje, close to where his mother lay. Everybody agreed. Gus had grown to be part of the family and would be buried with the family.

The shock had been magnified because the previous night had been one of happiness; not a planned organised celebration, just one of those warm times that spontaneously occur when people come together and a quiet contentment gently descends, a time when hope rears its head, hope that the bad things that have happened in the past are not forgotten but are finally consigned to their correct place in history.

In other circumstances it would have been different.

Six and a half years had passed. The date was indelibly fixed on all their minds: 12th June 1988. That was the day that James and Maggie had lost their mother and Duncan had lost Elizabeth, his African Princess and wife. The woman whom he'd loved so much, who had given him everything, had been stolen on that day in a violent terrorist explosion.

Duncan's quest for retribution had helped but could not nullify the deep feelings he had for Elizabeth. Somehow he could just not leave her memory behind.

Jane Ashton was an analyst with GCHQ in England. A consummate professional she'd had no time for personal feelings, only her profession had mattered, that was until she'd met Duncan. It hadn't been immediate; it was something that had crept up on her as she worked as part of the team that had tracked down Elizabeth's killers.

For James and Maggie it had been easier. Their youthful minds had healed more quickly than their father's. There was scar tissue of course but they knew with youthful wisdom that life had to go on. And they wanted their father to move on also.

Sometimes it appeared that Duncan was getting there. Sometimes it was as if he was ready and Jane's heart was filled

18

with hope. But then the very qualities that she so admired in him would appear once more. Even though Elizabeth had been dead for so long the cords of loyalty and love still tethered him to her. Jane never gave up hope just as she never pushed Duncan. Duncan would have to get there on his own steam. Not that others didn't offer encouragement.

She'd arrived from the UK that morning. Duncan's happiness at Jane's arrival was only surpassed by that of James' and his sister Maggie, who had both grown to love Jane. They knew Jane would never be a substitute for their dead mother. She had never tried to be that, but she had earned a place in their hearts in her own right.

After dinner Duncan and Jane had settled on the stoop with the children and watched as the sky put on its evening display, bright orange drifting to crimson and then dull red before finally succumbing to darkness. Mary, when she'd finished in the kitchen, had gone to fetch Gus from the annexe and the two had joined the family on the stoop. A quiet contentment permeated the evening as they sat in silence. Then out of the darkness came the sound of laughter and babbling chatter with the occasional curse as Tembo and Morgan stumbled through the scrub, sneaking from the Kraal to the farmhouse, like a pair of naughty school children even though that stage of life had long passed them by.

They'd brought with them a stream of funny stories that Duncan had said were taller than a giraffe's head and a torrent of naïve personal questions that made him flush with embarrassment and caused Jane to feign exaggerated coyness, to the amusement of the others.

Hours passed as they chatted together, the conversation a mixture of gentle anecdotes and hopes for the future. Jane had watched Gus from the corner of her eye as he leaned back in his chair, the curl of a smile on his lips. His eyes glistened with moistness and for a moment she fancied she saw a single teardrop forming before he quickly brushed it away with the back of his hand. Sometimes there are just magic moments and nobody wants to break the spell.

In the end it had been Gus himself that had made the first move.

It was a little after ten when he had used his arms to push himself out of the chair. "It's time for me to go," he'd said.

Beside Still Waters

With an unusual display of affection he hugged everybody and said goodnight, saving a kiss each for James and Maggie before stepping off the stoop and slowly walking off into the darkness, perhaps his back a little more stooped and steps more laboured than normal. James, in the future, would always believe that Gus had known he'd at last arrived at a good place and that it could be no better.

Sunrise was at six am and James got up as the first rays broke the horizon. He'd been warned by Mary often enough not to disturb Gus until at least half-an- hour after daybreak and so it was exactly six-thirty when he went to the annexe.

Gus was a slow starter in the morning but that was no excuse for James. He couldn't wait to get into the workshop and begin the working day. He loved his time with Gus. Gus was teaching him and Gus knew everything; there was so much to learn and there were projects to finish.

In the last month they'd been working on a pump system to take water six hundred yards from the borehole to the kraal so that the villagers could have running water where they needed it. It was only an interim measure. Gus had bigger dreams. There was a watering hole a few hundred metres from the farmhouse. It was full during the rainy season but was not very big. He had calculated that by blocking a drainage creek they'd be able to build a small reservoir, their own lake that would supply the farm nearly all the year around. It would mean they'd get two crops of melees per season instead of one. That would make a big difference. The dam was just about complete and the reservoir would fill in the coming months. The next stage would be to dig the irrigation channels.

They also had plans to install lightning protection over all the African huts. That would make it safer during the thunderstorms. And then of course, the year after or perhaps the year after that, they were going to get a bigger generator and everybody would have electricity. Those were just the big projects. The list of other jobs was endless and of course they had the ongoing maintenance of the pest control kit to carry out also. James didn't want to waste a minute – there weren't enough of them in the day.

He'd knocked tentatively on the door of Gus's room and waited for the usual gruff "What?"

James would giggle at Gus's attempt at anger. He knew Gus's humour would warm with the rising sun. But that morning there was no response. James had a bad premonition. Something

20

was wrong. He opened the door and saw Gus in bed, motionless, lying on his side. Peaceful, almost smiling, his eyes were open as if he were looking at the photograph that stood on the wicker bedside table, the family photograph with Gus in the centre surrounded by the people who had adopted him so late in life and who had become his family, the only loving family he had ever known.

The burial had been delayed for five days. It was a sudden unexpected death so the doctor had insisted on an autopsy before he would issue a death certificate. Duncan had argued.

"If it was one of the Africans from the Kraal you wouldn't have demanded this. We could have just buried him."

"Don't ask me to explain away the legacy of colonialism," the doctor had replied. "We have a system inherited from the British. Officially reported deaths are subject to the law but traditional African deaths are treated differently. If somebody dies in an African village and nobody complains then they can do what they have always done; bury the corpse. It's the accepted compromise when two cultures live side by side."

The body had to be taken to the hospital in Maun, three slow hours by ambulance. It had been returned four days later in a body bag that had been placed in an aluminium casket that had been packed with ice to slow decomposition. With the body had come the autopsy report. '*The subject, a seventy-one year old white European male had died peacefully in his sleep from heart failure*'.

James and Maggie had chosen the place for the grave. They'd picked a westerly facing spot near the top of the kopje, facing into the setting sun because that was Gus's favourite time of the day. The small party had climbed the hill. Tembo, Morgan and Duncan had carried the coffin. It had not been heavy. The party went slowly, the pace dictated by Mary Scobie's frail legs. James and Maggie walked together behind the coffin.

They hadn't known if Gus was religious or not, he'd never spoken on that subject but they suspected not. In any event they'd rustled up a Lutheran Minister. He said an incomprehensible prayer and spoke words that, despite the sincerity of the Minister, had to be meaningless because he'd never known the man Gus.

It had started off as a low murmur in the distance, almost a hum. As it got nearer the deep melodic tones got louder and louder. Eventually the Minister had to stop and the small assembly turned to see the sight of the Africans, many of them from the Kraal, slowly walking en masse up the kopje. They stopped twenty yards short of the grave.

Their traditional doleful melodic song was to say goodbye, in their own way, to the quiet man that for decades had been their silent friend. After a few minutes, without signal, the crowd had turned and started to walk slowly down the kopje, their deep voices gradually fading into the distance.

Back at the farmhouse the small group had gathered in the 'little used' living room. Duncan wanted to speak, something reassuring and positive but Mary, uncharacteristically had interjected.

"Gus and I had spoken of this moment many times," she'd said. "He told me what to say. Don't be so surprised, we were two old people together, very aware of the march of time. Gus knew his end was approaching.

For most of his life Gus had been troubled. His disappointment in people and life had forced him to Africa many years ago where he'd lived the life of a recluse. That long dark time helped make the last two years that much sweeter. He wanted me to thank you all for returning to him that faith and belief in humanity that had for so long been absent. He'd said that he was whole again and that, when the time came, he would happily depart and that he didn't want anybody to feel sad." Mary smiled at James and Maggie. "He simply said that I should thank you for the love you gave to him."

"Now," continued Mary in a more businesslike tone. "As you all know Gus was ever the practical man." Mary removed a sheet of paper from her handbag. "I don't think this constitutes the official will, that's with a Lawyer in Maun. Gus had a few thousand Pula in the bank. This he gives to Duncan to be used to make improvements on Stirling Farm, particularly for the Kraal. He specifically wants to see the current projects completed. I think it is a shame he will not see the lake filled, it is so close.

Now, Gus had a house in Oslo, Norway. It is his old family home and is managed by an agent and provides some rental income. The building held no good memories for him. He wants the house to be sold and the proceeds put in trust to provide university education for James and Maggie." Mary stopped for a moment and looked towards Jane and Duncan. "He recently amended his will stating that some of the proceeds be held back in case there are any children from the union of Duncan and Jane, which he was absolutely sure will take place!"

Duncan remained pan faced, Jane's mouth opened and everybody else laughed at Gus's prophetic assessment.

Finally Gus wanted to leave his tools and personal possessions to James. He was absolutely sure the tools would be put to good use. There is one special request though. Gus has two steel boxes. They contain personal documents, journals and what mementoes he has from his life before Africa. They are to go to James but he wants the boxes to remain locked for one year from his date of death. Gus said he was not proud of his former life and he did not want to immediately destroy any good thoughts people may hold of him. There was time enough for that in the future.

He asked me to thank you all for the kindness you showed to him and finally, to you Duncan. In you he saw something he would have liked to have been: a strong man who could distinguish instinctively the difference between right and wrong and always took the right path, even if it wasn't the easiest route. He hopes and asks that you never change."

Mary folded the paper and they all sat in silent contemplation for a while.

Chapter 4
Boma, Zaire.
3rd February 1995

Gunter Siegburg peered out of the window as the plane circled, swooping uncomfortably low over the river and town. The sight was unimpressive; a sprawl of ramshackle buildings, the largest being the cluster of dilapidated warehouses dotted along the rudimentary river bank berths. Half a dozen rusting ocean-going ships were tied up at the quays surrounded by a motley flotilla of indigenous boats plying their trade. At the remoter edges of the natural lagoon, dugout canoes, familiar to the eyes of explorers such as Livingstone and Stanley, held men that cast fishing nets into the murky brown water hoping to land some ugly and aggressive species of tropical fish that would keep their family free from malnutrition for another day. The only thing detracting from the scene of dilapidation and decay was the sight of a large impeccable white ocean-going motor-yacht slowly making its way up river, a dramatic sign of conspicuous wealth that appeared almost obscene amid such poverty. Gunter, with a wry smile, shook his head.

Travellers to Africa often saw cities that had an enticing appeal from the air but were disappointed when once on the ground they were confronted with the reality of endemic poverty: faded paint, stinking mould, potholed roads and the pervasive smell of equatorial rot. Boma was more honest in this respect; even from the air there was nothing alluring about the place; it had no redeeming features. Tourists did not visit Boma, not if they had any sense.

The runway was red, a dull earth red that characterises the landscape of central and southern Africa. It was nothing more than a large dirt landing strip comprising compacted earth that in the rainy season turned into a quagmire that was unusable for long periods. Boma, Zalre's only deep water port was often isolated from the vast hinterland that it was supposed to serve. Established by European traders in the sixteenth century it is located at the furthest navigable point up the Congo River, about a hundred miles from its mouth. It has a history as bleak as its current situation. For hundreds of years warring African tribes had marched their prisoners from the interior to Boma and exchanged them for manufactured goods; pots, pans, cloth, beads, trinkets but most of all weapons, weapons to help them dominate their rivals and perpetuate the slave trade. It became a place where an individual's prestige and power was measured by their ability to subjugate others.

The plane juddered violently when the wheels made contact with the ground. The only grader available, that was used on the runway periodically to level out bumps and smooth corrugations, had been broken for a month without serious prospect of being repaired. A shanty town, consisting of shacks made from disused bits of timber, old metal sheets and pieces of worn and torn canvas, had sprawled up to the very edge of the runway. Gunter saw the faces of the black children, standing in clusters, watching the Fokker turboprop quickly slow and pull up to the terminal building, a single storey construction little bigger than a double garage. Once it was painted blue and white but now it was just mud-stained and brown. Two officials, in khaki uniform sat on garden chairs unhurried by the arrival of the only scheduled plane of the day. In front of them was an old wooden trestle table, something that would not have been out of place in a 1950's English church hall. On top of the table was a rough cardboard sign with the words "*Customs & Immigration*" written in bold felt pen in both French and English. By their sides, leaning against their chairs were the ubiquitous AK47's, the only badge of rank and symbol of authority that meant anything.

Including Gunter there were six passengers on the plane. He was the lone European. They disembarked using the aircraft's steps and waited for the co-pilot to come and open the cargo hatch. He passed each of them their baggage. Gunter was the last to receive his holdall and so was last to join the queue for '*Customs & Immigration*'.

One of the uniformed men got up and sauntered around the trestle table, stopping at the first African in the queue.

"Passport?" was his single word question.

The man passed over the travel document. The guard flipped through the pages without apparent interest and then gave the document back before proceeding to the next passenger. He replicated the process until he came to the end of the queue. Gunter presented his passport. Tucked inside the back page was a fresh $20 note. The guard flicked through the pages and then began to feign a more detailed inspection, turning away as if trying to get more light on to the document's small print. After a few moments he passed the document back and pointed towards the trestle table, giving a nod to the guard still sitting there. A few moments later Gunter had cleared '*Customs and Immigration*' and was walking around the terminal building towards the exit. He quickly flicked the pages of his passport before putting it into the breast pocket of his shirt. The $20 dollar bill was gone.

Twenty yards clear of the terminal building were the remnants of the airport perimeter protection, a sagging chain-link fence, once more than three metres high but now, in some sections where the posts had broken, lying flat on the ground. The wide double gates were stuck in the open position, their hinges long since rusted and seized up. Despite the poor state of the barrier, the waiting crowd did not move forward and breach their symbolic rather than physical protection. They all knew the ramifications.

The crowd consisted of a hotchpotch of people: hopeful taxi-drivers, waiting family, vendors with second-hand plastic bottles filled with water of dubious origin and the pervasive child street beggars. Gunter immediately identified the man he was looking for, the only white face amongst them but what he saw was not quite what he expected.

Emrys ap Ewan was a good six feet one inch tall, his body so painfully thin, it could be described as emaciated. An ill-fitting light green safari suit sagged limply on his skeletal frame. His facial features did little to mitigate initial impressions. Pale sunken cheeks highlighted the deep eye sockets that were too close together and underscored with black shadows. Beyond the receding hairline was a tangle of dirty blond hair. Ap Ewan pushed forward his broad thin-ipped smile exposing yellow crooked teeth.

"Mr Siegburg?" The tone was confident and enthusiastic but the accent strange and unfamiliar. Ap Ewan offered his hand.

The handshake was damp and limp. Gunter felt the unyielding bone and knuckles that were so sparsely covered in loose fitting skin. "You are English? Your accent?"

"English!" The response was immediate but good humoured. "No not English man, I'm Welsh and proud of it too."

"Ah, Walisisch! I have never worked with a Welsh man before. But let us get away from here. You have a car?"

"Your limousine and driver awaits," joked ap Ewan. Gunter could not have immediately appreciated the humour.

On a nearby piece of scrubland, in the shadow cast by a lone tree stood the Peugeot 404 saloon. It had seen better days. The fawn paintwork had faded and cracked as a result of too much exposure to the African sun; rust decorated the wheel arches and the hub-caps were missing revealing a mix of odd grey and black steel rims.

"It's not as bad as it looks," said ap Ewan. "It's a great runner. I was lucky to pick it up. Get in."

Gunter tried the handle on the rear door. It was loose and non-functioning.

"I keep meaning to have a look at that," smiled ap Ewan. "Don't worry, the windows open. Put your hand inside and use the lever."

There was nothing inside the vehicle to raise Gunter's damaged confidence. The upholstery was torn, exposing bits of yellow foam. The foot-well felt soft under foot and Gunter thought his feet might break through the corroded metal and the smoke stained lining was coming away from the roof at several points.

Ap Ewan got in the other side. "Really it's a good runner, very reliable. I know about these things."

Gunter Siegburg wasn't sure.

Ap Ewan leaned forward and slapped the drooping black head that belonged to the body occupying the driver's seat. "Wake up Henry, you lazy bastard," he barked.

The black driver, wits instantly regained, turned to face the rear occupants, his broad smile exposing a set of perfect gleaming white teeth.

"Bas?"

"Paradise Hotel – quick as you can but keep it smooth."

Gunter doubted that the dual request of quick and smooth were compatible. He didn't see the cloud of black smoke that emitted from the rear of the car when Henry turned the ignition but he couldn't fail to notice the rattle from the engine and the loud metallic clunk as first gear was selected. Any negative thoughts on the mechanical condition of the car were quickly subordinated to the point of insignificance by Henry's novel driving technique. Unknown to Gunter, Henry was both short-sighted and too poor to afford glasses. Henry only ever saw the larger potholes and then only at the last second, resulting in constant sudden manoeuvres which threw the rear occupants from side to side. Another problem was the irregular throngs of people that congregated, for no obvious reason, at major crossroads in the precincts of Boma town. Henry, instead of slowing when approaching any such crowd thought it better to accelerate, apparently believing that the sound of a racing engine would sufficiently motivate the crowd to get out of the way. The strategy was partially successful but the occasional pedestrian was side-swiped or clipped by a protruding wing mirror. Neither Henry nor, it seemed, ap Ewan thought such occurrences necessitated a stop.

There was no proper road outside of the town. However this was actually an improvement. Although the way was rutted, at least the huge potholes were absent. Gunter, not having to hold on so tightly, felt better able to talk.

"I was told that I was to meet a well-connected former British Army officer. Was I correctly informed?"

"In a way yes, in a way no," was ap Ewan's cheerful reply.

"You must explain."

"I was a non-commissioned officer."

"*Shada, an Unteroffzier,*" Gunter's disappointment was clear.

Ap Ewan's defence was instant and sharp. "I worked hard for my rank; the British Army don't give away two stripes for nothing you know. It's an achievement."

"*Scheisse ein Korporal,*" the news was not getting better for Gunter but he knew there was nothing he could do. "Your unit, what was your unit?"

Ap Ewan straightened his back in half-hearted pride. "One-one-nine Company, 101st Battalion, REME."

"REME, what is REME?"

"Royal Electrical and Mechanical Engineers."

"A combat unit?"

"No – not really, more a support unit. But the guys in the line could never have survived without us," he defended. "And that's why I'm so good with cars by the way."

Gunter didn't try to conceal the disdain on his face. For him real soldiers fought. That was it, full stop. The journey continued in silence for a while. Gunter eventually broke the silence.

"When will we get to the hotel for the meeting?

"Two different questions," responded ap Ewan back to his perky self. "We will get to the hotel in twenty minutes. The meeting, I don't know. Africans don't like to be rushed. It could be tomorrow; then again it could be in a week."

"*WAS! Ein Woche!*"

"Calm down, calm down. In the old days the chiefs could keep visitors waiting for a couple of months – it's pretty quick nowadays. It's their way of showing who's in charge. If you want to do business in this part of Africa you have to get used to African ways." Ap Ewan's attempt at reassurance fell short of the mark. Gunter sank into more dark and quiet contemplation.

"You'll like the hotel," promised ap Ewan.

The person who had given the hotel its name had either led a very depraved life or had a well-developed sense of humour. It was situated directly at the bottom of the last cataract on the Congo River, alongside a slow moving shallow channel that was just about navigable by canoes and small craft. A multitude of small pools, filled with all but stagnant water, surrounded the place and were ideal breeding places for mosquitoes which inundated the area throughout the year. That alone should have been enough to put off any *'would be'* developers, but it had not.

The concept was good. It was built during the heyday of Belgium's colonial power in the late 1930's. It was meant to combine the most modern amenities of the day with an African feel. It was a single storey structure constructed of imported brick under, what was now, a weathered and sad looking reed thatch. Built in a horse shoe design, it was approached by a short drive. The entrance was at the 'head' of the horse shoe and the forty rooms, twenty per side, ran out along the arms, each with an en suite bathroom and patio door opening out on to what was once an ornate courtyard that had boasted a small but magnificent formal garden that was now just a bare patch with the occasional uncared for shrub and a few clumps of straw-like grass.

The interior too displayed only signs of former opulence. Gunter was disappointed but not surprised. The high glaze decorative green and white bathroom tiles were crazy-paved with minute cracks and reminded Gunter of a Belgian railway station waiting room. There was no shower only a bath, whose enamel was chipped at the edges and yellow stained around the drain. The brilliance of the chrome fittings had long since faded. The bed was big and sagging, the sheets threadbare linen once white but now grey and patched. An old stain on a pillow looked remarkably like dried blood. Gunter unhooked the mosquito net and pulled it around only to find that moths had rendered it useless.

A tray on the small writing desk held candles and matches. The reception clerk had informed him that the main's power was unreliable but went on to say that he needn't worry as the hotel had its own generator even if it was sometimes difficult to start. The candles were provided for the interim. Gunter took a torch from his holdall and placed it on the table alongside the candles.

Dinner had been uninspiring. Gunter and ap Ewan were the only customers in the formal carpeted wood panelled dining room. Despite a profusion of waiters scurrying about in white jackets with tarnished brass buttons, the service had been inexplicably slow between courses which would have been more annoying had Gunter been hopeful of receiving some culinary delight but in truth food was not what was preoccupying his mind.

After prodding the sweet a couple of times, a unique version of crème brûlée which appeared to have been made with sour curdled cream, Gunter pushed the plate to one side and drank the last mouthful of gritty coffee.

"I'm going to bed now. If I do not receive news of the meeting soon I will be making my plans to leave."

Ap Ewan responded. "No please do not go to bed just yet. I have a surprise for you. You'll really like it. It's all arranged, just come with me, we have a private lounge arranged."

The private lounge was actually just one of the rooms that had had the bed replaced with an old overstuffed suite. A waiter stood behind a drinks trolley which was overloaded with a variety of spirits and liquors. On the floor, plugged into a wall socket behind the waiter, was a cassette player.

"Do you recognize the music?" asked ap Ewan in hopeful anticipation.

Gunter shrugged his shoulders.

"It's James Last – James Last the German! I dug it out especially for you."

Ap Ewan, undeterred by Gunter's lack of enthusiasm, persisted. "Drink? What will you have, a cocktail, a liquor? I'm sure we have everything."

"Thank you for your efforts but I'm going to my room – unless the meeting is about to start?"

"No don't go!" said ap Ewan shifting slightly to block Gunter's way to the door, and sounding almost panicked. "Have one drink. Have a whisky. Chivas Regal. I have Chivas Regal. Do you know Chivas Regal? It's really good. Try one, trust me."

"I will have just one drink."

The relief was palpable. "I'll get it for you. Sit down. This is the most comfortable place, take this seat." Ap Ewan positioned Gunter on the couch.

Gunter sat. Ap Ewan came with the drink, a half-full lead-crystal tumbler complete with a set of the waiter's fingerprints clearly visible. "Twelve-years old, only the best, only the best." Gunter didn't bother to explain he didn't normally drink 'blends'; he preferred vintage single malts.

Ap Ewan ensconced himself in one of the armchairs with a smaller drink of his own. "*Prost*! That's what you say in Germany isn't it, *Prost* is the German for cheers isn't it?" He lifted his glass high into the air in a motion that was a little too reminiscent of a Nazi salute.

"It is. *Prost*" replied Gunter barely raising his glass.

"Are you comfortable then? Are you ready?"

"Ready for what?" asked Gunter.

Ap Ewan nodded to the barman who opened the patio windows. From out of the darkness, led by their waddling, overweight, middle aged matriarch, came a line of five young nubile African girls. They lined up in front of Gunter.

"Well," said ap Ewan, "what do think? It wouldn't be a party without female company would it?"

Gunter thought the sight reminded him of the girls that hung about on street corners on dark winter nights in the dock area of Hamburg touting for business.

"Not bad eh? Which one do you like the most?"

"None," responded Gunter.

"I know it is a surprise but don't be shy. The one in the middle, I reckon she's the best looking. You have her." Ap Ewan was now sitting on the edge of his seat, visibly perspiring and wringing his hands. "I like the one on the left. I'll go for her. That's if you don't want her that is, you get first choice."

Gunter got to his feet. "I'm going to my room," he said with finality.

"No don't go!" said ap Ewan in alarm. "You don't understand. They're a gift from General Lubala. If you don't accept he will be insulted. It could affect the discussions!"

"Tell Moses Lubala to fuck his own disease-ridden African whores."

The panic had now spread to the matriarch. She stepped forward. "You must take one. Lubala will be angry. He will blame me for offering bad girls." Her mind was working overtime. "You want more than one? You want two? You can have them all. They will do anything. Please choose someone."

Gunter looked blankly at the woman. He saw the expression on her face change, as if struck by a sudden inspirational thought.

"You want a boy? I have boys. Cherry boys, clean, untouched. Really good!" she smiled and nodded knowingly.

Gunter stepped forward and raised his hand to strike the woman but stopped himself before the blow fell. "I won't waste my energy on you. You're nothing more than the offspring of a lizard. Take your little boys to that Lubala arsehole. From my understanding that's what he likes." Siegburg turned and left.

Outside his room Gunter listened at the door and heard nothing. He slipped the key in the lock and pushed the door open just far enough to get his head in the opening. The sock was on the floor, where he had left it. Nobody had been in through this entrance – the sock would have been much further back. He went to the patio door. The tiny piece of cardboard he'd rested on the lintel had fallen to the floor. They had come in this way. He went to his holdall. It was where he had left it but the dead mosquito, carefully positioned on the zip now lay on the carpet. It was enough evidence for him. They had searched his room. He went to the torch on the desk. He pushed the switch. There was no visible beam of light but the tiny neon indicator flashed. "Good," he thought, "the game has started."

The two boats moved silently and slowly through the darkness. They had originally been Mercury assault craft, the type used by commandoes, but they'd been modified for clandestine night operations. They both sported 300 horse power V6 Evinrude outboard motors that had been adapted for silent running with the latest anti-vibration technology, an enlarged titanium silencer and extra sound insulation. They could make five knots fully laden in virtual silence but they still maintained the ability to make almost fifty knots with the throttle wide open in an emergency. The on-board technology was also pretty impressive; real-time super-sensitive forward looking sonar, infra-red night viewing optics, a super accurate electronic DF based navigation system and, for this operation, a unique underwater low frequency sound emitter, undetectable to the human ear but powerful enough to drive every crocodile within two miles not only mad but also out of the water. There were seven men on each boat, six highly trained special operations soldiers and a captain who never left the craft – all wearing black wet suits, night vision goggles and HF headsets for their personal radios.

The captain of the lead boat checked and re-checked his navigational position before choosing the waiting location amongst the tall reeds. He shut down the engine. They felt a slight bump but heard no sound other than the rustle of the reeds as the second boat came to rest beside them.

Gunter Siegburg guessed he'd get a pretty quick response. He knew he wouldn't have to wait long until ap Ewan or the old woman reported back to General Lubala. The bugging of the '*lounge*' had been crude, even laughable. They had made barely any effort to conceal the wires and the microphone was actually partially visible behind a curtain. Gunter was sure General Moses Lubala was both listening and nearby and he was also sure he wouldn't be able to keep his cool. African males didn't like to be accused of *'things'* with little boys. Gunter pushed the slider switch on the torch and carefully positioned it to face the patio window before checking his belt one last time. Then he sat down and waited.

There was nothing subtle about it. They came mob-handed. As the flat of a boot kicked opened the room door, a brick smashed the glass in the patio door and men, in army fatigues, piled in. Gunter offered no resistance but still there was pandemonium for a few seconds. Before the hood was pulled over his head Gunter counted at least six. One had a pistol, the others AK47's. They handcuffed him from the front. He felt strong hands hook his arms and partly carry, partly drag him through the patio windows and away into the darkness.

Gunter remained calm. Long training and experience had taught him that people who survived dangerous situations were the ones who didn't panic. He guessed he'd been pulled about one hundred and fifty metres before he was pushed through a door and felt the coolness of a functioning air-conditioning unit. He knew he must be near the General – only the leader would have access to such luxury. Hands roughly fumbled his body in a search for concealed weapons. He heard a door open and felt himself being pushed forward. He could hear the breathing and smell the foul breath of somebody standing close behind him. For a moment they stood silently, and then the hood was pulled from his head. Gunter's eyes began working immediately assessing the situation.

The house had at one time been quite grandiose. It had been designed and built for use by the manager when the hotel was in its heyday and it was necessary to provide accommodation of the highest standard to attract the best staff from Europe. The hotel had by now lost all such pretentions to greatness. So the house, and its outbuildings, with the tacit agreement of Mobutu, President of Zaire, was the current headquarters of the Cabinda Liberation Army. It was in the middle of what had once been the *'swanky'* main reception room that Gunter now stood. Directly in front of him was an apparition that would not have been out of place in Alice's Wonderland.

On a slightly raised platform, which had presumably been intended for a band during formal functions, sat the leader of the Cabinda Liberation Army, General Moses Lubala.

Lubala was a big man: heavy thighs, wide chest, bulging arms, thick neck and a full rounded black face. He wore a uniform that looked like it had been filched from the wardrobe department of a pantomime production. Braid, badges of rank, medals of honour, campaign ribbons were all in profusion making for a colourful display. His peaked military hat was so encumbered with gold piping that it made the wearer look top-heavy. He sat on a huge gold leaf fake Louise XIV wing-backed armchair as if it were a throne. Behind, as a back drop, hung red velvet curtains that would have been more impressive had they not been badly faded and covered in water stains.

Sitting cross-legged on the floor, almost in front, sat a hunched figure: a boy or maybe a young man, not a soldier, his head bowed, silently staring at the floor with a vacant imbecilic smile. To the left stood Emrys ap Ewan, complexion now ashen, smile absent, visibly shaking. Around the room were half a dozen armed *'soldiers'* lounging in faded battle fatigues, black berets and with assault rifles hanging loosely from their shoulders. Gunter thought they were most probably the ones that had fetched him.

He didn't wait. "You must be that savage Lubala!"

The punch in the kidneys was sudden but didn't hurt that much. Nevertheless Gunter took the opportunity and went down on to his knees. From behind a hand, the one that had just punched him, grabbed his shirt collar and pulled him upwards. For a few seconds Gunter struggled, grabbing the waistband of his trousers as though stopping them from falling. Nobody noticed him squeeze the switch on his belt that looked like a chrome stud. A few hundred yards away a dull neon light glowed on the control panel of one of the Mercury boats.

"Did nobody teach you manners?" said Lubala. "You are in my house now and I demand you respect me. I am General Moses Lubala head of the Cabinda Liberation Army, Head of State in waiting, and you will treat me as such. You will not speak unless I tell you to."

Lubala smiled, as if proud at the way he had conducted himself in front of his own men. "I am curious," he began. "You have been trying to contact me through my overseas agent," he looked at ap Ewan. "I understand you have an offer for me. Now tell me what do you have that I could possibly want?"

"I've changed my mind," replied Gunter. "I don't like the way you operate – I won't do business with you on these terms."

The fist was harder this time and Gunter's legs gave way on their own.

34

"Mr Siegburg you are very slow learning your manners. I have shown you great hospitality and leniency. But perhaps you will not learn. You are German I believe – perhaps you were born with arrogance in your make-up. It will be interesting to see if we can cure you but that will come later. First you will satisfy my curiosity. I want to know why you came here." Lubala nodded to one of the soldiers standing at the side.

In former times a crystal chandelier had hung from an eye-bolt in the ceiling. The chandelier was long gone but the eye-bolt remained and threaded through the hole was a rope with a shackle on the end. The soldier undid the other end of the rope from a cleat on the wall and lowered the shackle to just above Gunter's head.

"Hook him on," Lubala ordered before turning his attention to the boy at his feet. "Feliz, get me a whisky. We may have a long wait."

The boy at Lubala's feet got up and scurried away without a word. He returned after a few moments with a large glass filled with amber liquid and ice, handed it to Lubala without comment and retook his place on the floor. By this time Gunter was at full stretch, his hands above his head, toes barely touching the floor.

As a child Moses Lubala had been a lazy and arrogant student. It had been a struggle to get him to learn, as it often is for those who think all will come as a right of birth; the right conferred to the son of a powerful tribal Chief. Not that he'd had much of an education by Western standards. His father, a pragmatist, realised his heir needed to have some of the '*tools*' of the European world and that's why he'd named his first son Moses. A biblical name was enough to get him accepted into the remote mission school where he'd learnt the rudiments of reading, writing and counting and that was all his father wanted from the mission school. He didn't want any European version of history stuffed into his son's head, or any nonsense about '*gentle Jesus meek and mild*', nor notions of democracy or fair play. The part of education that was the formation of the mind was not to be trusted to foreigners. That was the domain of his father and he'd taught the reluctant boy well.

Moses had played in the jungle with the other village boys, just as his ancestors had done. Sometimes the children would divide into groups and pretend to be warring tribes but always Moses was on the victorious side. His father made sure of that. Sometimes they would hunt for wild animals. Moses always had the best spear or bow and arrow and he always carried the best catch to the village. No sooner had he begun to talk than he learnt to give orders to his mother and his father's other wives. He knew that if anybody disobeyed him his father would inflict punishment on his behalf – right or wrong – for the son of a Chief could never really be wrong.

Compassion and empathy were missing from his lexicon of words. He learnt never to pity others, never to give way to emotions. But he also learnt that he had to give; give on his own terms. Benevolence, as a reward for compliance, served to cement his position as leader; it conferred power, the power to give. He also learnt that he had to exercise the power to take away and to take away life was the most important sanction. It was at the beginning of puberty that he had faced the test that would signify his ultimate strength.

The transition from child to man was sudden, accomplished in a three day ritual. Moses had to do what the other initiates had to do to achieve manhood. He had to throw a spear long and straight, shoot an arrow true and stand there without wincing as his penis was circumcised by the witch-doctor in the traditional way, with a piece of sharp edged flint-stone. He had to sit in a hut for two days with the other boys without food or water as the smoke of burning grasses and forest herbs wafted through the loose thatch in a cleansing and empowering ceremony. When he'd emerged with the others, he was no longer a child but a man, a warrior. Only for him, the son of the Chief it had not been over. He'd had to demonstrate his worthiness to lead in the final act of the initiation, carried out at night in a clearing by the light of a giant bonfire.

Two men, young warriors from a rival tribe captured a few days earlier, were paraded in front of Moses, each held by two strong men. They were naked, with hands tied behind their back. In times past the strongest would have been chosen by his father and Moses would have had to fight them to the death. But Moses' father was not so willing to risk his investment. Instead Moses only had to choose: choose which of the two would live and who would die.

The men of the village sat silently and crossed-legged in a circle watching as Moses made his choice. First he picked, with a nod of his head, the one that was to live. The captive was forced to his knees and held strongly. His life may have been spared but he was still to suffer. Moses stepped forward. The knife was serrated. The jagged blade cut into the top of the left ear. Moses pulled the ear away and as he cut, bright red blood spurted high into the air. He pulled harder and tore the final thread of flesh away and held the severed ear above his head. The watching men howled their approval. Moses carried out the same procedure on the other ear before casually tossing both the severed organs into the fire.

The second captive was forced to his knees and Moses without hesitation slit his throat with the same knife. But the cut was not clean; the serrations were not strong enough to cut through the windpipe. Moses had to saw until the flowing blood began to foam as air from the victims lungs escaped through the slit and mixed with the free flowing red liquid. He fell forward and writhed on the ground. The cut was not deep enough to completely sever the artery to the brain. Only the returning vein was cut and the man bled to death struggling to free his tied hands in the forlorn belief that he would have been able to staunch the bleeding if only his hands were free.

Moses slowly walked around the man, smiling and goading until life was finally extinguished. Then he turned the dead captive on to his back and stuck his knife into the flesh, just below the rib cage and cut, as he'd practiced on a monkey, until he'd exposed the organ he was looking for. Plunging his hands deep into the chest cavity he wrestled free the still warm heart and severed the connecting blood vessels with his knife. He raised the organ above his head in triumph before sinking his teeth into the dark red muscle and tearing a large bite. He chewed and swallowed.

The seated men jumped to their feet and shouted their praise and adulation. Moses' father walked to his son and led him away to the Chief's hut, smiling and pleased that his son had passed the test. Inside the hut, with the curtain blocking the doorway, out of sight of the others, Moses heaved the contents of his stomach on to the floor of the hut. His father smiled.

"No matter, you have done what had to be done. Now drink this. It will take the taste away."

He passed his son a bottle of whisky. Moses gulped the liquid and again retched, but he took some more. Never again did he eat heart but his fondness for whisky never diminished.

From that day forward he was never far from his father's side. He learnt the importance of having a cause, a cause that would unify his followers, for there is no more powerful unifying factor than a common enemy or threat. He was by his father's side when Zairian troops had secretly crossed the border to Cabinda with American agents. He had been there when the Americans had persuaded his father to commit to the '*liberation of Cabinda*' in return for weapons, training and western goods. He had not understood at the time the Americans only wanted to sow trouble for the communist Angolans and occupying Cuban troops but he had been one of the first to receive modern military training and taste the Western luxuries that Kinshasa had to offer. He'd returned to the Cabinda jungle just in time to see his father succumb, not to violence but to Yellow Fever. He'd taken over. He'd learnt enough to maintain control without his father but he lacked the drive to achieve American objectives. When the Cubans left Angola the Americans lost interest and Moses became nothing more than a local dictator, dressed in a uniform and extracting only enough from the population for his own lustful needs. The knowledge that had been so hard to acquire slowly became diluted with alcohol and debauchery.

It happened quickly. It was a total surprise. The two boats moved forward in almost complete darkness and silence, the only noise from the fibreglass hulls scraping gently on the loose shale of the sloping beach. There was no guard. The men moved forward. The point man used infra-red glasses. It was not long before he picked up the beam of infra-red light from Gunter's torch. He stopped and crouched, flipping the lid off the mini DF detector display. Signal strength was four out of five bars, meaning less than one-hundred and fifty yards to target. The arrow on the LCD display gave the direction. He moved forward, the others followed. They closed in on the house using miniature periscopes to look through the windows. In minutes they'd found what they wanted.

Three men used the grenade launcher attachments on their CAR15 Assault Rifles to simultaneously fire '*flash-bangs*' through windows on two sides of the room before hurrying to defence positions to stop the arrival of reinforcements. The other nine men crashed through the patio doors, silencers fitted to their rifle muzzles. Three formed a ring around Gunter after shooting the one with foul breath; the other six focused their attention on the soldiers lolling around the room. In quick succession there was a series of sharp hisses. As the smoke cleared all Lumbala's men lay dead, Feliz was flat on the floor motionless and Lumbala himself had only time to drop his glass.

Somebody released the rope whilst someone else rummaged in the pockets of the dead man at Siegburg's feet and found the keys for the handcuffs. Two others dragged Lumbala from his seat and forced him to his knees in front of Gunter and pushed the point of a pistol into the back of his neck.

"Now," said Gunter, "do you want to continue our conversation on manners?"

Rivulets of sweat ran down the sides of Lumbala's face. The flab that was his neck shook like jelly. Without prompting he clasped his hands behind his head, "Don't shoot me, I surrender. I am your prisoner. Please don't shoot me."

"I have no intention of shooting you," said Gunter, "Although I find it hard to believe myself, you are too valuable to me. No, you are coming with me for some education and training."

One of the men shouted. "What about this one. He's alive but unarmed. What shall I do?"

Gunter turned to Lubala. "Who is he?"

Lubala bumbled. "It's Feliz. He's just an idiot boy, a camp follower. He's simple, he can't talk. He's my servant."

Gunter pondered and for a second or two Feliz's life hung in the balance. "Okay bring him with us. We'll make a decision when we get back to the motor yacht."

There was nothing clandestine about the Mercury boat's trip back to the motor yacht at Boma. The Evinrude outboards were opened up sacrificing quietness for speed. The hoist was ready and waiting. The two boats were lifted out of the water in minutes and shortly after that the yacht weighed anchor. Gunter now sat in the plush saloon of the luxury yacht he'd seen from the air that day when he'd been coming into land. General Moses Lubala had less to enjoy. Grim faced, imprisoned in a six foot by six foot windowless steel locker below the waterline he contemplated his future under the dull glow of a single sixty watt light bulb.

In three days the transformation had been little less than miraculous, testament to the effectiveness of German '*training*'. The yacht had spent a day sailing down the Congo estuary and out into the Atlantic, another day sailing up and down in the calm tropical waters and the third day meandering back up the estuary towards Boma. By that time the Cabinda Liberation Army had been changed to the Democratic Front for the Liberation of Cabinda (DFLC). General Moses Lubala, who would in future be known simply as Moses Lubala, would be the founding President of the DFLC. A declaration of the DFLC's aims and objectives would be published in the Correio da Manhã, Lisbon's main newspaper, Portugal being the former colonial power. The declaration was to state that all senseless atrocities, committed by either side should stop immediately. The DFLC would begin working on the hearts and minds of 'the people'. Above all the DFLC would promise to work peacefully to establish a democratic government and free Cabinda with a full constitution and Bill of rights. Additionally the DFLC would restore all nationalised property to its rightful owners and honour all international trade agreements. Negotiations to settle the detailed terms of the handover of the province from Angola were to be demanded immediately.

Gunter Siegburg and Moses Lubala had also signed a private protocol, more a contract really. The contents would not be published. In essence the DFLC had in perpetuity handed over the day to day '*management*' of its affairs to an '*independent consultancy*', for the time being headed by Gunter Siegburg. Security, finance, mineral rights (oil & gas production) and matters of policy would become the responsibility of the Consultant or his appointed representatives. In return the Consultant would ensure the prosperity and security of the new State and most importantly its President.

The two formal agreements were backed up by a very personal verbal understanding between Siegburg and Lubala. It was not complicated. Siegburg would make Lubala President of a '*free*' Cabinda. Siegburg would get assets returned and receive substantial ongoing management fees. There was no ambiguity on the final point; if Lubala tried to back out of the deal at a later date Siegburg would have him killed!

Moses Lubala, finally allowed into the yacht's saloon to taste the luxury that awaited him, finished his whisky as the anchor dropped into the waters off Boma town. The two men walked to the side of the yacht where the skiff was being launched, ready to take him ashore. They smiled at each other and shook hands, Moses nervous, Siegburg confident.

"Go and begin to organize your people," said Gunter.

Moses nodded. "I will and one day I will have one of these," he said referring to the yacht.

As he prepared to get into the skiff a man came forward pulling Feliz by the arm. "What about this one? What should I do with him? He's worse than useless."

Siegburg looked to Moses. "Do you want him?"

Once again Feliz's future, his very life, hung on the whim of another.

"I'll take him with me," replied Moses. "I will be able to afford better servants soon but for now he will do."

Chapter 5
8th August 1995
Long Island, New York

The weather could have not been better on the day. The sun was rising into a clear blue sky. It was a school day, but not an ordinary one. Melanie had gotten up early and prepared a special breakfast whilst Simon had busied himself around the front of their detached, double-fronted *postcard* house in Suffolk County, the most desirable part of Long Island. He hoped the surprise was total.

Together, Melanie and Simon had tiptoed up the wide staircase, their steps muffled by the thick pile carpet. On the walls hung enlarged framed photographs of animals in their natural habitat, the best ones they had taken, the ones that had been published in magazines all over the world and served as a reminder of how fortune had smiled on the photographer and his journalist wife.

Melanie opened the door slowly. They walked into the room and held hands as they looked at the child in the bed sleeping peacefully. They did not see a black- skinned African girl. They didn't see the colour of her skin at all; they saw the daughter they both loved so much.

Simon looked at his wife and was sure he saw a tear of happiness in the corner of her eye. He bent down and gently touched the child on her shoulder.

"Grace darling, wake up. Happy birthday sweetheart."

Grace opened her sleepy eyes and gently smiled.

"Your sixteenth! We have surprises for you."

At this perfect time Simon and Melanie never thought that Grace would have a surprise of her own for them by the end of the day.

Breakfast was early. As Grace got ready Melanie Shapiro prepared pancakes, waffles and peanut butter and jelly sandwiches, Grace's sometime favourite but unusual way to start the day. Simon placed the first wrapped present on the table, in Grace's place, together with a birthday card in a large pink envelope and another smaller envelope.

Grace came down, smiling, possibly a little less cheerful than on a normal day, but Simon and Melanie didn't notice.

"Sit down darling," said Melanie barely able to contain her excitement. "Open your card first."

Grace did as she was instructed. She looked inside the card and read the greeting. *"With lots of love to our darling daughter on her sixteenth birthday. Mom and Dad"*.

Grace smiled. "That's really nice. Thank you." She closed the card and put it on the table.

"Now the present. Open the present." Melanie's excitement was growing.

The package was big but soft. Grace carefully took off the gift wrapping to expose layers of tissue paper. Folding back the tissue she saw scarlet-red velvet material. She lifted it. "Oh, a dress Mom, it's beautiful. I love it."

"It's not just a dress." Melanie stepped forward and picked up the clothing by its shoulder pads, "Look darling, it's your first real evening gown. Isn't it beautiful?"

"It's beautiful Mom."

"Do you like it, I mean really like it? If you don't like it we can exchange it and if it doesn't fit properly the lady at Bloomingdales says we can take it back for a fitting and adjustment!"

"It's fantastic Mom, it really is," replied Grace taking the dress from her mother and carefully putting it back in the tissue paper. "I don't want it to get messed up," she explained.

"Just the envelope now," her mother pushed it towards her. "Then we can eat."

Inside were four tickets for *"Phantom of the Opera"*.

Melanie clapped her hands with excitement. "Daddy and I are going to take you to a Broadway show! You'll be able to wear your gown! There's a spare ticket so you can bring a friend! "

"It's great, really great. Thanks a million."

Simon was sitting at the far end of the kitchen table. "Do I deserve a kiss? I think I do."

Grace got up and gave her Dad a hug. "Thanks Dad, thank you Mom. The presents are fantastic. She returned to her chair.

"So what are you going to have for breakfast? I've made everything. Pancakes, waffles, ham and eggs, or.... wait for it .... peanut butter and jelly sandwiches."

Grace didn't reply.

"Cat got your tongue then?" asked Simon.

"Do you know what I'd really like?" said Grace in a quiet tone, looking at the table. "I'd like some porridge, just some porridge."

Melanie threw her hands up in the air. "What! Porridge, with all those nice things I've made?"

Simon saw the look on Grace's face. "Hold on a second. It's Grace's birthday. If she wants porridge, then porridge she shall have. Perhaps she's going through a Goldilock's phase," he joked.

Grace spooned the porridge into her mouth, eating it with quiet contemplation. She declined the offer of sugar or honey, eating it just as it came.

As soon as she'd finished Simon said, "Let's go, we've got to make a move. I need to get you to school."

"What's the rush Dad? We have plenty of time," replied Grace.

"I got a lot on today darling, I need to get you to school real early," lied Simon.

Grace grabbed her school bag and coat. "Okay, come on." she said making her way to the front door. Simon and Grace followed passing secret stifled sniggers between themselves. Grace opened the front door. A strange car was in the drive, a silver Honda saloon."

"Whose is that?" asked Grace turning to look at her parents.

Simon tossed a bunch of keys at her which she caught.

"Yours darling, it's your special present from Daddy and I," replied Melanie.

"But I don't have a licence."

"Yes you do," replied Simon handing over a New York learner's licence. "You can drive if I sit with you so long as it's not between the hours of 9 and 5 on a weekday. That's why I need to get you to school before nine!" Simon smiled.

"But I've never driven on the road!" protested Grace.

"You've driven my car up and down the drive enough times. This is smaller and it's automatic. It's only a couple of miles. We'll take it slow. Then I'll drive it back and pick you up at the end of school. You'll get a chance to show off to your friends."

"Okay, I'll drive there," said Grace nervously, "but I'll walk home from school. I don't want to show off in front of my friends."

Simon thought for a moment. "Okay that's good. I respect that."

"Good luck honey," shouted Melanie as Grace and her father tentatively pulled away.

Grace did walk home from school, not with a bunch of friends but alone. Not that she didn't have friends, she had lots of them. It was just that today she wanted to be alone. After school Grace sat with her parents and opened the remainder of her birthday presents each of which was received with gratitude. There was

44

just the three of them for the special birthday dinner. Her parents had said she could have friends, she could have had a party had she wanted, but Grace opted for the family meal. It was after seven when they'd finished eating and gone to the living room. Grace sat in an armchair alone, her parents on the couch. Despite all their efforts Simon and Melanie were unable to transmit their enthusiasm to their only child. It became too much for Melanie.

"Darling, we can see you're unhappy. We don't know why, we've done our best, we only want you to be happy. Did we do something wrong?"

Grace didn't reply; she didn't have to. Her eyes became suddenly moist and her head dropped.

Alarmed, Melanie sprang up and dashed over to her daughter. She went on to her knees and held her daughter's hand. "Oh sweetheart, you're breaking our hearts. Tell us what's wrong."

Grace began to sob. "That's what's wrong," she said looking at her hands."

"You don't like me holding your hand?"

"No, look just look. Your hand is white, mine is black!" the sobbing became uncontrollable. "You are the best parents in the world. Nobody could have a better Mom and Dad. I have everything any sixteen year old could possibly want, and it's all thanks to you. I love the two of you so much, nothing can ever change that and I can't bear the thought of hurting either of you. But I know I come from Africa and I had a real mother there. I know something bad happened to her but you never wanted to tell me much. Sometimes I think about her and then I try to put the thoughts out of my head. But today it's my birthday, the day my real mother gave birth to me. It's an important day for her too and I can't share it with her but I can't stop thinking about her." Tears were freely running down Grace's cheeks by now and Melanie could feel the flood welling up within her too.

Simon came over and put his arms around the two women in the world that meant the most to him. They held the embrace for a while before Melanie pulled away.

"Give me a moment," she said as she left and went upstairs.

She was only gone a few minutes and returned with a small paper wrapped package.

"Grace, I knew we had to have this conversation some time but I never thought it would be on your birthday. We know nothing about your real family. We found your mother when she was already dead. We can only be honest and tell you that what we saw was horrid. We took you from her side. When we were there I took this and kept it, always intending to give it to you one day. I guess now is that day."

Melanie gave Grace the package. She slowly unwrapped the yellow ageing paper. Inside was a rough necklace, unique, made from coloured stones panned from a riverbed in Cabinda.

"This was my mother's?"

"I took it from her neck," replied Melanie. "It's precious little, I'm sorry."

"No it's just precious," replied Melanie putting the necklace over her head.

"You know Grace you are right. Me and your mom have been selfish. We have tried to steal all your love just for ourselves. That's not right. We know you will always love us and will not abandon us but we also have to appreciate you do have a different background. In exchange for all the love you have given us over the years I promise, here and now, I am going to do my best to find out what happened to your birth mother."

For a long time they stayed together in silence, squeezing each other tightly.

The next morning, before nine, Simon Shapiro made the call that would start the family quest.

Burt Zimmerman had been through a tough time but it had come right in the end. It had started on a Monday morning. He'd been at his desk in the large open- plan office. He was reading some briefing notes and the supporting reports from young field operatives. It came on quite quickly. At first he'd begun to feel a bit hot and clammy. He loosened his neck-tie and wiped his forehead with the sleeve of his shirt before leaning over to his colleague at an adjacent desk.

"Hey Beth is the air-con working okay?"

"Yeah, I think so," she'd replied without looking up from her work.

A little while later Burt began to feel nauseous. He could feel the excess production of sour saliva in the back of his mouth.

"Gee I'm not feeling so good," he'd said.

Beth looked up. "You look really pale," she'd replied. "Want me to get you some water?"

"Thanks, but I'll take a stroll over to the water dispenser myself. Might make me feel better," he'd said.

They were his last coherent words for more than four weeks. He'd hardly taken six steps when the pain hit him in the chest like a sledgehammer. He'd wobbled for a second or two and then hit the ground and lost consciousness almost immediately. All in all it was to be his lucky day!

Dexter, the newest member of the office team, had been keen to get involved and had volunteered to become the office 'first aider'. With youthful enthusiasm he'd put his name down for every available course and, only the previous week, he'd spent a day in the basement training rooms learning about resuscitation and how to use the new defibrillators that were now positioned on every floor. Dexter had paid attention and by the time the paramedics had arrived he had, in textbook fashion, restarted Burt's heart and placed him in the three-quarter prone position. The paramedics had got a line into him as he lay on the floor. The trip to the Emergency Room at the local hospital had been short and swift. Because it was Monday morning it was quiet and the doctors and nurses were able to work on Burt without distraction. The emergency bypass surgery, which should have taken two hours at most, lasted for six hours – the complications primarily due to his excessive weight and poor physical condition. Burt had been placed in intensive care and kept so highly sedated that during the next days he just drifted in and out. Although the operation had been a success he had not responded for a long time and the doctors were worried that he was just going to fade away but somehow the constant presence of Faith, his wife, her kind words and soothing touch had gotten through to him and one morning he'd spoken his first word.

"Water." His voice was dry and husky.

The nurse had nodded and Faith had held the paper cup of iced water to his lips for him to sip. At last he'd got the water he'd set out to get four weeks previously.

From then on the going got better. The recovery had speeded up. Faith took Burt home and put him on a diet that'd he'd have laughed at previously – but he didn't laugh now. Burt, for his part, followed the exercise regime he'd been given to the letter. He got stronger as the pounds fell off him. Faith had to buy him new clothes; his waist measurement went from 42 inches to 34, a size he hadn't been since he'd joined the Agency. Within five months he was splitting logs in preparation for the coming winter and feeling better than he had since he was at high-school.

The Agency doctor had been effusive over Burt's condition but had said that his hands were tied. The CIA just didn't employ field operatives with his medical history. Personnel had been good and offered him several alternative desk positions but they all involved either a demotion or some mind-numbing repetitive position. At first when early retirement on medical grounds was suggested he'd balked at the idea but as time went on the thought had become more attractive to him.

He discussed it with Faith.

"Sure we'll have a smaller pension than we expected," she said. "but we can cut our cloth. We can downsize, move to the country. We can have a good life. I'll get the garden I always wanted and I'll still have you.

Simon and Melanie had picked Grace up at the school gates. The drive had taken the better part of three hours. They'd never been to the house before so they had trouble finding Teak Lane in the dark. In fact they'd never been to Bowie, Maryland previously.

It was a first for Burt and Faith Zimmerman too. They'd only moved to the house six weeks previously, Simon, Melanie and Grace would be the first family that were coming to stay, even if it was just for a weekend. Melanie was the daughter of Faith's sister. To say the families were close would have been an exaggeration. They met on family occasions, exchanged Christmas cards and occasionally, when they remembered, birthday cards. Simon knew that Burt had been something in the CIA and he'd been involved in Africa for a time; Burt knew that Simon was a pretty good photographer and made a nice living selling his work to glossy magazines all over the world. He also knew that they'd '*found*' Grace on one of their assignments and adopted her, which was pretty convenient as it turned out that Melanie was unable to have children of her own. The call had been a surprise as had been the request to visit. Burt knew there had to be a good reason. But they didn't talk about it that Friday evening. The conversation was just about Burt's health and how wonderful the new house was.

It was Saturday afternoon, when they were sitting in the garden after Burt had cooked the barbeque, before Melanie began to talk. She told the story of Grace's birthday and the family '*pledge*' they had made together. Burt and Faith listened without interruption until Melanie had run out of words.

"Oh darling," Faith had said to Grace. "That's really touching. It must be very tough on you. It's so nice you think of your real mother and about your roots. We just think of you as part of the family. I guess we didn't pay any attention to your feelings. Burt and I will help, if we can, won't we Burt?"

48

"What is it you would like me to do?" asked Burt, his words a little harsh, not out of a lack of compassion, but more a reflection of his innate common sense coming to the fore.

"I'd like to know about my Mom and my family, who they were and what happened to them," said Grace.

"I really don't want to be negative," began Burt, "but Africa is a big place. Where you come from, Angola, has been in turmoil for decades and they don't keep records like we do. What I mean is there's no public record's office we can just write to. Even the Agency with all its resources would have difficulty getting the detailed information you want, especially since the trail has been cold for sixteen years! More than that, I'm retired now and there are strict rules about the contact I can have. I can't even pick up the phone and see what they've got on record at Langley."

Grace, with youthful naivety, had been hoping for more. "I don't even know how Africans live, what life I would have had if it hadn't been for Mom and Dad, I don't know anything. I just want to share a little and understand."

"Do you know Burt," interjected Melanie, "for breakfast on her birthday she had porridge because she thinks that's what African's eat!"

"I like porridge in any case," chipped in Grace.

"Well I can help you on that one," he replied with a smile. "They don't grow oats in Africa; it's too hot. So no porridge, well not as you know it. What Africans call porridge is really what we call corn, corn-flour to be precise. They mix corn-flour with hot water."

Grace screwed up her nose, "That doesn't sound very nice. Do they mix it with anything, say honey or jelly?"

"I never had it myself, but I don't think so. They don't have larders and refrigerators like we do, not in the bush."

"I thought Africans lived in the jungle, why do you call it the bush? What's the difference?" asked Grace.

"Yeah, you really don't know too much do you? Maybe we can help with that a little."

"I'd like that."

Burt was thoughtful for a while. "This is really a long shot. There was a man, a Limie, Scottish to be precise. I worked with him and we became friends, well almost. He was very nice. I liked him. He married a real African Princess and went to live with her and all her family and I mean all. He bought a farm and moved the whole tribe in! They've really got a little community going the last I heard."

49

"A real African Princess! I didn't think they existed anymore," said Simon.

Burt shook his head. "Unfortunately this one doesn't, she was tragically killed by some very bad people."

"But he stayed on with the tribe?"

"Yep, I think so."

"He sounds like a nice man. Can you contact him?"

"I'll try, but don't get your hopes up."

Chapter 6
10th August 1995
Windhoek, South West Africa

The ritual began in the same way. Freifrau von Swartzstein fussed around her husband in the upstairs dressing room in front of the mirror. He walked down the stairs and the black servant with white gloves opened the door into the meeting room. The others stood and van Swartzstein took his seat. The meeting would normally begin with the reading of the prepared formal reports but today there was a slight deviation. Gunter Siegburg spoke first and without invitation.

"Excuse me please. I have just returned from an important visit and have not prepared a formal report. I can give only a verbal one."

Of the group only Gunter Siegburg could have got away with such an intrusion and break in protocol. But only just. Von Swartzstein frowned and reluctantly half nodded.

"You can give your verbal report after coffee. Let us begin with the normal reports."

Each of the men read from their prepared text with von Swartzstein hanging on to every mundane detail as if it were critical. Finally it was Hueber, the accountant's turn. He was unusually nervous as he began reciting endless figures and statistics relating to income and expenditure. One figure made von Swartzstein raise his eyebrows in mock shock, mock because he had already read the report and had prepared his response. He had decided to deviate from the norm and take the unprecedented action of questioning Hueber on his report before the coffee break.

"Herr Hueber, can you explain the sudden and large drop in our current cash accounts? It is quite dramatic."

Hueber was prepared. "The decline in our cash is indeed dramatic. The main reason for this is that Herr Siegburg has spent money far beyond his approved limit, some of it inexplicably on the charter of a luxury yacht! He has not been available to give me an explanation and I note he has not presented a formal report to this meeting. I am mystified and, like you, await with anticipation his verbal report."

The ball had been firmly placed in Gunter Siegburg's court.

"Coffee," said von Swartzstein.

There was none of the usual jockeying for position on the terrace. It was a relaxed break, smiles and jokes. Nobody need

51

worry, the focus of the second part of the meeting had been established.

The men followed von Swartzstein as he made his way back into the meeting room. On the table in front of each person was a blue cardboard folder. Hueber went to open his.

"Please wait a few moments," Siegburg said to the accountant with a tone of finality.

Von Swartzstein was curious and a little amused. "You may make your report now."

"I have recently made an important visit to Cabinda. I returned about two weeks ago and have been busy making arrangements as a result of the productive meeting that took place there.

As we are all aware it is off the coast of Cabinda that the oil fields lie that we have so heavily invested in and have now all but lost. The meetings I had were with the man who is to be the first independent President of Cabinda."

"Cabinda in not a country."

Gunter Siegburg didn't see who spoke, but it didn't matter.

"That is not strictly true," he continued, speaking without notes but with confidence. "Cabinda was inhabited by the Portuguese in 1482 but it was not until 1885 that it became a Protectorate of Portugal by formal treaty and became known as the Portuguese Congo. Angola was a physically and politically separate Portuguese colony. That was the status at the foundation of the United Nations in 1946. Then in 1956, Portugal, purely for convenience decided that Cabinda should be administered not from Lisbon in Portugal but from Luanda in Angola. The then Angolan colonial government treated Cabinda as if it was another province of Angola. When Angola gained independence from Portugal in 1975 everyone just assumed that Cabinda was going to be part of Angola. But the truth of the matter is that Cabinda is legally still a Protectorate of Portugal. Angola has no legal claim to the territory. Those are the facts."

"Why haven't the people of Cabinda pressed their case then?" asked von Swartzstein.

"In a way they have," replied Siegburg. "There is a liberation movement and it has popular support. It is led by a man called Moses Lubala. It is this man I have been talking to. He has made little progress however. Firstly his campaign is primitive and pays little attention to international considerations. He relies too much on African brutality. I have spoken to him on the matter and I think we have an agreement. Secondly he has met fierce opposition from the Angolan government who are of course anxious to maintain control of the oil fields."

"Do you think they will be any less anxious to hold on to the oil fields because you have become involved?" snapped Hueber, annoyed that Siegburg appeared to be wriggling off the hook.

"It is easier now not because I am involved but because the situation has recently changed." Siegburg's answer was ready. "The Angolan government is chaotic and unorganised, incapable of achieving very much. The reason they have managed to maintain control for so long is that Cuban soldiers have bolstered the Angolan Government and guarded the oil fields. But now the Cubans have been forced to withdraw by international agreement and the Angolans are vulnerable."

Hueber had not given up. "The International community will not stand for it."

"They will not only stand for it," replied Siegburg, "they will support a regime change because the new Government will promise to denationalise the oil industry immediately and give back to the oil companies, which are all American or European, their controlling interests. All the Western Governments will support the move."

"Hueber," said von Swartzstein, "unless you have a more valuable contribution to make it would be better for you to keep quiet." The humiliating put-down was complete. "Continue Gunter."

"Please excuse me Herr von Swartzstein I took the liberty of getting your wife to prepare some files whilst we were having coffee."

Von Swartzstein looked at his wife sitting in the corner making notes. She lifted her head and smiled.

"If you open the files you will find on top the contract I have signed with Moses Lubala. It is of course subject to ratification by this committee. It clearly states the direction Mr Lubala is to take and our part in the proceedings. I think you will find it in order."

There was silence for a few moments as the men quickly scanned down the main points of the lengthy document. As heads started to lift Gunter Siegburg continued.

"Also in the files you will find photocopies of a newspaper article recently published in Portugal's main newspaper giving details of the change in policy of Cabinda's liberation movement. It was published in Lisbon to ensure that the Portuguese are clear as to their position – they are still the international protectors of Cabinda – officially."

Siegburg continued talking for forty-five minutes explaining in detail what had happened and what he had achieved and finally concluding: "In summary gentlemen if we make a little effort we will recover all our lost investments and the costs associated with recovering them. Furthermore I have a contract binding us to this outcome."

Nothing can satisfy the almost innate desire for order in the German mind than a legally binding contract.

Freiherr Artur von Swartzstein raised his head, took a deep breath and smiled.

"This, gentlemen, is what we have been missing, divine inspiration and decisive leadership. This is what has been absent from previous meetings. We will consider this document for twenty-four hours. If anybody has any objections they must contact me within that time. There is no need for a formal vote; if nobody objects we will consider the contract accepted."

"I think that concludes our business and concludes it in a very satisfactory manner."

Gunter raised his hand. "There is just one small matter. It will be sometime, maybe a year or two before matters are concluded."

"I understand that," said von Swartzstein.

"There will be some expense in the meantime. We must stand ready to lend a hand and push the process forward. It may need *'decisive action'* and that will cost money. Of course a grateful Moses Lubala will refund all the expenses when he can."

"Of course. Hueber see that Gunter gets what he needs."

"What about the luxury yacht?" was Hueber's last futile attack.

"That's simple," replied Gunter. "I was concluding a major international agreement with a President elect. I could not be expected to have done that in some dingy hotel bedroom could I?"

"Of course not," said von Swartzstein. "Perhaps you would like to join myself and my wife for dinner where we can discuss the details of the project. The rest of you may leave."

Dinner was served outside on the manicured lawn. Gunter was excused for not having formal attire. When they had finished Freifrau von Swartzstein left the table and the two men continued talking over coffee, cigars and brandy.

"You have saved the fund Gunter. Veterans and their families will be forever in your debt."

"Thank you, Freiherr von Swartzstein. I am glad we are alone as there is something else I wanted to say that is not for other ears"

Von Swartzstein shifted uncomfortably in his chair. Under normal circumstances he did not like surprises. "Go on."

"What I have outlined is the return of our assets and the associated cash returns, as well as our expenses. But there is more. Moses Lubala is so pleased with our suggestions that it has been agreed that we should have an ongoing involvement in the running of his country; this includes the running of all the key ministries. There will of course be a reward for providing the service, a very substantial reward I believe. To my mind, and please correct me if I am wrong, your family have the experience of managing large estates and complex institutions. I believe the ongoing management of Cabinda should not fall to the committee – it is more appropriate that you personally take control of the country."

Von Swartzstein leaned back in his chair and placed both hands flat on the table. He allowed his mind to reminisce about the times his family had owned large estates and participated in the governance of Germany.

"I think that is wholly appropriate," he said. "I can think of no one better than myself for such a task. And to show my gratitude to you for your work so far I am going to raise your salary by ten percent immediately. How do you feel about that?"

"Most grateful," lied Gunter, his loyalty put into question for the first time by the miserly response.

Unaware of his mistake Freiherr Artur von Swartzstein of Brandenburg drew deeply on his cigar, blew a cloud of smoke into the still air and contemplated the glorious past and magnificent future.

Chapter 7
15th September 1995
LONDON

Ralph Foulkes left the Foreign and Commonwealth Office by the front door. He went to the top of Whitehall, crossed Trafalgar Square and took Charing Cross Road, passing the National Gallery on the left. St Martin's was across the road. The words of the children's rhyme sneaked into his mind as they always did when he walked past, *"Oranges and lemons say the bell of St Clements, I owe you five farthings say the bells of St Martins…"* . Just before the turning for Leicester Square he walked into the little boutique Italian restaurant. She was already there, waiting, seated at a table.

"Am I late," he asked with furrowed brow.

"No," she replied without getting up but offering her cheek. "I was early."

Ralph bent and gave her a reluctant peck before sitting down. "This is a bit of indulgence on my part really. We could have done this over the phone or you could have come to the Foreign and Commonwealth Office but I thought the phone a little too impersonal and quite frankly I'm fed up with our hospitality; there's only so many tea cakes and crumpets you can eat."

Jane laughed. "I'm with you on that and I was happy to get away. I'm only here for the grand tour of MI6's new building at Vauxhall. They invited a bunch of us up from Cheltenham. It reminds me of a school trip."

"Nevertheless an impressive building, very dramatic, right on the Thames, but not really in keeping with a '*secret service*' I'd have thought."

"It's the new philosophy. It's a service that deals in secrets. The organisation itself is not supposed to be secret. And have you seen our new buildings?"

"No I'm afraid getting to GCHQ wouldn't really fit in with my role."

"The Nissan huts have all gone and been replaced with something that looks like a spaceship. I liked it like it was before, sort of cosy. It's antiseptic now."

"Changing face of intelligence gathering I suppose."

"The electronic world is now in fashion; the new vogue phrase is *"Cyber Space"*. I don't know myself. Perhaps it'll just fizzle out."

The waiter came to them. "I'm having Hawaiian Pizza," said Ralph, "How about you?"

"Boring chicken and rocket salad I'm afraid," said Jane patting her stomach.

"And two cappuccinos?"

Jane nodded. "So how is it going with you, she asked. "I have to say you look completely different; I don't know bigger, more confident, I can't quite put my finger on it."

"Well I'm a Permanent Under Secretary now."

"Congratulations, that's great news, well done." Her enthusiasm was genuine. "And how's your, boss, Sir Basil?"

"Not so good there. He's 'Whitehall' through and through. Couldn't fault him on that but, and this is strictly '*entre nous*', he made a few bad calls. His judgement was coming into question in high places and he reacted badly. He was pompous at the best of times but he started to lose it with the politicians. It was suggested, in layman's terms, that he was losing his marbles and he wouldn't make sixty-five."

"Early retirement on health grounds?"

Ralph raised his eyebrows in horror. "Oh no nothing so drastic. No, he was awarded a peerage; he's in the House of Lords now. It's the best place for him. They're used to dealing with people in his condition."

Jane laughed aloud. "You're bloody magic you lot, I love it!"

Ralph smiled back. "And you? How are things with you and what's happening with Duncan and yourself?"

Jane shrugged meekly. "I'm sort of ready to give up GCHQ and move out there but I don't think Duncan is ready and I don't want to push him; I want him to get there on his own steam. But I get out there as often as I can and it's all good."

"I'd heard something to that effect - about you getting out there quite frequently that is. That's why I asked for this meeting."

Jane raised her eyebrows. "Go on, I'm intrigued."

"It's something that would normally go for routine analysis but I've got a feeling you might like to get involved. I'll tell you the story and if you're interested we'll go on from there.

Some time ago we got a routine report from our Lisbon Embassy. They'd picked up a newspaper article. It was about some place called Cabinda and some junior member of staff, trying to make a name for himself, sent out a briefing document on general circulation no less. Damn fool has caused us no end of trouble. I didn't even know where Cabinda is nor did anybody else in the office! To be honest the Minister doesn't give a hoot; he thinks that African politics are best avoided. I have to say I agree. We all hoped that it would just die a death. The gist of the briefing is that apparently there's some kind of separatist movement developing there. It's got nothing to do with us '*per se*', different sovereign states and all that guff. However it looks like some bright spark in the Exchequer had nothing better to do but delve deeper.

It appears that in the past, and I don't know how many years ago exactly but it was at the height of the Angolan war, the local oil industry was nationalised. All our big companies, Shell, BP and God knows who else, and of course all the American companies, had their assets confiscated and the Exchequer ended up paying compensation to the British companies because the Angolans wouldn't. The compensation figures went on to the '*to be collected later*' ledger in the Treasury – where they have stayed in peaceful bliss until now. According to the Lisbon briefing it appears this new liberation movement has declared that it will hand back all confiscated assets if and when it comes to power. That has made a few ears prick up in Number 11; nothing like the smell of cash to get the Chancellor of the Exchequer rubbing his hands. Now the Exchequer wants to know what is going on and when can it have its money back!

We have to be seen to be taking action so I thought you might take it up and give us a blandish report. In the meantime, if you felt you needed a field trip out to 'Southern Africa' I think we could support that."

Jane nodded. "So if I were to suggest writing up my report, say, at a farm in the Okavango Delta you wouldn't mind too much?"

"That would be fine by me," Ralph smiled.

Jane dropped her jaw in mock shock. "Ralph Foulkes, if I didn't know you were incorruptible I'd say you were offering me a bribe to brush something under the carpet. Am I right?"

Ralph's face reddened. He immediately went on the defensive. "No, no, not at all. If there is anything going on we'd want to be the first to know."

Jane mocked Ralph's reaction, Ralph smiled sheepishly.

Chapter 8
18th September 1995
Stirling Farm, Okavango Delta, Botswana

It had worked out for the best really. It's funny how things do that sometimes. It had been going on for well over a year and now it was starting to escalate.

Nobody had quite got over Gus' death; they were still going through the motions. No new routine had been established and it was strangely quiet, particularly after Jane had gone back to work in England.

The stalwart turned out to be Mary Scobie as usual who despite advancing years and visible frailty remained amazingly defiant in the face of adversity. Her brain was razor sharp and although she knew that it would be sooner rather than later that she would be following Gus she was able to talk about death with amazing candour and clarity. Her message was very simple really. There were many Gods and nobody knew for certain which of them, if any, was the real God. All that a person could do on this earth was to accept that the inevitable would come. In the meantime they should do all they could to make their life journey, and that of everybody else's they knew, a little better. That's what she did.

The first contact had been a short fax. Burt Zimmerman had asked if Duncan remembered him and wondered if he could help with a family problem. A few communications flowed back and forth. Duncan got enough information to get a handle on the problem but he felt he had to be honest and say right out that he would not be able to do anything to trace her family. The only way that could be done was to organise an expedition to the area and ask around. The chances of getting a result could only be described as remote. He felt bad about that but he had an idea he thought might help.

He told James and Maggie about Grace and asked if one of them would like to write to her. Maggie thought Grace was a bit old for her and James was not going to write to a girl – full stop. So he sent a fax to Burt Zimmerman suggesting that Grace wrote first. A week later two handwritten sheets came through on the machine. They lay in the tray for a couple of days. Finally one morning at breakfast Duncan asked would one of them please reply, even if it was just for the sake of good manners. Maggie said she'd write something the next day.

"It's okay I did it this morning" said James without raising his eyes from his plate.

Duncan and Mary Scobie exchanged quiet smiles without James noticing.

They started off at one a week but quickly escalated. James would make his way to the fax machine and hang about until the sheets came through and quickly scoop them up for private appreciation. One day an air-mail packet arrived. It contained photographs. James, judging by his reaction was not disappointed. He in turn took some photographs around the kraal: the huts the Africans lived in, the women and children and pictures of his uncles, Tembo and Morgan, messing about with toy shields and asagi. At the back of the pile of photos he slipped in a photo of himself. He was relieved when the fax messages did not stop. In a way it was a replacement for Gus, James had found his own friend and confidante; once again all was right with his world.

Grace had got her full driver's permit by the time she was sixteen and a half so for the last year she had been driving herself back and forth to school. As soon as she got home she'd make an excuse to go upstairs. In the privacy of her room she'd boot up her computer and see if there was anything in from James. Simon and Melanie didn't have to ask if she'd received anything; the atmosphere at the dinner table answered that question.

Today Grace never got to the stairs. Her Dad was waiting when she got in. He asked her to come into the lounge. Mom was already there, on the couch.

"Come and sit with me," she'd said patting her hand on the adjacent cushion.

"We didn't want to say anything before, not till we were sure," began her father enigmatically. "But now we have some news that will make you happy. We hope!"

Simon paused for what felt like a long time to Grace. "Well go on tell me," she prompted. "What is it?"

Simon continued. "We've got an assignment in Africa. I'm going to take photographs, Mom is going to do the articles and .... you are coming with us."

Grace could not contain her excitement. "Really, are we going to Africa, are we really going there!" The question was rhetorical; she never doubted them for a second. She hugged her Mom. "Oh thank you so much, thank you."

"Now just so we are clear and you don't get too carried away," continued Simon "we are going for four months. Your Mom and I will have to work and there will be a lot of travelling. Now this is important, Angola is not on the schedule, the commissioning editors don't think the situation is stable enough to visit there. Do you understand – we most probably won't be any further on in trying to find out about your real Mom."

"Yes Dad. But we still might pick up a little information?"

"I doubt that to be honest but you will find out about Africa first-hand."

"Is Botswana on the schedule?"

"Yes it is – the Okavango. And before you ask I've already spoken with Mr Murdoch. We'll be visiting; in fact we will be staying with them for a while."

Grace clapped her hands together in uncontrolled excitement.

Chapter 9
20th September 1995
Luanda, Angola

President Dr Jonathan Marobi was a calm man: a thinker, an academic. Recognised as a philosopher and humanitarian, he'd held the position of Professor Emeritus at Princeton University. It had taken him a long time but his sail was set fair in American academia. By nature he was not a man to rush or take hasty decisions but he was also a kind man with high moral principles.

After the Russians and Cubans had left Angola the country was left in a state of civil war that could have no victors. Neither of the competing factions was strong enough to defeat the other. SADAC, the Southern African Development Community, had sponsored a peace conference. It was decided at that conference that both factions, the MPLA and UNITA would form a government of national unity, under the control of a neutral and mutually respected President. There was only one candidate for the Presidency.

Dr Jonathan Marobi had moved uneasily into uncertain waters by accepting the proposal to become President of Angola, the land of his birth. His move was not motivated by vanity or a thrust for power, two characteristics completely absent from his personality. With, some said, a naïve view of reality, probably nurtured by a career closeted behind the ivy covered walls of America's top universities; he actually thought he might be able to make a difference.

Now the ageing man sat behind his opulent desk in the Presidential Palace waiting to be wheeled out into the public gaze once more, presented to the world as the respectable face of Angolan governance. Friends in America had urged him not to return to Africa saying that he was only adding a cloak of respectability to a corrupt regime but Jonathan, deliberating in his own mind, had not come to that conclusion himself – at least not yet.

Most of the time Jonathan Marobi trod delicately but recently he'd been forced to write to his friend, The Secretary General of the United Nations, to ask a favour. The reply, when it came, did not go to Dr Marobi's desk; it had instead been diverted to the real rulers of Angola.

The Central Committee of the military junta in Angola had little patience for the niceties and nuances of diplomacy. They accepted Jonathan Marobi on sufferance. They had spent the past twenty-five years fighting a war where violence was the final arbitrator. That is why their inclination was to reject the contents of the letter, the one that was formally addressed to the President of Angola and sent by the Secretary General of the United Nations but now rested on the table in front of them.

The reply was couched in unusually warm terms for a formal diplomatic communiqué. For those that understood, between the lines, there was an answer to the problem. For those who didn't or didn't want to understand it was more difficult:

> *To His Excellency President Jonathan Marobi*
> *Jonathan,*
> *You will understand the constraints of my office. I hope what follows is of assistance.*
>
> *Angola, in 1946, being officially an 'external province' of Portugal was not a founding member of the United Nations. However it has since become an independent member of the United Nations in its own right and agreed to accept all the points of the original United Nations' Charter and be bound by resolutions passed by both the General Assembly and Security Council. Its territorial boundaries remain unchanged since its original accession to full membership status.*
>
> *In direct response to your request, I, in my capacity as Secretary General of the United Nations, am forbidden to amend the terms of the membership of any Member State. I cannot add nor subtract, unilaterally, to the specified land mass of any State. Such amendments can only be accomplished by a majority vote in the General Assembly supported by a resolution passed by the Security Council.*
>
> *It is my opinion that any such proposals put before the General Assembly will only succeed if accompanied by a mandate of the people, acceptable to the United Nations, signifying that the occupants of any such territory agree, of their own free will, to the proposed territorial changes of any given Member State. Furthermore, I believe that changes will not be ratified by the Security Council unless there is unanimity in the Security Council and this can best be facilitated if the proposing country betters or matches*

*any substantive condition such as those offered by any
opposing party or entity.*
I hope that this clarifies the situation.
The General Secretary of the United Nations.

"What does this shit mean?" said General Morales, the
Junta's leader.

The Cubans had left Angola, nearly all of them. A handful of
political advisers remained and it was to Lawrence Rossie, one
such advisor, that Morales addressed this question.

Rossie was a short thoughtful man, clean shaven, pleasant
mannered and known for his ability to interpret and simplify
complex situations. He did not disappoint today.

"The Secretary General will not add Cabinda to official
Angolan territory but he recognises the *de facto* situation. If you
want to change your boundaries to include Cabinda in Angolan
territory, you need a mandate - that's a referendum of all the
people who live in Cabinda. He also thinks it would help to get the
change through the Security Council if you offered to give the oil
fields back to the Western countries just like the DFLC are offering
to ....."

Rossie was stopped dead in his tracks by the eruption of
General Morales who thumped the table and jumped to his feet.
"What fucking use is Cabinda without the oil fields! Are they
fucking mad? Do they think I am mad? I don't want a bit of land to
grow bananas – I want the fucking oil – that's what I want. They
are crazy, they are all fucking crazy. I'll kill them all..."

Rossie ignored the outburst and stood his ground impassively
until General Morales had calmed down and retaken his seat.
Then he continued.

"I personally do not agree with the Secretary General. It is my
experience, that when the time comes the Western Governments
will prove to be pragmatic. They will do a deal – a very good deal.
You might have to give them a piece of the cake that is all. But
you will have no negotiating position at all unless you have a clear
mandate. You must hold and decisively win a referendum calling
for the official unification of Cabinda and Angola. The Western
powers are quite stupid in this respect – they actually believe in
democracy. They'll respect the results of a referendum, no matter
how flawed. We just have to play them at their own game."

Morales became calmer but no less determined. "They want a
referendum they can have a referendum and I will win it because I

will kill everybody who doesn't vote for me. But they will not have the oil!"

Rossie smiled. "You won't have to do that. It's quite easy to win an election. Let Jonathan Marobi agree a referendum, let UN Observers come. Play by the rules and if you win it will all be yours legitimately."

"And if we lose the referendum?"

"You shouldn't but if you do there are other things we can do."

"So you are advising to leave it with Marobi? You are saying I should stand back?"

"That is exactly what I am saying."

Chapter 10
2nd January 1996
Stirling Farm

For weeks a growing air of expectation pervaded Stirling farm, but now as the moment drew close, James began to act quite nonchalantly, even disinterested in the main event.

The request by the Shapiro's to use Stirling Farm as their base for an extended 'photo safari' was accompanied with a generous offer of payment. Duncan had, possibly too hastily, agreed to the request, but not for payment. He knew how good the Shapiro's daughter had been for James. He believed both James and Grace had something to gain. It was not till Mary had asked about where the Shapiro's were actually going to stay that Duncan had questioned his own decision.

"Having house guests for a few days is one thing but for several months is a completely different proposition," Mary had said. "The annexe where Gus lived is totally unsuitable; it's just a shed!"

Tembo and Morgan had come up with a solution. They would get the women from the kraal to build an African rondavel near to the farmhouse. That would give the Shapiro's a better sense of real Africa. James was the only dissenting voice. He said the conditions would be too primitive and they should build a proper guest house. In his mind were the letters he had received from Grace and the lifestyle she was used to on Long Island, but he never said it quite like that. A compromise was reached. The size of the rondavel was increased, internal walls positioned for two bedrooms, a living area and a bathroom that had water and was connected to the main farmhouse septic tank. James then, without reference to anybody, proceeded to run an electricity supply to the building and it went on and on until what eventually emerged was what Mary described as "*a five star safari lodge*". At the forefront of the efforts was James, often working late into the night alone. Nobody dared mention his motivation.

Duncan, although pleased with the result, looked at what had been spent and muttered, rather gloomily, "Might as well have built a new house in the first place."

Everybody laughed.

Maggie had run over to the workshops and found James halfway through stripping a Briggs and Stratton petrol motor, his face and hands covered in oil and grease.

"Hey big brother. Are you not going to get cleaned up? The love of your life is about to turn up in less than an hour!"

James turned around sharply and uncharacteristically snapped at his little sister.

"What do you mean? You've been talking about me behind my back haven't you?"

"Hey, I only came to tell you it's getting late and our guests will be here soon. You don't have to get cleaned up for me; stay as you are. I like you stinking like an old oil can."

James calmed down. "Yeah, well I'll be along when I'm finished."

"Fine," replied Maggie turning away."

She'd only gone a few steps when James shouted, "Sis."

She turned to look at her brother. "What?"

"Sorry," he said without looking up from the motor.

Maggie walked on, "Kids!" she whispered under her breath.

There were only three people coming but from the stoop they saw two vehicles approaching, a car and a van. Not only had Melanie packed enough clothes to last the Shapiro's for a very long time, there was also Simon's photographic equipment that virtually filled the van on its own.

Duncan looked at the approaching vehicles and then the lodge.

"It's not going to be big enough," he sighed already beginning to wonder what he had committed himself to.

"They don't travel light do they?" said Tembo grinning.

"Perhaps they've brought all their food with them," chipped in Morgan.

More practically Mary said, "They can use the annexe for storage. It's good enough for that."

The car pulled to a halt a few feet from the house. The African driver got out and opened the door for Melanie. Simon got out of the front passenger seat and let Grace out. Duncan stepped down from the stoop, holding Mary by her arm. Tembo and Morgan followed a few steps behind. Before going forward Maggie looked around just in time to see James come out of the front door of the farm house, still wet from the shower, his hair parted on the wrong side.

"Hello, I'm Duncan. Welcome to Stirling Farm," He shook hands with Simon, Melanie and Grace in turn. "This is Mary."

Mary took a small step forward and held out a thin and weathered hand.

"You must be Duncan's Mom," said Simon.

"No," replied Mary."

"It's a long story," added Duncan. "She's not part of the family – she is the family. You'll find that out soon enough I'm sure. That's Tembo and Morgan standing over there, my brother-in-laws."

Grace smiled. Tembo and Morgan were the first '*real*' African Africans she'd met. A thought suddenly crossed her mind, something she'd never considered before. She whispered a little too loudly to her mother, "Do they speak English?"

The Twins overheard.

Tembo replied in a put on perfect Oxford English accent, "We started to speak English at about the same time as we gave up eating our enemies!"

Everybody laughed.

"They most probably speak it better than me," said Duncan.

Tembo and Morgan stepped forward. Grace held out her hand. The two big men ignored it, each bear-hugging her in turn.

"Welcome back to Africa little sister," said Morgan.

"And this is Maggie, my daughter," said Duncan.

Maggie shook hands with each of the Shapiro's in turn.

"Finally, this is James. Come and say hello James."

James reluctantly stepped forward and shook hands with Simon and Melanie. He turned to Grace, face flushed like a traffic light. He offered a hand so outstretched that he nearly lost his balance.

"How do you do?"

"I'm very well, thank you," replied Grace as coy as him.

"I have to finish a job in the workshop," said James, instantly turning and walking away.

For a moment there was a pregnant pause before Maggie stepped forward.

"You want to see my room?" she asked.

"Yeah, I'd like that," Grace replied.

The kids gone, Duncan looked at the visitors in an apologetic way. "That was truly cringe worthy wasn't it? He's actually been very excited about your arrival."

"We've been going through the same thing. Two miles before your gate Grace asked us to turn the car around and take her home!" replied Simon.

The magnitude of having somebody run a professional photo-shoot became clearer to Duncan. The afternoon was full. The

68

Shapiro family moved into the '*lodge*' and as anticipated the shortage of wardrobe and storage space was a problem. Maggie said they'd brought more clothes with them than the local shop had in stock. The photographic equipment was almost too much for the annex.

Duncan was amazed at the amount of stamina the visitors had. They'd flown from JFK to Jo'burg, only stopping in Jan Smuts transit hotel for twelve hours. They'd then taken an SAA plane to Gaborone before driving for five hours to Stirling Farm.

"Where do you get your energy from?" Duncan had asked Simon as together they carried a large aluminium case into the annex.

"Just running on adrenalin, we're so excited to be here. It'll catch up on us, be sure of that."

The sun set at six and James reluctantly emerged from his workshop. Food was simple; their first braai, their first experience of the South African barbeque. The meat was duiker served with pap, tomato relish and melees, the latter being the only thing the Shapiro's recognised, corn-on-the-cob.

"The meat is wonderful, what is it asked?" asked Simon.

"Duiker, a type of antelope – game meat," replied Duncan.

"Never heard of a duiker," said Melanie.

James, plucking up courage, attempted to make his first contribution to the conversation.

"They're tiny cute animals, fawn fur, about twenty inches high with huge brown eyes. About the nearest thing you will have seen to them is Bambi I suppose." He laughed.

Melanie put her fork down, her appetite for the meat suddenly diminished.

Mary, rarely one to criticise, shook her head and just said, "James!"

Simon broke the silence that followed. "What's pap?" he asked.

"It called different things in different parts. In Zimbabwe it's called Sadza. It's really just corn-meal mixed with water. It's the staple food for indigenous Africans; it's their main food – for all meals; at breakfast they mix it with a bit of milk, if they have it, and call it porridge. A far cry from what we know as porridge I have to admit. It's not much of a diet to be honest," replied Duncan

It was Grace's turn to put her fork back on to the plate, memories of her birthday breakfast and her mother flooding back. She struggled to stop the tears.

Duncan looked around helplessly. "I'm sorry; I didn't mean to upset you. What did I say?"

"It's a complex story," replied Simon, putting an affectionate arm around his daughter. "We'll tell you again."

Melanie had regained her composure, and abandoned the meat on her plate.

"Let's change the subject," she said. "When Simon suggested we ask you if we could come here I told him I thought it would be a big imposition and I was a bit nervous. But I feel so much better now. We didn't know you had that wonderful lodge available. I don't feel half as bad about asking now. I don't feel like we put you to too much trouble after all."

Duncan managed to force a smile, James was somewhat less successful. He stood up and said he was going to bed and left the table.

"What?" asked Melanie. "Did I say something wrong?"

Chapter 11
3rd January 1996
Windhoek, Namibia

Gunter Siegburg hadn't needed the distraction. He had a lot on his plate and because of the summons he might miss his flight to Pretoria. It would set his programme back a few days at a critical point but he knew well enough that when his boss, von Swartzstein whistled, he had to run.

The meeting was to be, as usual, at the house. That was unimportant; what was important was where in the house. If it were in the garden or in the Baron's private accommodation then all was good. If it were in the conference room or the Baron's private office then the Baron had concerns. Today the meeting was to be in the Baron's private office. Gunter waited impatiently in the ante-room, knowing full well the Baron was making him wait purely to demonstrate his own superiority. It was a predictable move as was the Baron sitting in a bigger and higher chair so that he could look down on his subject.

The Baron opened the office door himself and invited Gunter to follow after the briefest of formal handshakes. The Baron smiled, but it was not a warm informal smile, it was no more than good manners required. There were no pleasantries.

"I have the first draft of the last period accounts from Hueber? Have you seen them?

The Baron knew that he could not possibly have seen them. "No, but I am sure I will in due course," replied Gunter. "Is there a problem?"

"Hueber is concerned."

"Hueber is an accountant, he is always concerned. He needs to relax a little," Gunter smiled as he assessed the situation. He knew the mannerisms to watch out for; there were three main ones. If his boss put his hands flat on the desk, palm down, then there was to be no discussion. The Baron's mind was made up and there was no point in arguing. If the Baron leaned back in his chair and rested his arms on the arms of the chair or better still clasped his hands behind his head, then the argument was won. If the Baron was undecided or confused about an issue he would, involuntarily and unconsciously, gently stroke his chin. All was to play for in this situation. Gunter smiled inwardly. The Baron was stroking his chin.

"If you tell me Hueber's specific problem then I will try to help," continued Gunter.

"There is no specific issue. He is just concerned about the general level of expenditure and the lack of accountability – he doesn't know where the money is going."

Gunter smiled. "Ah, no receipts. That is a problem I have to admit, one that is hard to get around. But it is also not an unfamiliar problem in this part of the world. The type of people we are dealing with do not issue invoices. They deal in cash. There are advantages and disadvantages. Our investment is opaque as will be our dividend. Transparency means everybody can see what is happening and we don't really want that, do we? In any event I believe that I have not spent more than I indicated to you previously. Am I correct?" Gunter only asked the question because he knew the answer.

The Baron nodded gently, agreeing but unconvinced. He stroked his chin once more. "Is everything going according to plan?"

It was a leading question. Gunter knew that.

"No, it is not," he replied.

For a second the Baron let the neutrality of his expression fail but before he had a chance to speak Gunter continued.

"It is going far better than I had imagined."

The relief on the Baron's face was clearly visible. He took a newspaper from the top drawer and placed it on his desk, facing Gunter.

Gunter saw it was the *Frankfurter Allgemeine* two days old and opened on the financial section. Hueber got the newspaper sent to him regularly by post to *check investments*. He was clearly the one who was unnerving the Baron.

A small article at the bottom of the page had been circled in red. The headline was more dramatic than the dull text: *"Angolan Referendum for Control of Oil"*. Gunter read for a few moments, shaking his head from side to side. "I'm disappointed." Gunter looked his boss in the eye. "I wanted to tell you the good news myself!"

"What good news?" asked von Swartzstein, "How can a referendum be good news? The Angolan Government will hold a referendum that will allow Cabinda to become recognised as part of Angola. We all know that African governments never lose elections that they organise themselves!"

Gunter leaned forward and spoke quietly as if he was expounding a great confidence. "I had thought it would take a year or two for the Democratic Front for the Liberation of Cabinda to raise its profile. But this referendum catapults it right into the forefront and more than that it will be able to operate openly. The Angolan Government cannot be seen to persecute the opposition – not too overtly."

"Why? Why won't the Angolans just kill the Cabindan activists?"

"Because this is a referendum for UN recognition so there will be UN observers. If they, the Angolans, engage in illegal activity the vote will be null and void – and we win!"

"But they can carry out a '*black war*', do things secretly."

"We too can operate a '*black war*', but we will do it better."

"What do you mean?"

Gunter lowered his voice further as if he were betraying a deadly secret. Von Swartzstein leant forward to listen better and even began to speak in hushed tones himself. "Go on, tell me."

Gunter took a breath for dramatic effect.

"It is difficult. I have always believed that if it is better that you don't know the answer to a question, then it is better you don't ask the question!"

"What?" asked a puzzled von Swartzstein.

"Let me explain. Sometimes somebody is so important that they would like to do things but dare not do them because the moral standards they are judged on are much higher than those for ordinary people. For example the president of the United States wanted to take action against the Contras in South America. He could not do it because world opinion would judge him harshly. But luckily for the President there were people around him he could trust and they knew what the President wanted. So they did it without telling him. That way when it became news the President was able to say honestly that he knew nothing about it! The Americans even have a name for the system; it's called '*Plausible Deniability*'.

I think you are in a similar position. Some things need to be done for the greater good, but you should not ask too much. In that way your good reputation will never be put at risk."

Von Swartzstein leaned back in his chair and, smiling, rested his arms on the armrests.

"I have never been a great admirer of the Americans," he said "but sometimes I have to admit that they come up with good ideas. I think you are quite correct in not presenting me with a moral dilemma. You must do what you need to do."

"Thank you Freiherr von Swartzstein. I have a plane to catch. Is it all right if I go now?"

"Of course, go. Why are you waiting?"

As Gunter walked towards the door von Swartzstein said, "I will tell Hueber to make sure he assists you."

Gunter stopped and turned to face his boss.

"You know when this is over the financial gain will be tremendous. The sums involved are very large. I know it is not my business but perhaps you need to be making preparations for the control of the new finances. Hueber is fine for '*counting beans*' but perhaps he lacks the creativity or imagination to handle something that is as big as the expected dividends coming our way." Gunter didn't wait for a reply; he left the room knowing he'd stuck another nail in the coffin of that arsehole Hueber.

Gunter made his flight to Pretoria. It was just after seven pm when he walked into the impressive building that housed one of the last bastions of racism in the now multi-racial South Africa. The Club was situated right at the heart of South African politics amongst the impressive colonial buildings that constituted the administrative hub of the country. The German Club was a private members' establishment. It carried on in much the same way as it had done during the Apartheid era, it was just that there were no black staff or servants anymore.

Bernd Groelsh was already at the bar waiting. An impressive six-foot three, he was solid and muscular although his untrimmed moustache betrayed the undisciplined wild-side of his personality. He was no phoney. Bernd Groelsh was at the top of his profession. Initially trained in the German Bundeswehr he'd progressed to the paratroopers. Frustrated at the lack of opportunity for combat in the German Army he'd left and come to South Africa where he fought with relish against the Cubans in Namibia and Angola. When that war had finished he put himself up '*for hire*'. He'd since done stints in Rwanda and the Congo. He believed his skills would always be in demand in Africa. He was most probably right.

The two men hugged, hugged as only comrades-in-arms would.

"You're right on time," said Bernd.

"No thanks to the bastards in Namibia," replied Gunter. "Get me a beer and I need something to eat. Where can we talk?"

The high ceiling of the lounge bar was of ornate plasterwork, the walls panelled in Germanic fashion: heavy dark-stained wood, exaggerated carvings and private booths built into the structure.

The men took one of the booths and sat opposite each other with Bavarian steins and bratwurst on the table between them.

Gunter took a bite of sausage and spoke as he chewed.

"We may have to move faster than I first thought."

Siegburg produced a sheaf of handwritten papers and spread them out in front of Gunter.

"The plan is complete. I only need you to give me the go ahead."

Gunter Siegburg thumbed through the papers.

"I'll study them in detail later. I need to know will the plan give us what we want."

"It will give you Cabinda on a plate and what's more the world will think you are a hero or at least they will think that the African you have in your pocket is a hero."

"Lubala you mean. How many people will you need to complete the operation?"

"Shock troops, about forty-five. I will provide them. They will be expensive but they will be good. They will also have all the technical capabilities. Then I will need about three hundred and fifty native fighters. You are to provide them and I will train them. Some of them must be expendable."

"I have the numbers," replied Gunter, "But they are an undisciplined lot, they are the best of Lubala's guerrilla fighters."

"I will train them to the right standard," replied Bernd. "You will have a Cabindan Liberation Force. But do you have the base I requested?"

"I like that, we can call them the CLF and yes I have the base, Boma, in Zaire. And what about the equipment?"

"A list is included. The arms are easy enough. The other stuff a bit more difficult."

"What about logistics?"

Bernd smiled. That's been less problematic. I have a jump-off base identified, an isolated farm outside Louis Trichardt, near the Limpopo River. It has its own large grass airstrip, big enough for a DC3. Other transport I'm working on, but that won't be too difficult either."

Gunter smiled. "I need you to make a reconnaissance trip as soon as possible.

Bernd Groelsh smiled. "I've already been!"

"To Cabinda?"

"I went in with some oil workers. It wasn't too difficult. Spent two days in the city. I'm happy it will all work."

Beside Still Waters

Chapter 12
3rd January 1996
Stirling Farm, Okavango

"So this is where you work?"

James was startled by the unexpected voice that came from behind.

"Why do you start so early?"

James put his spanner down and turned to face Grace who was standing by the open workshop door dressed in tiny blue shorts and a white '*I love New York*' 'T' shirt.

"I always start at daybreak. I used to do it with Gus. It's cooler now and very peaceful, nobody disturbs me."

"Oh, I'm sorry I didn't know you wanted to be alone. I just wanted...."

James backtracked quickly, "I didn't mean it like that. You're welcome. Come in. You can see what I'm doing."

Grace stepped forward and looked around the workshop: at its benches piled high with oily tools and parts, at the floor space with its half dissembled machinery and at the rough old wooden desk, piled high with drawings and manuals.

"It's just how I imagined it, exactly how you wrote about it in your letters. It's lovely."

"Lovely? Lovely is not how most people describe it. A bloody mess most people say. But I know where everything is!" responded James wiping his hands on a filthy oily rag.

"I think you're putting more dirt on your hands than you are taking off."

James dropped the rag and wiped his hands on his overalls."

"That's better," said Grace, "Now your clothes match your hands."

They laughed together.

"Where are your parents?"

"Still in bed, I don't think we'll be seeing them for some time; they just collapsed last night."

"What's got you up so early?"

Grace shrugged, "I don't want to waste any time. Besides I was hoping for some breakfast."

"Breakfast normally comes from the kitchen – even in Africa. Nothing to eat here but I think Mary has got in some things you'll like. She's considering you as a challenge. Somebody told her that all Americans eat pancakes and syrup for breakfast, so that's what she's doing."

"She went to all that trouble?"

"That's Mary. Mind you she did get some pretty bad advice. She was also told that Americans eat bacon and eggs with their pancakes – on the same plate. That was really funny. She didn't fall for that one though."

"We do," replied Grace wondering what was so strange about that.

"What!"

"Well I don't, but some people do," Grace smiled. "You want to show me around?"

"You've seen most of it already. There's not that much really; the farmhouse, the workshops, the garden. We do have a swimming pool; there's a long story behind that."

"I thought you had an African village."

"The Kraal, you want to see that?"

Grace nodded.

"Let me take my overalls off first."

Grace followed James as he walked along the well-trodden path, around the base of the kopje. He took a shortcut and pushed through some light, lush scrub.

"It's not always this green," he said, "We have had some rain recently. That's unusual."

He was oblivious to the tentative way he was being followed, Grace being careful to put her feet in James's footsteps, her eyes darting back and forth, looking for danger but not really knowing what danger to expect. She sighed with relief when they broke out into the open, a few yards short of the edge of the Kraal.

"Here it is," said James turning to face her.

Grace quickly composed her anxious expression. "It's just how I imagined it. Like in the pictures you sent me."

"That's because they were photographs. Photographs do tend to look like the things you're photographing!" replied James, his voice tinged with sarcasm.

A flash of anger shot across Grace's eyes. "You picked the wrong subject there. My Dad's a professional photographer and I'm not blind or stupid. If you're going to be sarcastic with me better do it on a subject you're more familiar with."

James was taken aback by the sharp response. "I'm sorry. I didn't mean to be rude. It's just the way I talk."

"Not with me you don't. Just because I'm new here don't treat me like an idiot. Right?"

"Right." They were quiet for a moment. James broke the silence. "Are all girls in America so quick off the mark?"

"Just you worry about this one!"

The still morning air was suddenly disturbed by a piercing warbling screech.

James and Grace turned towards the source: the Kraal. On the edge of the village, a cluster of more than a dozen traditional thatched African round huts, stood a woman, short, fat, dressed in an old flowered frock, the front buttons of which struggled to constrain their contents. Her skin was black, very black covering a round smiling face, indeed it would be hard to imagine that a person existed with blacker skin.

"That's Mafutzi," said James. "She's sort of the village head busybody but she's very nice. She's Mary's best friend and she's just spotted us."

As they watched more women appeared, summoned by the call. One or two of the village men looked on from a distance, feigning disinterest. And then there were the children. They came running towards their favourite *'uncle'*. In a moment James was swamped by laughing children. They climbed on him and brought him to the ground by sheer weight of numbers. Grace looked on in amusement at the ridiculous sight of James, gently pushing and shoving, trying to break free from the infantile mob, the whole process shrouded in a veil of laughter.

The women walked slowly forward, Mafutzi at the front. She barked words that were incomprehensible to Grace but were in the language of James's mother; Matabele. The children got up, and ran away, laughing at the mock scolding they had just received.

"Grace this is Mafutzi and the rest of the village women. Mafutzi, this is Grace," said James stumbling to his feet.

Grace stepped forward with an outstretched hand. "How do you do?" she said, just as she'd been taught to do in polite society.

For a second the village women stood in bemused silence. Then Mafutzi came forward and hugged Grace, hugged her so tight that Grace could feel the air being driven from her lungs. The rest of the women surrounded them. When Mafutzi released her clasp the women, now suddenly a chattering herd, dragged Grace away with them, towards the village. Grace managed to look over her shoulder at James, unable to conceal her alarm.

"It's okay," shouted James. "They've been expecting you. They have never met somebody with skin like theirs that speaks with an American accent! Smile and you'll be alright!"

It was nearly two hours later that James, sitting under an Acacia tree with Tembo and Morgan, spotted Grace emerge from between the huts. She walked over to them.

"They said you were here," said Grace, her white 'T' shirt now dirty from a thousand hands and her hair grey with dust, her eyes full and moist.

James was apprehensive, wondering if he should have intervened.

Tembo and Morgan got to their feet.

"Now you have had your introduction to Africa," said Tembo.

"Was it as you expected?" asked Morgan.

"It must have been a frightening experience," added Tembo.

"Did they hurt you?" asked Morgan too quickly.

"Don't be stupid," replied Tembo. "They wouldn't hurt her. But did they scare you?"

"We can tell them off if you want," began Morgan, "One word from....."

"Stop!" said Grace. "It was so wonderful, so, so, wonderful. More than I could have imagined. I feel like I have come home."

James was now standing. "I better take you back to the farmhouse. Everybody will be wondering where you are."

They retraced their way along the path.

"How did the village come to be here," asked Grace.

"It's really a long story," said James.

"Well give me a short version for now."

"My Dad was a soldier in the Rhodesian Army during the Rhodesian war."

"Fighting for the whites?" asked Grace.

"Not really, he was with them but he was actually employed by the British to keep an eye on things."

"A spy?"

"Not quiet, but nearly. Not only were the whites fighting the blacks, the different tribes were at each other's throats. My Mum is a Matable and he saved her from being killed by some Shona fighters. They fell in love and when the war was over they got married. But things didn't work out in Rhodesia. A civil war started between the two tribes. My Dad wanted to leave but my Mum wouldn't leave her people behind. So my Dad bought this farm and brought the whole tribe with him. And that's how we're all here now."

"What happened to your Mum?" Grace asked. The mood changed.

"She died."

"How?" Grace's voice was softer.

"I don't want to talk about it now. I don't want to spoil a nice day. Besides we need to get back, Jane is arriving today."

"Who's Jane?"

The seatbelt light came on. Jane pulled the buckle together and heard the reassuring click. A white stewardess came down the aisle making sure that the trays were up and seats erect, ready for landing. It didn't take her long; the plane was less than a quarter full. Jane was worried, not about the landing, but about something else, something that would not normally concern her, her expenses.

She'd been away from her desk at GCHQ in Cheltenham, England for seven days and would not be back there for a further six. That was a long time for so little in terms of result.

She'd started off flying from London to Lisbon. Two days there had given her precious little. The British Embassy had nothing for her that she'd not have been able to get over the phone. The man at the Portuguese Ministry of Foreign Affairs shrugged his shoulders and shook his head but did offer to take her out to dinner. As for the offices of the '*Democratic Front for the Liberation of Cabinda*', they were just nowhere to be found. All she managed to get was a phone number that had a more or less incomprehensible message on the answer machine. The overnight TAP flight from Lisbon to Luanda had been uncomfortable in the extreme; turbulence was constant, food rubbish and cabin staff rude. The tipsy fat man beside her in business class joked, a few times too often, that TAP stood for 'Take another plane'.

Luanda airport was terrible and it only got worse when she got outside. The driver had demanded $25 over and above the fare just to let her into the shed he called a taxi. The roads were crowded and potholed, the car's air-conditioning didn't work but the driver insisted on the windows being shut and doors locked to deter thieves. There were no seat belts, but they seemed superfluous as the car stank of petrol and all she thought about was fire and the need for a quick exit plan. Her back was bathed in sweat from the shiny plastic seats by the time she arrived at the Ambassador Hotel and she slid around constantly.

At some point in the past the Ambassador Hotel was most probably acceptable. That was the highest accolade she could give it. The embassy had booked her a standard room on the first floor. At the reception desk the smiling male reception clerk had offered a free upgrade to a suite. She'd accepted willingly, hopeful that her luck had changed. The formalities complete she enquired about the lifts to get her to her 'seventh floor room'.

"Sorry," the clerk had replied, "The lifts haven't worked for several weeks. We're waiting for parts from Germany."

She'd asked for her old room back. The clerk, suddenly forgetting all his English and apparently suffering from sudden onset amnesia, somehow managed to convey to her the message that there were no rooms available on lower floors and no, he did not have a record of her previous booking. Eventually she gave up arguing and traipsed up the seven floors to her 'suite', carrying her own suitcase, the bellboy, expecting very little by way of a tip, having suddenly disappeared. She was not disappointed. The air-conditioning was non-functioning, the mini-bar fridge was empty and the amount of mould on the walls was surpassed only by that on the tiles in the bathroom. Jane was too tired to bother; she finished off a bottle of water she'd carried from the aircraft and fell asleep on the bed.

It was late afternoon when she was awakened by a knock on the door. She rubbed her eyes and tried to orientate herself. The knock came again, this time a little harder. Jane went to the door and opened it to find a young woman from the British Embassy standing there, flanked on either side by large Africans.

The woman introduced herself and asked to come into the room. Jane looked at the two men only to be told that they were bodyguards and that they would wait outside. The woman produced two large bottles of water and handed them to Jane explaining that drinking water was a major problem in the city as repairs from the war were still underway. That was about the extent of the good news.

An Under Secretary at the Palace de Justice wanted $500 for an appointment, Jane declined the offer. Nobody was available in the Foreign Affairs Department to give a statement never mind have a meeting. Everywhere there was poverty, except in the Government quarter, the exclusive beachside area where Government officials, diplomats and corrupt businessmen lived in luxury compatible with the French Rivera. The British Ambassador was, in his own way, no better. Frustrated by the insurmountable obstacles that were continuously placed in his way he had given up trying. Weekday receptions, private dinner parties, Saturday golf and Sunday sailing were his prime concerns, in that order, whilst he worked out the remaining time of his posting. Last but not least Jane was unable to obtain a travel permit to visit Cabinda itself.

In frustration Jane had bought a ticket from Luanda to Gaborone on one of the twice weekly flights. She'd paid more than twice as much for that flight than for her long-haul journey from Lisbon. That was going to be hard to explain on her expenses. As the plane made its final approach she could only hope that Ralph Foulkes at the Foreign and Commonwealth Office was going to be as good as his word and sign off on the account.

It was mid-morning when Jane stepped off the plane at Gaborone and took the short walk to the waiting light aircraft that was to carry her, and a few tourists to Maun Airport in the Okavango. Another four hours she thought. Then she'd be at Stirling Farm.

Chapter 13
10th January 1996
Boma, Zaire

There was no repeat of the first performance for Gunter Siegburg's arrival at Boma Airport. This time he'd come from Kinshasa, the capital of Zaire, in a private plane. The '*Customs and Immigration*' people had been squared off before his arrival. No money had changed hands; the guards knew better than to interfere with anybody who was travelling under the personal protection of President Mabutu of Zaire.

Feliz, General Lubala's dumb servant boy was there when the plane came to a standstill. He collected Gunter's bag directly from the plane's small hold and carried it to the car that was waiting inside the airport's dilapidated perimeter gate, engine running, air-con switched on. This time it wasn't a wreck of a vehicle but a new Land Cruiser station wagon. The only thing that had not changed was the presence of the intrepid Welshman, Emrys ap Ewan who once again appeared to have overdosed on a cocktail of false confidence and exaggerated enthusiasm.

"Good to see you back again," he began with an outstretched hand. "It's changed so much since your last visit. It's fantastic isn't it? Fantastic what a bit of organisation can do. Get in the car, it's nice and cool for you. We'll be on our way in a jiffy."

As Siegburg got into the back seat ap Ewan went to the rear of the station wagon where Feliz was waiting. He pulled open the tailgate and lifted in the suitcase. Feliz climbed in and lay flat on the floor, as low and inconspicuous as his small body would allow.

Ap Ewan joined Siegburg in the back seat. He slammed the door shut. "Right driver, off you go then. Paradise Hotel, as fast as you like."

Gunter Siegburg interjected. "Drive at normal speed and get me there in one piece."

"There you go then, you've had your instructions, do what Mr Siegburg says." Ap Ewan turned his attention to his charge.

"Good trip then was it? Comfortable?"

Siegburg was looking out of the window. He didn't bother to look at ap Ewan. "Nothing is comfortable in this place. I wouldn't be here if it wasn't necessary."

There was finality in his tone, as if to say don't disturb me. Ap Ewan was not sensitive to such nuances.

"Kinshasa, now there's a place for you. Central to the history of Africa it is. A lot of people don't realise that and it was a

Welshman, one of my compatriots, who opened the place, that's another thing people don't know."

Ap Ewan had hoped that his titbit of historical information would arouse Gunter's interest. It didn't. But undaunted and unwilling to travel in silence, he decided to tell Gunter the story anyway.

"I'll tell you what happened. Everybody has heard of David Livingstone haven't they now? Well David Livingstone was a missionary and not a very good one. After spending his whole life in Africa he only made one convert! Now that's not very impressive is it?" Ap Ewan's question was rhetorical. "I don't know how he became so bloody famous to be honest.

When you mention Livingstone everybody says "*Dr Livingstone I presume.*" Nobody ever thinks about the man that actually said those words. Nobody knows his bloody name now. Well I do and his story is far more interesting. His name was Henry Morton Stanley and he was not only a Welshman he also came from my neck of the woods. What do you think about that then?"

Siegburg made no response.

"Well, I say his name was Henry Morton Stanley, it was in the end but in the beginning it was John Rolands. That was his birth name. Born in Denbigh, North Wales and put in the workhouse in St Asaph. His mother had a pub near Abergele and guess what? It's Abergele I come from. There's a coincidence for you isn't it?

Well John Rolands got out of the workhouse and went to America on a ship and he changed his name to Henry Morton Stanley. He fought in the American Civil War, on both sides actually. Funny that. Then he became a newspaper reporter, writing exciting stories about the American native wars. That's cowboys and Indians to you and me. Did well didn't he? Ah, but he didn't stop there. He persuaded an important newspaper owner to send him to Africa to look for Livingstone, who by then was completely lost. Silly bugger. Gordon Bennet didn't give Stanley much money. That was the name of the newspaper man, funny name isn't it?

Stanley went to Africa and found Livingstone. But that's not the end of the story. At the time everybody was looking for the source of the River Nile. Stanley had an idea from his first trip and so went back and followed a little river he'd found. Now, at this point, I have to admit he dropped a bit of a bollock. He hadn't found the source of the Nile, no, he'd found the source of the River Congo. What do you think of that then?"

84

The station wagon hit a pothole and lurched widely from side to side.

"Steady on," shouted ap Ewan, his comment directed at the driver. "Now as I was saying, Stanley discovered the River Congo, followed it all the way to the Atlantic Ocean, making him the first man to cross Africa, an impressive feat by any measure.

He went to England and tried to persuade the Government there to take charge of the Congo River and its lands. Well let me tell you, not a bloody chance! Stanley hadn't been to one of them fancy schools see, Eton or Harrow or whatever. That didn't put Stanley off though. He got a ferry to Belgium and gave the whole lot to the king there; a fellow called Leopold. A real rum bugger he turned out to be. Screwed the Africans into the ground. I mean he was really not a nice man, not that I'm a kaffir lover now, but there are limits you know.

Just to pull it altogether now, Stanley established a settlement at the toe of the river, at the very beginning; he called it Stanleyville after himself. At the bottom of the river, well at the cataracts really, he made another settlement and called it after the Belgian king, Leopoldville." Ap Ewan's voice went into a low whisper. "He had to do that if he wanted more money you see.

Well in any case let me finish my little story now; pull in the loose ends so to speak. Now, as you know, the Congo, that's the country not the river, became independent and the blacks, the ones that took over, they changed the name of Leopoldville to Kinshasa. And blow me isn't that where you've just come from and the same place where my compatriot made his name. Now isn't that a coincidence and a nice way to finish my little story off?"

How much further? asked Siegburg.

Ap Ewan had hoped for a slightly more effusive response but, as one who had learnt to cope with life's little disappointments, he carried on seamlessly.

"Should be there in a few minutes now. Comfortable enough are you?"

The Paradise Hotel had changed beyond all recognition since Bernd Groelsh and his five man training squad had arrived. There was a high chain-link fence surrounding the whole property. A red and white barrier prevented free access to the property. It was manned by what had been Lubala's rag-tag guerrillas but who had now become, after training, Cabindan Liberation Front soldiers. Gone were the dilapidated hotel signs. They were replaced with a new, freshly painted, sign: *'Ministry for Natural Resources,*

Research Establishment, Government of Zaire. STRICTLY NO ADMITTANCE'.

The red and white pole was raised as the station wagon approached and the CLF soldiers stood to attention and saluted as the vehicle passed. White painted stones bordered the weed-free gravel driveway. The tyres crunched as the driver pulled to a halt outside the main entrance. A double row of African CLF soldiers formed 'a guard of honour, in the square in front of the building. Outside the main doors, separate, in dress uniform, were Groelsh's five European Shock Force soldiers, the training squad, standing to attention. A few steps apart was Bernd Groelsh. Gunter smiled for the first time since his arrival.

The former manager's house was now termed Force HQ. The room where General Lubala tried to string up Siegburg had changed; it was now the Operations' Room, in effect the planning and conference centre. Freshly painted with functioning air-conditioning it was a comfortable place to meet and work. Somewhere in the distance a V12 Mann diesel generator hummed away, providing a secure electrical supply. Siegburg and Groelsh sat at the planning table.

"So, first impressions?" asked Groelsh.

"Good," replied Siegburg. "But I expected no less from you. Brief me, what are the physical arrangements?"

"We, the SF soldiers, live in this house."

"SF soldiers?"

"*Shock Force*, that's what I call the mercenaries. A term you would recognise from the German Army I'm sure."

Siegburg nodded.

"General Lubala stays in the old deputy manager's house. We allow him a small staff and we watch him constantly. Some of the CLF men, the one's we trust and have made NCO's stay in one of the old hotel wings. The rest of the men live where we can put them, some in outbuildings and some in tents. The hotel's kitchen and dining room provides good messing facilities and the old ballroom is an infirmary and medical centre. The medical officer is doing a good job. General health and fitness of the men is improving markedly."

"And what about the men, the CLF men?"

"We are just about at strength. In total we have three-hundred and fifty men."

"Are you sure it's enough?" asked Siegburg. "I could get more."

"I prefer to have fewer better trained men. Taken together with the experienced Europeans we will be strong enough, believe me."

Bernd continued. "The men are divided into five operational sections each with a specific task."

"What about the 'special' section?"

"We keep them isolated, twenty-five of them. They're billeted in what used to be the old hotel gardens. They're a bad bunch, resistant to discipline, difficult to control. Most of their minds have been pickled with drugs and alcohol."

"When the time comes will they do what we want them to do?" asked Gunter.

"Oh most certainly they will."

"Good."

"And what news do you have for us?" asked Bernd.

"The business is concluded in Kinshasa. Mabutu's lot will continue to support this camp and everything within Zaire. How is that going by the way?"

"Fine now but we did have some difficulties in the beginning," replied Bernd. "The Governor of Boma got his chaps to ask for an *'import tax'* for each delivery we received; in US dollars."

"How did you get around that?"

"We went down to one of the Government warehouses at Boma docks where our stuff was being held. We had discussions with half-a-dozen of the staff there and it worked out okay."

"No problems?"

"Not for us. Two of their 'negotiators' didn't survive the meeting, regretfully, but the sudden shortage of manpower didn't impede them in loading our trucks. Since then supplies, diesel, food, etc. have arrived just about on time and in the requested quantities. They have been very co-operative."

Both men smiled.

"That's as Mabutu's people promised. I have also arranged for the Zairian Army to occupy the strip of Zairian land that separates Angola from Cabinda. That should stop the Angolans being tempted to make a land dash to Cabinda when it all kicks off."

"Sounds good. "You want to have a look around?"

"Later, first I need to talk to Lubala. "How is he getting on?"

"We give him whisky, women and reassurance. That's it. He doesn't know the plans and doesn't ask."

"It's amazing the effect that an ocean cruise can have on a man!"

Gunter Siegburg waited on the patio in the shade of a sun-umbrella. The second chair had been intentionally placed not only to be out of the shade but also with the sun shining directly into the eyes of its intended occupant. Lubala was kept waiting for a few minutes before being brought through. Siegburg didn't stand when his guest arrived, he just pointed at the vacant chair. Lubala sat without complaint, maintaining his smile.

"It is good to see you again Herr Siegburg. Indeed you have done everything you said. I for my part have done as you asked. Am I fulfilling the terms of our agreement?"

"So far," Siegburg's words were curt. "Soon more will be expected of you. You are going to move to Cabinda City. You will be based there."

Lubala's eyes opened wide with alarm. "That is the home of the enemy. They will kill me. I cannot go there!"

"You will go there and you will be safe. You will be under the protection of the United Nations and you will also have a *security team*', ten of my SF troops. You will be there to run and organise your referendum."

Lubala was unsure.

"You can take one or two people with you. You are allowed a small entourage. That is all."

"I have no experience of elections. You know my background; it is not in the democratic ways. If you leave it to me we will surely lose. I do not understand why you would want that."

"How well you prepare for the elections is of no relevance, just as long as you do what you can. You cannot just sit, drink and womanise. Do you understand that?"

Lubala did not answer.

"You will do it and you will trust me. Is that clear? All will be as I said. Germans fulfil their contracts; I will make sure you fulfil your obligations."

Chapter 14
12th January 1996
United Nations Building, New York.

André Piet was no stranger to ethnic diversity and nationalistic fervour. He was born and brought up in New Brunswick, that Canadian province that struggled to peacefully combine twin French and Anglo Saxon cultures. His first language was French which he spoke with a heavily accented Canadian accent, an accent that the people of France found crude and slovenly. Not that there was anything slovenly about André Piet. At six foot one he had an athletic build that was the envy of many people who were younger than his forty-three years. His bearing and manner was more in keeping with a military vocation rather than his actual diplomatic career. He'd always wanted to be a diplomat but couldn't stand the bitter and often petty bickering of French Canadian politics, which is why his chosen career route was within the United Nations. He'd progressed well in the organisation because he possessed qualities that at times could be contradictory in nature. He was able to operate with apparent objectivity, yet in practice he was not so objective as to have given up his judgement. His was a unique type of subjective objectivity, if such a thing could exist. He was not easily hoodwinked. He was a democrat by nature, always willing to solicit the opinions of those with whom he worked and sensitive to the majority view, but at the same time he could implement a policy with ruthless efficiency, steamrolling objectors and obstructions like a true autocrat. But his real unique talent was his ability to correctly decide when and where to allow which of his various personality traits dominate a situation.

He didn't like the feel of his latest assignment. His gut reaction told him it was spawned by cynical politics and more than that it was being needlessly rushed. Nevertheless he was determined to do the best he could given the difficult circumstances.

The Angolan Ambassador and his group were already in Meeting Room seven on the tenth floor of the United Nations building on Manhattan Island when Piet walked in followed by his team of four. Piet knew immediately his visitors were going to be no match for the skilled bureaucrats of the Electoral Assistance Division of the Political Affairs Department of the United Nations.

The hastily assembled Angolan/Cabinda Referendum Committee, led by André Piet, had clear ideas about how a

89

referendum should be organised. The Ambassador was given little opportunity to talk or suggest alternatives; he had no option but to acquiesce to the demands of M. Piet.

"Mr Ambassador," began M. Piet with a bluntness that was unfamiliar to the diplomat, "your ideas of fairness are very different from those of this committee. In deference to your obvious inexperience let me lay out the general process for you. There will be some guiding rules. Firstly, and most importantly, your Government will recognise the main opposition and its leadership. In this instance that is General Lubala and the Democratic Front for the Liberation of Cabinda. Further you will protect them. Let me assure you that if any harm should come to General Lubala or his associates the finger of suspicion will immediately fall on the Government of Angola and to ensure that there is some substance to the UN protection, Mr Lubala and his close associates will be issued with temporary UN diplomatic passports for the duration of the project."

The Ambassador didn't respond.

Piet continued. "Whilst the Committee recognises your Government's anxiousness to settle this matter we insist that an election cannot take place until an electoral register has been established. We do not believe that this can be done in less than twelve weeks in the best of circumstances. Notwithstanding that, for our part, we are willing to act immediately. Any delays will be solely down to your Government's failures."

"Furthermore the opposition, as you see it, will be allowed to canvass publicly without hindrance. It will have fair access to the media and be permitted to organise public meetings. There will be no intimidation or coercion of the opposition or of the electorate. To ensure this point there will be no build up of Angolan military forces in the Cabinda Province. From this moment no new troops will be allowed to enter Cabinda and those that are there will be confined to their barracks for the duration of the referendum. Security will remain in the hands of the civil police force. Is this clear or do you require further clarification – do you understand what I have said?"

The Ambassador simply nodded.

"In recognition of the fact that your country has little experience of the democratic process, we will supply experts from the United Nations, technical people who will assist you in the general organisation of the referendum. In fairness we will supply the same technical assistance to the Democratic Front for the Liberation of Cabinda. Furthermore you as the existing power are established in Cabinda and have at your disposal all the administrative means to conduct and administer a referendum. Therefore in the interests of fairness you will allow, without hindrance, the Cabindan Liberation Front to either acquire locally, but if necessary by importation the necessary equipment, including the likes of vehicles, printed matter, office equipment etc. Their supplies will have the same status as diplomatic transfers of goods and you will not interfere."

As well as the technical assistance the United Nations will also deploy independent election observers. These individuals, accredited by the United Nations and having full diplomatic status will have full freedom of movement. It is the report that these independent observers make, at the end of the process, which will determine if the United Nations General Assembly recognises the result of the referendum as free and fair.

Those are our conditions Mr Ambassador; they are more fully detailed in this document."

One of Piet's assistants produced a comb bound folder and pushed it over the table in the direction of the Ambassador.

"A copy of this document is already on your President's desk," continued Piet. "If you have any questions or queries I suggest that you hold them till you have read the document. Is that all clear to you?"

"I feel that I am being pushed," responded the Ambassador. "This is not the normal manner for negotiations. Why is there so much haste?"

Piet put on his best surprised expression. "Because it was your Government that requested the matter was settled as soon as possible. We are as unhappy as you at the undue haste. I suggest you take the matter up with your own Government."

Chapter 15
January 14th 1996
Stirling Farm, Okavango, Botswana

Jane had arrived after dark, exhausted by her epic journey from Luanda. She was too tired for anything but the most cursory of introductions to the visitors at the farm; she didn't even manage to talk with Duncan other than to say "Good night!" She took a shower and slept and slept and slept.

The sun had traversed more than half the sky by the time she emerged on the stoop, still bleary eyed. For others the day had started earlier. Grace was at the workshop doors even before James.

"What's wrong? Can't sleep?" he asked, smiling.

"No," replied Grace. "You said that this was the best time of the day. So I thought I'd try it out."

"So you came here to watch me then?"

"No."

"So what did you come for then?"

"I want to help."

"You!" James's expression quickly turned from surprise to scepticism.

"Yeah, well why not. Don't you think a girl can do the things you can do?"

James shrugged his shoulders. "I just thought you'd be happier ... doing something else."

"Like what?"

"I don't know, painting your fingernails or something."

"What!" Grace exploded, stepping closer and playfully hammering his chest with clenched fists. James turned his back on her and covered his head in defence.

"Okay, okay," he shouted. "I'll show you. Just stop hitting me will you?"

For the next three hours Grace learnt about the intricacies of a 5hp Lister diesel generator that he'd already started stripping down.

"This is going to be a back up for the Kraal when it's working properly. They've got electricity now but it keeps cutting out. It's not so bad with lights, they've got candles and oil lamps but it means they can't have a refrigerator, or more importantly," he paused for dramatic effect, "TV to watch the football!"

"They want to watch TV?"

92

"Yeah, why wouldn't they? Why wouldn't they want refrigerators, cookers, washing machines?"

"But they live in a real African village, they have a real culture. Don't they want to keep it?"

"Yes of course they do. But they're not stupid either. They are being really clever in fact. They're trying to keep the good bits but enjoying what's available at the same time."

"Who decides what's good and what's bad. Who's the boss?"

"That's a funny one," replied James wiping his hands with an oily rag before passing it on to Grace. "It starts with my grandfather, on my mother's side that is,"

"Well I didn't think it was on your Dad's side," interrupted Grace

"His name was Dingeswayo. He was one of the great Matable chiefs. His first child was my mother. Elizabeth was her name. Then he had two sons, twins, Morgan and Tembo. You've met them. In our culture the first born male is always the next chief. My grandmother died at their birth and the only people who knew who was first born was my grandfather and my mother and they're both dead."

"So how do you pick a chief now?"

"We don't. But that's not as bad as it sounds. Tembo and Morgan are so close to each other, inseparable, they're like eh..."

"Twins?"

"Yeah, very clever." They both laughed.

"So who's in charge? I still don't know."

"Nobody really. Tembo and Morgan I suppose. Everybody just gets on, we just respect each other. It doesn't seem to be that important."

"It sounds a bit funny."

"It works," said James.

"And you. What about you? Are you African or European? With your colour you could be either."

"Officially I'm a coloured, at least that's what it says on the official forms, child of mixed race."

"But what do you feel? What do you think you are? Where are you most comfortable?"

"Never thought about it really. I'm comfortable everywhere."

"You have to be one or the other."

"Why?"

Grace started to say something but James cut her off. "Come on let's go. We're done here."

They walked from the workshop towards the farmhouse. Grace suddenly stopped.

"Can we walk towards the Kraal again, just for a bit? I liked that path."

"You want to go to the Kraal?"

"No, I just don't want to go back to the lodge yet."

James wanted to ask why, but he stopped himself. "Okay."

They walked along the path, slowly, Grace at first following. When the path widened a little James slowed to let her come alongside him.

"I didn't help you did I?"

"What do you mean?"

"I didn't answer your question," replied James.

"What question?"

"About being black or white. I think it's you who is confused."

"No, I'm not!" the response was too hasty. "What do you mean by that?"

"You're black and your Mum and Dad are white. Are you black or are you white is the question you want answering. I thought I knew you from our letters but really I don't. Just now I think you're black on the outside and white on the inside. That's difficult I suppose. It's easier for me; I'm just all mixed up, inside and out."

"At the Kraal yesterday, the people, they just took me by the hand, brought me right in, it felt so natural. It felt for a while like I belonged there."

"Didn't that make you feel good?"

"No. I felt like a traitor, like I was being disloyal to my Mom and Dad." There was a quiver in Grace's voice.

James stopped walking.

"Do you want to go up there?" He pointed to what was a barely recognisable path.

"Up the hill?"

"Yes. But we call it a kopje here; it's the name for a small hill in these parts. It's pronounced copy but spell kopje."

He didn't wait for her response; he just set off, slowly climbing. She followed. The ground became difficult after a few yards; stony in parts, pebbles and dust on the path that made tiny avalanches every time a foot failed to find proper purchase and slipped. The vegetation changed too. Hardy succulents and aloes dominated, randomly dotted between scattered round boulders, the scene only broken by the occasional spreading Acacia clinging on to the hillside and appearing to achieve little more than an austere life.

94

They had to concentrate on keeping their footing and, in the steep early section, getting their breath as the moved forward with the ever rising sun on their backs. It was good that they couldn't talk. It meant that each could be alone with their own thoughts for a while without being conscious of the other.

Suddenly Grace let out a scream, high pitched and loud. James turned to see Grace standing, still as a statue, her gaze fixed on a large boulder a few feet to her left. He laughed.

"It's only an iguana," he said smiling.

Grace didn't take her eyes off the animal; her words were little more than a mumble. "It looks like a dinosaur to me."

"It is quite a big one. I'll give you that but they're harmless, nothing to be scared of."

"Why is it staring at me then?"

"Well actually he is more scared of you than you are of him."

"I doubt that very much," replied Grace.

"They're reptiles, cold-blooded animals. They have to lie in the sun when they can to get their temperature up. Then, when they are warm they can hunt for food which I assure you consists of small insects and flies."

"I really don't like him."

"Most Africans don't. It's not because they're dangerous though, it's because they think they contain evil spirits. So you're in good company."

Grace began to relax a little. "Do all reptiles lie in the sun to get warm?"

"Just about. Shall we move on a little?" James turned to continue the climb. He hadn't taken a step when Grace asked another question.

"Snakes are reptiles, right?"

"Yes they are." James' nonchalant response was not reassuring. Grace was once again frozen to the spot.

"There are snakes here?"

"There are snakes all over Africa. But it's quite safe, don't worry."

"So nobody gets bitten by them?"

James' response was quick. "No, it's really safe." Then he had second thoughts. "Well actually Jane got bitten by an Asp once, right outside the farmhouse. Nearly died; she was ill for a long time. But she's okay now! You just have to keep an eye out and be aware."

The answer was not what Grace wanted to hear. She couldn't conceal her nervousness.

"If I hold your hand and lead the way will that help? I can look out for both of us."

Grace didn't need much thinking time; she moved quickly to take James' outstretched hand. Tentatively at first they began to move forward and upward again, Grace's grip not so much a hold as a clasp of desperation. He could feel her nails digging into his flesh. He glanced at her.

"Don't look at me," she said through clenched teeth. "You just keep looking out for them snakes!"

James turned away, not wanting her to see the smile on his face.

It took forty minutes to make the journey, a walk that James would normally have made in fifteen. Just shy of the summit he stopped and turned around. Grace stood beside him.

"Look." he said.

Throughout the walk Grace had kept her head down, looking out for predators; the steady rise had gone unnoticed. When she lifted her head the view caught her by surprise. Spread out before her was an African vista to move the heart. In the distant horizon was a landscape both wild and beautiful; a thousand colours, natural, almost untainted by human hand, a sight that was breathtaking, a sight that was Africa and the type of sight that had captured the heart and minds of so many visitors for many years.

"That's beautiful, so beautiful," she said in a hushed voice. "And it's so quiet, peaceful, yet powerful and inspiring. It makes you think there might be a God. A view like that has to have had a maker!"

"When you see Africa like this it is magnificent. That's why people come here. It's so sad, that when you get down to the detail, life here is not always so good."

James pointed to a place at the base of the Kopje, almost hidden by vegetation.

"Look, there's the farmhouse and the workshops."

He swept his finger in an arc and pointed to another place.

"That's the Kraal. They're not so far apart are they? It's only a couple of hundred yards really."

"Wow," replied Grace, "they are not that far away but it's hard to see them."

"Gus used to say that life, like Africa, holds a lot of secrets. It's often hard to see things that are right under your nose but it helps if you know what you are looking for."

"I know from the way you wrote about Gus that you miss him don't you?"

It was difficult for James to talk. He just led Grace by the hand a few steps along the contour of the hill to where there was a small raised mound of uniform stones. They stopped.

"Gus' grave?" whispered Grace.

James could only nod.

They stood there for a while, then without saying a word James led Grace by the hand to another place, not far away. There was another mound of stones; this time there were also flowers.

"My mother," said James in quiet reverence.

"The flowers are fresh," said Grace.

"They always are, sometimes its people from the Kraal, sometimes Maggie, sometimes Dad."

"And sometimes you?" asked Grace.

James nodded.

"This place must be so sad for you."

"No not really. Sometimes I'm sad when I arrive but I always feel happier after being here. I can talk to Gus and my mother and they help me. I love them both. It's good that I know where they are and I can visit any time."

James looked at Grace; her eyes were transfixed on the grave.

"You don't have that do you, a place to visit? That's really sad. This isn't sad at all."

They walked the few steps to the very crown of the kopje.

"I play a little game sometimes," said James. "If I want something I make a wish when I'm standing here. Then I slowly turn around, a full three-sixty degrees with my eyes shut. I know it's stupid but it always seems to me that my wish comes true."

"I don't think it's stupid at all," replied Grace.

James smiled. "You want to make a wish?"

Grace nodded.

James let go her hand and moved away a few steps.

"Go ahead, but don't tell me, it's bad luck."

The walk down the kopje was easier and faster, Grace's clasp on James' hand less fierce. They laughed at each other when they lost their footing and when their eyes met it was now somehow different.

Grace's parents were sitting with Duncan when they got back to the farmhouse. Grace let go James' hand and ran forward, smiling. She skipped up the steps to the stoop and hugged Simon and Melanie in turn.

97

"Love you Mom and Dad," she said without embarrassment.

"Wow what did we do to deserve that?" asked Simon. "No don't tell me, I'm just going to enjoy it!"

Duncan looked at his son.

"What?" he asked.

All eyes turned to James.

"Oh, alright then. I love you too Dad. But you're not having a kiss or a hug!"

"Were you two holding hands?" asked Duncan.

James and Grace looked at each other, alarm clearly evident.

"Grace is scared of snakes; I was just trying to make her feel more comfortable"

Grace nodded vigorously in agreement. "Yeah, I'm really scared of snakes."

James and Grace were flushed with embarrassment.

Everybody laughed.

A smiling Jane came from the house carrying a tray of cold drinks. "What am I missing?"

"He looks like somebody who found a penny and lost a pound," said Jane with a smile on her face.

Duncan laughed. "You're not far off the mark there. James won't be better till the Shapiro's return I think. They're away for six days; Victoria Falls and then Hwange Game Park."

"Bit on the well trodden tourist trail isn't it? They're unlikely to get anything special there."

"I think it's just a warm up photo-shoot to be honest," replied Duncan, "possibly with a bit of personal sightseeing thrown in as well. Still it's convenient; you'll have some peace to write your report."

"Well that's not going to take too long. I've precious little to report."

Mary Scobie came through from the kitchen. Outwardly Duncan smiled but inside he knew she was getting older: frailer, stooped, thinner, sunken cheeks but nevertheless still resilient. In her hand was a piece of paper and an envelope.

"Mafutzi just brought me this," she said holding up the envelope. "She found it in the lodge."

"What was Mafutzi doing in the lodge?" asked Jane.

"The Shapiro's didn't ask for it but I thought the lodge should be cleaned whilst they're away. Mary arranged for Mafutzi and a couple of others to do the work," said Duncan.

"What's in the envelope Mary?"

Mary passed the envelope to Duncan without a word.

It had '*Mary S.*' hand-written on the outside. It had already been opened.

"It's for you," said Duncan.

"Look inside," said Mary.

Duncan withdrew the folded note from inside. As he unfolded it several bank notes dropped to the floor. Jane was quickest; she gathered the cash from the ground.

"Wow, eight hundred dollars," she exclaimed.

Duncan read the scribbled note out loud:

> "*Mary,*
>
> *Your welcome and hospitality has been fantastic, more than we expected or could have hoped for. We offered to pay Duncan some time ago but he refused any money.*
>
> *However as we are here on a commercial venture, in all conscience we cannot stay at the lodge without paying something. The cash enclosed represents our monthly 'budget'. If Duncan is still refusing to accept our money will you please ensure that it is put to good use somewhere around the farm.*
>
> *Thanks,*
>
> *Simon & Melanie.*
>
> *PS, if the sum is insufficient please let us know and we will adjust it accordingly.*"

"That's very nice of them," said Jane.

"Nice!" replied Duncan. "That's more than they'd pay in a safari lodge!"

"Well actually it isn't too much. It's just on the very generous side of right," replied Mary, the canny Scot not yet totally eradicated from her character. "What should I do with the money?"

"I don't mind. Cover their costs I suppose and if there's anything left over do what you want with it. I suppose it would be nice for Mafutzi and her gang to get something. What's that other piece of paper in your hand?"

"Oh yes I nearly forgot," replied Mary handing the single sheet of paper to Jane. "It's a fax that came in for you a couple of hours ago."

Jane read the one-line message. "Ralph Foulkes from the Foreign and Commonwealth Office is going to phone at ten. What time is it now?"

"Five to," replied Duncan looking at his watch.

"God, that doesn't give me much time to prepare. He most probably wants a preliminary verbal report. I don't know what I'm going to tell him; there isn't anything to tell him actually. Duncan what am I going to say?"

Duncan laughed at Jane's concern. "Well in my experience, when all else fails, tell the truth. That'll be a shock for the Foreign Office."

"It's no joke Duncan; you want to see my expenses!"

The phone rang.

"Shit!" Jane went through to the house.

Ralph Foulkes was looking out of his office window, on to Parliament Street, still thinking about how he was going to guide the conversation when his phone rang. He sat down behind his desk and picked up the receiver.

"Ten o'clock Mr Foulkes," said his secretary, "Your scheduled call to Botswana. Miss Ashton is on the line."

There was a click. "Hello Jane, is that you?"

"Yes it's me. Hello Ralph."

"Glad I got hold of you. It's coming on to rain here, dull and overcast. Make me jealous; tell me what it's like there." Ralph was going to lead her in gently.

Jane had a different intention. "Ralph, I'm not going to beat about the bush. I've run around all over the world, achieved bugger all and spent an awfully large amount of money. I have nothing of value to report. I'm depending on you to cover me on this one."

Ralph smiled to himself. "Oh, that's no problem at all. Of course I'll cover you, it's not that important. I really do hope you have not been worrying unduly."

It was too easy. Jane hadn't lost any of her sharpness. The hairs on the back of her neck stood up.

"If it wasn't that important, why did you send me in the first place?"

"Don't get me wrong. When I asked you to go in the first place it was important, very important. It's just that things move on, circumstances change. You know what foreign affairs are like."

"So no report needed, I can just come home?"

Ralph contemplated his response for a moment. "Well, yes and no."

"What do you mean Ralph?"

"Well yes, you don't have to write a report but no, you cannot come home just yet."

"What are you talking about Ralph?"

"Can I be perfectly frank with you?" he asked her.

Jane sighed. She knew that when a civil servant said '*can I be perfectly frank*', what it really meant was he was either going to lie through his teeth or drop you in the shit, possibly both.

"I think you better had," she responded.

"Well," said Ralph, "Firstly I should say that the Exchequer is still rather keen to get their hands on the '*outstanding balances*' from the Angolans. They're a bit short of the readies."

"When aren't they Ralph?"

"Exactly. It's like this you see. The Angolans are getting nervous and are keen to sort out their territorial anomalies, with reference to Cabinda, that is."

"You mean they have realised that legally Cabinda Province doesn't actually belong to them?"

"In a manner of speaking. They have now decided that the best way to progress the situation is to have a referendum and give all the people of Cabinda the opportunity to formalise their relationship with Angola proper."

"A land grab?" said Jane.

Ralph considered the question to be rhetorical and ignored it. "The United Nations have indicated that they will endorse the correction of the border '*anomalies*' if they hold a referendum and it is found to be free and fair."

"You're rambling Ralph. What's that got to do with me?"

"In a nutshell, the Secretary General is an old friend of the President of Angola, a man called Jonathan Marobi. Now's he's a decent chap by....eh."

"African standards?"

"I never said that! The Secretary General, as a sort of favour I suppose, is giving the Angolans technical assistance with the referendum and they are pushing it through very quickly, fast by any standards. Looks like the whole thing could be done and dusted in twelve weeks."

"You still haven't told me what it's got to do with me."

"Well I'm sure you know that all votes, elections and referendums, are monitored by independent international observers?"

"Oh no you don't Ralph! Don't push that on me. The place is a hell hole. I'm not getting involved."

"Bit late really, you're down as one of the two independent observers that Britain is to supply. Now don't worry about anything, all the arrangements have been made. GCHQ are happy to release you, your accreditation with the UN is finalised."

"Are you telling me this is a '*fait accompli*'?"

"Oh no, I wouldn't put it as strongly as that."

"So I have a choice."

"To be honest? No, not really."

Jane was getting angry and responded with her characteristic bluntness. "Ralph the fact is that it is a '*fait accompli*' just like the fact is you are an arsehole!"

Ralph struggled to stifle a giggle.

"Are you laughing at me?" demanded Jane.

"No."

"So what are you laughing at?"

"I know what's coming."

"What's coming? What do you mean?"

"You never asked who I nominated as the second British observer."

"All right smart arse, who is the second observer?"

"Duncan!"

There was silence for a while. Ralph was the first to speak.

"Hello, hello. Can you hear me, can you hear me. Think the line is breaking up. Hello. I'll call back later!"

Ralph put the receiver back in its cradle thinking it might be appropriate for Jane and Duncan to have a little time to absorb the information he'd just imparted. He went back to the window and watched people hurry up and down the street as the rain began to fall. He allowed himself a smile, inwardly a little excited about the situation; life was normally so boring in the Foreign and Commonwealth Office. He remembered the last time he'd been involved with Jane and Duncan, in South Africa, and wondered how he might involve himself a little further in the present situation.

BOOK TWO

Chapter 16
Cabinda City, Cabinda Province
2nd February 1996

Jane was providing a running commentary, instantaneously translating from Portuguese to English for Duncan's benefit, not that he was overly interested. The sounds echoed hollowly around the empty spaces of Souza Park, carrying across the open ground, amplified by an archaic public address system. They'd stumbled on the rally and were watching at a distance. Their vantage point, a small area of raised ground in the shade of a tiny copse of trees, gave them a perfect view.

They looked over the crowd. It wasn't big. Duncan thought that there might be a thousand people at most: men, women and a few children. About half the men wore bright orange 'T' shirts, the colour taken from the little known flag of free Cabinda. In front of the crowd, standing on a make-shift platform, constructed from old scaffolding pipes and planks was the speaker, a tall African who looked uncomfortable in his European suit. Jane thought he spoke hesitantly, possibly because he was not used to public oratory. She didn't immediately realise that she was watching Moses Lubala, leader of the Democratic Front for the Liberation of Cabinda, giving his first public address in the city he would see as his capital, if he won the referendum.

Jane was right in thinking he was nervous. He had good reason to be. Up until a few days ago he'd been a wanted man. He only dare show his face in Cabinda now because of the UN sponsored amnesty and a diplomatic passport. He knew that only time and events would prove the value of the promised safe passage. Despite his nervousness he laboured his way through the prepared text.

"Fellow Cabindans, you have been cruelly subjected and you will continue to be cruelly subjected as long as the thieving and lying military Junta in Luanda dominates your country. They are no better than the colonialists that came before them. They do not care for you. They only want to take what is truly yours.

Cabinda is only small but it has oil, lots of oil, more than almost any other place on this earth. Yet Cabinda, with all its revenue and all its potential is a poor place. Just look around you at this city. This is no Kuwait; it is no Dubai nor is it a Burundi. We have no towering skyscrapers; we have no cars, no swimming pools. Our

104

women are not draped in jewels; our children do not attend expensive foreign schools. No. We have only bare feet to walk on, old sheets of corrugated iron for shelter and not enough food to eat or medicines for our sick.

But yet it is true we have more oil than Kuwait, Dubai and Burundi put together.

So what is happening to our wealth?

I will tell you. The wealth of our country never gets here. It is whisked away to our masters in Luanda who live lavish life styles and stuff private overseas bank accounts in places like Switzerland. But it is worse than that. What they can't use themselves they spend on fruitless wars, wars of domination and suppression, wars that go on for decades and bring nothing to you, the people, but misery and fear."

"It's well written if badly delivered," said Jane, breaking her running commentary to remove the cover from her camera. "I think I'll take a few photographs."

Duncan didn't respond. Jane turned to look at him. "Are you okay?"

"There's something not quite right," replied Duncan his eyes scanning the empty parts of the park, unsure, for the moment of what he was looking for.

"What?" asked Jane.

The hint of an answer came almost immediately, but not from Duncan. In the distance could be heard a sound, at first just a deep murmuring, a growling that was steadily growing louder. Soon Duncan and Jane were able to identify the noise as the rhythmic sounds of chanting African voices.

"They're coming in this direction," said Duncan.

"Who?" replied Jane.

"The opposition I'd guess."

"Won't the police keep them apart?"

"That's what's wrong," replied Duncan. "When we arrived there were police milling around; they're not here now, they've melted away!"

Perhaps because they were listening to Lubala or maybe because they occupied lower ground, Lubala's supporters didn't hear the approaching mob, not until it was too late.

The loyalist Angolan crowd was entirely composed of young men dressed in black trousers and red shirts, the colours of the

105

Angolan flag. They'd entered the park on the far side in a long column, six or seven people wide, chanting as they snaked their way at a rhythmic trot.

From their vantage point Jane and Duncan could see the inevitability of what was going to happen. Jane raised the camera and used the zoom to focus on the approaching crowd.

"They're all carrying weapons of some kind, sticks and clubs mainly" she said. She took a couple of quick snaps before swinging around to Lubala's supporters. Duncan kept his attention focused on the approaching column. He watched as they stopped singing and, as if at the behest of some unseen signal the column broke and spread to form a wide line, two to three persons deep. Slowly and deliberately they walked forward, restrained and ominously quiet, waiting for the order.

The line was only a hundred yards away before it was noticed by people at the back of Lubala's crowd. A ripple of disquiet spread forward towards the platform. Lubala, at first oblivious, continued to read from the prepared text. Four white men, his security, SF men from Bernd Groelsh's group clambered on to the stage and began to bundle him away. The men, without ceremony pushed Lubala towards the back of the platform. For a moment there was silence in the crowd, silence enough to hear the bark of a Jeep engine growling to life. The vehicle sped off, away from the mob; Lubala's crowd was left to their fate.

The ominous line was only fifty yards away when a spontaneous cheer was raised and the line broke into a charge.

The panic amongst Lubala's supporters was immediate. Men women and children looked frantically for an escape route but there were too many in the confined area in front of the platform. Within seconds the mob had fallen upon them. Blows rained indiscriminately, women howled, children screamed. A few men tried to stand their ground, attempting to protect the women and children. Without weapons they were quickly overcome. The milieu lasted only a minute or two. Once the mob had felled or chased off all of Lubala's supporters they re-formed their column and trotted away in the direction from which they'd come.

Jane, from the cover of the trees, had been taking pictures of the scene as fast as she could roll on the film in her camera. She was focused; anxious to make a record of what was happening. She continued even when she felt Duncan's hands pulling her away.

"Jane stop! We have to get out of here." There was urgency in his voice. "Jane we've been seen. We have to go!"

Duncan's warning was too late. An Angolan police vehicle, a battered Soviet four-wheel drive, was racing toward them, bumping and jolting over the uneven ground. A ragged bunch of policemen clung on precariously, one stood, gripping the anti-roll bar tightly. He wore black framed roll-around mirror sunglasses and the tail of his red bandanna fluttered behind. Even before it had stopped policemen were jumping from the sides of the vehicle. They ran forward wildly waving their assault rifles at Jane and Duncan. It was clear that escape or resistance was futile. Duncan raised his hands above his head exposing open palms. Jane stood motionless, holding on to her camera. The one with the red bandanna, the leader, came forward shouting incomprehensible words, not in Portuguese but in an unrecognisable African dialect. His attention was on Jane. He screamed at her. Jane stood motionless. The policeman pointed at her camera. Jane still didn't move. The leader grabbed the strap and tried to tear the camera from Jane's hands. As a reflex she resisted the snatch and for a moment the two tussled for possession. Duncan lowered his arms and stepped forward. He'd barely moved when he was hit by a kick to the back of his legs that forced his knees to buckle. As he went down he felt a heavy blow to his back that emptied his lungs of wind and left him lying face down on the ground. The flat of a boot came to rest on the nape of his neck stopping him raising his head. The unmistakable feeling of the tip of a gun barrel pressing on his head ended any thought of further resistance. Jane immediately abandoned her resistance also. The leader gave a final yank and wrenched the camera clear of Jane's hands. In victory he smiled exposing a row of green stained teeth.

The leader examined his prize and one of the men standing over Duncan bent down and began to undo the strap of his wristwatch. Duncan felt hands probing in his pockets, the contents being rifled. The policemen's chatter raised in intensity as they fought over their prizes. Even though the words were foreign, it was clear the men were discussing the fate of their captives.

Duncan's mind raced as he desperately sought an opportunity. He knew that with excitement came unpredictability. This was not a situation where reason would prevail. The policeman standing over Duncan removed his foot from his neck. Duncan, now free to twist his head, looked and thought about trying to disarm one of the policemen and taking control of the

107

situation but he knew it was a plan born of desperation. As his mind sought a more practical alternative he became aware of another vehicle approaching. He twisted his head further and saw the arrival of an olive green Peugeot 404, an army staff car with a tiny Angolan flag fluttering wildly on one of the wings.

The army officer that emerged from the car was different. His camouflage battle fatigues were clean and pressed, his boots polished and regulation. His epaulettes boasted three pips and he wore a bright red beret with a centred chrome cap badge. Hanging from his canvas belt was a brown leather holster, its flap open. The officer's hand rested on the butt of his pistol. But it was not the weapon that gave him authority. There was an aura about this young tall soldier, something in his confident demeanour and handsome clean features that exuded a sense of superiority.

He immediately barked orders, the words incomprehensible the meaning clear. The rabble of policemen had been almost oblivious to his arrival, but his commanding words and tone got their attention.

The policeman with the bandanna turned to face the officer. He stepped forward with both hands on his rifle. The officer stood resolute and unflinching apart from an almost imperceptible tightening of his grip on his pistol. For a second or two the men stared at each other. The policeman with the bandanna was the first to blink; he lowered his eyes almost reluctantly accepting the authority of the officer. He released the hold on his rifle and let it swing loosely on its shoulder strap. He made a half-hearted attempt at a salute. The other policemen, acknowledging the situation, slowly came to a ragged and silent attention.

The officer having gained control of the situation turned towards the captives. He bent down and put his hand around Duncan's arm. He spoke in heavily accented American English.

"Please stand." Almost gently he helped Duncan to his feet. Jane came and stood beside him. "You are American? Journalists?" he asked.

"English," replied Jane. "We are here with the United Nations. We strongly protest at the treatment we have received. We demand an apology."

Duncan was surprised at Jane's sudden bravado and hoped she did not push her luck too far.

"Do you have identification?" asked the officer.

Jane produced her UN accreditation card.

"Mine is in my wallet," said Duncan pointing to one of the soldiers. "He has it together with the other things they have taken."

The officer took the wallet from the policeman's hand and removed Duncan's ID. He examined it carefully and not looking up spoke some words in Portuguese. Duncan's watch and the change from his pockets were returned. The officer smiled for the first time.

"Many people have come to Cabinda for the referendum. Not all of them would like to see it succeed; many have come from the international press, a press that wants to show only the dark side of Africa. I apologise that you were mistaken for such people and for the treatment you have received. I hope you will accept my apology and it will be an end to the matter."

"Who will apologise to those people?" asked Jane pointing to the scene of the rally where there was once again some sign of life as the ones who had been lucky enough to escape came back to help their fallen and injured comrades.

"Democracy is a strange concept to this place. Western standards will be many years in arriving. It took you centuries in Europe to develop your systems – and I think I am correct in saying a lot of people sacrificed their lives before those high standards were achieved. We here need time." The officer's words were neither aggressive nor grovelling, merely matter of fact. "If I had got here earlier it would not have happened."

"Nevertheless….," continued Jane.

Duncan intervened. "Jane, leave it. There is a time and a place and it's not here and now."

"You are staying at the Maiombe Hotel? I will take you back there."

"That would be good," replied Duncan.

The officer turned to the rabble whose discipline had lapsed and were now whispering amongst themselves. He briskly dismissed them.

"Wait!" said Jane. "My camera, I want my camera."

The officer stepped forward and retrieved the camera. Carefully and deliberately he removed it from its brown leather case, clicked open the back and pulled out the film, exposing it to the light and ruining the pictures that Jane had taken. He snapped the back shut and handed it to Jane.

"You need a permit to take photographs in this area," said the officer.

Jane's face reddened. "You cannot stop me reporting the matter to…"

"Jane, stop now!" Duncan's words were firm.

"It's best that we go," said the officer opening the rear door of his car for Jane to get in.

The drive to the hotel was short. The officer was relaxed. "That was a difficult situation you got yourselves into. Those policemen are reservists, from a local unit. They are not as disciplined as they might be. They know that if the referendum is lost then they are finished; a new regime would punish them severely. More than that, they are unpredictable. Did you notice their teeth?"

"I noticed," replied Duncan.

"Notice what?" asked Jane.

"They're green. That is because they have been chewing Khat."

"Khat?" asked Duncan. "That's more associated with East Africa isn't it?"

"What's Khat?" asked Jane.

"Khat is the leaves of a tree that is native to Somalia," replied the Captain. "Unfortunately local farmers are cultivating it here now. It's a cheap drug; the local police lives on it. They chew the leaves all day. It's a stimulant, that's why they are so excitable and their teeth are green. The local officers turn a blind eye as it keeps them happy. At night time they smoke marijuana."

"That's terrible," said Jane.

"I think the Americans started the custom in Vietnam," replied the Captain not disguising his sarcasm.

"You're army," said Duncan. "Are you supposed to be around town, I thought you were confined to barracks?"

"The Army is confined to barracks," replied the officer. "Strictly speaking my unit is not army. We are the Presidential Guard. We only answer directly to the President."

"The Presidential Guard is supposed to be providing protection when we go up country," said Duncan.

The Captain smiled. "That is correct. I will be protecting the observers. We need you here. It would be bad if the UN was to pull out."

The Captain stopped the car. "We're back at your hotel now."

There were a few scattered patio tables on the pavement in front of the hotel.

"I think I need a drink," said Duncan. "Would you like a beer? A drink for saving us is the least we can do."

The Captain smiled. "I'll have a drink with you now if you promise not to leave the hotel again today, especially not after dark. And perhaps I should introduce myself. I am Captain David Marobi."

Jane took a seat on the hotel's veranda next to Duncan. "You sound more American than Angolan," she said.

"I spent some years of my childhood in America," replied the Captain sitting and removing his cap to reveal tightly cropped black hair.

They ordered beer from a waiter that had sauntered over.

"Well we're back where we started," said Duncan. "All told our experience of Cabinda in the last few days has not been that good."

"Why don't you tell me about it," said the Captain.

Jane began. "Three hours ago we were standing outside this hotel wondering what to do for a few hours. It was quiet. It was really hot. I guess the humidity was high."

David nodded. "There was a thunderstorm building. It's cleared now, it's much more pleasant."

"Duncan had heard that there was going to be a political rally but we didn't intend to go. We were killing time and decided to walk to the centre; somebody had told us there was a nice church in the square."

David smiled, "It's common in this part of the world for events not to turn out as expected."

"That's for sure," replied Duncan his mind flashing back over the last few days. It was true that his mind harboured doubts from the beginning but it was turning out to be worse than he'd imagined and he chided himself once more for succumbing to Jane's reckless attitude, particularly when her motivation was based on nothing more than a romantic notion.

It was less than three weeks since Jane had received the phone call from Ralph in London. Since that time a lot had happened. Duncan and Jane had stayed in hotels together previously but they had never shared a room. It wasn't a progression in their relationship that had put them in a shared room now.

The Maiombe looked like a reasonable hotel from the outside. A seventies characterless concrete construction, it had been built during the final days of Portuguese rule. It was one of the last 'new' buildings to be constructed in the city, that and State House. Nothing much had been built after the Portuguese pulled out, the

111

ensuing civil war made sure of that. The hotel was located on the city's main street, Rue de Dr Agostinho Neto.

Typically, Jane had somehow found time to do her homework.

"The street was named after Angola's first President," she'd told Duncan. "He died prematurely, not violently in the normal African way but riddled with cancer. He passed away in a characterless Moscow hospital, undignified and alone. He'd been the country's first President but hadn't achieved international statesman status; far from it. His only claim to fame was that the Bulgarians named a street in Sofia after him. His successors in Angola were embarrassed into a reciprocal action but didn't want to establish a focal point for opposition in Luanda so they named the main street in Cabinda City after him. Bit ignominious for what was essentially a good man, don't you think?"

"That's really interesting," responded Duncan, not even convincing himself, his thoughts elsewhere. In his mind neither the street nor the hotel amounted to much, nor did Cabinda City for that matter. First impressions had not been good and it hadn't got any better. They'd arrived at the airport on Thursday night aboard a chartered UN flight that had come in from Jo'berg. Jo'berg being the only decent place in southern Africa with a truly international airport had been the chosen assembly point for the hastily assembled UN monitoring and observer delegation.

The speed of the operation ensured that there was going to be organisational chaos. At the best of times any type of decent accommodation was scarce in Cabinda City, premium accommodation was non-existent. There were only two hotels worthy of the title '*hotel*' and both of them had optimistically rated themselves as three stars. Their normal trade was a trickle of foreign oil workers staying overnight, either waiting for an early morning flight out of the place or having arrived too late in the day for safe transfer to their secure camp north of the city.

Cabinda City was known as Tchiowa to the locals and it was clear that if Cabinda did get independence then Cabinda City would become the official name but until that time the Angolans made sure the old colonial name stuck. Currently the city was only a provincial capital; there were no embassies or consular facilities with their associated guest accommodation. That's why the UN had snapped up every suitable and many unsuitable hotel rooms or other places to bed down their staff.

Duncan and Jane were listed as independent observers in their own right; the two observers that the British Government had been allowed to nominate. Because of that they'd been allocated separate accommodation. Jane was given a precious room in the Maiombe Hotel whilst Duncan had been allocated a cubical in a nearby Catholic seminary that had been hastily made available by the Abbot who'd not hesitated in sending the hapless novices home so that he could avail himself of the US dollar windfall going begging.

Jane's hotel room was small but it did have two single beds. Duncan's main reason for agreeing to accept the assignment was so that he could accompany Jane and keep an eye on her. So it wasn't much of a decision for them to share the room.

Duncan was disappointed by the place but Jane, after her recent experience of hotels in Luanda, had found the place to be acceptable, not because it had any particular redeeming features, more because her expectations were so low in the first place. Once again there were no working lifts, but that was not so bad as the hotel had only six floors and their room was on the fourth. Surprisingly the air-conditioning did work, even if the control was limited to simply on or off. The noise of the fan was disturbing but not as bad as the alternative of sleeping with windows open and being subjected to the din produced by millions of crickets throughout the night, not to mention the hordes of mosquitoes that had little regard for repellent creams no matter how liberally applied. As a bonus the linen was acceptably clean and there was hot and cold water most of the time. It would do; it was not as if they were going to spend much time in the room.

The first few hours after their arrival had been a scramble sorting out living arrangements; the next day, Friday, was spent arranging an operational HQ. A secondary school, simply named K11, had been seconded for the duration of the referendum. The first problem they'd encountered there had been dealing with the parents whose children had been sent home. It gave the task force an insight into how the authorities dealt with dissent in Cabinda. The parents wanted a refund of the schools fees they'd paid in advance and had gathered outside the school. With no cash forthcoming the crowd had shown signs of turning into a mob. André Piet, the UN delegation chief, had returned urgently the short distance from State House where the Angolan authorities were chaotically trying to administer the referendum. He tried to reason with the crowd. He'd stood on a small wall and addressed the parents through an interpreter. Sympathetically he agreed they should get a refund of school fees but said it was the responsibility of the local Junta as the UN had paid handsomely for the use of the school. He told the expectant faces he'd go back to the Junta at State House and sort out the confusion. Before he had a chance to go two dilapidated open backed Mercedes trucks had arrived. Quickly they disgorged forty policemen in riot gear: long boots, padded jackets, helmets and Perspex shields. In a surprisingly well practiced drill they'd fallen on the crowd with raised batons. The hapless parents had been dispersed in a few minutes. M. Piet had tried to intervene as the batons fell on people who were unable to get away quickly enough. The Officer in charge just shrugged his shoulders and turned his back. The parents never returned to the school. Later that day M. Piet complained to the Governor who unreservedly offered his profuse apologies for the misunderstanding. Against his own better judgement M. Piet decided there was no time to or value in dwelling on the matter. Already containers full of supplies and equipment, including vehicles, were arriving from the docks and they had to be dealt with.

Saturday was spent on explaining the objectives, the operational plan and handing out individual assignments. The UN observers were to be split into two teams; one would stay in Cabinda City and monitor the administration of the referendum and its preparations, the other team would go out into the rural areas to carry out spot checks and talk with the local population. Jane had been roistered for admin, Duncan for up-country.

"I don't want office based duties," protested Jane.

"It's not like South Africa you know, it's not even like Botswana," Duncan had said. "If you think it is bad here wait till you get up country; nothing much has changed since the nineteenth century. Outside of town there aren't even any proper roads. "

She'd gone directly to André Piet.

"Why do I have to stay in Cabinda City?"

"Because we need you here. You speak several languages and your specialisation is in information analysis. I have more important work for you than looking down lists of potential electors and checking ballot boxes. I simply can't afford to let you go."

Only gradually had she acquiesced to the order and then only on condition that Duncan promised to do his best to fulfil the promise she had made to herself.

Chapter 17
Villa de Santa Maria, Cabinda City
2nd February 1996

Gunter Siegburg laughed to himself. It had been so easy. The last of the containers had arrived. Now they had all the equipment and vehicles they needed and the buildings had been prepared too, all under the nose of the Cabindan authorities, achieved by the diplomatic protection given by the United Nations. Gunter Siegburg even liked the story behind the villa. It gave a link to German history even if it was a bit tenuous.

Modern Italy was established in 1870 due in no small part to the efforts of a secular revolutionary, Giuseppe Garibaldi. The Vatican, a mere suburb of Rome, was incorporated into the Italian State. Various Popes were rightly alarmed; Garibaldi and his associates were not supporters of the Church. Garibaldi himself had famously said *"God did not create man, man created God"*.

The Church in Rome looked for a way out of this secular prison. It was not until the mid-1920's that an opportunity presented itself. Pope Pius XI was quick to recognise a rising political figure – Benito Mussolini. Mussolini, a firebrand, operated on the fringes of Italian politics that is until Pius XI intervened and negotiated a secret pact with him. For his part Pius XI encouraged all Catholics in Italy to vote for Mussolini, in return for which Mussolini agreed to grant the Vatican City independence if and when he came to power. With the Catholic vote secured Mussolini, much to his own surprise, was swept to power becoming the first Fascist leader in Europe. Mussolini kept his word and the Vatican was declared an independent state on 11th February 1929. The *Vatican State* also received a substantial cash subsidy in return for continued Papal support. The future for the Papacy in Rome had been secured at the cost of releasing the scourge of Fascism on Europe.

Not everybody was convinced it was such a good deal. As the practical implications of Fascism became clear and the doctrine spread – specifically to Germany – some people within the Vatican became uneasy about the *'secret pact'* and the potential for papal embarrassment. Pius the XI was succeeded by Pius XII who was terrified by the whiff of a scandal. Cardinal Pietre Gussipi was identified as the individual most likely to *'spill the beans'* about the secret pact so Pius XII decided to make an example of him as a warning to others. Exile was the chosen punishment and the place chosen for this exile was unusual – Cabinda at the mouth of the Congo River. Cardinal Gussipi was unable to resist the Papal edict and so resigned himself to his fate.

Cardinal Gussipi may have had a conscience over geo-political matters. However that characteristic did not stretch as far as things personal. It was said that it was difficult to know what the Cardinal would eventually die of but everybody agreed it wouldn't be self-neglect.

He began to build a residence that would be comfortable and befitting of his status. Pius XII agreed that the Cardinal could stay on in Rome until the residence, the Villa de Santa Maria, was completed. The good Cardinal didn't rush which in hindsight was a mistake. He was still in Rome on 8th September 1943 when Italy surrendered to the Allies. The Germans, not standing on ceremony, took over the Government in Rome and the Cardinal, believing he was protected in the confines of Vatican City, decided to exercise his vocal chords once again. The response was swifter this time.

A few days later he was found dead in his Vatican apartment with three bullet holes in his head and no gun present. The official Vatican report on the matter informed the world that Cardinal Gussipi had committed suicide.

The Villa de Santa Maria, by now almost complete, remained the property of the Church in Rome. The authorities there quickly forgot about it, they had other things on their mind in 1945/6. The Villa was never occupied by its intended resident nor any other resident for that matter. It had stood there slowly decaying until spotted by Bernd Groelsh on his reconnaissance mission. It had taken Gunter Siegburg only a few minutes to get the Deacon of Cabinda to give '*his permission*' for the place to be used as a Head Quarters for General Moses Lubala and his delegation. A few minutes and a thousand dollar donation with no receipt required, that is. It was to this place that the Jeeps had whisked Lubala from the rally in the park in Cabinda City.

The location was ideal. It was not just a house, it stood on six acres of land just north of the city, between the sea and what passed for the main highway. On either side were a few subsistence farmers and a lot of unusable scrubland. A three metre high perimeter wall was part of the original design and it hadn't taken much work to put it back into reasonable order. New extra wide steel gates had been fitted and scrub cleared, behind a huge wild bamboo, to provide parking for several vehicles, out of

116

sight from the road. A track led another forty metres to the main buildings. It was built on a rectangular design. There was a front archway, leading into a yard, surrounded with cloisters. Straight on was another archway, leading out of the courtyard and on to the path that led to the shore line, eighty metres further on. On the left of the courtyard were the '*cells*' for the monks that were to have accompanied the Cardinal. To the right was the refectory and what would have been kitchens, if they had ever been finished. At the far right hand side was the only part of the building that had a second storey. On the top floor was the Cardinal's Apartment, planned to be a lavish and spacious affair but it had never been completed. The only substantial building outside the confines of the courtyard was to the right, standing on its own, the Cardinal's private chapel. It was this building that Gunter Siegburg had chosen to be the Operations Room and to where he walked now. He needed to know if other parts of the plan were progressing.

Chapter 18
BOMA, ZAIRE
2nd February 1996

The MV Brilliant Star hardly lived up to its name in appearance. Two hundred and ten feet long, one thousand five hundred tonnes in weight, it looked every day of its twenty two years at sea. Maintenance was not a priority for the owners. They considered painting to be an expensive decorative luxury, not an essential anti-corrosion procedure. From the funnel down to the waterline, brown rust streaks were the predominant visual feature. But it was not just the visual appearance. Had a Lloyds inspector ever managed to get on board he surely would have gone down with a fit of apoplexy. The main deck, once well coated with protective red-lead paint had been penetrated by the constant lashings of rough seas and salt water. Not only was the paint flaking but in areas the very steel had blistered and could be forced free by hand. Below decks the situation was worse. Had the inspector used his tapping hammer around the main intake for the cooling water he would have heard a dull thudding rather than a crisp clear ring. He would not have needed a crystal ball to predict that before too long the hull surrounding the flange would give way and that event would signal a catastrophic end for the vessel.

It had not always been like that. The vessel had been built on Clydebank in Scotland and launched as the MV Fair Bank. For sixteen years it had served as a small but proud part of the Bank Line fleet. It had been classified as a coastal vessel by the original owners, intended for trade in relatively safe '*home waters*' around Europe. The new owners had however re-classified it, with the stroke of a pen, as an ocean-going vessel capable of the longest and most arduous of voyages. Not that the administrative change had altered the commercial viability of the ship. Potential charterers were scared off by the high premiums requested by insurance companies for their cargoes. For the past few years the vessel had been relegated to infrequent voyages carrying low value bulk commodities along the West African coast and even those charters were drying up. That is why the owners didn't ask too many questions when an anonymous customer contracted to take the vessel on open charter to undisclosed African destinations for an indefinite period. They were just pleased to receive the initial payment and security bond from a South African bank. With the formalities complete the captain had received his first orders; to sail light ship from Freetown in Sierra Leone to Boma in Zaire with special instructions to ensure that the single hold had been thoroughly cleaned out and fumigated.

Eight days after it had started its journey the MV Brilliant Star hung on its anchor, just outside the main channel off Boma, the river current trying vainly to push the vessel back out into the open ocean. The Master, a thirty year old native of Monrovia was dressed in his normal 'T' shirt and dirty blue jeans. The only nautical reference to his attire was a battered white captain's hat whose peak was pulled low to protect his eyes from the dazzling sun. Now he stood on the bridge wing and waited patiently, patience being an essential qualification in this part of the world.

"The ship has arrived," announced the soldier who'd come into the '*operations room*' at what was once the Paradise Hotel a little further up the river. "The Harbour Master phoned and said that it has cleared customs."

The latter piece of information was unnecessary. Gunter Siegburg knew the ship would clear customs the second he'd paid over $500 to the Harbour Master. In fact he fully expected the $500 to ensure that there would be no interference or undue delays with the arrival or departure of the vessel due to '*bureaucratic*' problems.

"Thank you, that is all," was Siegburg's response to the messenger who turned smartly and left the room. "You've trained them well," his next comment was directed to Bernd Groelsh.

"Discipline in the camp is one thing. We'll see how they perform under battle conditions."

"You don't sound confident."

"Oh they'll be fine, I have my methods. They might not like it but they'll do as they're told – in the end."

Siegburg nodded fully aware of what the methods would be. "So this is our last meeting before the operation. Are you clear about everything?"

"Perfectly. Today and tomorrow we make preparations on the ship. I have all the equipment that is necessary. The next day the ship sails."

"Is it big enough?"

"Three hundred or so men in the hold will be a tight squeeze but it will be alright as long as the weather is not too rough and we are not kept waiting for too long."

"I'm glad I'm not going on the journey," replied Siegburg.

"At least I won't have to make the whole voyage myself. Once the ship has departed I will escort the *'special squad'* to the Cabinda border. I have the transport prepared, two trucks. Then I will set them loose," said Groelsh.

"What about the uniforms?" There was a taint of alarm in Siegburg's voice as if he'd suddenly remembered a forgotten detail. "Do you have them?"

"Yes, don't worry, they are safe but I won't distribute them till the very end. Where did you get them?"

"It's a long story, a story better told over a beer when this is all over. What are your arrangements after sending off the *'special squad'*?"

"I go by road to the Congo River and then a fast Zairian motor patrol-boat will soon catch up with the *'Brilliant Star'*. And what about you?"

"From here to South Africa, one day to check the plane and airstrip at Massena, then to Cabinda to await the news from you and the *'special squad'*."

Groelsh's expression became more serious and his voice lowered, "And the Baron, does he have any idea?"

The reply was less cautious, even confident. "He suspects nothing. He is too naive and the people around him are too stupid. It will be too late before he realises."

"Good. It's only fair that if we take the risks we get the reward."

"Then it's all good. I will see you in Cabinda."

The men hugged as comrades.

"Good luck," said Groelsh.

"And good luck to you," replied Siegburg.

Chapter 19
Stirling Farm
3rd February 1996

Although her body was becoming increasingly frail Mary's spirit and mind remained undiminished and she retained her matriarchal position easily on Stirling Farm, particularly so when Duncan was away. She was rarely still. *"The devil makes work for idle hands"*, she would say when prompted to slow down. Nothing fazed her; all issues were met head on without fuss. She was even stoic in the face of calamity, something that had visited her life often enough. She had merely nodded when Duncan had told her that he was going to Angola with Jane to help monitor the upcoming referendum. It meant little to her beyond managing the simple practicalities of their absence.

Simon, Melanie and Grace had arrived back at the farm the day after Duncan and Jane had left. Mary had offered Duncan's apology and made sure that they were comfortable. Simon and Melanie were disappointed to have missed Duncan and Jane; Grace was less disappointed, James was there.

Three days after Simon, Melanie and Grace had returned Mary was surprised when they had all appeared in the garden.

"Is there any news from them yet, from Duncan and Jane?" asked Melanie.

Grace hung back a step wearing a face of doom.

"No," replied Mary. "But I wasn't really expecting anything so soon. Is there anything wrong? I might be able to get a message through to them in an emergency; they have left a telephone and fax number for some chap in London."

"No, no, don't do anything like that. It's not that important. We'll leave our plans as they are."

Mary saw tears welling in Grace's eyes.

"Well it might not be that important to you but it is to her," replied Mary pointing at Grace. "Shall we go inside, I'll make a cup of tea and we'll talk about it if you want."

"I always find that problems look a lot less daunting after a cup of tea and a chat," said Mary sitting herself down on a kitchen chair to face the others. "So what is the problem?"

Her gaze was on Grace but it was Melanie who replied. "We have to go away soon on another assignment. It's to do a photo shoot of Ugandan gorillas; it's going to be the gold nugget of our trip. We were really lucky to get special permission and can only go on the specific dates they gave us. Access is extremely limited. We think it's a great opportunity for Grace to see some really endangered animals."

The clue is in the name of the *'Bwindi Impenetrable National Park'*, situated in the south-west of Uganda. The 128 square miles of tropical forest is both dense and remote. That is the most probable reason why three-hundred and forty gorillas live there, half the world's population. They co-exist with one-hundred-and-twenty other species of rare mammals, 348 bird species, 220 types of butterfly, one-thousand flowering plants and one-hundred-and-sixty types of tree. The park has the world's highest concentration of rare and endangered biodiversity.

There are no roads in the Bwindi National Park, no hotels, no telephones; in fact there is basically nothing to do with mankind there. Access is severely restricted and when allowed it is on foot under strict control. Visitors leave this world when they enter the park.

"I take it Grace is not that impressed." said Mary.

"I think that's the nub of it," replied Simon. "She's very upset to be leaving again so soon. She has other things on her mind."

Mary smiled at Grace. "So what is it you would like?"

Grace looked uncomfortable and spoke shyly, her gaze fixed on the floor.

"I'd like to stay here." She paused for a moment. "I didn't really enjoy the trip to the safari park. It was full of tourists jostling around in the hotel and when we did get away from the hotel we just bumped around all day in a truck."

"It won't be the same with the gorillas by the sound of it," said Mary. "And I expect your parents would be disappointed if you don't go with them."

Grace was finding her voice. "I am only just getting to know the people here."

"James?"

"No!" her protest was firm. "I mean the people in the village, my people. I'm more interested in people than in animals and plants."

"So you'd like to stay on here?" asked Mary.

"We told her that would be a terrible imposition," interjected Melanie.

"Oh she's a big girl," said Mary, "I'm sure she wouldn't be too much trouble."

122

"I'd help around the house," said Grace sensing a ray of hope.

"It's really down to your parents," said Mary.

Simon broke in. "There's a bit more to it. There is something I should make you aware of before you agree to anything. I think he was only trying to be nice, but James told Grace that he'd spoken with Duncan and Jane before they left. He got them, well Jane at least as I understand it, to promise to try and find out about Grace's birth family whilst they were in Cabinda. I think her motive for not wanting to go is that she doesn't want to be away if any news comes through. That's the real truth."

"Ouch, the silly boy. I knew about that. He wasn't supposed to say anything to Grace." Mary shook her head gently. "Duncan and Jane did say they'd look at what records there were but I have to be perfectly honest they were not very hopeful." She looked Grace in the eye. "It would be very wrong for you to get your hopes up but if you wanted to stay here that would be fine with me. I already have James and Maggie; one more won't make a difference. Morgan and Tembo are always fussing about and I get help from Mafuti from the Kraal."

"So can I stay Mom?" asked Grace.

"We'll be gone for a couple of weeks. You've never been away from us for so long and you most probably won't be able to contact us for most of the time. Won't you miss us?"

Her response was a little too enthusiastic for Melanie. "No, I'll be fine."

"Well that's it then," said Mary, "It's settled but you can't stay in that lodge on your own. You can move to the house and share with Maggie."

Chapter 20
UN HQ, School K11, Cabinda City
3rd February 1996

The United Nations has a reputation for being an inordinately cumbersome bureaucracy burdened with the niceties of international diplomacy. However in practice, field operations can have a surprising degree of flexibility and spontaneity, even a raw edge; provided the Head of Station has both the authority and guile. The Cabinda operation, having André Piet as its Director, was fortunate in both respects.

M. Piet looked over the two documents that were laid on the table before him; one was a map of Cabinda with rural polling stations marked in red felt pen; the second was the itinerary, a list of the stations and dates for visits. He thought it was a good plan, but he had concerns. Was it acceptable to carry out joint inspections with the Angolans? He didn't dither for too long, a deep breath signifying the end of his deliberations.

"Okay Mr Murdoch, I am agreeable for you to travel in the company of the Presidential Guard. I must ask if you are aware of the potential difficulties and dangers? You will be alone with the Angolan monitors and out of our immediate protection. You will be dependent on the Angolans for communications with this office. Do you feel comfortable with that?"

Duncan nodded.

"Will Miss Ashton be comfortable during your absence?"

"Of that I'm sure," replied Duncan. "She has a habit of making life interesting for her colleagues, I'm sure you will enjoy her company."

"I'm not sure I understand what you mean by that. All I can say is that you should not worry about Miss Ashton. As long as she obeys instructions I can assure you of her safety. She will be under the UN and my protection."

Duncan wanted to say, "Obeying instructions is not her strong point," but resisted the temptation. Instead he concluded, "Then that's fine, we're on. I'll join Captain Marobi outside and we'll get going. See you in eight days or so."

"I expect you to try and phone or radio in at least every forty-eight hours, better still every twenty-four." He offered his hand to Duncan. "Good luck."

124

Jane would have liked to have been going along but had accepted Piet's decision. As they parted she had given Duncan her notes. "Promise you will at least try. It's important to her."

The distances were not great and the coastal road was the best that Cabinda had to offer but progress was not fast. Captain David Marobi drove the lead Nissan Pathfinder at a sedate pace doing his best for the comfort of the troops in the rear of the Hino three tonne truck which was following. Marobi was conscious his men had to sit on un-cushioned outward facing wooden bench seats; his consideration was indicative of how the man's mind worked.

Alongside Marobi sat Duncan dressed in plain sand-coloured fatigues which stood in contrast to the dark green jungle camouflage battle dress of Marobi and his men. The United Nations' light blue berry and shoulder sash distinguished Duncan even more. As they trundled along the badly paved road that weaved its way through the outer environs of Cabinda City, Duncan looked out of the window at the seemingly endless mass of shanty town.

It was an unplanned and chaotic African suburbia characterised by ramshackle buildings, tiny alleyways, open sewers and the stench of decaying humanity that even permeated the Nissan's air filtration system. Yet in Duncan's mind there was something strangely alluring about the place. It was not without hope. Perhaps it was the dense concentration of people pressed together in their squalid warren-like habitation that inadvertently acted as a social leveller. Duncan thought that people didn't live in the shanty town, rather they belonged to it and he imagined there was something perversely comforting and reassuring to be a member of the community. He mused how a similar development had risen, like a Phoenix out of the ashes, collectively raising its inhabitants. Once Soweto had been like this yet the people had come together, coalesced into a powerful social force to the extent that the label '*resident of Soweto*' had become a badge of honour recognised throughout the world. But deep down he knew the chance of that happening here was small.

"Does it disgust you?" asked Marobi, bringing Duncan back to the present with a jolt.

Duncan focused his mind. "No, far from it. There is something there worth preserving."

"What do you mean?" asked Marobi.

125

In my country Scotland, in Glasgow, we once had living conditions like this. We called them tenement blocks, places where people lived in inhumane conditions; squalor, poverty, disease and every conceivable immorality abounded. In the name of progress new developments were constructed, the people moved out and the tenements were pulled down. Now if you talk to the old people who used to live in the tenements they will agree that they are better off, there is less disease, they are warm, they are secure but in the same breath they will say that something has gone. The new places have no community; they are cold characterless concrete places without a sense of belonging."

"Ah that is the view of a romantic and it ignores reality. You live in the world of Emile Zola."

"Who is Emile Zola?" asked Duncan.

"A thought provoking French thinker and writer of the nineteenth century," replied David.

"How do you know about him?" asked Duncan not disguising his surprise at Marobi's knowledge.

David Marobi took one hand off the steering wheel and held it up for a second displaying the blackness of his skin.

"You are surprised that a black man, particularly one that wears a uniform and carries a gun should be capable of knowing about French philosophy. That my friend is a thing called inherent prejudice. But don't be alarmed. I don't think badly of you. It's something you can't help. All that can be hoped for is that your conscious mind tries to fight it and I can tell already, from what I know of you, that is what you try to do. Besides I went out of my way to find out a little of your background. I know what is in your heart."

"What!"

"Well do you think I'm stupid enough to go gallivanting around the jungle with somebody I don't think I can trust?"

Duncan stared out of the window again but now his thoughts were not on what his eyes could see.

The Angola of the mid-1960's was relatively speaking a docile and backward colony of Portugal, kept in line by the hard-line right wing Salazar dictatorship in Lisbon. Officially it was an external province of the mother country, just another province of Portugal proper. Generally speaking this designation had little consequence for the poverty stricken majority black population. They were still considered to be an inferior breed fit mainly for manual labour.

But it had not always been like that. Luanda, the capital of Angola was one of the oldest European settlements on the African continent being able to trace its origins back to Henry the Navigator in the 15th century. For a century the Government in Lisbon considered Luanda as nothing more than an underperforming trading post. The big money was to be made in India and the Far East. It was events in another part of the Portuguese Empire that was to shape the future of the African outpost.

Brazil had been discovered and colonised by the Portuguese in the early 16th century. The first explorers had spent their time searching for gold and looting the natives. Revenues soon dried up and the prospects for the colony looked bleak. Until it was discovered that sugar, a much sought after commodity, would grow well in the Brazilian climate. Unfortunately the indigenous Brazilian population proved *'unsuitable even for slavery'* on the new plantations. However Africans were considered to be excellent *'slave stock'*. At first slaves were transported from Luanda to south Portugal and sold at markets before being transported to Brazil. Soon the Portuguese market was cut out and they were transported directly from Africa to Brazil. For a long time Portugal became the biggest slave trading nation in the world.

In Africa, the Portuguese had no need to establish a vast colony; instead they exploited tribal differences and an African propensity to be inhumane to their own. Warriors from favoured tribes and clans were sent out from Luanda to capture slaves and bring them back to Luanda to be exchanged for beads, brass wire, textiles and most of all modern weapons. For more than two hundred years lands deep in the African interior were stripped of the flower of their youth. Ironically it was not only the Portuguese traders that grew rich on the system; a few African clans also became wealthy. Some were prudent and grew into minor dynasties, African aristocracy. It was into the remnants of such a dynasty, a heritage of African exploiting African that David Marobi was born in 1964. For David Marobi and his father, the guilt of their ancestors would reside in the back of their minds forever. They were wise enough to know there was nothing that could be done to expunge the sins of former generations but, almost without ever discussing the issue, they were of one mind in their desire to eliminate the Africans' ability to be cruel to their own. They became part of a rare and lonely breed.

127

David's father Jonathan was a non-violent man. Not one to pick up arms. His war had been an intellectual one, fighting for the contents of peoples minds. His Portuguese passport and residual family wealth had enabled him to study not only in Angola but also in Portugal and then later in the United States where he had shone like a star and won many over with his reasoned arguments on liberal democracy.

David, his son, never had the intellectual capacity or potential of his father but that was not a disappointment to either because he did share the same values. David's way was not that of the theoretician, he was to propagate practical and direct methods. His secondary schooling took place in Portugal and he attended university in Lisbon, passing but not excelling in a degree in English. After his studies he could have gone to join his father in the United States but decided to stay in Portugal for his National Service. His degree and declared willingness to sign on for a couple of extra years ensured his officer status. From a distance he watched as his country, Angola, tore itself to shreds in a bloody and bitter civil war. When it concluded and the corrupt leaders looked to his father to act as figurehead President, David had resigned from the Portuguese Army and joined his father in Angola as head of the tiny independent Presidential Guard.

David Marobi and Duncan travelled north, crossing the Lulondo River and following the coastal road with the sea on the left. Not that they could see it for much of the time as the road twisted, following the natural contours of the land. There were small intermittent patches of barren rocky land, subsistence farming where it was fertile enough to scratch a living but it was mainly undulations with thick vegetation that crept up to the very edges of the metalled roadway that had once proudly born the title highway. Now, due to years of neglect, it could no longer justify that description. The traffic was minimal. In the first hour they'd met an African bus trundling in the opposite direction, listing heavily to one side as if the suspension was damaged, the situation not helped by overcrowding and a roof stacked with an assortment of luggage and crates clinging precariously as the vehicle rocked from side to side. A little later two lorries came towards them each bellowing plumes of black smoke as the engines laboured to haul their loads of hardwood that had undoubtedly been illegally felled in the rainforest. Otherwise traffic was limited to occasional ox drawn carts, a rickety bicycle and two or three women in colourful cotton prints carrying bundles on their heads invariably followed by scantily clad infants almost trotting to keep up with their mother's hasty steps. Just before the town of Malembo they came across their first roadblock. The barrier consisted of two fifty gallon oil drums, one on either side of the road with a slender pole, a trimmed tree branch, connecting the two. Four men manned the barrier dressed in worn battledress and black berets. Incongruously they wore not regulation boots but rubber soled sandals manufactured from defunct car tyres.

"You stay in the vehicle," said David as he drew the vehicle to a halt a few yards short of the check point.

He got out and approached the men that were now holding their weapons if not threateningly, at least in a more attentive manner. Duncan couldn't hear the words spoken but by angling his head he looked into the rear view mirror and could see that some of the Presidential Guard in the following truck had disembarked and were readying their weapons.

After a while David came back to the Nissan and fired up the engine. The barrier was removed and the vehicles moved forward. As they passed the check point Duncan noticed to the left, previously concealed by the undergrowth, three large Yamaha trial bikes each bearing a helmeted man presumably ready to pursue anybody that tried to '*run*' the roadblock.

David was the first to speak. "They're unofficial militia. You can never tell if they're going to be drunk or high on khat. It makes them potentially erratic and dangerous."

"Can you be sure they are not Angolan soldiers?" asked Duncan.

"Some of them might be former soldiers. But along the coastal road we should be alright. When we go into the jungle there is always the chance there are separatist rebels setting up an ambush. It's rare but it does happen."

The procedure was to be repeated several times over the next few days.

The method of local government and administration in Cabinda was a replica of the Portuguese system. Cabinda was split into districts; each district was governed by a '*Camera*', the Council. Councils were further split into sub-districts which were administered by a '*Junta*'. It was one of the jobs of the Junta to maintain the '*citizen list*' but it was a function that had been neglected over the years. A whole new register had to be established for the referendum. Normally each Junta office was open from nine in the morning to midday and then from 3pm to

5pm but for the duration of the registration period they would be open from 8am to 8pm. Only people who were on the register would be allowed to vote in the actual referendum.

"So my friend this is Malabo, our first stop," said David as he drew up the vehicle on the dusty shoulder of the road.

"The Junta office is just over there." He pointed to the only brick-built two storey building. "The truck and my troops can wait here. We'll walk the remaining distance."

Duncan got out of the vehicle and suddenly appreciated the air-conditioned cocoon he had been travelling in as the hot humid air hit him in the face. He looked around taking in the view.

Malembo was not an overcrowded place with cramped shanties. The houses were large by African standards, most of the private dwellings were of mud-wall construction, the better ones built from cinder block. All had corrugated iron roofs and substantial gardens boasting not flower beds and decoration but tiny plots for the cultivation of vegetables and the keeping of chickens. The side roads were just tracks in the compressed red soil. On dry days, like today, even the light breeze lifted dust into the air. On open ground miniature tornadoes suddenly formed but disappeared quickly and did nothing to alleviate the sultry feeling that enveloped the settlement.

The two men walked towards the Junta Office. Outside the building were the only two visible vehicles, a couple of white pickup trucks. Duncan noted that the idea for the emblems painted on the doors of the trucks had been borrowed from the Soviet hammer and sickle. The picture was of a half-gear wheel crossed by a machete with a star to the top left. As they walked Duncan became aware of approaching traffic. He turned to see a long white bus being driven along the highway. It was not a typical ramshackle African bus but a new, white painted vehicle, pristine except for the red dust that clung to the sides in defiance of gravity. As the bus drew closer it slowed and Duncan could see the symbols painted on the side: two big "V's", one red the other blue. Above the "V's" written in capital letters was the word "*Chevron*". The bus slowed, turned off the road and pulled up outside the Junta offices. The occupants, well dressed Africans, started to get out and began to form an orderly queue outside the office door.

David didn't wait for Duncan to ask. "This is oil country; the whole coastal strip owes its prosperity to the oil industry. Good jobs, good pay, those are the lucky ones. The oil company is providing transport for them to come and register."

"Why would they do that?" asked Duncan.

"The oil companies are on to a good thing. They don't want any change in the current arrangements, nor do the people who work for the oil companies. The whole coastal strip will reject independence. But the situation may well be different in the interior."

It took Duncan about half-an-hour to go through his check list with the head of the Junta, a thin smiling middle aged African in safari suit, crumpled white shirt and thin red necktie. The register was being compiled in accordance with recommendations and Duncan watched as the line of smiling bus passengers shuffled forward, patiently waiting their turn. It crossed his mind that the event was so smooth that it might even have been orchestrated specifically for his observation.

Light was beginning to fail by the time they had reached the last settlement before the Congolese border. They had gone through several roadblocks and inspected four Junta Offices and everything was in order. That night Duncan stayed at the guest house belonging to Angola Oil at Chicamba. A steady flow of American and European oil workers passed through the place and it provided good accommodation and decent food.

"You should get an early night," was David Marobi's parting advice before he left to spend the night with his troops in the local barracks. "Tomorrow we go inland. It will be slower and less comfortable."

Beside Still Waters

David Wooding unlocked the door to his secure office and walked into the room. He went over to the electronics stack and pushed the power button on the server even before he'd taken off his soaked winter coat. He knew he'd have time to dry himself off and even make a cup of coffee before the green screens on his desk lit up.

David hated this duty which he had to do one week in every four. His house was only five minutes from his normal office in Cheltenham. The drive to Portishead however was forty-five miles down the M5 and could take an hour on a good day and more like an hour and a half on a bad day. Today was a bad day. Winter persisted. A freezing fog had descended over the West Country overnight and the roads were shrouded in winter gloom. The side roads were treacherous with unseen patches of black ice. To cap it off freezing rain had begun to fall as he pulled into the car park, forcing him to run the one hundred and fifty yards from his car to the building's main entrance. The ice cold droplets of rain burnt his cheeks on the short dash.

A few minutes later he sat down at his desk cradling a mug of coffee in the palm of his hands. His screen glowed; green writing on a black background. He put his finger on the *'down'* arrow on the keyboard and shook his head. Not that long ago the system had been state of the art but now DOS systems had been superseded by the Windows operating systems. He guessed that Portishead, as a remote outpost, would not be a priority for an upgrade any time soon.

He looked at the right-hand column of the tabulation that was rolling before his eyes. Page after page went by with nothing. Portishead processed literally millions of communications a year. Every day there were thousands. After a while it became mesmerising; he blinked and almost missed it. He had to press the *'up'* arrow and go back a page or two. Instead of a number there was, a *'flag'*, actually a capital 'X', on the column headed IMEI. IMEI stood for International Mobile Equipment Identity. A new unregistered transmitter had come on line. He punched a few keys; the screen changed; he waited for the computer to catch up.

"Ah!" he thought to himself. "No actual IMSI number. This boy doesn't have a registered SIM card."

David went to another screen and tried to get a location lock. The best he could get was somewhere around South-West Africa. Only two satellites got a lock on the transmission; that wasn't enough. Three were needed for full triangulation. The location was only accurate to within a radius of a hundred miles. He couldn't even determine if the transmission was land or sea based but he did know it was within the footprint of the Foreign Office *'watch'* list.

David set the computer to automatically record further transmissions from the flagged IMEI and at the same time scan for other equipment responding. Then he sent a message to his usual office at GCHQ in Cheltenham, along the dedicated optical fibre line. Before he'd finished setting up the connection his screen flashed. Another unidentified phone had shown up. Before he had time to check it out, a third piece of unidentified equipment flashed up on his screen. The three pieces of equipment were communicating with each other. He modified his message to GCHQ. The status of the incident was automatically upgraded to *'alert'*. David cursed under his breath knowing that he'd now have to stay at Portishead until he'd identified the transmissions or somebody came to relieve him, and there wouldn't be many volunteers for that job. He settled down for a long day.

Arthur C Clarke had first published the idea. He reckoned that if a satellite was pushed into a high enough orbit it would spin at the same rate as the earth itself. It took a full gaggle of scientists and mathematicians to work out what that orbit was: 22,236 miles. At that altitude a satellite would appear to be standing still to people on the earth; geostationary was the term they coined.

The next step came from an even more unlikely source. Singen Fetherstone-Hore had come through prep-school and Eton unharnessed by convention and a love of the Classics; his interest lay in adventure and science or more precisely science fiction. After Cambridge he'd followed his chosen career path, with the help of his well-connected father, and joined the security services, MI6 to be precise. His enthusiasm and motivation had indicated a promising future. Unfortunately Singen had an Achilles heel; he *'batted for the other side'* as his controller had delicately put it in his report. Not that preferring the company of gentlemen over that of ladies was considered to be particularly bad or even unusual in his circle. The problem was that he had a particular passion for public toilets. He could not avoid mixing his sexual preferences with his insatiable desire for risk. That particular behavioural trait

133

did not fit in well with his position at MI6. It was suggested that his future might be best served in a different environment. That's how he ended up working, somewhat reluctantly, in the City, for Lloyds of London as a maritime insurance broker. That was in the early 70's. He never stopped yearning to return to MI6.

As a maritime broker he'd learnt to listen with dread for the Lutine Bell. The Lutine Bell hung in the great hall at Lloyds and was rung whenever news of a ship's loss came through. It was at a time when even great ships had only short-wave radios and Morse code with which to communicate. Many ships went missing for two or three weeks at a time, some vanished without trace. It was an expensive problem for Lloyds.

Somebody suggested that if there was a network of geostationary satellites in space, then ships in any part of the oceans could have constant contact with their owners and emergencies could be better handled. Unfortunately nobody was willing to pick up the bill for a network of expensive satellites. That was until Singen had a brainwave. He felt sure that every ship owner in the world would jump at the chance of having continuous information as to their vessels' whereabouts and to have the ability to talk shore to ship at any time. He also knew that whoever controlled that system would know the position of every significant ship in the world and have the ability to eavesdrop on their communications. The intelligence potential was truly staggering. He penned a missive about his ideas and sent it off to MI6 in the hope of rehabilitation. His idea was taken up and his rehabilitation became a distinct prospect until a further conviction for lurid behaviour in a public place and indecent exposure put an end to discussions on the matter. Singen never saw what his basic idea developed into.

By 1996 Inmarsat had nine satellites in orbit and about 95% of the world's shipping companies as subscribers. They would have had ten satellites if a French Arrian rocket had not malfunctioned on launch. Ostensibly Inmarsat was funded by Lloyds of London but actually most of the money had come from the British Foreign Office, in much the same way as BBC World Service was funded, not by the licence payer but by the security services.

It was a great asset as it was, but then a US company, Motorola, took it to another level. They came up with the idea for a mobile satellite phone based on the Inmarsat system. Sure it wasn't totally mobile, it required a small parabolic dish and an external power source but it was a winner, not only for Motorola but also for British Intelligence as all messages could be intercepted. Inmarsat stood for International Maritime Satellite System. Because of the *'Maritime'* in the name a bureaucrat decided it would best be located in Portishead, the traditional home of the Merchant Navy radio system. It was on the Inmarsat system that David Wooding was now operating at Portishead.

By six pm David had intercepted no less than eleven messages. Unfortunately he had no idea what they said. The mysterious units were using a state of the art system, SBDT, *'short burst data transmission'*. SBDT was a sophisticated system only used for two reasons: when somebody had so much information to transmit that connection to a satellite became prohibitively expensive or, as David suspected in this case, when somebody wanted to minimise their time *'on air'* so as to reduce the chance of detection.

The *'short burst'* information David had intercepted was decoded by a technician at GCHQ and then graded by an Intelligence Analyst. The Reviewing Supervisor decided it was important enough to pass on. He directed an alert to the African Desk of the Foreign and Commonwealth Office. The Duty Officer at the Foreign and Commonwealth Office couldn't make head nor tail of the telex message from GCHQ so he put it in his pending tray to await further developments.

Chapter 22
Windhoek, South West Africa
4th February 1996

The technician had arrived in jeans and 'T' shirt. Von Swartzstein was unimpressed.

"I didn't want to stand out," he explained.

"I would prefer it if you dressed properly," replied Freiherr von Swartzstein.

The technician didn't argue. Before he started work he changed into his fatigues, making sure that his tunic was properly buttoned up.

Four hours later von Swartzstein followed the uniformed technician to the roof terrace of the villa to inspect the installation.

Von Swartzstein looked at the parabolic dish and the cabling that ran around the terrace and disappeared over the wall.

"It looks like a TV satellite dish and the cabling looks very untidy," were his initial comments.

Fortunately the technician had been warned about van Swartzstein's idiosyncrasies.

"I agree Freiherr von Swartzstein." The technician had been told always to agree with the Baron, even if the Baron was wrong. "What I have done now is just to see if the system works. When it is proved I will make it so you cannot see the cables and I can put a fibreglass *'golf-ball'* cover over the parabolic dish. It will then look really impressive, distinctive. Nobody else will have an installation like it."

The comments removed the scowl from the Baron's face. "I look forward to seeing that. Now take me to the room I have assigned to you."

The technician had taken care to cover the French polished table, that the Baron's wife had supplied, with some green baize material to prevent scratching. The equipment did not look very elaborate. There was a phone set, something that did not look dissimilar to an ordinary table top phone, an electronic box that meant nothing to the baron and a computer with an attached dot-matrix printer. It looked makeshift but was neat enough. The technician had done all he could to make the multitude of connecting cables look tidy.

"Explain to me what this does," ordered the Baron.

The technician smiled and tried not to be patronising. "The parabolic dish on the terrace is pointed at a geostationary satellite twenty-two thousand miles above us. It is also connected, via a high volume super-fast fibre optic cable, to this processing unit. The processing unit has several functions. It is able to take analogue data transmissions from the handset." The technician pointed at the phone. "It converts the analogue to a digital signal, the only type of data that can be transmitted along a fibre optic cable of this sort. Additionally it can both receive and transmit SBD's, that is short burst data transmissions."

Von Swartzstein was looking perplexed.

"Put simply you can type a message on the computer using the keyboard. It will be sent to the box that will compress the message and send it to the recipient via the satellite.

"So I can send a written message to anybody in the world instantly?"

"Yes you can," replied the technician, "as long as they have the same equipment as you that is."

Von Swartzstein frowned.

The technician sensed disapproval. "With the phone your voice will be sent up into the heavens whenever you wish and the satellite will send it back to any place on this earth. For that the recipient only needs an ordinary phone.

Von Swartzstein appeared pleased at the thought of his voice being relayed via the heavens.

"But that is for the future," said the technician. "In the meantime we must only use the equipment for the task in hand. The time is approaching for our check in call. Then later you will give the signal for the formal start of the operation. Perhaps you would like to compose a message."

Von Swartzstein was not completely convinced by the technology. He recalled that Gunter Siegburg had said he need not be in contact during the operation. But von Swartzstein felt differently. As leader he wanted ultimate control so, Siegburg had come up with the present system which was much to the Baron's liking. It offered the prospect of him sending an inspiring message to his foot soldiers on the eve of combat. He felt that was appropriate.

The Baron straightened his shoulders, turned sharply and departed for his study where he would contemplate the words he would use for his '*address*'. The technician sat at his computer and stared at the screen trying to remember the password but the only word that would come to mind for the moment was '*prat*'.

A plume of black smoke spurted from the funnel of the '*MV Brilliant Star*' as the engineer '*blew*' the engine over with compressed air and it hesitatingly came to life. It was a full thirty seconds before the engine settled into a steady throb at 185 rpm and the black smoke gave way to a light grey plume that rose vertically in the still and humid air of the Congo River. The Captain walked on to the bridge wing and waved his hand at the bo's'n who was on the ship's forecastle waiting. It was the signal for him to engage the windlass and raise the anchor. The clanging of chain as it fell into the chain locker below the forecastle rattled throughout the ship and was amplified in the hold, audible even above the drone of the noisy ventilation fans that laboured to keep an air flow for the three hundred armed men that were doing their best to make themselves comfortable in a bad situation.

Bernd Groelsh stood on the quay two hundred yards away, watching as the vessel slowly came about and set off down the river. It would be three days before he made the rendezvous and rejoined his men on the ship.

He drove himself back to what had once been the Paradise Hotel but had been his training base for the past few weeks. It felt strangely quiet, empty now that the majority of his men had left. All that remained were the ruthless, undisciplined ones. Groelsh parked the car and pondered for a moment; the next phase was going to be critical. He too would have to be ruthless and decisive but first he had to send his signal.

Everything was at the farm near Louis Trichrdt, a South African border town near the Limpopo River. The men had been arriving in a steady trickle. They needed no training; they did what they knew they had to do. Equipment was checked and then checked again. Maps were studied and plans gone over. Each man became familiar with his own assignment. There was no doubting them. They would do their job.

In the late afternoon, as the sun was slowly sinking in the western sky the drone of the aircraft's engine grew louder, a sound familiar to all the men. Some came out into the open and watched as the twin-engine propeller-driven aircraft made a wide circle as it descended slowly. The wing profile and bulbous nose were as familiar as the noise. The plane touched down at the very beginning of the grass strip and taxied to a halt close to the farm buildings.

The plane had first seen service in the last years of the Second World War. On D-day it had simultaneously carried a troop of the American 101st Airborne and towed a glider across the English Channel at the very beginning of the operation. For the next five days it had made countless journeys back and forward from France to England. A few months later it carried British paratroopers on the failed attack on Arnhem.

At the end of the war the Americans couldn't be bothered to take it back State-side; they just had too many of them. It was sold to a war surplus dealer who really had no need for it but hoped something would come up. For three years it stood idly on a Cambridge airstrip. Its airworthiness certificate ran out and the dealer began to fear that his investment was not going to mature. But then the Russians decided to blockade Berlin and the allies got together to mount a massive airlift to supply the city. Anything that could fly was commandeered. For almost a year the plane ran to and fro Berlin Templehof Airport carrying goods in and people out. Each trip netted more profit than the dealer had paid for the aircraft in the first place.

When the airlift ended the plane again stood idle until the South African Air Force decided it could do with a few more transports. They held on to it until 1964. By then it was twenty years old and as far as the South African Air Force was concerned beyond its useful life. Then history intervened again.

On 11th November 1965 Ian Smith declared UDI in Rhodesia. Suddenly that country was at war. A friendly South African government did what it could to help and the plane was rescued from the scrap heap and repainted in Rhodesian Air Force colours. For sixteen years it took part in countless special operations, often flying four sorties a day to drop paratroopers from the Rhodesian Light Infantry in '*hot pursuit*' operations.

Not long after the war was lost, and Rhodesia had become Zimbabwe, the plane was sold to a small Harare based freight company. From then on it was chartered, mainly to mining companies to ferry goods and sometimes people around Southern Africa.

Throughout its long career the aircraft had sustained no damage whatsoever, not even a single bullet hole; never had there been any accident or injury on board. In fact many of the original features from its US Air Force days remained. One of the features was a small metallic strip stuck to the bulkhead just above where the radio operator normally sat. In the phonetic alphabet was written the plane's original call sign: LIMA, UNIFORM, CHARLIE, KILO, YANKIE: spelling LUCKY. The plane had certainly been lucky both in operation and name.

The arrival of the plane was almost the last piece in the jigsaw. All that remained to be done was loading up and to send a satellite message indicating readiness.

Chapter 23
Lulia, Cabinda Province
5th February 1996

The openness of the coastal strip was far behind them. They were now in the rainforest, the green canopy still and motionless high above them. Occasional spear-like shafts of bright sunlight broke through the uppermost foliage generating an almost cathedral like atmosphere. The track was deeply rutted and hardly warranted the title of road. The odour was a strange mix of new growth and rotting vegetation. It was as if it were almost possible to smell the cycle of life; new nubile vegetation optimistically clinging on to the promise of life, emitting sweet odours, before maturing and then giving way to the challenges of nature, wilting and finally rotting with a pungent vengeance.

The snail like progress came to a halt as David Marobi stopped the Nissan in deference to a troop of baboons occupying the centre of the track. In front was the largest of the group. Initially the primate was unperturbed by the arrival of the vehicles, ignoring their presence, pretending that they were a natural part of his day. David selected first gear and slowly edged forward. At some point he crossed the invisible line that signified entry to the animal's personal space. The baboon turned to face the challenge, lifted his arms high and came to full stretch, pushing out his chest. He bared his teeth, displaying menacing fangs. The other animals in the troop stopped their foraging and playing. Each looked intently and expectantly at the alpha male, waiting for a signal. A mother to the rear moved deftly and quickly scooped up her tiny offspring. David inched the vehicle forward a few more paces. The alpha male stood his ground staring intently at the threat as if deciding what to do. Suddenly he let out a great roar of defiance, turned his back on the intruders and waved his bare backside, a gesture of indecency common to both the human and primate worlds. The rest of the troop took their signal from the alpha male and quickly scrambled away to the left of the track each emitting screeching cries. Slowly and deliberately, in a final display of defiance, the alpha male sauntered after his charges and disappeared into the undergrowth.

Duncan Murdoch moved his gaze to David Marobi. "They're an intimidating bunch aren't they?"

"I'd like to say their bark is worse than their bite, but it isn't. They can be really nasty."

141

Both men laughed.

They were now into the third day of their tour. Duncan had grown to like David Marobi more and more. Between jolts, bumps and delays they talked. Duncan learnt the young Angolan Army Officer had a great respect for his father and the ideals he stood for. It was clear that David saw his father as the man to set the conditions for a better society and himself as a tool to assist – a man of practicality and kindness thought Duncan.

The previous night they'd stayed at the police depot at Bucco Zau. The accommodation was rudimentary: camp beds in a shared room, cold water from aluminium jugs for washing and out of date Cuban Army rations for food. When darkness fell there was nothing to do but talk. The two of them sat alone with only the dull yellow glow of a hanging kerosene lamp to break the darkness. The men discovered each other there.

"My father became President at the time when the Angolan Government wanted to present a respectable face to the world. It was a difficult choice for him. He knew that by becoming President of Angola after the war he would be offering legitimacy to a corrupt and brutal regime. In the end he decided that he would have more chance of changing things from the inside, so he accepted the post.

One concession he drew was that he could have his own Presidential Guard. This was to be a small unit, free of the Army command structure that was to protect him but would also have freedom of movement and the ability to report to him directly. He asked me to take charge of that unit. Many said he was guilty of nepotism, that he was as bad as the governing junta. And it is true that I would not have got the job if he had not been my father but I promise you we do what we can for the people.

I am here because my father wants the referendum to be as free and fair as possible. I am his eyes."

"Your father agrees that Cabinda should become independent then?" asked Duncan.

"No not at all. He thinks it will be bad for Angola and Cabinda."

"Why?"

"The problem is not that the Angolan Government takes the oil money. The problem is that a group of corrupt leaders are in control. All that independence would achieve would be to replace corrupt leaders in Luanda for corrupt leaders in Cabinda City. There would be no benefit to the people of Cabinda. What needs to be changed is the method of government. Everything is about the battle to eliminate corruption – wherever it occurs. More than that, Cabinda has oil wealth now but one day that oil will be gone. But Angola is vast; it has huge amounts of minerals much of which have not yet been discovered. He believes it is better for Cabinda to share its current oil wealth with the rest of the country and then, when the time comes, the people of Angola will share their wealth with the people of Cabinda."

"Your father has a good mind if he truly believes that but he has challenges ahead of him."

"He knows that but he says that big problems are only made up of lots of small problems. We will just keep solving each small problem as it comes along."

Duncan contemplated the next question. "So did your father send you to make sure you win the referendum?"

There was no anger in the response but it was emphatic. "No. My father believes in democracy. He says it's not a perfect system but it's the best we have. He is anxious that the referendum is fair. He is worried that others do not share that opinion."

"You told me what your father thinks. What do you think?"

"I don't think we're ready yet. Everything is going too fast. The people in New York, in the United Nations, they sit in nice calm offices and profess on principle. They don't understand reality. This election will never be fair in my view. You have seen for yourself. In the coastal areas where support for Luanda is strong, it is organised. The people are comfortable; buses will bring them to vote. But here in the interior the support is for independence. Here it is not organised. The people are scared. They believe the government will penalise them if they vote for independence but if they don't vote there is a danger that the liberation movement people will attack them. They are in an impossible position."

"So who will win the referendum?"

"Clearly the government. In truth our presence here is pointless, we are wasting out time, it's a foregone conclusion. People will vote to stay with Luanda. But what about you Duncan? Why are you here?"

"I don't want to be here at all," replied Duncan honestly with a smile. "I cannot claim to be acting on any high moral principle. I'm only here to keep an eye on Jane, to look out for her. She is the one that wanted to come."

"So she is the one with romantic principles."

"Not principles like you but she does have romantic notions which, if I am truthful, can get her into difficulties at times."

"Only the naive have romantic notions about this place."

"I'm not sure about that. She's not naive," replied Duncan. "Not in the sense you mean."

"I don't understand, tell me," said David.

Duncan gave David a "*potted history*" of his relationship with Jane, explaining the type of person she was: loving, caring, idealistic and very clever but daring in an almost childish way. He concluded by telling David the latest torch Jane was carrying, the story about Grace, how her mother and been killed, how she'd been rescued and taken to America and the struggle she was having with her own identity.

"The young lady Grace has been both fortunate and unfortunate," said David at the end of the story. "She has a life that is beyond the dreams of most people here yet it sounds as if she feels guilty for what she left behind. It will be difficult for her to enjoy what she has but it is good that she doesn't forget. Do you have any details about her beginnings?"

"I have some handwritten notes in my bag," replied Duncan.

"Show me."

David read the two A4 sheets, the ones that Jane had given Duncan when he'd left Cabinda City. He held them close to the kerosene lamp for light.

"In this part of the world they do not keep very good records. It would be useless trying to get information from a government office."

"We already found that out," replied Duncan.

David thought for a while. "We are not so far away from where the baby was found. We could go there tomorrow, ask some questions, if you would like that."

"Go into the jungle and just ask some questions? That doesn't sound very promising."

David smiled. "We may not have very much in the line of official administration but what we have never been short of are missions and churches. The people in those places tend to have a long memories. I'm happy to go and see and you may never be here again. Maybe something good will come from this trip after all; perhaps we can solve one of those small problems my father talks about."

It had been an early start but now they were near. The last two kilometres of the journey were easier. There were breaks in the forest, places where men had hacked away at the undergrowth and established small areas for cultivation. They

144

passed close to a clump of huts, a small village. Smoke from a cooking fire rose into the air but there were no people.

"Where are they?" asked Duncan. "Aren't the villagers curious? It can't be often that vehicles come this way."

"Visitors are uncommon in this area and rarely bring good news, particularly those that turn up in army trucks. They'll have dashed off into the jungle but you can be sure that somebody is watching us."

David carried on the pace and passed the settlement without slowing. The ground started to rise gently and the track widened and gave the appearance of having had some recent attention. Fifteen minutes later they rounded a bend and were met with the incongruous sight of a church that would not have looked out of place in a nineteenth century Mediterranean village. The building boasted a terracotta tiled roof and gable-end bell tower, with missing bell. The potentially idyllic sight was spoilt by black streaked dirty white paintwork and an abundance of weeds in the cobbled square that fronted the building.

Duncan smiled and shook his head. "How did this get here?" he asked.

"Monuments such as this we are not short of," replied David. "It was in the name of the Church that Cabinda was opened up in the first place."

David stopped the Nissan and the truck pulled up behind. The soldiers spilled out arching backs and stretching limbs trying to find relief from the pains inflicted during the arduous journey. A few lit cigarettes, others took swigs from canteens of water.

The front door of the church opened slowly revealing only darkness. From the gloom came an African, a monk in brown cassock. Slowly he stepped forward into the light. He stopped, folding his arms, tucking his hands into the folds of his cassock.

David walked towards the man.

"What do you want?" asked the monk.

"I want to seek your help Father."

The monk's suspicions were not allayed by the softly spoken words. "How can we help you? We have nothing here."

Chapter 24
Villa Santa Maria, Cabinda City
6th February 1996. Early Morning.

There was a big flat spider on the ceiling in the corner of the room, motionless between the cracks and flakes of yellowing paint. Ap Ewan's gaze had been fixed on the arachnid for a long time but his mind was elsewhere. In the next room he could hear everything that was going on and it disgusted him, not only because of what it was but because he had facilitated it. With each sound he conjured up a new mental vision.

He'd arrived at this place willingly yet he hadn't applied for the job that had been assigned to him. It had been forced on him. He'd not been given the opportunity to refuse and now he was too scared to cross the people in charge. He knew he'd just have to sit tight and see how things panned out. His normally inexhaustible reservoir of optimism was running dry.

The grunts next door grew. There was a sound of cracking wood, most probably breaking furniture, followed by garbled words, not in a language he understood, some African dialect or other. But the tones transcended interpretation; they were words not of love and passion but of trepidation and fear. One of the girls screamed. Ap Ewan heard a hard slap, hand on flesh, then the momentary silence and finally the cowering sobs. He heard Lubala's voice, gruff and loud, insulting and sneering and finally the clink of glass.

"At last," thought ap Ewan. "Lubala's back at the whisky; he'll fall asleep soon or fall into a drunken stupor more like."

The Germans scared ap Ewan. It was as much what they weren't doing as what they were doing.

Ap Ewan longed to go back, back to Boma. He was something there but here he was nothing. True at Boma, Lubala was both erratic and ruthless and there wasn't a plan but in a strange sort of way ap Ewan felt he belonged and was useful. More than that ap Ewan had always felt he had control over his own destiny and could get out when he wanted to. It wasn't like that here.

From the beginning the Germans had been in control at Villa Santa Maria. It was a cold antiseptic control. Ap Ewan had arrived as Lubala's aide-de-camp, or so he thought. For Gunter Siegburg, and he was the one giving the orders, that came down to keeping Lubala out of the way, incommunicado until the time he was needed. Ap Ewan's method was to keep Lubala supplied with girls and whisky.

Ap Ewan rolled over on the flop mattress that was laid out on the floor, trying to make himself more comfortable. It could be worse he thought looking at Feliz who had no mattress but had to sleep on a bed of corrugated cardboard with only a piece of rotting curtain material for a covering.

"Poor Feliz," he thought, "There is nothing for him. He will live and die just as he is now. Poor little bugger doesn't even have his voice." Ap Ewan wondered what went on in the mind of Feliz. "Sometimes he listens like he understands but at other times it's like talking to an empty vessel."

"Hey Feliz," ap Ewan's voice was soft, not harsh.

Feliz opened his eyes and looked at ap Ewan without expression.

"Hey, Feliz you need to go down to the kitchen and boil water. The Germans will want their coffee soon. It wouldn't be good if you were late with that. I'll give Lubala time to go off. Then I'll get the girls out and you can take them back into town. You understand that?"

Feliz smiled and pushed the old curtain off his body.

When Feliz had left ap Ewan put his ear to the wall adjoining Lubala's room. He heard tiny whimpers and, more importantly, laboured heavy breathing. Lubala was asleep. Ap Ewan moved. He listened at Lubala's door, a final check. He pushed the handle and the door gave easily without noise. Ap Ewan had used some cooking oil to lubricate the hinges not long after they'd arrived. It had worked a treat.

Lubala was belly down, naked, stretched out on the bed. One of the two young African girls that had been brought to the house the previous night sat on the floor by the window, eyes open, naked and shaking. The other, also naked, lay on her back in the middle of the floor. There was an open gash on the side of her face; a result of the slap he'd heard thought ap Ewan. But what sickened him most was the pool of blood that was spreading from her open genitals, evidence of how Lubala had brutally forced himself on her.

Ap Ewan put a finger to his mouth, signalling the girl by the window to remain silent. He motioned her to get up. Without a sound he went around the room collecting anything he recognised as part of the girls' clothing. He handed them to the girl that was now standing. Gently he picked up the motionless one, feeling the sticky warm blood on his fingers. He carried her to his own room

147

and the other girl followed. Ap Ewan pointed to a plastic bucket filled with cold water and gave the conscious one a rag. She took it and started to clean the other one who was beginning to stir. He left them alone; it was the only morsel of dignity he had to offer them.

It was no more than a basic field kitchen set up in one of the better downstairs rooms. Feliz had been taught how to fill the water urn with clean water and switch the appliance on. Fresh coffee was a non-negotiable demand for the ten German SF Troopers, or so it appeared to ap Ewan. He even admitted to himself that it wasn't half bad. He promised himself that if he got out of the place and things picked up he would always have fresh filtered coffee, not that instant shit he'd been brought up on.

He'd just started his second cup when heard the commotion outside. He looked through the window. He saw the hand go down with force and strike Feliz on the head. Dazed the youth staggered a few steps before falling to the floor. The uniformed German stepped forward. He was about to kick the prostrate body but was stopped by the loud shout.

"Stop! Leave him alone."

Ap Ewan, who had made it to the door in two steps, dropping his mug on the way, was surprised not only at the tone of his own commanding voice but also by the fact that the German actually did stop.

"What did he do," shouted ap Ewan going forward.

"He was in the Operations Room poking around. Everybody knows that is forbidden."

"He's an idiot. You can see that. He doesn't understand rules, besides it was me that sent him to prepare the coffee for you. He was most probably just trying to tell you it's ready."

The SF Trooper hesitated. "You just keep the little shit under control in future. It'll be more than his life is worth if I catch him poking around again." He turned and went.

Ap Ewan rushed over to the still body and gently lifted him. He felt Feliz pushing with his own legs. He half carried him to the kitchen and got him to a chair. Feliz pushed himself free of ap Ewan's helping hands. He smiled and touched his head where the guard had hit.

"You crafty little bugger. You were just playing possum weren't you?"

Feliz smiled.

"You were lucky then. He could have really hurt you. What were you up to?"

Feliz looked blankly.

"Just go and get those girls and get them out of here before Lubala wakes up. They don't need another session with him."

Feliz left the field kitchen.

The SF Trooper returned to the Operations Room in the old chapel.

"So what was that about?" Gustav asked.

"I found that little African shit poking around in here. I gave him a good hiding!"

Gunter didn't lift his head from reading some pre-prepared press releases. "What was he looking at? Did you find that out?"

"I don't know. The Welshman said he was just coming to tell us coffee was ready."

"So?"

"So what?" replied the SF Trooper.

"So where is the fucking coffee?"

Chapter 25
Foreign and Commonwealth Office, UK
6th February 1996 Mid-Morning

The Duty Officer had come on early at 7am and spent the next two hours checking the log and going over the previous night's dispatches. Britain may no longer have an Empire on which the sun never sets but certainly the rest of the world was busy when England slept. Only when he'd finished going through the classified messages did he turn his attention to items that had been unclassified and stuck into the pending pigeon-holes. Mostly he discarded the reports as background chatter. One group of messages caught his attention though. GCHQ had sent several notifications requesting feedback. They were in the African hole. The Duty Officer thought that one or two unidentified intercepted satellite messages would not be considered as suspicious but there were now more than six of them. What was of more concern was that the unidentified units appeared to be communicating only with each other. That suggested there was some kind of co-ordination. He thought about it for a while before banging off a reply to GCHQ. He asked them to intercept further transmissions and pass on not just the meta data but also the message contents. He knew that this would mean a lot more work for them but felt that knowing the content of the messages might be important. Then he decided to pass on a note upwards, to cover his back, in case anything came of it. Under the circumstances he had no choice other than to change the status of the messages from unclassified to classified. The lowest appropriate level of classification was the fourth level of importance, '*restricted*'. That was just about enough to get it on to Ralph Foulkes' desk on a quiet day. Today was a quiet day.

Ralph had lunch in the '*Senior Dining Room*' at the Ministry. It was quiet; most of the tables were empty. He sat alone enjoying the attention of his own formally dressed waiter.

"As you are having the Filet Mignon can I recommend a wine sir? We have a particularly nice Châteauneuf-du-Pape available," the waiter smiled to the point of ingratiation.

"Châteauneuf-du-Pape?" was Ralph's surprised reply.

The waiter nodded with a sickly sweet smile.

"Yes I know it is a rather common wine nowadays, taken over by the masses so to speak. However I can promise this is a particularly good vintage from grapes grown high on the south side of the valley, only five bunches per vine, in the traditional manner. I don't think you'll be disappointed."

Ralph thought about his predecessor for a moment, Sir Basil Parker-Smythe. No wonder he ended up at twenty-two stone and with a pickled brain by the time he was sixty.

"I think I'll just have the steak with a glass of water and no sweet and I'll take my coffee in my office later before you ask."

"Sir," the waiter bowed and withdrew two steps backwards before turning and heading for the service desk thinking of how standards were slipping with the younger generation.

It was a beautifully prepared piece of meat and Ralph knew he hadn't done it justice. Wolofing it down as he did, it might just as well have been a burger. He was slightly miffed with himself; something was bothering him.

Back in the office he sat at his desk sipping his coffee and thinking. He decided to bounce it off an old friend. He picked up the phone and asked his secretary to get hold of Lieutenant Colonel Cameron at MI6.

"Can I say what it is about Sir?"

"Just say it's personal will you."

A few moments later the handset on his desk rang. He lifted the receiver.

"Ralph?"

"Yes. How are you Stuart?"

"Better if it wasn't for the weather."

"You should be here in this building; overheated, claustrophobic, rain lashing against the window, almost like a rainy day at prep school, stuck in the classroom, bored."

"Bored! Is that why you're ringing me?" There was a chuckle on the other end of the line.

"Not at all, but I have time to think for a change. I'm not sure it's important but I'd just like your opinion on something."

"Go on."

Ralph explained about the satellite transmissions that had appeared on his desk. "Don't suppose you're aware of them?"

"Something at restricted level wouldn't normally get to me, not from that part of the world. We've got nothing going on there so far as I know nor have our friends across the pond. The Russians are out of Africa and the Chinese haven't arrived in West Africa – yet. I can't see anything to be bothered about."

"That's what I thought really. I suppose I was just crossing the '*t's*' and dotting the '*I's*'."

"Must be more than that," replied Stuart sensing something in Ralph's voice.

"Well there is a referendum coming up in Cabinda."

"Cabinda!"

"Yes, a province of Angola."

"I know that. What's it got to do with us?"

"We've got a couple of observers out there – assigned to the United Nations monitors."

"Well, that's not out of the ordinary."

"It's just that one of them is Duncan Murdoch, your old friend."

"What! That's not his line of work. How did he end up there?"

"He had no choice I suppose."

"Had to, why?"

"Well he's the only one that can keep Jane Ashton in check."

"What! Jane Ashton is there as well. She can find a conspiracy at a children's party. What idiot assigned them to the task?"

Ralph replied with silence.

"Ah, I understand your concern. She does rather attract trouble doesn't she? Leave it with me; I'll see what I can find out," finished Stuart.

Chapter 26
UN HQ, Cabinda City
6th February 1996 late afternoon

André Piet was not one to subscribe to conspiracy theories. He dealt in facts and made his decisions based on them. Second guessing the future was not part of his repertoire. Nevertheless he'd agreed to sit down and have a chat with Jane. It was not as if they didn't have time, it had been quiet, too quiet. It was as if nothing was going on yet, well certainly not in the Lubala camp. That was part of the problem for Jane.

The school was set out in a square. In the middle was space intended for assembly and recreation. The four sides were bounded by the classrooms connected together by a covered walkway opening on to the square. André and Jane walked along the walkway, carrying polystyrene cups of coffee. They found an empty classroom. André pulled up a couple of chairs alongside a child's desk. He looked around the room top to bottom, from the bare corrugated asbestos roof to the cement floor that had been polished to a shine by countless feet. A two-inch thick-red line was painted around the walls about four feet off the ground, like an imaginary dado rail. Below the line the walls were painted dark green, above light green. There were a few torn and faded posters on the side walls and a giant Mercator projection map of the world on the back wall. The wall behind the teachers table was dominated by a solid blackboard that ran the full width of the room. It was utilitarian and scruffy but useable. By standards in this part of the world it would be considered to be a good teaching environment.

André drank from his cup, placed it on the table and leaned back. His smile was warm, almost fatherly. He gave the impression of being open and easy to speak to. That was most probably one of his principle assets thought Jane. A diplomatic non-combative manner and the ability to smooth out difficulties without conceding on principle was an essential characteristic for the leader of such assignments. Jane knew he would listen to her. At the end of the referendum all the UN monitors had to sign off on the final report so he needed to keep everybody on side as far as was reasonably possible.

"You have concerns Jane?" His French Canadian accent combined Latin smoothness and American practicality.

"This is just not correct; what is happening here. There is no evidence that the Liberation Movement is taking part in the referendum. It's as if they don't care: no rallies, apart from the one that was attacked in the park, no posters, no meetings no free 'T' shirts, no attempt to participate. We have all seen that. Does that not concern you?"

"We don't know what the Liberation Movement has in mind. Cabinda City only accounts for thirty per cent of the votes and the Government is strong here. Perhaps they are concentrating their efforts in the country, where they are strong. We have to wait till we get reports from those outlying areas."

"I don't think that is the case," replied Jane. "The leader, Lubala, is holed up in his HQ. He never comes out and that HQ is like a fortress according to the reports getting back here."

"We can't force him to participate. Our job is just to ensure he has a fair opportunity. If he wants to stay in his headquarters that is his choice."

"Do you worry about his headquarters?" Jane didn't wait for a reply. "I do. It's like a military installation."

"That is a bit of an exaggeration I think," countered André. "Nobody has been inside to see what is happening there. We don't have evidence of anything wrong."

"Lubala has surrounded himself with white security guards, Germans I believe. It is possible, in fact probable; that these men are mercenaries and I think that it is quite possible they are up to no good, possibly military preparations!"

"Jane you must be careful with your choice of words. '*Military preparations*' is an evocative phrase. It could inflame a situation, particularly coming from a member of the UN monitoring team. Please don't use those words unless you can substantiate them."

"I think I can." Jane withdrew a folded piece of paper from the breast pocket of her shirt. She spread and smoothed it on the desk between them. In pencil was a sketch diagram. This is a rough plan of the '*Villa Santa Maria*' and shows what they are doing inside. Look at the amount of dormitory space they are making and the logistical supplies. And just look at the location and size of the communications room and the number of electronic aerials. To me it looks like military preparations not an election campaign."

"Where did you get this," said André picking up the paper and scrutinizing it in detail.

"A youth passed it to me through the gates late this morning, then he ran off without saying a word."

154

André thought about it for a while. "I think this paper does indicate possible military preparations but I have to ask is it genuine. It could just be somebody making mischief – maybe somebody from the Government side."

"If it is true it is a problem for us, the United Nations. It is we that have negotiated extraterritoriality status for the building they are using. It is possible that the Liberation Movement is planning a military operation from a UN protected area. They may also have smuggled weapons into the country using immunity from search organised by us. That could have tremendous diplomatic repercussions."

"The only way we could validate that concern is if we were to gain access to the buildings and conduct an inspection."

"I agree," said Jane.

"But we can't get access without an invitation."

"Not necessarily," she replied.

Chapter 27
Nazareth House, 10 miles north-west of Lulia, Cabinda
Province
8th February 1996 7am

They'd slept outside the previous night, bivouacked in the square near the church. Captain David Marobi had organised the camp and taken the precaution of setting overnight sentries. It had been strange lying there, under the African sky. It was so clear that Duncan felt he could almost reach out and touch the stars. He forgot about his physical discomfort and fell asleep awe inspired, wondering which one of the twinkling lights was Elizabeth, his dead wife. He awoke with the first light feeling strangely refreshed.

Duncan walked towards the church which didn't look so forlorn in the early morning light. A rotting wooden sign with flaking paint clung to the wall near to the front entrance. He tried to make out the faded writing, *'Casa Nazareth'*, Nazareth House. He could barely make out the words.

"You appear surprised at the name." Although the voice was deep and gravelly it hinted at compassion. Duncan turned to see the cassock-wearing African.

"Your English is good," said Duncan.

The man bowed his head slightly in recognition of the compliment. "Is something troubling you?"

"No not really. It's just the name brings back memories. A long time ago things were bad for me. I was in a city called Glasgow, living in a YMCA. Do you know what a YMCA is?"

The man nodded.

Duncan continued. "The physical hardship, the pain of being poor, was not the worst thing; it was the feeling of being alone, abandoned that was worse. I used to go to a building down the street. They gave me tea and more importantly time. It helped. It to was called Nazareth House. That's all I was thinking."

"I hope we do the same here."

Duncan changed the subject. "Do many people come to the church?" he asked.

"Lots," replied the monk. "When life is so precarious people try to find hope wherever they can. We have the best offer around, the only offer; paradise in the next life - but precious little for this life. This is a forgotten place."

"At least your church hasn't forgotten this place."

"Oh yes it has. They abandoned this place years ago."

"What do you mean?" asked Duncan. "You're here."

"I'm not a priest; I'm not even a monk." The man in the cassock smiled. "There used to be monks here at one time but they got old and there were no replacements. Eventually the last ones left to die elsewhere. Before they left they told us not to worry, God would find a way to help us. We waited but nothing happened so I put on these; they were left behind." The man pointed to the cassock he was wearing. "Somehow they give the people comfort."

"So what are you?" asked Duncan.

"Really I am nothing, but the people here call me Father. Before the real monks left I worked in the kitchen and gardens, I did the work the monks couldn't do. I was a servant of God, well not of God exactly; I was a servant of God's servants to be precise.

Now tell me why have you come here with soldiers? Do you mean to harm us?"

"No not at all. The Captain over there," Duncan pointed to David Marobi, "He is a good man and he brought me here as a favour. I wanted to do something nice for somebody but I think it is a waste of time."

"Tell me what nice thing you wanted to do."

"Something happened close to here, a long time ago."

Duncan went on to explain Grace's story and about the emptiness that existed in her life.

The monk listened without interruption till Duncan had finished his tale.

"A young lady, a very lucky young lady who lives in that great city of New York and benefits from material things that are beyond the wildest expectations of people here, needs help. Then other rich people, like you, combine to help her. Even our own army goes out of its way to assist. There is hope in this world."

Duncan began to feel ashamed that he was on such an errand when there was so much need here.

The monk smiled. "It's wonderful that so many people recognise material wealth is not everything, that fulfilment is more than material things. Normally we have little to give but perhaps in this instance we can help. What do you think we can do?"

Duncan smiled. "I would like to try and trace Grace's family but there are no Government records, not in this part of the world. I was perhaps thinking that if Grace's mother was a Christian there might be church records?"

The monk shook his head. "When they withdrew from this place the church officials took all records with them. There are no records here. There is nothing in writing."

Duncan nodded in recognition of the fact. "It was a stupid thing to expect. I am sorry to have troubled you. I'm sorry you couldn't help."

"I didn't say that," replied the monk. "All I said was that there was nothing in writing. There are other types of records, records in people minds, memories."

"I think the incident I want to know about occurred a long time ago, even before you came here."

"That is true but that is not everything. There is an old man, we look after him. His body is damaged beyond repair but his mind is as sharp as ever. We could talk to him."

David Marobi was not sure. "You don't know the man. He admits to being an imposter. Going off alone with him is a grave risk. I can provide a guard, otherwise I take no responsibility."

"I trust him," Duncan had replied, scribbling a note. "Take this," he said passing the note to Marobi. "It excuses you of any blame should something go wrong."

Marobi read the note. "Do you know how to use a firearm?"

"I do," replied Duncan.

"Then take this," Marobi offered Duncan his pistol.

"No I don't need it."

For twenty minutes Duncan had followed the monk along paths that criss-crossed like a maze, through increasingly dense jungle.

"It would have been better if he'd offered me a compass and map," thought Duncan knowing that the greatest danger was getting lost in this place. Eventually they came to the smallest of clearings, barely a hole in the jungle canopy that let in light for a couple of hours a day. In the middle of the clearing was a round thatched hut. Close to the hut door a woman, naked except for a beaded string holding a rectangle of cloth over her genitals pounded cassava seeds using a large mortar and pestle. She didn't hear the men approach and only became aware of them as they entered the open space. She smiled at the sight of the monk.

"Come," he said, lowering his head as he entered the hut. Duncan followed. Even when his eyes had adjusted to the gloom it was not bright inside. There were a couple of folded blankets to one side and a motley collection of dinted aluminium cooking pots.

Leaning against the back wall, knees raised, sat an old man straining to read a large worn bible that rested on his knees, his only aid the flickering yellow light from a tallow lamp. He raised his head exposing a black haggard face which bore a ghostly grey hue. He smiled a feeble smile.

"Banda, somebody has come to see you. He is a good man and wants to test your memory. Are you willing?"

The old man nodded without expression. Duncan stepped forward and offered his hand. The old man simply raised his previously unnoticed arms, exposing just stumps where his hands should have been. He shrugged his shoulders and smiled almost apologetically. Duncan froze, embarrassed and unsure what to do.

"It happened a long time ago," said the monk. "The shock is over, he has learnt to live and accept. Sit down and tell him your story."

Duncan sat cross-legged in front of the old man and told his story of the little African girl, his gaze fixed on the ground to avoid looking at the old man's stumps. Duncan only raised his head at the end of the story. The old man's eyes glistened. Duncan somehow knew he wasn't sad, he was happy.

"You should tell him the girl's name," said the monk.

Duncan didn't have time to reply. Instead the old man spoke.

"He doesn't have to. Her name is Grace and only God knows how I have prayed for that little girl and for this moment. My name is Banda Sitole. I am the one who found her."

"You are the priest in the story?" said Duncan shocked beyond belief.

Banda nodded.

For two hours the three men sat together. Duncan had to explain in detail what he knew about Grace and her family. In turn Duncan learnt how Banda Sitole had come to be in his present state.

"Men found me walking between villages; bad men in uniforms. Maybe they were government soldiers or maybe rebels, or perhaps just bandits. I never found out. They wanted to know what I was doing. They accused me of being a spy. I tried to tell them I was just bringing the hand of God to people who needed it. They were drunk and wild; they said who were they to refuse the hand of God when it was offered. So they cut my hands off and laughed when they told me that from then on they would always march with the hands of God.

Then they left me in the jungle; perhaps they thought I would bleed to death. I didn't. Some villagers found me and brought me here where I have always been looked after."

"They are only repaying you for the good you have done," said the monk. "And the story you have told just demonstrates that goodness. You never told that story before. I knew nothing about it."

Banda laughed as if he was about to reveal a guilty secret. "Oh but you have celebrated the event, many times."

The monk look confused. "What do you mean?"

"What is the most important day for Nazareth House, your church?"

The monk thought for a while. "March 23rd, isn't it?"

"What do you do, what do you celebrate?"

"We have a thanksgiving service and then a procession where we put flowers on the monument to the blessed Virgin."

"No you don't. Well it is not a monument to the Blessed Virgin that you put flowers on. After the journalists had taken the baby away I decided it was not good to just leave the mother in the jungle to rot. I went back to the village and collected the body and brought it to Nazareth House. I had it buried. I didn't want it to lie in an unmarked grave so I chipped a headstone to mark the place but I didn't know what name to put so I just wrote on the stone '*Mother of Grace*', that is because it is the place where the mother of Grace is buried! I also inscribed the date. I was away for a long time. When I returned you were celebrating the 23rd March. I let you do it because I thought it was somehow appropriate."

"So the grave of Grace's mother is at the church we have just come from?" asked Duncan.

"It is smiled Banda Sitole. Perhaps if Grace comes to see it she will visit me?"

"I will do what I can," promised Duncan.

At that moment less than twenty miles away, on the other side of a river that marked the border with Zaire, Bernd Groelsh struggled to maintain discipline amongst his men. They were champing at the bit, eager to get on with the task, to unleash their pent up frustrations and complete what they had to do and then enjoy the promised rewards. Their anxiety made them oblivious to the fact that their actions were actually just one part of a greater plan. Groelsh had set up his mobile satellite receiver and now waited for the '*go*' message.

160

Chapter 28
Windhoek, Namibia
8th February 6pm.

He'd toyed with the idea of wearing his Colonel's uniform but decided against it in the end. Not because of the military connotations but because he thought he should have been a General. In his heart he truly believed he deserved the rank and had only been denied it by the premature ending of the Second World War.

Prussia, unlike Bavaria, had never developed a formal national dress for men. So von Swartzstein had been forced to revert to a black-tie dress code, which he disliked because it reminded him too much of the British. Nevertheless he believed that the occasion was worthy of the effort.

He checked his watch for the time. "I have ten minutes to spare, mien liber," he said to his wife who stood attentively two steps behind him. "Leave me alone and I will read the text once more. It must be correct. I am sure these words will go down in history for future generations to read."

Freifrau von Swartzstein left the room without speaking, shutting the door behind herself. The Baron picked up the two pages of double-spaced words, stood in front of the mirror and began to read. Sometimes he stopped and re-read certain phrases until he had got the intonation as perfect as possible – as far as he was concerned. He was worried that the message was too short, after all he thought, "It is hard to be inspirational in too few words."

There was a gentle knock on the bedroom door.

"Come."

"It is time my dear," said his wife. "They are ready and waiting for you."

The Baron made his usual deliberate journey from his dressing room to the meeting room, not forgetting to look at the stain glass window with its depiction of Fredrick the Great on horseback in battle. He wondered if that great hero of Germanic folklore had felt like he did today. The doors opened and he walked to his seat at the head of the table. The other men, seven of them, were standing, also dressed formally. Only one chair remained vacant, the chair of Gunter Siegburg.

"Sit gentleman," von Swartzstein commanded.

The men took their seats. Von Swartzstein remained standing.

"Today is an epic day in our history." Von Swartzstein's voice was loud and confident, his demeanour expansive, unusually expansive. He bore the broad smile of somebody who had just won a great victory.

"In a few moments I will be sending a message by satellite communication. Satellite communication!" He repeated it for emphasis waving the two sheets of paper in the air. "This message will authorise our forces to implement our bold plan that will not only restore our fortunes but also mark the beginning of resurgence, a resurgence of our people."

Worried glances shot around the table.

"I do not need to tell you about our journey to this point, you are all aware of our history. However I cannot let this moment pass without saying something.

For more than an hour von-Swartzstein spoke, without pause, reiterating the already well known history of his family, starting at the Second Crusade in Palestine and ending with the '*heroic*' battle of Stalingrad, which according to his version was a great victory for the spirit of Germany. His audience sat in attentive silence, none daring to say what they were thinking.

Eventually he came to the end of his soliloquy. "Now gentlemen I will go to the '*communications room*' and send the message to our outlying stations. Whilst I am completing this important task I want you to enjoy yourselves and look forward to the future with some champagne."

He left the room clutching his sheets of papers. Waiters, dressed in black came in with ice buckets of Champagne and plates of hors d'oeuvres on silver platters.

Hueber turned to the man next to him. "Is he drunk?"

"Intoxicated by his own words I would say," was the whispered reply.

"Well I'm getting drunk," said Hueber with uncharacteristic bravado. "I think the English have a saying that would be appropriate on this occasion, '*It's shit or bust now!*'.

Gunter Siegburg sat next to his '*telecommunications officer*' in the Operations Room at Villa Santa Maria.

"I only intended it as a formality; inviting him to give his approval for the beginning of the operation. He's turned it into an epic set piece; he thinks he's part of some Wagner Opera."

The telecommunications officer looked at the clock and punched some pre dial numbers into the digital set in front of him. "I can make the connection okay. The Inmarsat system allows

GSPS conference calls. Technically it is not difficult. The problem is we will have five units connected simultaneously, four of them illegal unregistered units. There is a real risk that somebody will pick up on the calls."

"It's time. Okay?"

Gunter nodded. The telecommunications officer turned on the transceiver and put it on to loud speaker. At the same time in the radio room, behind the bridge on the *MV Brilliant Star*, in the farm house at Louis Trichardt near the Limpopo River and in the Zairian jungle close to Kimongo and the Cabinda border other transceivers went live.

Gunter Siegburg, sitting at a trestle table, buried his head in his hands as he listened in despair to the words of Baron Freiherr von Swartzstein of Brandenburg. After what was a painfully long period the voice stopped.

"He's finished," said the telecommunications officer.

"Cut the connections and let's get on with the operation, everybody knows what they have to do."

The Telecommunications Officer turned his back on Gunter Siegburg and pulled a few switches. "Our leader is very enthusiastic."

"Well he might not be our leader for too long," was the caustic response. "His head is so far up his own arse he's in danger of giving himself tonsillitis!"

Proud of his performance the Baron returned to the meeting room, duties complete, ready to join in the celebrations and indulge in adulation from his supporters. Each man present knew that the lifestyle they enjoyed was beyond what they could expect back in the Fatherland and was anxious that it continue; they were more than ready to '*lick arse*' for their privileges. The Baron, now joined by his wife circulated the room, accepting congratulations from each man in turn. With the appetite of his ego fully satisfied he prepared for the final duty that would bring a welcome conclusion to the evening's event. Champagne glass in hand he brought everybody to order.

"Gentlemen, gentlemen, now we have nearly finished it is time to drink a toast to our absent colleague." Von Swartzstein could not resist offering a few more words. He changed the theme from Germanic folklore to Christian loyalty.

"All great leaders need loyal and true followers. That has been true from the very beginnings of Christianity. I like to think of you as my disciples, the people I can rely on to assist me in my

163

arduous tasks. But tonight one of my disciples is away, busy on a task that is for the greater good of us all. I would like to offer a toast to our friend and colleague who today I consider to be to me what Peter was to Jesus." Von Swartzstein raised his glass. "Gunter Siegburg, gentlemen!"

Each man repeated the name Gunter Siegburg and sipped from his glass. To the rear of the room stood Hueber. Lubricated by earlier drink, he was unable to stop his tongue forming the words: "More like Judas I think!"

Hueber never noticed Frau Swartzstein standing behind him or realised that she had overheard his comment.

Chapter 29
Buco Zau Army Base, Cabinda Province
9th February 9am

Captain David Marobi made sure that Duncan got privacy by chasing the men out of the Officers' Mess. The Mess lived up to its name. Despite the presence of orderlies, there was no evidence that the worn carpet had been cleaned in recent history or that anybody had bothered to clear away the empty bottles or full ashtrays from the previous night. The place stank of stale tobacco smoke and Duncan had to open the window just to make the air palatable for his throat.

Buco Zau Army base owed its origins to the days of Portuguese colonialism. All the rudiments were there but, as is so typical of infrastructure that is handed over by one country to another it suffered from lack of maintenance and basic care. Duncan often mused to himself that there must have been a dearth of paint factories in central Africa and that the ones that did exist concentrated their production on garish colours.

The old black Bakelite phone rang once. Duncan picked up the receiver before it had a chance to ring a second time. André Piet was on the other end of the line.

There was no requirement for Duncan to make any kind of formal report at this stage. He was happy about that as he could not be certain about security; anybody could be listening in.

UN observer teams normally only issue a formal report after an election, declaring the result either valid or invalid, or as was more commonly the case, valid with caveats. During the election process they have no executive power although they may offer '*advice*' if they come across questionable activities. They would, as in this case, be permitted to offer procedural and organisational advice if it was requested and facilitate the competing parties.

"You failed to make contact yesterday, any problems?" Piet began.

"There was no means available. We camped out near the Zaire border."

"Is everything okay with you?"

"Perfectly fine," replied Duncan.

Piet ignored the response. "And what is the weather like there?"

"Good. Better than in Vancouver I'll wager."

That was what Piet wanted to hear. They had a simple code. If Duncan wove the word *Vancouver* into the conversation then everything was in order; *Montreal* meant there were irregularities or difficulties. *Alaska* was the emergency code word, only to be used in the direst circumstances but Duncan didn't need assistance.

"I'm sure it is," replied Piet. "Anything you need."

"If Jane is around I would like to speak to her for a moment."

"Hold on."

Piet put his receiver down and went to look for Jane. Duncan could hear chatter in the background; the office was busy. Somebody picked up the receiver.

"Duncan?"

"Yes. Jane I can't say too much. Everything is fine here. What about with you.

"Fair to middling. We'll talk when you get back."

Duncan knew that Jane would only use that phrase if she was uncomfortable with something.

"I have some news for you. I've found where Grace's mother is buried!"

"WHAT!"

"I found where Grace's mother is buried. I can't tell you more than that at the moment but its good isn't it?"

"Are you really sure?"

"I also found the man that rescued her."

"No!"

"That's all for now Jane, you'll have to live with that till I get back."

"When will that be?"

"Tomorrow evening or the evening after I think but don't worry if I'm a day later again."

"I can't wait. That's such fantastic news."

"Okay, see you then."

Duncan hung up. Jane held the receiver in her hand, excited and wanting to do something – but she wasn't quite sure what.

Chapter 30
Foreign and Commonwealth Office, London
9th February 2pm.

Ralph Foulkes held the two sheets of typed paper in one hand and the telephone receiver in the other, pressing it to his ear as he leaned back in his chair. On the other end of the phone, close to Vauxhall Bridge, the headquarters of MI6, Stuart Cameron looked at copies of the same document.

"It's nonsense, the ramblings of somebody who is quite deranged," said Ralph. "I'm beginning to feel a little embarrassed that I brought this to your attention."

"Don't be," replied Stuart. "There may be more to it than you think."

"You have read it?" asked Ralph.

"It's in front of me now."

Since the issue had kicked off, his supervisor had used it as an excuse to keep David Wooding at the Portishead listening station.

"You started it, you can run with it," he'd said.

But David knew it was just an excuse, nobody liked being sent to the outstation. The only good thing was that there was no overtime limit and as long as he stayed on station till at least 10pm he could claim for an evening meal and overnight allowance so he was going to make sure he milked it for as much as he could. That's why he was there when the automatic recorders had come to life, not just one but all four of them simultaneously. David knew immediately that he'd captured a linked call and that this time he would not just have the meta-data, he'd captured the full conversation as well. There was also a little bonus, in his mind at least. The operation was now classified, so he could forward it to Cheltenham and demand that the translators get to work immediately.

"That'll piss them off," he thought. "Bang goes their quiet night."

As a result the transcripts were on desks in London first thing the next morning.

"I agree it's quite bizarre," said Stuart. "Maybe something is lost in translation but it does rather sound like the ranting's of somebody who is deranged. However, there is something quite interesting about the whole episode. It was a complex five-way connection. I'm informed that is technically quite difficult to achieve."

"I thought there were only four unregistered receivers," replied Ralph. "Did I miss something?"

"There are only four unregistered receivers but it appears a registered set was also linked into the call. There is a transceiver aboard a Liberian registered ship, the '*MV Brilliant Star*' that was also linked in. Now I do agree with you about the content of the transmission, but there is just something too organised about the whole set up. I'm going to dig a little deeper. I'll keep you informed." Stuart hung up.

Chapter 31
Stirling Farm, Okavango Delta
9th February 5pm

"Sometimes I feel my age," said Mary putting a hand to the small of her back. "Not long before I join Gus," she added with a smile.

"Oh Mary! Don't say that," replied Maggie stopping in her tracks, aghast at the thought.

"It comes to everybody darling, you can accept it or resist it but the event is inevitable."

"Stop, I can't bear the thought of this place without you. You've been here all my life."

"Then be thankful, others haven't been so lucky." Mary sat down on one of the wooden chairs surrounding the kitchen table which she'd just finished setting for the evening meal.

"Are you talking about Grace?" asked Maggie.

"She has a lot of unanswered questions. She has a troubled mind, don't you think?"

"You'd hardly notice it at the moment, it's like she's stuck to James's hip with glue."

"You don't think she's missing her parents then?"

Maggie shrugged. "Maybe, I was a little harsh. Actually she's worried for her parents. She thinks because she wants to find out about her real mother it is upsetting them."

"It's a difficult situation to be sure."

The kitchen door flew open. James came in, closely followed by Grace, both filthy from a day in the workshop. "So what were you two talking about? Not us I hope."

Maggie reddened but neither James nor Grace noticed.

"So what's to eat then?" asked James

"Nothing," replied Mary, "Not until you two have got yourselves cleaned up at least."

The transformation in Grace had been dramatic. When she'd arrived she had been shy, even reserved. The thought of spiders and snakes had scared her and she picked tentatively at the '*strange*' food that had been on offer. Now she was confident and adventurous, willing to try anything, even Mary's Scottish dishes that were out of place on anybody's table.

Eventually the four of them were seated.

"What's it today?" asked Grace.

"Faggots and potatoes with cabbage," replied Mary. "Just like we used to have in Glasgow."

"Faggots?" asked Grace looking into the pot where the meatballs were swimming in a sea of gravy."

"Don't you have faggots in America?" asked Mary.

"Don't answer that," replied James a little too quickly. "It's a linguistic thing. Just eat, they taste good."

"Mary does a lot of Scottish food," said Maggie. We even have haggis on Burns nights."

"Burns nights? Is that when you've been in the sun too long during the day?" asked Grace.

Everybody burst out laughing. Grace sat in silent embarrassment.

"No dear, it's the 25th January, the day we celebrate the Bard of Scotland, Robbie Burns."

"I'm not going to guess what a Bard is," said Grace in a more subdued tone.

"I read that Winston Churchill once said that America and Britain are two countries divided by a common language," said James. "I'm beginning to see what he meant."

"Is there anything from my Mom and Dad?" asked Grace changing the subject as quickly as she could.

"I'm afraid not dear," said Mary. "But they have only been gone a few days and they made it quite clear that communications were going to be difficult. The forest in Uganda is a remote place. There's nothing from Duncan or Jane either. I'd be more pleased to hear from them if the truth be known."

As if to order, hardly were the words out of Mary's mouth when the phone rang. Two rings then it stopped.

"Fax," said Maggie.

They could hear the paper rolling out of the machine in the next room, the one they used as an office. When the message finished coming through, the machine gave a short ring. James went to fetch the transmission. He was away longer than expected. He walked back into the room; there was a look of shock on his face. Without speaking he retook his seat and passed the sheet of paper to Grace who read it silently, her complexion greying.

"What is it," asked Mary. "Is it your mother and father? Is something wrong?"

"No, it's from Jane," replied James. "She says that Dad has found the grave of Grace's mother!"

170

"Oh dearie me," said Mary, "Isn't that wonderful, isn't that what you wanted? I expect you can't wait for them to get back here and tell you all about what they have discovered!"

They finished the meal passing the single handwritten fax between them each scrutinising it before offering an excited opinion. Only Grace was not excited or joyful; she began to shake.

"I imagine it's a great shock to you my dear," said Mary putting a reassuring hand on Grace's arm, "Sometimes when we are looking for something it is a big surprise when we find it."

Grace didn't finish her food. Instead she got up. "I'd like to go outside for a while."

"Can I come with you?" asked James, half expecting a rebuke.

Grace simply nodded and James followed her.

For a while neither spoke as they walked to the back of the house and sat on the swing next to the pool. James wanted to say something, something positive and strong but couldn't find the words to match Grace's mood. He could only reiterate Mary's words and add a thought of his own.

"Perhaps you will be able to go there one day and see for yourself."

"I don't want to go one day," said Grace. "I want to go now!"

Chapter 32
Miconze Village, Cabinda Province
10th February 7am

Juba was always happy in the morning. In fact she was happy most of the time. She never complained about the work she had to do. Wherever she went she took her smile with her. She liked the morning particularly because her first job was to take her plastic bucket down to the riverside. The bucket was a valuable possession but it had had a previous existence. With careful inspection it was just possible to make out the faded print on the side. It said 100% maize cooking oil in large letters and in smaller writing underneath: a Proctor & Gamble Product. There were traces of a picture and nutritional information but they were too far gone to make out. Each morning Juba took the bucket with her down to the river to collect the early morning water for the family.

The path was well trodden; it was used by all the women of the village every day, not only to collect water. The little rapids, with their large boulders and small pool beyond, was the place where the women-folk did their washing as well. It was also the social centre of the village, where women, away from the men-folk talked and laughed, often about the stupidity of their male counterparts. It was the place where news was exchanged; sometimes good news, a birth or a marriage, sometimes bad, sickness or death.

From Juba's house to the river was only about three hundred yards, a short distance by African standards. The twisting path was bounded on either side by tall trees and was in shade for most of the time. That was good because it meant that the women-folk were out of direct sunlight on the arduous uphill journey back to the village with full buckets of water precariously balanced on their heads.

That morning Juba did not participate in the conversation, she didn't understand what it was about. She didn't know what a referendum was and could not understand why people would be so concerned about where 'the big chief' lived, or even who the big chief was. She'd heard about Cabinda City and Luanda but as far as she was concerned they were places that might as well have been on another planet. And so she continued to smile as she waited her turn to dip her bucket into the moving water and thought about her secret, the secret that was neatly wrapped up in her bedroll, the secret she looked at last thing at night and first thing in the morning, the secret that filled her dreams, her most cherished possession.

Juba was twelve years old and her first blood had come so now she was considered to be eligible. She of course knew she would not be a real woman, not until she had been found a husband and he had broken her '*skin*'. She also knew her father was wealthy enough to be able to afford a good man for her because Juba was the daughter of the wealthiest man in the village. Getting married would mean moving to another village. She would have to go and live with the family of her husband. That was not upsetting to her because she had been brought up with the knowledge that that was the way things happened. All she hoped was that her husband's village was not too far away and that she would be able to visit her '*birth*' family now and again.

Peoples own perception of poverty is relative. By most Western standards Juba would have been considered very poor, but Juba did not measure herself by Western standards; she compared herself with the people who surrounded her. The village consisted of about thirty buildings laid out randomly, not according to any plan. Most of the buildings were of traditional construction, made from the products of the forest: round huts made from sapling trees and thin branches woven together with lengths of vine and thatched with long dried out grass to the roof and sides. Only two buildings differed. One was the '*community building*'. This was a small garage-sized block-shed. It had been built a few years previously by European volunteers that had arrived without notice and gone just as quickly as they'd arrived. They'd brought all the material with them. They'd come from something called VOS. They were mainly young people and they didn't intermix much. A few weeks after they left a black nurse and doctor had arrived from something called '*Save the Children*'. The doctor had examined a lot of people and given out white medicine and the nurse had stuck needles into all the babies and children. They said they were going to come back every year and do the same thing but they had never returned. They had said the village could use the building as a school when they were not there but as there was no teacher that never happened and because the building was in a clearing and had a bare shiny corrugated iron roof it was very hot inside; it was, in practical terms, useless.

The other '*different*' building was where Juba lived with her family. It was square. It had a thatched roof for coolness but the walls were mud-coated and there were even windows and doors. The windows had shutters that could be shut. The building was not just a house. It was also the village store. It didn't sell much: sacks of grain, kerosene for lamps, cooking oil, sugar, sometimes tinned fish and infrequently Coca-Cola. Juba's father dreamed that one day they would have electricity and a refrigerator and cold Coca-Cola. They would then become really rich. But that was only a dream.

Juba's mother did the cooking under a lean-to at the back of the shop and that is where they ate. At night time the shutters would be closed and Juba, with her mother and father would get out their bed rolls and sleep on the floor. Juba also had two brothers. They were much older than her and it was they that were the source of the real family wealth. They had broken with tradition and gone off to the coast when they were old enough. One of them was lucky to have got a labouring job on a building site run by an American oil company. He'd worked so hard the Americans had kept him on when the construction had finished. A few months later he'd managed to get his young brother a job too. Between them they earned nearly $40 a month. As the oil company supplied accommodation and food they didn't need all that money so every three months they bought '*goods*' at the market in Cabinda City and paid a man in an old Peugeot pick-up to take them to their village. It was a good arrangement.

Juba had returned to the store with her water. Her mother had just finished making their breakfast of sorghum porridge which they ate with honey their father had collected from a wild hive he'd found in the jungle a few days previously. It tasted good but Juba remembered that once she had the porridge with honey and condensed milk from a tin that her brothers had brought back from the city. They'd brought back a lot of things on that visit – including Juba's prized possession, a shiny magazine called '*Ebony*'. It had writing that she couldn't understand but the pictures, pictures of pretty African girls dressed just like European girls, evoked dreams of another world in Juba. She heard the word 'glamorous' and thought that it was a word used to describe these girls. Sometimes she day-dreamed; one day she too might appear on the pages of a shiny magazine and be famous. She had no idea that her ambition was about to come true, but not in the way she expected.

To catch most people in the village they needed to strike early, before people went to work in the field or went into the jungle to hunt. That had meant crossing the river, still in darkness, before five-thirty am. Only one man had been left behind to guard the vehicles and protect their clothes and personal possessions, such as they were. Bernd Groelsh had inspected every man personally. They wore the uniforms he'd provided, uniforms that had been stolen over a month ago from an army base just outside Luanda. Everybody had to be in Angolan Army uniform and none were allowed to carry anything that could identify them as anything else other than Angolan Army soldiers. The one exception was himself. He was wearing an old Cuban Army uniform; a uniform that would identify him as one of the few remaining Cubans that had stayed on to advise the Angolan Army.

It wasn't a difficult or complex plan. It couldn't be. The men he was commanding were not capable of following difficult instructions. Miconze Village had only one track capable of supporting vehicles leading to it. There were a number of paths leading into the jungle, to the small areas that had been cleared for cultivation and down to the river. It was about as remote a place as you could get. That's why it had been chosen.

They intersected the road at about eight-thirty. Groelsh split his squad into two groups, one to surround the village clockwise and the other anti-clockwise. He would remain on the road and allow twenty minutes for the men to get into position, and then he would blow the whistle. That would be the signal. From then on their only order was not to kill each other.

Groelsh looked at his watch. Three minutes to go.

Joining a rebel army is not a normal career choice in most parts of central Africa. Many of the hardened soldiers started their *'military careers'* as children orphaned by the very group they had become part of. Others had simply been kidnapped and forced into service. Rebel leaders liked to get children when they were young. Their minds had not been corrupted by moral standards; they became obedient to the authority of their leader but were otherwise without control. As they grew older some detested what they had become and wanted to escape but most of them relished their elevated position, a position in which the general population respected them. They did not care that that respect was born of fear. To some there was prestige in having power over life and death, for others brutality had become an aphrodisiac. The fringe elements of the groups became dangerous because the means had become the end to them; they enjoyed the kill and they enjoyed the torture. Inflicting terror and mutilation often became a cathartic experience. They did what they did because they wanted

175

to. Their minds had become permanently distorted; there was no hope of redemption. It was this group of fanatics that Bernd Groelsh had identified and weeded out of the general company of men he had inherited from Lubala and was moulding into CLF soldiers. It was they who had been earmarked for this special task. They had been kept separate from the others. The fact that they had lost any moral perspective made them very useful.

Juba had sneaked into the back of the shop after breakfast for a secret look at her magazine and to inspect, for the hundredth time, the latest present she had received from her brothers: a bright red cotton *'T'* shirt with the *Coca-Cola* logo printed in bold white letters, back and front. She smiled as she put the treasured item back into her bed roll and remembered with anticipation her brothers' promise to get her a pair of blue jeans one day. The whistle was shrill and loud. Juba looked up. It was not a sound that she was used to; she wondered what it was, but wasn't alarmed. She was still an innocent. Not so her father and mother; age, stories and experience had made them more attuned to the danger of things that were out of the ordinary.

Juba heard her mother call from the front of the shop. The young girl thought she was to be scolded for her vanity and hurriedly finished putting her bed roll away. Barely had she got to her feet when her mother came rushing to the back of the store.

"Quickly Juba!" she cried urgency in her voice. The older woman grabbed her daughter's arm and pushed the child towards the back window of the building.

"Juba, listen to me. You must go out of the window, run to the forest as fast as you can, hide there and do not let anybody see you. We will come to find you when it is safe."

Her mother pushed open the louvered window shutter.

"Let me see that the way is clear." The older woman looked through the opening whilst Juba peered over her shoulder. Juba saw the figure of her childhood friend, Shara, running barefoot away from the village towards the hunter's path. A few steps ahead of her ran Sigway, her younger brother. To Juba it looked as if Shara was trying to catch Sigway in a game of 'catch me if you can'.

Then came a succession of evenly spaced cracks, crisp and distinct. Shara fell forward on to her face. For a second Juba did not associate Shara's fall with the cracks. She thought her friend had just tripped. Then Sigway fell too. He lay completely motionless but Shara started to move, crawling forward on all

176

fours towards her brother. There was another succession of cracks and Shara's body shuddered before arching in its final death throe.

Juba became aware of voices outside shouting. Some were familiar, people she knew, but there were also strange voices, excited men screaming in a strange dialect, words that Juba could not understand. Her mother pulled her away from the window and pulled the shutters closed.

"It is too late to escape that way, you must hide," she said pushing her into a corner where sacks of corn were stacked almost to head height.

"Climb on top, go to the back and cover yourself with this." Her mother picked up some rough hessian material and threw it towards her daughter. "Be still, don't make a sound."

By now Juba knew that something was terribly wrong. Her mother's fear was contagious and the sense of panic sharpened her mind. She became acutely aware of her surroundings: the roughness of the sack cloth on her bare legs, the dry dusty smell of the hessian that was now covering her head and body but most of all the shouting and screaming.

The shouts came from men and the women screamed. In the milieu of noise Juba could hear her father, issuing commands, giving orders. His voice alone appeared to be strong and calm and stood out above the rest. Her mother gone, Juba tried to push herself deeper into the recess of her hiding place.

The ring was closing; the CLF soldiers were now out of the jungle, walking forward across the narrow strip of bare land that separated the village buildings from the wild vegetation of the jungle. An occasional single crack or short burst would silence the voices for a second or two. But soon the hysteria returned with a renewed intensity. The village people were systematically being herded towards the village centre.

The villagers didn't have a plan. What happened next was purely instinctive. The men pushed the women and children into the centre. They tried to form a protective cordon. Some had had time to pick up their machetes; others had been too slow or too far away. Juba's father ran forward from the shop, a handful of hoe handles in his arms; quickly he distributed them to the unarmed men but it was a pitiful and useless gesture. One or two of the village men stepped forward, waving their impromptu weapons as threateningly as they could; each was silenced in turn by a single shot.

No order was given to surrender. It wasn't necessary. It quickly became apparent that resistance was futile. The noise subsided and men began to drop their machetes and hoe handles on to the dusty ground. They maintained the protective ring around their women whilst at the same time acknowledging their capture. They realised that their only hope lay in the humanity of their captors. They would have to beg for their lives but unfortunately humanity was not a common character trait in Cabinda and certainly not amongst this unruly bunch of soldiers.

Bernd Groelsh stood back from the fracas. He looked at his watch. From when the whistle had been blown only seven minutes had elapsed. One or two of the CLF men, almost surprised at the lack of resistance and speed of their victory looked to Groelsh for orders.

Groelsh shook his head. He had thought that the men would not need orders from this point.

"Do as you will," he shouted. "It would be better to separate the men from the women first. Here," he said throwing a canvas pouch towards one of the men. "Share this."

The soldier picked up the pouch and undid the buckle. He stuck his hand inside and withdrew a handful of green leaves. "Khat!" he shouted. A cheer rippled through the CLF men.

Groelsh turned his back on the crowd and walked to where the bodies of Shara and Sigway lay. He let his rifle swing on its shoulder strap and took out a camera from his hip pocket. It was new to him. He had never heard of a digital camera before but he'd been assured it was foolproof. He'd been told there was no film to worry about; he just had to point it and press the button and it was good for over a hundred photographs. The first one he took was of Shara, in death still reaching out for the body of her dead younger brother. Blood had spread around her and what had not soaked into the sandy ground made a scarlet puddle that was even then attracting flies. Groelsh hoped it would show up well. He was not the artistic type but he thought the picture told a story.

The soldiers had begun splitting the men from the women and children. There was little resistance, merely pleading, pitiful bleating, as women were forcibly separated from husbands and children dragged from father's arms.

Freiherr Artur von Swartzstein was still in his pyjamas and dressing gown as he took breakfast on the terrace of his villa outside Windhoek. Although it was early in the day the temperature was already rising as the sun blazed through a clear sky. The Baron and his wife were thankful for the purple bougainvillea that shrouded the pagoda and covered them with shade.

Freifrau von Swartzstein leant forward in her seat and wiped the side of the silver teapot with a lace handkerchief.

"It is almost impossible to teach these people anything," she complained, referring to her black domestic staff. "I can think of nothing more disgusting than finger marks on silverware. I have told them over and over again that they must always wear white gloves but they take no notice of me. It's as if they're not grateful for all that we do for them."

The Baron did not respond. His mind was elsewhere.

If von Swartzstein had little liking for the British people he had a positive loathing for their food. He considered it to be both crude and barbaric. There was however one exception: breakfast. The Baron loved to start his day with a cup of Earl Grey tea, taken not in the German way but in the English style, with milk and sugar. The tea was always accompanied by hot toast and marmalade. Not any marmalade but Burlington Breakfast Marmalade that he had specially sent from Fortnum and Mason's in London.

"I've prepared you toast and poured your tea darling," his wife continued.

Still he ignored her. Hueber the accountant had been different in the private meeting yesterday. He was not the usual subservient and compliant 'bean counter'. It was as if he'd had an injection of spinal fluid. His words had been firm and clear.

The accountant's opening statement was stark. "Baron I have complied with your instructions. Gunter Siegburg has been supplied with all he has demanded even though some of his requests have been questionable. The situation is clear now. We have almost no liquid funds left and I am running short of investments that I can easily liquidate. If we do not receive funds soon we will be bankrupt. This venture had taken us to our financial knees."

There followed a period when the two men poured over the accounts in detail. The Baron was unable to find fault with Hueber's work and interpretation of the situation. He agreed that the bleak financial assessment was correct but he remained confident and self-assured that the situation would improve. The operation had already started and victory was within their grasp he assured Hueber.

179

This only prompted the accountant to expound his next worry.

"Freiherr von Swartzstein I have to remind you that this whole endeavour hinges on a single man. This makes us vulnerable. How sure can you be of him?"

For the Baron loyalty was a two-way process: loyalty would be rewarded with loyalty.

"You are of course referring to Herr Siegburg. Let me assure you that this man has my complete trust."

"That is quite clear," replied Hueber. "Let us hope it is not blind trust."

"What do you mean by that?"

Hueber did not cave in. "Just like you I too know my history. There are instances in the past where a single man has become a heroic figure in German folklore. But let me remind you of something. Invariably heroic figures come from Germanic aristocratic blood. For a man to become a hero and a legend I believe he must be of pure blood, a man of breeding from a family that has proved themselves down the generations. You are such a man. But let me also remind you that Gunter Siegburg is the son of a peasant Saxon farmer. No pure blood runs through his veins. Only two generations ago his family were serfs and servants; the man has no pedigree. It is a risk to put so much trust in a man with so little breeding. I would be failing in my duty if I did not tell you I do not trust him. I have nothing more to say on the matter."

Hueber did something he had never dared to do before. He gathered his papers and left the room without permission. This bothered von Swartzstein. Hueber had never previously behaved in such a way; it was the action of a man that was motivated by more than petty jealousies. Perhaps there was something in Hueber's words.

"Your tea is quite cold darling. Shall I pour you a fresh one?"

Von Swartzstein didn't answer his wife's question. Instead he asked his own. "Do you think there can be such a thing as a man of destiny?"

His wife didn't hesitate in her response. "Yes my darling. You are such a man."

"Could Gunter Siegburg be a man of destiny?"

This was a more difficult question for her, one that she could not answer directly.

"You have doubts darling and you ask me questions that I am not qualified to answer. But I can tell you something; your lieutenants do not share your confidence in the man. I have seen their faces, heard their whispered remarks. It is for you to answer that question for yourself because you are the real leader; you are the one with the heritage and pedigree to make the right judgement."

The Baron sipped from the cold cup of tea and took a bite from his toast. The two sat in silence for some time. Eventually he spoke.

"It is time for me to demonstrate my leadership and let my people recognise my qualities."

"How will you do that darling?"

Bernd Groelsh felt an inkling of tiredness by mid-afternoon. He knew it was just the first of many barriers he would have to overcome. It would take all his determination to remain alert for the next sixteen hours. He didn't have the same concerns for his men. At that moment they were pumped up. The Khat was doing its job. The hallucinatory effect of the leaf not only gave a feeling of self-confidence but it also acted as a stimulant that mitigated the need for rest. If all went according to Groelsh's plan, by the time they got back to the vehicles the men would be coming down and be at their lowest level of alertness. But that was for later. Right now Bernd needed evidence, evidence of an atrocity.

He walked along the track that led out of the village. The guard that had been posted was there, he was awake but not alert. His mind was on joining his colleagues back in the village, nothing more. Bernd made his way back. The women and small children had been herded into the store, Juba's home. A few women had been allowed out, women who would not flee because they had small children. They were forced outside to cook.

The men of the village had been crammed into the largest of the wood and grass huts, crowded in so tight that there was no room to sit. CLF soldiers, the ones that were not guarding prisoners or just lolling about, went from hut to hut looting and wrecking, seeking out any treasure that might be of value. Their search was destined to end in disappointment in such a poor community, but this did not diminish their anger at such a miserly return for their efforts.

Bernd looked in at the store before walking to where the village men were being held. Two soldiers, high on Khat, one holding a bottle of whisky taken from the store, were arguing over a string of beads.

"Why are you fighting when there is more important work to do?" he asked.

The men looked blankly at him.

"The beads are nothing in comparison to the reward that is waiting for you back at the camp in Boma. Share the whisky and burn the hut," he said nodding in the direction of the place where the village men were being held.

The men dropped the beads and smiled at each other, their argument quickly forgotten. One of the men grabbed a handful of loose thatch from the roof of a hut and set it alight from the open cooking fire. He walked over to the men's hut and held the naked flame to the dry straw thatch. The flames caught and began to crackle. Like moths attracted to the light the soldiers surrounded the burning hut. Some prepared their weapons.

"No!" shouted Bernd Groelsh above the increasingly noisy crackle of the flames. "Not guns use your machetes. Save your ammunition."

Inside the darkened and crowded hut there was a mixed response. Some men literally froze, stiff with fear, others screamed in anticipation and some clawed at the walls of the hut with bare fingers. But all immediately knew in their hearts the final and imminent outcome that awaited them.

In the end ironically few died of burns. The few that did manage to get out through the door or break through the walls were immediately set upon. Machete wielding CLF men, acted with uncontrolled enthusiasm. Inside the hut, once the flames had broken through, the available oxygen was immediately consumed by the flames. All that was left to breathe was acrid smoke. Unconsciousness came with a few gulps of the life denying gaseous mixture. Less than ten minutes after the flame was put to the hut the last feeble scream faded to a whimper.

Inside the store the atmosphere was calm resignation. That was until the first of the men's screams pierced the air. Those women that were sitting got to their feet. Mothers gathered up their children. They couldn't see what was happening as all the shutters were closed but their imaginations were true to events. In the near calm air outside, smoke from the burning hut slowly drifted and enveloped the store.

Juba, although no longer concealed, had retained her position on top of the hessian sacks. She looked over the heads of the milling women and saw her mother, alone amongst them trying to maintain calm. It was an increasingly pointless task as fear spread and the women screamed and wailed. Some cried for the loss of their men folk, others in anticipation of the terrors that were soon to be visited upon them. Calm was never restored although the peak of the feverish panic subsided with the fading screams of the men. Some mothers turned their attention to comforting their terrified, sobbing children. Resignation infected others; all that they could do was wait for Fate to reveal her grim hand.

The soldiers were different now; all discipline and control had gone. The fire and excitement had taken them to a new high. None lolled around; all were induced into an adrenalin fuelled frenzy. Some, the ones who had over indulged on Khat or had been fortunate to find some alcohol to enhance their euphoria, danced around the dying flames waving their machetes, gratuitously reigning blows on already dead bodies and charred remains. The air was thick with the smell of burning flesh. Bernd Groelsh calmly walked around taking pictures.

Juba's mother realising that the soldiers were beyond control attempted to make a plan. She guessed that the noise and excitement would have drawn away the guards from the back of the store. She pushed her way through the throng of women and forced open the rear shutters. She was right. Her first thought was for her daughter.

"Juba!" she shouted. "Come!"

Frantically she motioned her daughter to climb down from the pile of sacks and make her way to the window. The few steps might as well have been a hundred miles. Other women quickly realised the opportunity and soon the window opening was choked with scrambling fighting women; women willing to forget family bonds and a lifetime of friendships in their frantic scramble for survival. A few got out, others unselfishly pushed their children through the opening and urged them to run, forsaking the opportunity to save themselves. It seemed to go on for a long time. Finally Juba got close, it was her turn. Her mother pushed her forward with force. Juba, scrambled, looked up and got a fleeting glance at the beckoning jungle. With a final effort she would be free. And then suddenly the laughing face was in front of her, a laughing grotesque face expounding teeth green with Khat and bulging red-rimmed eyes, signalling the end of hope. Rough hands pushed Juba back into the building. She landed on the floor and the shutters slammed shut. Looking up Juba saw only the hopelessness on her mother's face.

Often in chaos a vestige of organisation can remain. Even in such a situation a ring-leader can emerge. One of CLF men entered the store. He dragged out a woman, one that was unfortunate enough to be closest. Outside the soldiers gathered. The self-appointed leader held the hapless woman by the arm.

"Who wants this one?" he shouted.

The terrified woman was not old but her body had not worn well. Her skin was already cracked and wrinkled by the sun, her breasts hung loosely and her teeth were stained brown and crooked. Nobody came forward for the prize.

"Take her around the side," said the man.

Somebody dragged her around the side of the building. There was a single shot. The woman had been sent to her maker not realising how lucky she had been. Another woman was dragged from the building and received the same treatment. The process was repeated five times. The waiting soldiers were growing impatient.

Different men went into the store. They were more selective; they pushed their way through the throng of women, looking, searching for something that would be desirable. Finally they found what they wanted and dragged the screaming child, no more than twelve years old, to face the crowd.

The leader grabbed her by the hair and tilted her head back so all could see her high cheek bones and smooth complexion. She stood there shaking only the fear in her eyes spoiling her beauty.

"Who wants this one?" he shouted.

This time the response to the question was different.

There was a cacophony of shouts as the CLF surged forward, breaking the invisible barrier that had kept them from the store. The leader, to avoid being overwhelmed pushed the girl forward. She stumbled into rough clutching hands that drew her toward an empty hut. On it went, some women being immediately despatched with a single bullet while others had their inevitable sentence delayed.

Soon the remaining CLF fighters became restless, concerned they would be left with the dregs. They pushed forward. Two older women were dragged out and quickly despatched to the jeers of hopeful and expectant men. There was another surge and what scant order that had existed evaporated. There was an uncontrolled scramble to get into the store.

Juba and her mother had remained at the rear of the store, mother and daughter entwined in each other's arms. Juba had asked what had happened to her father. Her mother replied that she thought he must have escaped and would soon be coming back with help, her response not only to calm her daughter but also a wish born of desperation, the last remaining grain of hope.

When the soldiers rushed the building Juba's mother knew the end was close.

She whispered to her daughter, "When the time comes you must spit on your hand and wet yourself. Do you understand?"

"Yes," whispered Juba although she did not understand. They were the last words between mother and daughter. CLF men came forward; unyielding hands pulled them apart. Juba's mother made a last pathetic attempt to save her daughter; she scratched her attacker across the face. The soldier, enraged by the trickle of blood that ran down his face, withdrew his side arm and shot her in the head. She slumped to the floor. As she was being dragged away Juba heard the shot but saw nothing.

She didn't know where she'd been taken. She knew she was lying on the floor, the pressed mud floor of a hut. She was naked. The man came upon her. At first she felt no pain, her senses overwhelmed by the rank breath of her assailant. For a second her eyes locked with those of her attacker, her's soft brown and deep, his bloodshot and raw. He forced her legs apart and she felt him enter her, rough and hard. He began to pump. Too late she understood what her mother had meant but the advice would have been useless in any event, her arms were pinioned, she could not have spat on her hand and lubricated her vagina. In seconds the dry friction caused the membranes of her most intimate organs to bleed as she was ripped and torn. The pain subdued as she felt the warm trickle of liquid running and soaking her legs and backside. She was being lubricated with her own blood.

When the man had finished, when he collapsed on her knocking the breath from her lungs, she thought it was over but it was not; it had only just begun. Throughout the night men came to her. Gradually her senses dulled and she began to drift in and out of consciousness, sometimes not even realising that yet another one had violated her.

Her final memory came just as day was breaking. The last one came to her. He was young and small. For a brief moment her mind cleared. He had abandoned his tunic; he wore a 'T' shirt, a red one with the 'Coca-Cola' logo on it. Before he'd finished she closed her eyes and was no more.

Just before sunrise Bernd Groelsh tried to rouse and marshal his men. He was anxious to leave now that the job was done. The effects of the Khat was wearing off. Some of the men were showing signs of fatigue. He needed to motivate them.

"The bonus is being raised from $1000 to $2000 per person," he shouted, "But only if everybody gets back to the vehicles."

There was just enough alert and greedy men to respond. They took on the task of getting everybody together. They kicked, cajoled and dragged the unit into order. They no longer resembled a fighting unit, many had lost items of uniform and some had even lost weapons but Bernd Groelsh didn't care about that; he just didn't want any witnesses left behind, mouths that could tell the truth about what had happened. Before leaving he had a final look around. He didn't know why but he went into one of the huts, it was just one of those chance things.

The sight before him made even his hardened stomach churn. It was clear that she'd been a beautiful girl but now her face was grotesquely contorted as if still racked in agony. Her eyes, wide open, exuded pure terror. Her arms lay on the ground, blood covered palms now open to heaven. Groelsh noticed her fingertips were raw flesh; during her trial she'd clearly dug her fingers into the baked mud so hard that she'd ripped her own fingernails out. Her legs were spread, her young womanhood just a bloody mass.

Groelsh fumbled for his camera hoping that there was still room for more pictures. He didn't have time to check the settings. He just pointed and clicked. He didn't even realise that the camera was set to auto and that he was about to benefit from nearly a million dollars' worth of technological investment made by the Sony company in Japan. All he knew was that when he pressed the button the flash went off on its own.

Finished he put the camera carefully away in its pouch fully aware of the importance of the images it held. But he did not know, could not have known, that what he had done was to ensure that by his action Juba's ambition of appearing in a glossy magazine would be fulfilled. Her picture would be seen by countless millions, a picture that would horrify the world. It was a shame he didn't even know her name.

Chapter 33
Cabinda City Airport
11th February 9.30 am

It had been a torrid 24 hours for Jane and it was not as if the problems were over. Just now all she knew was that she had mixed emotions: feelings of great relief mingled with a raging anger. As she watched the plane make its final approach she didn't know how she was going to respond. It wasn't just the inconvenience of their arrival it was the fact that they'd buggered up her plans too.

It had started well yesterday morning. She'd had a hunch that the youth that had passed the message to her through the railings before might come back. So she made sure she was outside again, in the same position. Sure enough he turned up. She saw him coming; she made eye contact and smiled. He didn't return the smile; instead he hesitated for a moment. Jane thought he might turn tail and run, but he didn't; he continued coming forward but perhaps a little wearily.

When only the railings separated them she spoke, "Do you speak English?" she asked.

The youth just stared at her blankly.

She tried Portuguese, then Spanish, French and even German. The expression never changed on his face. Having failed to find a *lingua franca* she reverted to English.

"Do you have something for me?"

The youth stuck his hand into his pocket and pulled out a sheet of crumpled paper and passed it through the railings. She took it and he immediately turned and started to walk away, disappearing into the crowd. But she was prepared, she'd made a plan. She'd seen the way he'd left the previous time; he'd gone across the rough land and then taken the first left turning. She reckoned, that if she was quick, she could dash around the school, leave by the back gate and then follow a parallel street before taking a right at which point she should intercept her target. She'd tried the route previously and was confident it would work.

Folding the note she turned and set off, walking quickly, almost breaking into a trot. She'd got around the building and was just approaching the rear gate when she became aware of hurried footsteps behind her. She turned her head to see André Piet gaining on her.

"Jane stop," he shouted.

"I can't," she shouted back over her shoulder. "I'm doing something important."

"Jane I need to speak to you."

"As soon as I'm finished I'll come right back." She was almost at the gate.

André stopped his pursuit. "Jane it's personal, it's about your family and it's very urgent," was his final plea.

It was enough. She stopped and turned. "What's happened? Is it Duncan?" She began to walk back, fearful of what she was about to hear.

"No, he's fine, as far as I know. It's about his children, they've gone missing."

"James and Maggie?" she asked as they began to walk back to his office.

"James and Grace are the names I have written down," he replied. "Isn't that right?"

"James is Duncan's son; Grace is a house guest at the farm."

"Well whatever their names they're missing."

Back in his office André got Jane to sit whilst he explained about the call he'd taken. He concluded by saying, "I've kept an open landline so you can speak to the people at the farm yourself."

Maggie's voice lacked its normal buoyancy. The 'Hello' was tentative.

"Maggie, its Jane. What's happened?"

"James and Grace have gone; they left a note to say they're coming to see you and to see the grave of Grace's mother."

"What! How are they going to do that?" was the immediate response followed by, "Didn't they say anything before they left?"

"No just the note. Mary's worried, she's blaming herself and she doesn't know what she's going to say to Duncan or Grace's parents."

"I doubt it's her fault," said Jane. "I should never have sent the fax. I should have waited till Duncan had got back to Cabinda City before I passed the news on."

"Dad's not with you? He doesn't know yet?"

"You got it Maggie. Who's there with you at the farm?"

"Tembo and Morgan are at the house, so is Mafutzi, she's with Mary. We're okay here. It's just James and Grace."

"Do you have any idea what their plan is?"

"You better speak to Tembo. He's here with me."

There was a slight pause. Tembo didn't waste time on pleasantries.

"Jane, I checked, they didn't take much luggage but their passports are gone, so is James' bank book, the one with the money Gus left him and they've taken Duncan's mail as well. I suppose they mean to pass it on."

"What possible route could they take to get here?"

"I don't know. There are no direct flights from Maun to Cabinda. It's not even that easy to get to Luanda. I suppose it's possible to get to the Caprivi Strip and use native buses but that's one hell of a trip. It would take days if not weeks! They'd be stupid to try that."

"They've been stupid already," was Jane's instant response. "How are the Shapiro's taking it?"

"They're not here. They have gone to see the gorillas in Uganda. We won't be able to get hold of them, at least not easily. Do you think James and Grace might just come back?"

"I wouldn't count on it."

South African Airways ran a daily shuttle flight from Jo'burg to Maun. It was intended for tourists visiting the Okavango Delta. Buying tickets had been easy. There were no visa requirements between Botswana and South Africa and it was common for passengers to just turn up at the gate and buy a ticket on the spot.

It was when they tried to pass though immigration at Jo'burg that their problems started.

A good immigration officer has an eye for detail and a nose for trouble. Futhi Molov wanted to be a good immigration officer. At first her supervisors had thought she was carrying too much personal baggage. One manager had once written on her appraisal that Futhi was well balanced: she had a chip on each shoulder. That comment had to be struck and the supervisor had to apologise but the sentiment had been difficult to shake amongst management. Although people had to be careful what they said, the consensus was that Futhi had been struggling with being black and a woman in what was still a white male dominated environment. But Futhi hadn't been deterred by the bad report. She'd kept her head down and got on with her job. It took time but eventually people had started to come around and realise that her style was not confrontational or aggressive, it was actually meticulously correct and fair, to the point of bluntness. There was no sudden defining moment, it was a gradual process but after three years everybody realised she was a good immigration officer and her views began to gain respect. Her current appraisals recommended promotion and suggested suitability for the accelerated management training programme.

James didn't know this as he led Grace to the raised kiosk in the arrivals hall at Jo'burg International Airport. All he'd seen in the kiosk was a smiling immigration officer. Initially he'd felt confident as he handed over both passports to Futhi.

Tucked inside each passport was the obligatory landing card that they'd filled in on the plane. Futhi looked at James' documents first and then Graces'. She ran her eyes over the passport bio-data before flipping through the pages to check current and spent visas. Then she checked the landing cards, struggling to read some of the writing that had been done in mild turbulence as the plane was coming in to land.

The officer lifted her head, continuing to smile.

"You are travelling together?"

"We are," James replied for both of them.

"You are a British citizen living in Botswana Mr Murdoch and you, Miss Shapiro are an American citizen?"

James thought it was a stupid question as the officer was holding the passports in her hand but he resisted the urge to make a flippant comment. "Yes, that's correct."

"And the purpose of your visit?"

"We are in transit."

"And your intended final destination?"

"Cabinda, Angola."

"Do you have tickets for the onward part of your journey?"

"No. We are going to buy them here. We have the money, cash."

James knew that last word was a mistake the second he said it but it was too late once it had left his lips."

"Can I see?" asked the officer.

James withdrew a wad of cash from his wallet; Grace rummaged in her back pack and dug out more. They handed the bank notes over.

"This is South African Rand?"

Again James thought it was a stupid question but didn't over react. "Yes."

"How much is here?"

"Nearly three thousand Rand."

"That's a lot of money," said Futhi handing the cash back. Then, after a brief silence she said, "Can I ask you both to take a seat over there. I just need to check a couple of things." She pointed to a bank of black plastic and chrome chairs pushed up against the wall to the side of the arrivals hall.

"Do you have any baggage to collect?"

"No," replied James. "Grace just has the back-pack and I've only got this holdall," he replied pointing to his bag on the floor.

"I'll be with you in a few minutes."

Futhi hung on to the passports and landing cards. Before she slipped out of the kiosk, to see the senior duty officer and flag up an anomaly, she pressed a concealed button under her desk which alerted the operator in the control room and let him know he needed to train the covert cameras on the suspects.

Futhi Molov moved quickly. She didn't want time for her 'suspects' to collude. She just told the duty officer she was closing her kiosk to investigate two new suspicious arrivals and then went to fetch James and Grace. She led them into the Immigration suite via a long corridor.

"Mr Murdoch you wait in there," she said pointing the way into a small side room. The plaque on the door said 'Interview Room 1'. "Miss Shapiro you come with me."

"But we're together," protested James.

"It's our policy to carry out interviews on an individual basis," was the bland response.

James' interview room was furnished with two grey plastic chairs either side of a formica topped table. He heard the door shut behind him and the lock turn.

Futhi led Grace further along the corridor, into an identical interview room.

"Please sit Miss Shapiro."

Grace tried to think what her father would do in such circumstances. Her response was possibly a little over dramatic.

"I want to see the American Ambassador!" she said firmly.

Futhi struggled to conceal her smile. "Just sit down."

Disappointed at the response and with no 'stage two' to her plan Grace complied.

"Firstly I imagine the Ambassador of the United States of America to the Republic of South Africa is quite a busy man. I doubt that he would drop everything to come and see you. What you should be asking for is Consular access."

Grace jumped in. "Alright then I want Consular access."

"Sorry no can do."

"I'm a citizen of the United States and I'm sure it's my right to have access to diplomatic advice when in a foreign country. I'm sure my Dad said that's International Law!"

"Let me explain," said Futhi. "This airport is what's known, in international law, as a port of entry. Now until you get past me you have not entered the Republic of South Africa. Technically you are still in transit and as such you are not entitled to the protection of the accredited representatives of your Government in South Africa – because you are not in South Africa."

Grace was silent for a moment. "Well surely I'm entitled to make a phone call or something."

Futhi shook her head. "You've got no rights in South Africa if you're not in South Africa and you my dear are not in South Africa. I suggest you answer my questions and we'll see what transpires." Futhi opened her note pad and began to write. "Now.....let's begin."

It was more than an hour before she entered the room where James sat. It had been a long hour and James' mind had been racing. He was agitated by the time Futhi sat down in front of him.

"What did she say," asked James.

"Oh you don't need to worry about that. Concentrate on answering the questions I have for you," was Futhi's response.

James ignored the advice. "Why have you detained us? You have no right. South African law says that we don't need a visa if we are not staying for longer than ninety days. That's your law."

"I think it would be better if you remained calm. Don't exacerbate the situation; I assure you it's not in your interests. I will explain why you were stopped, if it helps. Before the plane landed you filled in an entry card." Futhi held the card up for him to see. "This is your signature isn't it?"

James nodded.

"Good. Do you see the declaration written above the space for the signature? It means that you understand that this is a legal document. It is important. On the card you stated that your reason for entering the country was for reason of transit. Yes?"

"Yes."

"I asked you were you able to produce onward tickets but you couldn't. Correct?"

"Yes, but I explained it was our intention to purchase the tickets here. I even showed you the money I had."

"Yes you did and that is the problem."

"What problem?"

"Well firstly you didn't declare how much cash you were carrying on the entry card. That's not so bad; we could find a way around that. What is a problem is that South Africa has strict foreign exchange laws. There is an absolute limit to the amount of cash that can be carried across our borders. Currently that limit is 2500 Rand unless you have a bank certified stamp in the back of your passport. You have no such certification. There is little discretion allowed on these regulations."

James screwed up his face. "What does that mean?"

"In practical terms? Well first of all I am empowered to confiscate all the funds. Additionally I am permitted to impose up to a one-hundred per cent penalty charge; finally I can refer the matter to the Prosecutor's Office which may result in criminal charges. The penalty on being found guilty of such charges is typically five years imprisonment. However I have a considerable amount of discretion on the matter. Now do you feel like co-operating with me?"

James didn't respond but his expression was enough.

"Okay, but before we get started I'm going to pass your luggage on to one of my colleagues for inspection."

"You can't do that. It's got my father's mail in it. It's private."

"Not here it isn't. Let's get started."

"Can I make a phone call first?" James tone was becoming more conciliatory.

"Who to?"

"Mary."

"Who's Mary?"

"She's sort of my grandmother. She'll be very worried."

"Sort of," said Futhi. "I'll think about it when we've finished."

Dane Akai was pissed off. By this time he'd expected to be mid-Atlantic, well on his way home. The exercises had gone well with the South African Air Force. He'd been sent to South Africa from his base in Maryland to practice working with the South African's on the mutual support programme. The US as part of the programme was to supply the South Africans with logistical support in the event of natural disasters that occurred anywhere on the continent but in truth it had just been a bit of flag waving and a jolly. Job done, Dane wanted to be home for the big ball game on Saturday. Now sitting on the apron at the freight terminal at Jo'burg International, in the pilot's seat of his C130J Hercules, all hope had evaporated and he was sulking. That's why he'd sent Marie to sort out the paper work in the co-ordinating office instead of going himself. He just knew it was going to be some bull-shit job, why else would he have been diverted to a civilian airport?

Maria Zane was one of the few female cargo marshals in the US Air Force and she was good. As a female she felt she had to be better than the men on the job just to be considered equal. Not that she minded that much.

She found the temporary UN co-ordinating office easily enough. She knocked and went in. There were two desks. To the rear of the room a man and woman were talking.

A woman sat at the front desk.

"We've been expecting you," she said eyeing up Marie's flight overalls. "We opened the office especially for you today. Hopefully they'll be loading you soon. Here's the manifest. It's not that complicated." She handed Marie a single sheet of paper. In the column marked 'Items' was a single line: Four-hundred and fifty empty metal ballot boxes.

"Empty ballot boxes?"

"Yeah, it's a real cock-up," said the woman. "They're having a UN supervised election in Cabinda. One of our guys discovered that the Cabindan's, or whatever you call them, were going to use old cardboard boxes or something to collect the ballot papers. That's not allowed. All ballot boxes need to be lockable and uniquely numbered. Apparently they don't have any proper ones of their own so the South Africans are giving them some. I suppose elections and democracy is a bit new to them. We had no means of getting them there so some guy in Washington offered your service. At least it's not a dangerous job."

"The skipper's going to be really pissed off when he finds he's missing the ball game to deliver a load of empty tin boxes."

"Nothing I can do about it. You got the plane's documentation? I need to fill in the forms and sign you off."

Marie handed over the plane's registration book and the woman started filling in a sheaf of forms in longhand. Marie leant back in her chair. She began listening to the conversation that was going on at the other desk.

The man had been reading a stack of documents that the woman, Futhi Molov had given to him.

"Yes they appear to be all in order. Just wait a moment. He pulled open the top desk draw and withdrew a file. He thumbed through the paper until he'd found the sheet he wanted. He ran his finger down a column.

"Yes that's absolutely fine," he said. "But can I ask you how you came by these papers? They're the official accreditation documents for Mr Duncan Murdoch and Miss Jane Ashton. Both those individuals are currently in Cabinda and should have these papers with them."

"I just spent the last couple of hours interviewing two kids we pulled coming into the country. The letters were in their baggage. I'm glad it all checks out. They told me a story; it's interesting and sweet. I would have been disappointed if it was a pack of lies."

"Don't leave it like that," said the man.

Futhi gave an abbreviated version of the story she'd put together, from when Grace was found in the bush as a baby to when the two of them were pulled at the gate.

"And do you know what's really sad? They're so close and I haven't got a choice but to send them back to Botswana. I can't give them a 'happy ending'."

Marie, who'd been listening couldn't resist butting in.

"I do happy endings," she said. "Or at least I might be able to do something. We're going to Cabinda. I might be able to organise a ride for them."

Futhi turned around to face Marie. "What would it cost them?"

The woman who'd been filling in the forms for Marie had stopped writing and was listening to the story.

"Nothing," answered Marie, "We're going that way and we aren't exactly overloaded. We've only got four-hundred and fifty empty metal boxes on-board. Reckon I can charm the skipper. Bet he'd be pleased that missing the ball game was at least for a good reason. I just need the travel requisitions. You issue them here right?"

"Well I don't know if I have the autho...." The man began. Something made him look up. The three women were staring at him. He paused and realised there could only be one answer.

"I don't suppose it would be that difficult," he concluded.

The three women smiled.

James and Grace had been re-united. They'd been put in an interview room together. Subdued they sat holding hands, resigned to their fate. They were startled when Futhi Molov came into the room and sat opposite.

"I've concluded my investigation. I'm going to tell you what I have decided and arranged. If you disagree with my conclusions you will be given the chance to appeal. Do you understand?" Her demeanour and tone offered little hope.

"I'm sure by now you realise the magnitude of what you have done. Not to mention the trouble you have put the department to, you have also, potentially, broken several laws and regulations."

James and Grace nodded. He squeezed her hand lightly; it was scant comfort.

Futhi continued. "But more than the trouble you have caused the official world you have put your families through a nightmare. The anxiety and anguish you have caused is astounding. You have acted with total irresponsibility and I'm sure they will come up with an appropriate response of their own. That is for later. In the meantime I have to inform you that you are being refused entry to South Africa and I have therefore arranged for your deportation at the earliest possible opportunity."

"You're sending us back?" asked Grace.

"That's not what I said. I said I was arranging for your immediate deportation. The first available flight is not to Botswana."

"Where are you sending us?" asked James, alarm bells ringing.

"A plane is leaving here in just over an hour's time; you will be on it. It is bound for Cabinda City."

James and Grace looked at each other. After a few astounded seconds James turned his attention back to the Immigration Officer.

"You're sending us to Cabinda? Really?"

Futhi was no longer able to suppress her smile. "Yes you're going to Cabinda. That's unless you want to appeal my decision?"

"No. No we don't" said Grace, "Do we James? We don't want to appeal do we?"

James smiled but only for a moment.

"Now Mr Murdoch, your currency issue," said Futhi, turning her attention to him. "Just to be clear you were carrying 3000 Rand which you claimed was all your money, is that correct."

James nodded grimly.

"As I understand it you had split the funds for security reasons, you and Miss Shapiro carrying 1500 Rand each. You split the money whilst still in Botswana. I also understand that the money was to be used to purchase onward air tickets for yourself and Miss Shapiro. Is this correct?"

James nodded unsure where the Immigration Officer was going with her questions.

"So really the half of the money that Miss Shapiro was carrying was a gift from you to her that you had made before entering South Africa?"

"Yes," his answer was less hesitant this time.

"So really it was not your 3000 Rand? Actually you were carrying 1500 Rand each?"

"Yes," replied James finally getting it. "And 1500 Rand is within the permitted allowance?"

Futhi smiled. "It is. You did however make a false declaration, which is in itself an offence. However I am willing to let you rectify the matter."

Futhi produced two fresh landing cards. "If you'd like to fill these in correctly my paperwork will be in order and I will be able to return this to you." She held up an envelope containing James's cash.

"It's not a great place, so I hear," said Futhi Molov as they walked towards departure security. "I hope you find what you're looking for."

James shook Futhi's hand. Grace hugged the Immigration Officer.

"Our work is to enforce the law. It's not always that pleasant. Occasionally it's nice to help people out. Now hurry. There's a car waiting to take you over to the cargo area and your plane."

There was not much to the security check-out. Within seconds they were through and walking towards the gate.

Just when they felt they could breathe easily again they were stopped by a man with a '*Department of Parks and Wildlife*' shoulder badge sewn on to his khaki shirt.

"Hello," was his innocuous greeting. "That's an interesting necklace you're wearing. Can I ask you where you got it?"

"It was my mother's," replied Grace. "It comes from Angola."

"Do you have a '*CITIES's Certificate*' for it?" he asked.

"What's a CITIES certificate?"

"It's permission to carry restricted items across international borders."

Grace and James stared blankly.

"The white beads, they may be ivory. If so the necklace requires a CITES certificate. May I examine it?"

Grace reluctantly removed it from her neck. "It's the only thing I have that belonged to my mother."

"It's a quick chemical check."

"If it's ivory?" asked James.

"Then it's confiscated I'm sorry to say."

The man walked off but returned within five minutes. He was smiling.

"I told you it was quick. Good news. The bits I was concerned about are actually inorganic. That's fine, you may keep the piece."

They'd cleared the last obstruction.

Jane watched as the C130J touched down at Cabinda City Airport. The giant sky-grey aircraft disappeared into a cloud of dust as the pilot put the propellers into negative pitch. The plane slowed dramatically without the pilot even touching the brakes. A few minutes later it was parked up on the apron. The throaty roar of the main engines died away; all that remained to break the silence was the high pitched whining of the tiny auxiliary jet engine, buried deep within the plane's tail section that provided electrical power for the plane on the ground.

Jane braced herself for the encounter.

Chapter 34
Cabinda Border (Zaire side)
11th February 10.30 am

The march back had been as hard as Bernd Groelsh had anticipated. The Khat was all gone, the effects of the drug wearing off. The weaker men and those who had over indulged were hardly able to walk near the end. The promise of the enhanced bonus motivated the more able to help the laggards.

Groelsh was happy to see the vehicles. The driver of the truck, the one that had been left behind to guard them was fresh. His hands helped push soldiers over the tailgate.

Groelsh drank from his water bottle and splashed some of the tepid liquid over his face. For him there was work to do and he needed to be alert.

"We will leave immediately," he said to the truck driver. "I want to get back as soon as possible. I will drive the Nissan myself. You follow close behind."

"It's a long drive," replied the driver. "We cannot make it today. Where will we stop for rest?"

"Just follow me. It's not for you to worry about that."

The truck jolted wildly but still made steady progress along the rutted jungle track. Some of the men in the back slept, the others occupied that hazy zone between consciousness and unconsciousness. For two and a half hours they continued without pause. For a while Groelsh doubted himself, he thought he'd missed it and then there it was. Just as hope was fading he spotted the secret advance marker he'd left on the roadside a week previously. Two hundred yards further on he slowed the Nissan to a crawl. Finally he spotted what he was looking for and stopped.

The driver of the truck got out of his cab and walked forward to find out what the problem was. Groelsh met him halfway.

"I have a short-cut," he said. "It will save us more than ten hours. You will need to follow me."

Groelsh pointed in the direction of, what appeared to be, impenetrable thick bush.

The driver shook his head. "Impossible."

"No it's fine. The undergrowth is only twenty yards thick. We can force our way through. After that there is a dried riverbed. It's rough but if you follow me we'll get there safely."

The lorry driver briefly considered protesting but in the end just went back to his cab.

Groelsh selected low gear ratio, four-wheel drive and differential lock on the Nissan. He moved the vehicle forward, swinging it in an arc until it was head on to the vegetation. Revving the engine he slipped the clutch until the bull bars came into contact with the undergrowth. The bushes were soft and sapling trees weak. They yielded under the force of the three and a half litre diesel engine just as Groelsh had promised. The truck followed the path that had been opened up. In minutes they were on the dry riverbed. Progress was slow; it took them twenty-five minutes to reach their destination.

From 1870 onwards the great empires of the world had scrambled to grab a share of the Dark Continent: Africa. In the absence of a navigable river they thought that railways would be the best way of gaining access to the interior. The French dreamed of a great East West railway, dissecting the continent. They'd planned a railway from Massawa on the Red Sea to Dakar on the Atlantic Coast. The British had ambitions of a Cape to Cairo railway. Belgium's King Leopold, owner of the Congo, also had an ambitious plan. His idea was to link the mouth of the Congo River with the headwaters of the River Nile.

Britain came closest to succeeding; the French were defeated by the shifting sands of the Sahara; Leopold simply ran out of funds – but not before he'd already made a start on his venture. Leopold was inspired by Cecil Rhodes who had diverted his railway line and built a bridge over the Zambezi Gorge so that travellers could *'observe with awe'* the spectacular Victoria Falls. That is why he'd commissioned the building of a bridge by Dorman Long Ltd of Middlesbrough, England, the same company that was subsequently to build the Sydney Harbour Bridge. Leopold had nothing as grand as the Victoria Falls but he did have some mighty chasms and gorges the most dramatic of which he modestly named after himself, the Leopold Gap.

The gorge that had taken nature several million years to create was 300 feet wide and two hundred and eighty feet deep. The bridge over the gap was finished in 1895, the same year that Leopold went bankrupt. It was never connected to a railway system and had stood there ever since, a rotting hidden monument to a single man's megalomania. It was at the South side of that bridge that the two vehicles now stood.

The lorry driver protested. "It is too dangerous. It cannot take the weight of the vehicles. Nothing heavy has crossed that bridge in my lifetime."

"I have crossed it," replied Groelsh truthfully. "Less than two weeks ago I came here. I have checked it. I have even been underneath and looked. It is safe. If you do not believe me I will go first. You can watch. If you are happy you can follow, if not you can go back alone and I will meet you in Boma."

The driver didn't respond.

"Don't worry," added Groelsh, "I will wait at Boma with your bonus money. You get there when you can." He didn't wait for a response. He went back to his vehicle.

Traversing the bridge was slow. Originally railway sleepers had formed the roadway. Over the years many had decayed, some had fallen into the river far below. Gaps had appeared. Local people used the bridge as a footpath and had made rudimentary repairs with crudely hacked tree branches held in position by lengths of jungle vine. The Nissan heaved itself over the bumpy way slowly but without incident, only picking up speed once it had cleared the last log. Groelsh stopped, got out of the vehicle and looked back. He smiled as he observed the lorry starting its journey. He knew the driver would not be parted from him, not whilst the bonus remained unpaid.

The lorry lumbered forward, inching its way onward, the confidence of the driver increasing the further he progressed.

Groelsh dropped the tailgate of the Nissan and removed the moulded plastic cover of the compartment on the right. He withdrew the bundle of cloth and from inside the bundle he withdrew a small electronic box, extended the telescopic aerial and flicked the chrome toggle switch. A green light flashed. He paused to look at the truck.

The driver lifted his eyes for a moment to check how far he had gone.

"Halfway, maybe a little further," he thought. He dared to think of arriving in Boma than night. It was his last thought.

Bernd Groelsh pressed the red button. The explosions were text book. The charges at either side of the main arch, where the steel work butted up against the concrete mounts, did their job of shearing the giant corroded, fixing bolts. The third charge, positioned under the roadway, at the peak of the bridge's steel arch, lifted upwards and effectively broke the bridge's back.

For a last few seconds the structure tottered as if reluctant to obey the laws of gravity. It didn't resist for long. With protesting groans from buckling metal and the high pitched snaps from popping rivets, the bridge gave up the will to exist and folded in on itself, cascading deep into the gorge taking with it the lorry and its contents. Groelsh's smile was this time accompanied with a sigh of relief.

Six hours later, still in daylight, he pulled up outside the chain-link fence. The security guard was expecting him. He opened the gates, raised the red and white pole barrier and pointed to the well maintained prefabricated office building that was a remote outpost of Nordrhine Hansahaus Gmbh, a German trading company whose African HQ was situated on a small quay on the banks of the Congo.

Two circumstances had drawn Groelsh to this place; firstly Baron Freiherr Artur Swartzstein was a shareholder of the company and secondly it was one of the rare locations that had an internet connection to the rest of the world. Not that Bernd knew anything about the internet other than that he had been reassured that if he delivered his camera to this place then the resident technician would be able to send a '*digital*' copy of his pictures. Bernd Groelsh was sceptical about new technology but he was putting that scepticism behind him on Gunter Siegburg's word.

Two hours later the technician made his declaration. "So, it is done. Everything is sent. What else can we do for you?"

"Give me something to eat and find me somewhere to sleep."

Chapter 35
Lisbon, Portugal
11th February 1996 4.30pm

Neither at the offices of Associated Press in New York nor, even more so, at the offices of Reuters in London did they have much time to spend on the matter. Uncorroborated stories had to be checked out. Hard evidence of a reliable second source had to be established. That was not going to happen for two reasons. Firstly there were just not enough resources on the ground in remote parts of Africa and secondly everybody was busy with another breaking story.

A few hours previously somebody had driven a white van into a giant construction site on the east side of London, parked it up and walked away. A few minutes later it had exploded creating devastation in the surrounding area. It was regarded as one of the most audacious and successful terrorist attacks ever made by the IRA. It would become known as the *Docklands Attack*. It was news not only in London but all around the world. The wires were buzzing. Every available hand was busy trying to glean every little detail.

That's why the anonymous report of an atrocity in a province of Angola received scant attention. The editors in both news agency offices made more or less the same decision: let a junior researcher make a couple of phone calls but otherwise wait for evidence or a second source to come forward. The story didn't make the '*wire*'. Within twenty-four hours the executive editors of both agencies had to change their mind.

The editor of a Portuguese newspaper, '*Correio da Manha'*, was interested. His paper had received the same anonymous despatch as AP and Reuters but he had given it more weight, possibly because he was monitoring the progress of the referendum in Cabinda. It was, after all, a former Portuguese colony. He ordered a copywriter to knock up an article for consideration at the editorial meeting that was to take place at six pm. His decision paid unexpected dividends. Just before the end of the editorial meeting a secretary had come into the office with a picture of a young African girl, a heart wrenching picture that depicted the extremes of human barbarism. The picture was of Juba, although the editor didn't know her name. Everybody at the meeting agreed it was going to be their front page story. The only decision to be made was how much of the picture would have to be cropped because they knew that the public would not have the stomach for the full gory image.

Just after the newspaper went to press both AP and Reuters were ringing '*Correio da Manha*' vying for syndication rights to the lead picture together with the sixty accompanying photographs. Some speculated there could be a Pulitzer Prize winner there.

The story of Juba didn't surpass the '*Docklands Explosion*' story in London but it did make people in other parts of the world take notice. It wasn't long before the Chief Press Officer in the United Nations was inundated with information requests. And it didn't take long for people to remember that it was the United Nations who were supervising the Cabinda referendum. The UN Press Officer contacted Operations and not long after André Piet had an urgent fax on his desk asking for corroboration or denial of the event. It had come as a major unpleasant surprise to him. He called an urgent and impromptu meeting of his staff. He had no idea that the origin of the original anonymous report and the photographs was the Headquarters of the Cabinda Liberation Campaign based at Villa Santa Maria, less than a couple of miles from where he was now sitting. If he'd have had time he might have thought it through, but it was not long before another potential bombshell dropped on his desk that was going to distract him. The conclusion of Piet's meeting was that everybody would gather what information they could overnight and the meeting would be reconvened in the morning. Piet, in the meantime tasked himself with getting hold of Duncan Murdoch. He was the observer closest to the scene of the alleged atrocity.

Chapter 36
Villa Santa Maria
11th February 6.00pm.

He didn't look much like a President in waiting. Unshaven, his clothes gave the appearance of having been slept in, which they had been. He peered at his visitor through barely conscious dull eyes. His visitor wasn't too worried though. He knew that Lubala had the ability to recover quickly from the effects of alcohol.

Gunter Siegburg was annoyed at being forced to make the trip from the Operations Room to Lubala's '*apartment*'. He'd initially ordered the man to be brought down but Lubala had refused to get out of his bed. Siegburg would normally have reacted angrily but he needed Lubala to do something for him so he held his tongue.

"This place is a mess," said Siegburg looking around the room. It was the opposite of Germanic cleanliness and order. "A pigsty," he added.

"My father used to say 'treat a man like an animal and he will behave like an animal'," was Lubala's unexpected gasp of a reply. "What do you want? Are you ready to free me from my prison; have you come to tell me when I will be President or have you come to order me to clean the toilets?"

There was no tone of apology in Siegburg's response. "You have no part in this bit of the operation. When you are required you will be informed but I warn you, in this condition you are of no use to me.

For now I need you to do something simple." Siegburg cleared a space on a dressing table by sweeping the mess of ashtrays and empty spirit bottles on to the floor. He placed two neatly typed pages in the cleared space and produced a pen.

"Sign!"

"What are they?"

"It's of no consequence to you. Just sign."

"And if I don't?"

"I'll get somebody else to do it. It would be inconvenient but not impossible."

"Things cannot stay like this," responded Lubala.

"That is true," replied Siegburg, already ahead of Lubala with that thought. "Now sign."

Scratching his name at the bottom of each page Lubala made no attempt to read the documents.

"I want you to send me a woman and more whisky."

"There will be no more women or alcohol." The reply was final. Siegburg picked up the papers and left the room.

At his desk in the Operations Room Gunter Siegburg read the documents for a final time. The first one was addressed to André Piet, leader of the United Nations monitoring group. It was headed '*Official Protest*':

> "*The Cabindan Liberation Front abandoned the armed struggle in the hope of a fair negotiated settlement with the Angolan Government. It has entered into the spirit of the democratic process whole-heartedly and without reservation. Our behaviour has been faultless.*
>
> *However the Angolan Authorities in Cabinda, whilst expounding fine words, have acted in complete contradiction of the agreement we all entered into. Throughout the election process my organisation has been subjected to obstruction and physical attacks. Until now we have not complained about the methods employed by our opponents.*
>
> *Recently unconfirmed reports have been received stating that a massacre of my supporters has occurred, carried out by the Angolan Army. It is claimed that many of the victims were women and children and it appears that their only offence was to support the creation of a 'Free Cabinda'.*
>
> *Should the reports be confirmed, I have to inform you that the Cabindan Liberation Movement will have to reconsider its position. Whilst it is desirable that matters are settled by recognised democratic means I cannot, in all good faith, abandon my first duty to my people, which is to offer security and protection.*
>
> *I now demand that the United Nations carry out immediate enquiries and confirm or deny the actual facts concerning the alleged massacre.*
>
> *General Moses Lubala*"

Siegburg was satisfied with the content of the message. He scanned his eyes over the second sheet which was almost identical in words but headed '*Press Release*'. He called one of his SF men over.

"I want you to deliver this by hand to the United Nations Headquarters at 10.00 hours tomorrow. It is important that they receive it directly and promptly. Take a car, no rifle, only a concealed side arm and go in civilian clothes. Clear?"

"Sir. I don't know where the Headquarters are located; I'll take that Welshman to show me the way."

"No. I need him to get to work on straightening out that arsehole Lubala. Take the African kid."

"He's dumb, he can't talk."

"He understands well enough and he's got fingers. He can point the way."

Chapter 37
Miconze Village
12th February 9am

André Piet didn't manage to get to speak to Duncan Murdoch on the phone till after 9pm the previous evening. André explained about the newspaper reports and the queries from the UN in New York. He asked if there was any way Duncan could get to Miconze Village quickly and confirm or refute the allegations.

David Marobi had been more shocked than Duncan. It was not a feigned shock, it was real.

"There are no army units in the area. All soldiers are confined to barracks till the referendum is over."

"Could somebody have disobeyed orders?" Duncan had asked.

"It's possible," was all that Marobi could reply.

"We will go and see in the morning," said Marobi. "You and I, it will be quicker if we go alone."

Duncan didn't hesitate. He'd grown to trust Marobi. They'd set off as soon as there was light to see. They went quickly despite the condition of the tracks. In three hours they were there but even before they'd arrived they knew that there was at least some truth in the reports. High in the sky they saw vultures circling.

They walked the last hundred yards. At first there was a faint whiff of sweet burnt wood in the air. It was quickly overtaken by the smell of charred flesh that would have been pleasant had they not suspected its origins. The worst was awaiting them. Marobi walked a few paces ahead; he made directly for the store. He stepped through the doorway but quickly stepped backwards as if pushed by an unseen force. As Duncan arrived the repugnant stink of rotting flesh assaulted his senses. Not only was it revolting to smell, it was so strong it attacked his taste buds and he instantly felt the flow of saliva at the back of his mouth, the precursor to a severe vomiting fit. Those who experience the stench of death never forget it.

Duncan was sure that if any human had been to the village since the massacre they had not lingered or left any evidence of their visit. But animals had not shown the same respect or restraint. Most of the bodies lay more or less where they had fallen. Some showed signs of dismemberment. Footprints suggested a pack of wild dogs. They were not there now but Duncan suspected they had only left as their vehicle approached and it explained why the vultures had not dared to land either. Both David Marobi and Duncan knew that scavenging animals, big and small, would return to finish their macabre feast.

The two men walked around the village separately. Duncan first tried to count numbers. When he got to the burnt-out hut, where the men had been kept, he could only make an estimate. It was impossible to distinguish individual bodies from the tangled mess. He spotted clothing on the ground and picked it up. He had seen enough. He searched for Marobi. He was standing motionless at the entrance to a hut that at first sight appeared to have escaped involvement in the atrocity. Duncan approached from behind and put a hand on his shoulder. Marobi stepped back and let Duncan see inside. The ghastly sight of Juba in her death throes, told a story that was beyond description. Helpless the two men walked away in silence. Duncan watched as Marobi took his turn to vomit.

It was some time later, back at the vehicle that the men spoke but not until they'd drunk from the water bottle. The liquid did nothing to alleviate the lingering rasp that clung to the back of each man's throat.

"Before we leave we should agree what we have seen here," said Duncan.

Marobi nodded.

"I've counted more than a hundred dead," he said. "Some shot, some hacked to death and a substantial number of bodies burnt in huts. About thirty of the victims were young children. There is evidence of torture and rape of the women. Do you agree?"

"Without a forensic examination I think that's a fair description. "Do you recognise these pieces of uniform? I found them on the ground. It's the only physical evidence I've collected." Duncan held up a soldier's battle blouse and a camouflage cap, the clothing he'd found as he walked around.

David didn't really want to look. He feared they were going to tell him something he didn't want to believe. It pained him to admit that the items looked like bits of Angolan Army uniform.

Duncan didn't push for an answer. "I need to get to a telephone and report this as soon as possible."

"That's clear," replied David. "We'll go. But I want to come back. I want to follow the trail the attackers left. I want to know who they were exactly. Something is telling me that this is not what it appears to be."

"It's true we shouldn't jump to hasty conclusions but neither can we ignore the evidence."

James had slept on the floor of the tiny hotel room. Jane and Grace had taken the beds. It had been cramped but there wasn't any choice. Jane had lain awake for much of the night, thoughts flying through her mind, not the least of them was how she was going to explain to Duncan about James' and Grace's arrival. She still blamed herself for sending that fax about Grace's mother. At least now she had been able to send a message to Stirling Farm and assure them of the children's safety.

Jane's guilt stopped her being angry when Marie had escorted her charges across the airport apron. Empathy made her believe that she, if put in the same position, would most probably have done the same.

The previous day's conversation with Marie had been brief.

"Thank you for pulling our coals out of the fire. That was a kind thing for you to have done."

"It was nothing, we were coming here anyways. Take it compliments of the US Air Force."

"Thanks a million. You're going back to the States now?"

Marie raised her eyebrows. "You shouldn't have asked. On the run up here we suffered a partial instrument failure. We gotta go back to South Africa for repairs. Andrew's wouldn't clear us transatlantic."

"Andrew's?"

"Andrews Air Force Base, our bosses."

"Is it safe? To fly back to South Africa I mean." asked Jane.

"Not in the cockpit. The Skipper's really pissed, like a bear with a sore head. You don't need to get too close to him," Marie laughed. "I ain't in no rush to get back though. Weather's really bad Stateside."

"Well good luck."

Marie turned to Grace. "Hope It comes right for you, you deserve it. You all take care now."

They didn't want to move. Perhaps the tiredness was just catching up with them but Jane persisted.

"You're not staying in the hotel on your own."

"Don't you trust us?" moaned James from his floorboard bed.

"What do you think? Get up you're coming with me."

They'd picked at a breakfast that would have been better avoided and got the hotel reception to get them a taxi to take them to UN HQ just before 9am.

"You'll have to wait here." said Jane leaving them in the classroom that served as admin office. "There's a big meeting I've got to attend. Don't wander off."

André knocked his knuckles on a desk to bring the meeting to order. The meeting was in another classroom and all the available UN staff were there.

"I'll keep it as brief as possible," began Piet. "International newspaper reports are circulating about an incident that has possibly occurred near the border with Zaire. Before you get carried away I can tell you that the reports, although horrific in nature, have not yet been confirmed. New York have asked us to investigate. One of our men, Duncan Murdoch, is in the field and we're waiting for him to get back to us. I think most of you knew that already.

What you are not aware of is that last night I received a confidential fax from New York. Just so we are all clear, what I am about to tell you is confidential and doesn't go out of this room. Apparently the British Ambassador to the UN has informed the Secretary General's Office that they have credible intelligence that there is some type of covert and co-ordinated activity in this region, most probably military in nature which may or may not be connected with the referendum. I know that's not very specific but I need you all to be aware and on the look out for anything that might be considered suspicious."

"What's the nature of the activity?" somebody asked.

"I think it's intercepted radio communications or something like that. It may be nothing but it's enough to get the British interested.

Now moving forward. What's the general feeling on how things are progressing? I need to get a consensus so I can report back to New York."

There followed about fifteen minutes of questions and answers. When the chatter started to degenerate and people began to talk over one another André Piet interrupted.

"That's enough discussion I think. Let me summarise.

Barring an incident in the park when an opposition meeting was disrupted by loyalist civilians, there have been no noted problems. The pro Government campaign is organised and well advanced. On the negative side we are surprised at the lack of evidence of any opposition organisation. It almost appears that they are not even trying to mount a campaign. On the plus side they do not appear to be using any form of coercion themselves. Is that succinct enough?"

A murmur of acceptance spread throughout the room.

"Right that's it. I'll bring you all up to date as and when. Please bring anything you get straight to me?"

Everybody got up and moved towards the door except Jane, who hung back.

"André, can I have a word?"

"What is it? I heard about your problem. You got it sorted, you need help? Does Duncan know?"

"Yes and no. Yes I have it sorted but no, Duncan doesn't know. That's not the problem I want to talk to you about though.

This might be something or nothing, I'm not sure. A couple of days ago a young lad, it's hard to tell his age, stuck a note into my hand and promptly disappeared. I thought he might come back so I hung around the gates. He did reappear and gave me another note. I'd intended to follow him. That's what I was doing when you stopped me going out the rear gates."

Jane handed the notes to André. He scanned them quickly. "And what else did he tell you?"

"Nothing, he didn't say a word?"

"The notes are really scruffy and the writing looks like the person is only semi-literate."

"That's true," replied Jane, "But they do indicate that somebody thinks the opposition are not sold on the referendum."

"Okay, let me think about it," replied André handing Jane the notes back. "In the meantime if you could get hold of the lad again it would be good."

"Okay, I'll see what I can do. Separate subject. Is it alright with you if I take one of the trucks? I've got accreditation documents organised for my visitors but I need them signed at State House. I don't want my visitors trailing around on foot without proper documents."

"Yeah go ahead." André looked at his watch. "Hey it's ten, the morning's flying, I need to get going."

Feliz had never sat in the front of a Jeep, It was something he'd always wanted to do but he'd rather it wasn't in these circumstances. The German had come to the courtyard and shouted incomprehensible words at him. In frustration the man had grabbed his arm and dragged him roughly towards the vehicle.

"United Nations," he'd said.

Mistaking Feliz's silence for stupidity he shouted, "UNITED NATIONS!" Feliz still looked at him blankly. "U-N-I-T-E-D N-A-T-I-O-N-S" he'd almost screamed. In frustration he clipped the boy across the head with the back of his hand. He was about to deliver another blow when ap Ewan appeared.

"Whoa, what's the trouble?" Ap Ewan put a protective arm around Feliz.

"The stupid idiot understands nothing," said the German SF man.

"What are you saying to him?"

"United Nations."

"What about the United Nations?"

"I want him to show me the way to their Headquarters."

Ap Ewan put a hand on each of the boy's shoulders and looked him in the face. "This man wants you to go with him and show the way to the United Nations building. Can you do that?"

"Feliz nodded."

"Get in the car and point the way."

"He's an imbecile," repeated the German grudgingly getting behind the driver's wheel. "He better get it right."

The drive was short; the man drove aggressively yielding to none. Outside the school with the UN flag the man parked on the open ground in front.

"Stay here." He was gone for only a minute or two.

Jane edged the four-wheel drive through the gate. James sat beside her with Grace in the rear.

Grace had been plucking up courage to ask a question. Finally she just said it.

"Will I be able to go to my mother's grave?"

Jane didn't respond, her mind already elsewhere. Her eyes were fixed on the vehicle parked on the waste land, or rather on the occupant of the passenger seat. She was going to park up and approach on foot when a man jumped into the driver's seat and fired up the engine. It was an instinctive decision of hers to follow.

The German drove no less aggressively on the return journey. Jane had difficulty keeping up; following in a clandestine manner was an almost impossible task. Even so it wasn't until they were only a few hundred yards short of Villa Santa Maria that the German SF trooper became suspicious. He took one hand off the wheel and withdrew the concealed pistol from his waist band. He wedged the weapon between his legs.

The German slowed but did not turn in towards the gates of Villa Santa Maria. He passed the gates seeking an opportunity. It came soon. To the right, a track cut through the middle of a copse of trees. He turned the vehicle off the road and ran along the track, stopping after the first bend. In a second he was out. Feliz felt a surge of panic; definitely something bad was going to happen. Almost instinctively he got out of the vehicle and started to run back down the track intending to warn Jane. The German SF man was too quick. Feliz felt the trip but there was nothing he could do to stop himself falling face down into the gravel. He pushed himself up and began to scramble away. He didn't see the blow coming, the flat of the pistol butt travelling towards his head. It connected just above the temple, almost a glancing blow, but not quite. There was a second of dizziness and an instant of hopelessness. Then blackness came as he collapsed on to the floor.

The man stepped forward. He heard it before it appeared. He was right, the vehicle had followed him.

Jane was taken by surprise. She was speeding up towards the bend, attempting to get closer. She hadn't expected to find it stopped, her way blocked and she hadn't expected to be face to face with the barrel of a gun. She hit the brakes. The vehicle's wheels locked and the truck slewed to the right before coming to a halt.

The man came forward, training his gun on her. He pulled open the driver's door, grabbed her by the hair and dragged her out of her seat. He spun her so she was facing the bonnet.

His words were clear. Jane put her hands on the bonnet. Although she felt the tip of the gun's barrel on the back of her head she had the presence of mind to give a warning to James and Grace.

"Stay in the car, don't do anything." Her next words were in German. "I am an accredited United Nations' observer and have diplomatic protection. If you do anything to me or my companions it will have serious consequences."

She tried to sound confident but was sure she'd failed.

"Empty your pockets. Put your things on the bonnet." A rough hand frisked her body, looking for a weapon. He found nothing.

"Why were you following me?"

She almost said, "I recognised the boy that was with you," but was quick enough to stop herself. If he was covertly helping the United Nations it could be a death sentence for him. She stayed quiet.

For the SF trooper the silence was damning. He rummaged through the items on the bonnet: hotel keys, a wallet more suited to a man, a few coins and a couple of pieces of folded paper. One of the sheets slid on to the floor. The man picked it up and unfolded it. It didn't take him long to recognise the sketch plan.

"You are a spy!" he growled as he glanced at one of the pieces of paper Feliz had passed to her. He waved his gun. "Get back into the car, into the driver's seat."

The tone of the order was severe enough for Jane not to protest. She complied. The man got in the back seat, alongside Grace.

"Turn the car around. Follow my directions."

Feliz had regained consciousness but had decided to stay prostrate on the ground and listen.

Chapter 38
MV Brilliant Star, Congo Estuary
12th February 12 noon

The Congo estuary is several miles wide at the point it joins the Atlantic Ocean. For most of the year it is a steamy hot place. It is the zone where fresh water from the interior, the product of a thousand tropical rain storms, races into the salt water of the open seas. The currents are always treacherous, the conditions often rough. The river banks are low and flat and the lofty tropical rainforests have given way to inhospitable mangrove swamps with their grotesquely twisted and gnarled root systems which become exposed at low water. The flats conceal numerous hidden inlets and inferior tributaries; creeks, places where it is possible for even a large ship to remain unnoticed.

Bernd Groelsh clung to the bridge rail as the thirty foot launch bounced its way across the choppy waters, pitching and rolling alarmingly as it fought against the residue of Atlantic swell that was trying to force its way up river. The trip from the dilapidated wooden jetty at Soyo on the south bank to the remote deep water creek seemed endless. He was relieved as they rounded a headland and the MV Brilliant Star came into view, swinging on its rusty anchor chain. The journey had put him in foul humour and that humour was not to improve when he finally got to the Brilliant Star.

In the lee of the headland, the waters around the Brilliant Star were calm but dirty brown, laden with sediment. A pall hung over the vessel, the pungent smell of rotting eggs. Whiffs of poisonous swamp gas drifted over the waters. It took a great deal of effort for Groelsh to drag himself up the rope ladder on to the deck. Sweat made his shirt cling to his body whilst insects attacked his exposed flesh. The captain was waiting, the greeting unceremonious.

"We have been here for nearly four days now," he protested. "It's too long, the men are not doing well. It's impossible to keep them hidden in the hold. It's too hot, no matter how much ventilation there is. I'm only circulating the same hot putrid air. Soon your men will be capable of nothing. I need to move the vessel out to the open sea immediately."

Groelsh looked around. On deck several men lay prostrate under whatever shade they had found. They were lethargic and drenched in their own sweat, the scene only confirming the

Captain's words. It was a dilemma. Groelsh knew moving now, before the command had been given, would risk premature detection but to stay might render his force useless even before the fight had begun. He made his mind up quickly.

"You may move the vessel but keep it away from any busy shipping lanes. Remain as inconspicuous as possible."

Minutes later the relative silence was broken as the main engine throbbed into life and expelled a cloud of black smoke from the funnel. It was soon followed by the eerie metallic clanging as the windlass began its job of pulling in the anchor chain. An echo ran through the hull as the heavy chain links dropped into the steel storage chamber. The tone of the engine deepened as the ship got underway, the propeller churning up the water, leaving a wake of dirty grey foam behind. The effect was immediate. Clear of the headland and pushing forward, a cooling breeze of salt laden Atlantic air swept across the deck and soon men began to stir and lift their heads.

A rota was organised. Each man got the opportunity to come on deck, to get respite from the humid stinking hold. Appetites returned, the men were fed. Within hours they had recovered sufficiently for Groelsh to start cajoling them. Equipment needed to be prepared, ammunition distributed and weapons cleaned. He thought he'd probably made the right decision. Now all they had to do was wait for the signal and hope that they remained undetected.

There was an air of confidence and excitement, even relish, for the fight amongst the thirty men waiting at the farm near Louis Trichardt in South Africa. They were all mercenaries that fought for money but at the same time enjoyed their job. There may well have been eve of battle nerves but that feeling shouldn't be confused with fear. These were men whose chosen career was combat and they were going to do their job. They enjoyed being referred to as Shock Troops.

The pilot of the waiting DC3 had done his calculations over and over again and got the co-pilot to check them. No matter how he worked it out the figures didn't quite add up. As he approached the CO he knew something was going to have to give. He stated the problem in simple terms.

"The distance from here to Cabinda is 2500 miles. We've got a refuelling stop halfway, in Zaire. It's about 1250 miles per leg. The range of the plane is just about 1400 miles with a payload of 6000 lbs. Six-thousand lbs is normally ample for thirty men. The problem is you want to bring so much extra kit with you. We're more than five-hundred lbs. overweight. Even by dropping my navigator I can't make it work. The only way I can carry more than a six thousand pound payload is by reducing the amount of fuel on take-off and if I do that I can't reach the destination. It doesn't matter how I work it out I can't do what you're asking."

"Come on, you always got a bit of reserve," replied the CO. "You can always squeeze a bit more in."

"We'll be really heavy on take-off. I'm even nervous that I'll get the thing off the ground before I run out of runway. There isn't any slack."

"So what's the bottom line?"

"You take four men or five-hundred lbs. of kit out, your choice."

The CO thought about it for a while. "Okay I reckon we got a chance of 'capturing' equipment when we get there but I ain't going to find no trained men there, that's for sure. So I'll tell you what we'll do. We'll strip all the packing materials out and if that's not enough we'll ditch half the shoulder launched missiles. Okay?"

"I don't care how you do it so long as you do it. You got to do it quick though. We're on an hour's stand-by from midnight. I guess your guys at Cabinda wouldn't appreciate it if we were late."

At Villa Santa Maria Gunter Siegburg was feeling the pressure building up. Like all military men he liked things to go according to a plan. When the plan got disrupted, or even threatened with disruption, they got agitated.

"I'm guessing that dumb African kid was passing on information," said the trooper, "I wasn't left with much choice, take them prisoner or kill them on the spot."

"You might as well have done that," replied Siegburg. "If you'd have thought to blindfold them before you brought them here it might have helped. As it is they've seen everything; including our faces. What have you done with them? Where are they?"

"I got them locked up in the monk's cells. If it's a problem I'll go and deal with them now."

"No. I'll deal with them later. We've enough on our plate. We're so close I don't think the UN having a few of their people taken hostage will wreck the operation. It might even spur them on in the short term, particularly if they don't know who's responsible. Where's the African kid?"

"I left him unconscious on the track. When I went back for my vehicle he was gone. I reckon he's that scared he's run for it."

Siegburg shook his head, "I'm not sure what you base that assumption on other than hope. If he's found I want him killed."

Siegburg turned and went to where the Electronics Officer was sitting. "Anything?"

"No, nothing on Reuters or AP."

"They should have had time by now."

"The press release will have to go to New York for approval," answered the Radio Operator.

"Just let me know as soon as we have something. UN confirmation that the atrocity was real and carried out by the Angolan Army is the trigger event. Twelve hours after that it will all be over and there will be no world condemnation. It will just be seen as Cabindans protecting themselves from brutal Angolans."

From his desk at the Foreign and Commonwealth Office in London Ralph Foulkes tried to phone Stuart Cameron. He wanted to talk about the way events were panning out in Cabinda. The woman who picked up put him on hold. He hung on to the receiver, waiting and waiting. Eventually a different female voice answered. I'm sorry I had to check that I could talk to you. Mr Cameron has left the office. He went suddenly and told me he would not be back for several days.

"What!" said Ralph.

"It's not all that uncommon."

"Where's he gone?"

The line went dead.

Chapter 39
Secretary General's Office, United Nations, New York
12th February 9am (Eastern Standard Time).

The Secretary General would have preferred it if Dr Jonathan Marobi was not a personal friend that he held in the highest esteem. There was little he could do for him without discrediting his own position as Secretary General. Even making this call, and giving him forewarning of the UN's preliminary judgement, was politically risky. The Secretary, receiver to his ear, heard the ring tone twice before it was answered. On the other end of the line in Luanda was Dr Jonathan Marobi, President of the Republic of Angola.

"Jonathan, before I begin I want to say that I would not be making this call if I thought you were in any way implicated in recent events. However although I count you as a friend you are the Head of State so beyond this phone call I cannot and will not afford you any further privilege."

"I understand that and I appreciate your call," replied the President. "The position I find myself in is entirely of my own making and I take full personal responsibility for all events, without exception."

"I doubt if the events are of your making but I knew you would do no less than accept responsibility. Now you must listen, I want to read you the press statement that I will sign and that will be issued in the next few hours:

> *Reports of a massacre of men women and children began to circulate in the International Press on the 11th February. The location given for the event was Miconze Village in the remote north region of Angola's Cabinda Province. The United Nations have no permanent presence in the area but are currently involved in a referendum monitoring exercise in that province.*
>
> *On hearing about the alleged event a member of our monitoring staff was despatched to the village and I have subsequently received a preliminary report.*
>
> *Our inspector found that the press reports are substantially correct. A massacre did occur at Miconze Village. It would appear that the majority of the people of that village, if not all, have been butchered and there is strong evidence of acts of torture and rape. Additionally physical evidence was found linking the atrocity to the Angolan Army.*

It has been further alleged that the motive for the attack was that the village was viewed, by the Angolan Army, as being part of the pro-independence movement. At the present time we are unable to substantiate that claim but further investigations will need to take place.

Acts such as this deserve universal condemnation. Furthermore they will throw doubts on the credibility of the forthcoming Cabindan referendum.

The United Nations urge all parties involved to exercise extreme restraint and avoid taking any action that might jeopardise the democratic process or inflame the current tense situation.

That's it Jonathan," said the Secretary General. "I cannot tell you how much it pains me to issue such a statement. Can you give me any reason why the United Nations should not issue the statement?"

"You know I am speaking honestly when I say that I have only limited power," replied Jonathan Marobi. "I can only tell you that my own son is actually in Cabinda as we speak trying to feed me with accurate information so that I can react to the situation. If I believe it will help and not inflame the situation I will visit the Province myself to try and assure the people there that I wish to seek a peaceful resolution to any difference. Beyond that I have no further comment."

"That could be a very dangerous move for you. Be careful, you are a cherished friend." The Secretary General hung up.

At the same time as the Secretary General finished his phone call a scheduled Air France A340 Airbus touched down at Libreville Airport, Gabon. The flight attendants rushed off their priority passenger as soon as the steps were in position. A car was waiting at the bottom of the steps to whisk the man across the airfield to another part of the airport where a Lynx helicopter was waiting, it's rotors already turning. The roundels on the tail boom were the insignia of the Royal Air Force. The helicopter lifted off as soon as the passenger was buckled in. It banked left on full power, gaining height and speed at the same time. Land was quickly left behind.

On the bridge of the ship the captain ordered a change in course so that the vessel was running straight into the wind. Men on the helicopter deck waited, ready to dash forward and fasten the restraints on to the helicopter's skids as soon as it touched down. Landings with the ship at full speed were hazardous but it was something for which the pilot had been trained and it went smoothly. As soon as the helicopter was secured the captain ordered the ship back on to its original course.

The two Rolls Royce Olympus engines were pushing the ship along faster than the published maximum speed of 30 knots. Its true top speed was a closely guarded secret. HMS Liverpool, a type 42 destroyer, was a loved and reliable part of the British Royal Navy.

Chapter 40
UN HQ Cabinda City
12th February 6pm

André Piet was shaken. Responsibility never weighed lightly on his shoulders but this was of a different magnitude. When Jane had not returned from State House he'd sent somebody to look for her. They'd come back with the news that she'd failed to arrive for her appointment. That was worrying and prompted a general search and even a visit to the hospital. He knew telephone enquiries in this place were less than useless. The police response was not helpful either. Piet wasn't sure if they were being deliberately obstructive or just ignorant. Whichever, he was not optimistic that they would be able to make any type of valid contribution. Then came the bombshell. The note from the mysterious youth thrust through the railings. It was written in poor English. '*Your people taken. They is in danger*'.

He'd sat down at his desk to weigh up the situation. In the end the decision had not been difficult: a major atrocity, rumours of unrest in the city, an intelligence warning passed on by the British and now three people gone missing. He was going to evacuate everyone he could. He acted decisively once his mind was made up. The message was sent to New York requesting emergency transport and the staff were ordered to collect what they could and wait at the Maiombe Hotel.

André had decided that he would close the HQ down. The building could revert to being a school. He would stay on but move to the hotel. There'd be plenty of spare rooms once the UN team had departed. He couldn't leave himself until he had resolved the situation of Jane and of course he had to ensure that Duncan got back from his trip. He shook his head, realising that Duncan didn't even know that his son was here with his girlfriend. "Shit," he thought. "This is really bad."

Marie had to leave. She knew if Dane saw her giggling it would only make a bad situation worse. She crept to the back of the briefing room and slipped out of the door, leaving it ajar so she could hear what was going on from the corridor. Not that she really needed to leave the door open, most people in the building could hear her Skipper screaming profanities.

"They have to be fucking joking! This is ridiculous! Why did they send you with the message? Are they too fucking scared to tell me themselves?" Dane kicked a metal waste paper bin as hard as he could; it flew across the room, landing with a clatter in the corner.

The wing commander of the South African Air Force remained calm but couldn't help wondering how the pilot would react to an in-flight cockpit emergency and speculating that '*temperament*' might just be a bit of an issue. Actually he would have been reassured if he had spoken to Marie; she'd been on board as Cargo Master when Dane was handling emergencies. She'd have told the Wing Commander that Dane was a different person when he was in the air with a C130 strapped to his backside.

Dane started to calm down. The Wing Commander took his opportunity. "By the way, I suppose I should mention that it might take more than one round trip."

Dane re-erupted.

The Wing Commander noted that Dane was struggling to find enough profane words to fill his sentences and was having to resort to duplication. He counted 6 'F's' in one sentence. But by then he was even beginning to enjoy the spectacle.

Dane's second rant began to run out of steam and eventually petered out with a final, half sighed, "I've just come from that God forsaking, fucking hole! Fuck the fucking United Nations!"

The South African Wing Commander was almost feeling sympathetic. "It is an emergency and we will provide whatever backup we can."

"Well I can tell you one thing, I'm not taking that plane off the ground till the avionics spares have arrived and been fitted. So tell them it's going to be a good twenty-four hours before we get there."

Initially, when the news came through it had been a concern to Gunter Siegburg but now he was more relaxed.

An hour previously he'd gone over to the Electronics Desk. As he was standing there the printer started churning out paper. It was what he'd been waiting for, the UN statement of condemnation of the massacre, distributed through the news agencies worldwide. That was the trigger he'd wanted.

Without fanfare he said, "Send the code word to everybody on the list. Make sure you get confirmation. We have now passed the point of no return; there is no stopping us now."

Almost nonchalantly he'd leaned over the operator's shoulder and, with his pen, struck a line through one of the numbers on the list.

The operator looked at him as if seeking confirmation.

"No more communications with Namibia. Von Swartzstein is off the list. He is no longer our concern."

It had been so easy he thought as he walked back to his own desk. "That superior egotistical arsehole had been easy to dupe."

No sooner had that thought passed through his mind than the news came that the UN were leaving because some of their staff had gone missing. A brief wave of panic washed over him before he realised it might not be all that bad. Not only was there a massacre but the UN was pulling out as well because of safety concerns. If the UN staff were to die, as die they must, he could blame the deaths on the Angolans. Not only would the world allow a coup, they would positively encourage it!

Chapter 41
Windhoek, Namibia
12th February 10pm

"Do you really think I will need so much my dear?" asked Von Swartzstein alarmed at the amount of baggage that his wife was packing for him.

"My darling you must be prepared for all eventualities. This is going to be your most glorious moment. You must look the part, whatever the situation. I want to be proud of you."

Von Swartzstein, partially reassured ventured a little further. "Do you think I should take appropriate dress for a formal occasion?"

"Already packed my dear."

"And my ceremonial sword?"

"That too."

"I can't think of anything else I might need. I don't know what I would do without you," he admitted. "My life feels so complicated at times."

"That's the burden bequeathed to you at birth."

"You're right. But now I think I should rest. Tomorrow will be a long day and I will need all my fortitude."

"At least you will have your own private plane. That is so much more convenient than common travel."

Only for a moment did the Baron's thoughts drift from his own arrangements.

"It's strange that I have heard nothing from Gunter as yet," he mused as he headed for the bedroom. "Do you think there is anything to worry about?"

Chapter 42
Villa Santa Maria, Cabinda City
12th February 11pm

It was the first day of the full moon. The celestial body hung large over the clear African sky. It's pockmarked and patterned surface was clear to the naked eye almost as if it had deliberately come closer to earth so that people could get a better view. The reflected light cast eerie shadows across the courtyard and cloisters in much the same way as it had for the decades the building had been unoccupied. The truth of what was happening was shrouded by a veil of heavenly tranquillity.

In the shadow of the eastern cloister walkway, the guard almost hidden, one of Gunter's SF men, sat on a hard chair, cradling an assault gun in his lap. Sleep got nowhere near his eyes; he'd been trained in a place where falling asleep whilst on lookout was a serious offence. He guarded one of the cells, a cell originally intended for a monk's private meditation and prayer that had become an impromptu prison.

Inside the cell Jane sat on the hard stone floor, facing the door, back to the wall, knees raised almost to her chest. A protective left arm was wrapped around Grace whose head rested on her chest. The girl slept uneasily, worn out by nervous exhaustion. To Jane's right sat James. They held hands, each trying to comfort and reassure the other. The tiniest whisper echoed around the cell. Conversation, without the guard outside hearing was almost impossible. The process worked both ways.

Both Jane and James heard the low whistle followed by the scrape of the wooden chair legs. Jane let go of her charges and crept to the locked door, trying to peer through a crack to see what was happening.

Outside the cell the guard now standing, returned the whistle. From the archway, the wide archway that broke the cloister on the southern side, another SF soldier stepped out of the shadows. He'd just walked up the seventy-five yard long path from the beach. He approached the cell guard. They spoke in whispers, Jane could hear but not see the men.

"How did you get on?"

"It's done," said one. "The direction finding lights have been set and switched on. Both the boats are ready. It will be okay, the sea is calm we should be able to fetch ten men per trip in each of the boats. Disembarkation time should be less than two hours."

"That's still a long time."

"We'll start moving them out from here before they're all landed."

"Any sign of the ship yet?"

"It's not due for another four hours. I expect they're waiting off shore. What about those?"

The soldier nodded towards the locked cell door, referring to the prisoners inside.

Jane didn't hear a response. The guard didn't reply, he simply made a cut throat gesture that was a clear indication of the prisoners' fate.

"Getting rid of people from the UN is going to get a lot of people's back up."

"Yeah well that is okay as long as somebody else gets the blame."

Both men smiled.

Jane was not the only one secretly listening. The words sent a shiver down the second listener's spine.

"You better get some rest. The action will be starting soon enough," said the cell guard ending the conversation.

The hidden figure in the shadows slipped away knowing that he must do something.

Ap Ewan knew them as DT's. He'd never previously seen them but he'd heard about them. He didn't know the proper Latin term was '*Delirium Tremors*'. He didn't even realise that they were a recognised and serious medical condition. To him they were just what an alcoholic went through when they couldn't get a drink.

Gunter Siegburg had stopped Lubala's women and drink two days previously and ordered ap Ewan to get the General into some kind of presentable shape. Initially it appeared to be going well. Lubala slept for most of the day in his filthy bed. The symptom ap Ewan noticed was that Lubala appeared to be shaking in his sleep. He thought it was because he was cold, so he covered him with a blanket. Later he noticed the sweat rolling down Lubala's head and neck and his skin was glistening like a man with a fever. Ap Ewan removed the blanket. The shaking continued, getting worse. His concern increased. As darkness fell on the second night he heard Lubala talking. He thought he must be coming out of it but when he tried to speak to the General most of the words were incomprehensible gibberish. At that point ap

Ewan thought he needed to tell Siegburg so he'd left the Bishop's Apartments and gone down to the Operation's Room.

Siegburg had kept him waiting whilst he issued instructions to one of his men. Ap Ewan overheard the orders but didn't understand their significance.

"Don't kill the prisoners yet," he'd ordered. "We'll make it look like the Angolans killed them when we take the Governor's Office."

Siegburg turned suddenly to face ap Ewan. "What do you want?"

Ap Ewan's confidence had long since deserted him. He spoke nervously. "It's Lubala…." He never got to finish the sentence.

"Don't bother me with that idiot now. There's no more women or drink, I just want him ready at the right time. You take care of it."

He was about to try and explain that Lubala was unwell but Siegburg stopped him with his next words.

"Where's that dumb African kid. Have you seen him? I want him dead."

Ap Ewan shook his head. "No. He's been gone for a long time."

"If he turns up grab him and bring him to me. I don't care if it's alive or dead." There was no mistaking the tone of Siegburg's voice.

Ap Ewan returned to the Bishop's Apartments. Lubala was still rambling, garbled words, nonsensical sentences. Then the hallucinations began. Lubala could see spiders on the wall and begged ap Ewan to kill them. Sometimes he asked for water but wouldn't allow ap Ewan to put the glass to his lips. Mostly he just ranted on about the past, issuing orders to non-existent men, recounting acts of bravery and holding imaginary conversations with his long dead father. Ap Ewan decided that there was nothing he could do for Lubala other than sit and wait it out.

The hours passed slowly. In the shadow of the flickering kerosene lamp, he had time to think about his own life. He recalled how he'd once both feared and respected the man that now lay helpless before him. He remembered how he'd once hoped that he'd bask in Lumbala's reflected light, how he'd hoped people might come to respect him too and how that reality had actually played out. He realised that in the end Lumbala had no more respect for him than anyone else. He looked back, almost with a tinge of nostalgia, to the times in Boma when he'd wanted to get near to the man even though he was dangerous and scared him. Lumbala didn't scare him now nor did he command any respect; the man had been exposed for what he was.

His mind went back to his past and his desire for acceptability and success. He remembered his dreams of returning to his home village, a hero a man that people would look up to. It slowly dawned on him that reflected glory was not glory at all. Glory was something you had to earn on your own. It was Siegburg and the other Germans that had finally made it clear. They just saw him as an idiot, somebody only fit to fetch and carry, to do their bidding. They would never consider him as an equal. Ap Ewan knew things could not stay the same. In his frustration he spoke out loud, "How could I have made such a mess of my life, why can't I accept that I'm fucking useless, good to neither man nor beast."

A shudder ran through his body as he realised that somebody else was in the room. He turned to face the door. It was open and he could make out the silhouette of Feliz standing silently in the gap, listening. Ap Ewan's thoughts came rushing back to the present.

"Feliz, come in, close the door, be quiet. They are looking for you. What have you done wrong? You are in big trouble."

He was not expecting an answer; he always spoke to Feliz and never expected an answer.

"I like you. I think you are a good man, I respect you," were the first words he heard from the lips of Feliz.

Ironically Ap Ewan was himself dumbstruck. Never before had he heard words come from the mouth of Feliz.

Chapter 43
Dinge Army Camp, Central Cabinda
13th February 2.00am

A strain had developed in Duncan Murdoch and David Marobi's relationship; shadows had been cast by the atrocity at the village. Marobi was convinced that others were responsible whilst Duncan believed only what he'd seen and the evidence he held in his own hands. He believed it was Angolan soldiers that had been responsible and that is what he'd said in his report. But that is not to say he hadn't given Marobi the opportunity to present his case.

Duncan had agreed to come to the army camp at Dinge with Marobi and witness his investigation even though he felt that Marobi would be swayed away from the unpalatable truth. After all it was clear to both Duncan and Marobi what the implications would be if the outside world thought that Angolan soldiers were guilty.

Marobi had been almost desperate to get Duncan to make a positive report to the UN and he'd failed in that quest. Duncan had gone to bed disappointed that they'd not come to the same conclusion.

By Angolan standards the base was well ordered. For the past four weeks all the troops had been confined to barracks in compliance with the United Nations referendum resolution. It had been difficult to keep the men occupied; they were becoming restless. But Murdoch believed that the Soviet trained Commanding Officer at the base did things '*by the book*'.

"I promise you, I give you my word, there have been no patrols sent from this or any of the outlying bases that I control," he reiterated time and time again when questioned by David Marobi.

"It is possible," the base commander conceded, "that a few men may have got out into the surrounding villages without my knowledge. It is difficult to maintain complete discipline. Some men will want to get close to drink and women but I can assure you no force, and especially no unauthorised vehicles, have left this camp for weeks."

Duncan Murdoch had remained unconvinced but alone in his room he went over the matter again. He held the tangible evidence in his hands, the bits of uniform they'd collected at the scene. As he examined them it dawned on him, something was suspicious that had been niggling at the back of his mind. In the end he decided there was nothing to do for now; he would bring it up with Marobi in the morning. But events were soon to overtake his thoughts.

His sleep was light and uneasy. It was not difficult for the orderly to rouse him.

"Captain Marobi needs to see you urgently in his office."

Duncan hastily pulled on his clothes and rushed to join Marobi who was sitting behind a desk waiting.

"What's happened that can't wait till the morning?" asked Duncan.

"Quite a lot has happened but the main things affect you personally."

The hairs on the back of Duncan's neck began to bristle.

"I have just finished a conversation with André Piet, your head of mission in Cabinda City. He will attempt to get through on the phone again in half an hour so you can talk to him directly."

"Well if it's about my report I've had second thoughts. It has occurred to me that all the evidence, the bits of uniform and equipment we found, they are all brand new. That's strange. It raises the prospect of a setup."

Marobi smiled, "Thank you for that but that's not the problem. Let me brief you so you can be prepared. Firstly he has been trying to get hold of you for some time. There is news about your family."

Duncan listened with quiet unease as Marobi spoke, telling him about the unexpected arrival of James and Grace at Cabinda city and then their unexplained disappearance with Jane. He resisted breaking Marobi's flow by asking questions till he'd finished. But then the questions came.

"How did James and Grace get from the Okavango to Cabinda?" he asked.

Duncan was looking straight ahead not expecting an answer, merely thinking aloud, trying to clear his mind.

"Disappearance, what does that mean? Are they harmed? Have they been taken? Who would kidnap them? Had Jane found something out; was it a deliberate pick up? What do the British Intelligence reports mean?"

Marobi broke Duncan's chain of rhetorical questions only to pose more questions. "Could it be that events in Cabinda City are connected to the atrocity at the village? There may be a reason

232

why the Cabindan Liberation Front is not campaigning. Could they have a different plan?"

"There are too many things happening for it all to be a coincidence," replied Duncan, "But I know my priority is my family."

"Absolutely," replied David Marobi. "I understand that and I promise you that I will do whatever I can to help."

Duncan was about to say something but was interrupted by the ringing of the phone.

"You take it," said Marobi. "It can only be your HQ."

Nobody was resting; the foyer of the Maiombe Hotel was full of baggage. People were chaotically milling around. To an outsider it would appear that organisation was breaking down. UN vehicles were parked pell-mell at the front of the hotel, in preparation for the run to the airport when word came.

Two floors up, in the rooms that André Piet had commandeered and made into his new impromptu Headquarters, the situation was calmer. André waited for information about when the evacuation plane would arrive. In the pit of his stomach he felt that something was going to happen. He hoped the plane arrived as soon as possible, but there was nothing he could do about that at the moment. He just had to wait, it was in the hands of others. His mind was more on the missing people. He wasn't overly concerned about Murdoch, it was Jane Ashton, together with Grace and James that had to be his priority. He knew Africa and was savvy enough to realise that kidnapping was a best case scenario. In truth they might already be dead. The only bit of he had that would give him a glimmer of hope, was the scribbled note. Piet knew there must be a friend out there.

He looked at his watch. It was time to call back, to speak to Duncan at the army camp. The call went straight through.

"André?"

"Yes. I take it you've been briefed by Captain Marobi? It must all be a shock to you."

"That's an understatement."

"An evacuation is being organised for UN staff. I need you to get back here. Are you able to do that on your...."

"Stop!" interjected Duncan, "Before you go any further I'll make it very clear to you. I'm going nowhere without Jane, my son and Grace. Don't make any plans for me."

"I anticipated that response," replied André, "I'd feel the same way myself. Tell me what I can do."

233

"Give me an up-to-date run-down. What's your situation?"

"I've ordered an evacuation of all staff. A plane has been assigned but I don't know when it will arrive. In the meantime I've got everybody marshalled, after a fashion, in the hotel lobby. I plan to stay on here till there is news of the others. I've been trying to get the local Cabindan authorities moving on the search. They don't appear to be very interested and even if they were I'm not sure what use they'd be in any case."

There was a pause before André continued. "I'm sorry to be so blunt about this. The best I can expect from the local police is that they find the bodies and tell us. My real hope is that they are alive, kidnapped and that we receive a ransom demand or something. Basically all that I can do is wait to hear from the captors and see if I can deal with their demands."

"Do you have anything at all for me to go on?"

"It's tenuous."

"Tell me."

"Jane had a couple of scribbled notes passed to her – more or less anonymously. They were vague but she thought she might be on to something. I know she wanted to check them out but she'd been distracted because of the arrival of James and Grace."

"Is that it?"

"After they went missing another note was left at hotel reception. It's just made its way to my desk, in the last few minutes. It's in the same handwriting as the ones before and it says they're alive and being......"

There was a click and the line went dead.

It's taught in every military school throughout the world. The lesson differs little: in conflict, communication is key to victory. If possible, control the methods of communication. If you can't control them at least deny them to the enemy. It follows that if you are expecting problems they will in all probability appear first in the communication systems.

The central telephone exchange in Cabinda was an easy target. There was no security guard and only two technicians worked there overnight, or more truthfully one read a book whilst the other slept. There hadn't been a battle just a bit of gun waving. One man could have done it on his own. As it was there were five attackers, all Siegburg's SF men. Quickly the two technicians were bound with cable ties and stuffed into a dark cupboard. It didn't take long to find the switchgear for the incoming electrical supply, throw the breakers and remove the heavy duty ceramic fuses. As an additional measure the fuel supply to the backup generator was cut. Not only was Cabinda City, and a good part of the rest of the province now without telephones, but international calls were no longer possible.

Only one of the SF men remained at the telephone exchange. His orders were simple. Stay till relieved, if attacked destroy the main circuits with explosives and get back to Headquarters at Villa Santa Maria by any means possible.

The remaining four men got back into the Land Cruiser and headed off to the second of their three targets.

Chapter 44
DC3 Transport Plane, Above Zaire

The trip had been uneventful. They'd been challenged over Zimbabwe. The pilot hadn't responded but had turned off the plane's transponder. They were out of Zimbabwean airspace before the Zimbabwe authorities had a chance to respond. The Zambians hadn't even noticed they were there, the night time radar operator at Lusaka Airport totally failing to notice the small white blip at the bottom left hand corner of his screen.

The re-fuelling airfield was surprisingly good. Constructed by the Belgians in the late fifties before they lost their colony, the concrete strip hadn't subsided at all. The truck with the fifty-five-gallon drums of aviation fuel had been ready and waiting. They were finished ahead of schedule.

The pilot smiled to himself as he set the altimeter to twelve thousand feet. The higher a plane flies the more fuel efficient it is, there's less air resistance. But as the cabin was not pressurised, the higher he went the more difficult it was for the men in the back to breathe in the rarefied atmosphere. He'd had to fly at seventeen thousand feet for the first leg of the flight, just to make sure he got there, but now he had plenty of fuel. Dropping the cruise height by five thousand feet would help the soldiers be alert and ready for action as soon as they landed. He looked at his watch, "Not much more than an hour and a half to go," he thought to himself.

Bernd Groelsh stood in near darkness on the starboard bridge wing looking down the twenty feet to the main deck. Men were climbing out of the hold and the deck was beginning to look cramped with soldiers struggling to put on their combat clothing and ready their weapons. The captain was next to him, his eyes looking into the darkness. In the distance he could see the lights of Cabinda city. He'd already picked out the red and green shore navigation lights that marked the entrance to the harbour and gone past them. Now he was looking for something else. And he soon found it, the two direction finding lights that had been turned on by the German SF soldier a couple of hours previously. The captain took the bearings of the two lights every thirty seconds. As the two bearing lines converged on his target position he slowed the main engines. Just as the two lines intersected the pre-marked position on his chart, the captain rang 'engine stop' on the

236

telegraph and picked up the intercom to speak to the bo's'on waiting on the forecastle.

"Drop anchor," he ordered. The quiet of the air was broken by the rattle and clanging as the anchor chain unravelled itself from the chain locker. The men on deck surprised by the sudden noise quickly realised they had arrived at their point of disembarkation.

Chapter 45
Bishop's Apartment, Villa Santa Maria

Ap Ewan was incredulous, even now after he'd heard the story. In a way he thought it was funny but he was also full of admiration for the deception that Feliz had pulled off so successfully for so long. Somehow it was unbelievable.

"Run that lot past me again will you," he said.

"There isn't much time," responded Feliz. "You just have to believe me for now. My life is a blank before they found me. I don't have any memories. I don't even know my name or how old I am. I just knew that they had found me one day. I think I can remember men dragging me up from a river bank. Then I was in a camp in the jungle. I knew they'd saved me but I also knew I had reason to be scared. Inside I felt the men were bad. I just lay there, not making a sound. I didn't speak. I lay there for hours. Slowly my strength came back and I was hungry.

It was getting dark; the men were sitting around, drinking. One man was at a fire cooking. I heard him say food was ready but none of the others moved. They shouted at the one that was cooking, telling him to bring the food to them. He swore. I thought that if I did something nice they might give me something to eat. I got up and started carrying food to the men that were sitting down drinking. They liked that. When they'd finished I collected the plates. The man cooking let me finish what was left.

One of the men who'd eaten called me over. He looked at me and felt my arms. 'He might grow into something,' he said.

The he looked at me. 'If you grow a bit you can join us and learn how to fight.'

I didn't know why, I just knew I didn't want to be like them but I was too scared to tell him that. So I just stood there looking at the man. He got angry. I thought he was going to hit me. Then one of the others joined in.

'The kids dumb, he can't talk.'

'That makes him useless,' said the first man. 'We might as well finish him now.'

The cook disagreed.

'Well he just brought you your food didn't he?'

The ones by the fire joined in. 'He'd be good enough for fetching and carrying.'

'Let him stay whilst he's useful,' said another.

That's how it started. I thought if I didn't talk I'd be safe."

238

"How old were you then?" asked ap Ewan. "You must know that."

"No I don't, I told you."

"Where did you learn to speak English?"

"I don't know. I could always understand different languages, not just English. I understand Portuguese and German too. I don't know how. I can write a bit in them, but I don't think it's very good."

"Somebody must have taught you," said ap Ewan. "And tell me, if you didn't like it there why you didn't run away."

"Where would I run to?" Feliz wanted to change the subject, time was pressing. "But that is in the past. Bad things are happening now. Things are changing quickly."

Ap Ewan looked at Lubala, still in his bed, now slowly writhing as if in pain. "That's for sure. Things will never be the same for him – or us. It doesn't look good."

Feliz shook his head. "That's not true. The United Nations are here, in Cabinda City. I have heard they are good people."

"We have been with Lubala, they will see us as bad people," replied ap Ewan.

"No," said Feliz. "I have been helping them. I have been giving them information. Ever since I knew what was going to happen I have been giving them information."

"Is that why Gunter Siegburg wants you?"

"Yes, I think so."

"You know he will kill you if he catches you?"

"More people than I could lose their lives soon. They have three prisoners in the monk's cells. I know they plan to kill them and blame the Angolan people. And they are going to take over the country, and then a lot of people will die."

"There's not enough of them to take over the country," replied ap Ewan.

"They have an army coming. It is nearly here."

"What are you talking about?"

"Look out of the window, to the sea. There is a ship. It is full of soldiers. Soon they will be on land. They have boats ready to bring them ashore. Then it will be too late."

Ap Ewan opened the window shutters that looked out to the shore. The moon was still low in the sky, silhouetting the '*MV Brilliant Star*'.

"Well bugger me, you might be right. But what can we do?"

"I have told the United Nations people that their people are here. They will come to fetch them soon I am sure. I think it would

239

be good if you and me got them from the monk's cells and hide them till their people come."

"I don't know about that. It's most probably better not to get involved."

"The UN will thank you for it if we succeed."

"And if we don't succeed we will be dead."

"Then you will be a hero. You're a soldier aren't you? All soldiers want to be a hero."

Lubala groaned in his bed then babbled a few incomprehensible words. Ap Ewan looked at him and recalled the long night he had spent with his own thoughts.

"We don't have any weapons?" he said, "We're powerless."

Feliz shook his head. "They gave me jobs. They made me clean the guns. I have been in the armoury room often. I have hidden some guns and ammunition. I know how a gun works, I have stripped them down and cleaned them many times. And you have been in many battles, you told me that, you will know what to do."

Ap Ewan reflected silently for a moment: firstly on how his lies had caught up with him and then on how useless his life had been. He remembered how he had prayed for an opportunity to demonstrate his usefulness and now, when that opportunity was presenting itself, all he could feel was fear and the desire to hide. From the depths of his mind a resolve surfaced. He knew it was the time to prove himself, his opportunity had finally arrived.

"We will try, but firstly I have to tell you the secret I have. I'm not going to risk my life with you thinking I am something that I am not.

My name is not Emrys ap Ewan. My real name is John Rolands. Emrys ap Ewan is the name of a man who died a long time ago, a man I learnt about. He was a man of principle who I admired, a man who was everything I am not. By taking his name I thought that I would be gaining his qualities. I would become him. But that didn't happen. The truth is I'm not the soldier that I let you think I am. I was only a reserve soldier in the Territorial Army. When it started I was a bread van driver but at the weekend I put a uniform on and ran around the country. I liked it so much I got carried away and lived a fantasy life. After a while I used to pretend that my bread van was the point vehicle of a convoy on a special mission. People in my village used to laugh at me and call me a fantasist. I wanted to prove them wrong. I came to Africa wanting to do something good and planned to go back home a hero, a man that they really would respect. But I only proved that

240

they were right; that's why I can't go back. It would be a humiliation. I have nowhere to go. So I suppose I might as well do something good.

Now that's it, my mind is clear. You don't have to call me ap Ewan anymore, use my real name, John."

"I always liked you," said Feliz. "You were the only man that ever showed me kindness, the only one that did things for me and expected nothing in return. I have always known you are a good man. You have nothing to prove to me and you will always be ap Ewan to me."

It was an attempt to replicate the grandeur of the Vatican's Papal apartments. The Bishop's residence was situated on the first floor. The main entrance, on the southern side of the courtyard, was through a wide double door archway into a large entrance hall. A sweeping marble staircase led up to the mezzanine. From the mezzanine another set of arched heavy double doors was to have led visitors into the apartment's main reception room. The marble for the staircase had either not been installed or had been looted during the long period the building had been empty. There was a second entrance to the apartments, an external stairway. The steps were situated outside the courtyard, on the external walls. They were supposed to have led down to what would have been formal gardens between the apartment and the beach. The gardens had never been fully developed; they were now just scrubland, dotted with giant wild shrubs, land that had been reclaimed by nature.

Ap Ewan left Feliz alone with Lubala for a few moments. Feliz looked down on the helpless man, the man that he'd spent so much of his life fearing. Ap Ewan returned.

"Right I am ready."

They left the apartments by the external stairway, in what remained of the moonlight. They moved silently, keeping to the shadows. At the bottom of the stairway Feliz grabbed John's arm and led him to a barely visible door that hung lopsidedly on a single corroded hinge. Feliz pulled at the rotting wooden door. It yielded easily as if it had been exercised recently, which it had. He disappeared into the darkness and emerged a few seconds later carrying two assault rifles. He thrust one at ap Ewan.

"M16 carbines," whispered Feliz.

John fumbled the weapon with complete unfamiliarity.

"You do know this gun?"

241

John shrugged his shoulders.

"You have shot a rifle haven't you?"

"Oh yes, of course I have," whispered ap Ewan with indignation. After a short pause he added, "On an army firing range in Chester twelve years ago!"

Ap Ewan could just make out Feliz's smile and little shake of the head.

"It's loaded; I've set it for short burst, that's three rounds when you pull the trigger. This is the safety," he said, adding, "keep it switched on until you're ready to fire."

"I'm not stupid you know," was the whispered response.

They crept forward, crouched, keeping to the cover of the wild undergrowth and bushes that dotted the area. They came in line with the archway and got an angled view. A kerosene light hung from the wall in the shade of the far cloister where the Monk's cells were. From its yellow light they could make out the guard sitting upright on the chair, cradling his rifle. Feliz lay on his stomach; John crouched beside him only a few feet from the path to the beach.

"We will have to wait for an opportunity," whispered Feliz.

"You stay here I have something to do first," was John's near hushed response.

Feliz tried to put a hand on ap Ewan's arm but was too late, he'd stepped backwards quickly and disappeared into the darkness. Feliz had no option but to stay and wait. The minutes ticked by.

The SF guard stood up at the sound of voices. From around the corner came two men familiar to him. They carried their weapons across their chest and walked with purpose.

"On schedule?" asked the guard as the men came alongside him. At first it looked like they were going to pass by the guard without a word. Then one of them stopped.

"The ship's in position, we're going to start ferrying the men ashore now. You can help carry some of the field handsets to the shore line. The men will need them when they come ashore, everybody else already has their's. We'll most probably need a hand launching the boats too."

"What about the prisoners?"

"It'll only take a few minutes, they'll be alright."

"That's not my orders."

"Don't be an arsehole, come on."

The guard shrugged, took one look into the cell through the Judas hatch and hurried to catch up with the other two that were now a couple of steps ahead.

Feliz lay frozen, not even daring to breathe. He heard the crunch of the men's boots on the gravel. He closed his eyes and pushed his head down and listened as they got closer. It felt as if they were going to walk right over him. He expected to feel the tip of a boot in his rib cage. It didn't come. Not until the footsteps were fading did he dare to breathe or lift his head. In the distance he saw the empty chair and unattended cell door. He was about to move when from behind came a rustling sound. For a second he thought the men were back, then he saw ap Ewan coming toward him in a low crouch.

"Where did you go?" demanded Feliz too loudly.

"Shush, you'll find out later," he responded, "That was a close one wasn't it? Come on let's make our move. By the way how are we going to open the lock, have you thought about that?"

"Don't worry. I've seen what they have done." Feliz was up and running forward, ap Ewan close behind.

Jane's eyelids were heavy; she'd been struggling to stay awake. Both James and Grace slept either side, leaning on her. The Judas door opening had roused her. She was fully alert when she heard the fumbling at the door. "When people came in the dead of night it wasn't necessarily a good thing," she thought to herself, preparing for the worst. She shook the two beside her. "Wake up, something is happening."

"They couldn't find a padlock. I heard them cursing," said Feliz. "They just fastened the hasp with a loose nut and bolt. Look it's easy to open. You take the three of them back the way we came. I'll follow later, after I've put the nut and bolt back. With a bit of luck they won't realise they're missing for a while."

The door opened and ap Ewan stepped forward.

"I'm here to rescue you, or at least try. Don't say anything, be as quiet as possible and follow me."

Jane was up. "I've never been so pleased to hear a Welsh accent," was all she said. She pulled James and Grace to their feet.

As the four disappeared into the darkness Feliz hurried to refasten the nut and bolt. In his haste he dropped the nut. As it was too dark to see properly he had to search on his hands and knees. At last he found it and with fingers that felt like sausages he tried again. Just as he was finishing he heard the sound of the returning guard's footsteps on the gravel. It was too late for him to get back the way he came without running straight into him. He picked up his weapon and made his way to the north end of the cloister, towards the main entrance, the entrance that led to the Cabinda road. Crouching, keeping in the shadows as much as he could, he darted from pillar to pillar. At last he made the cloister exit and disappeared into the blackness.

The guard, bemoaning the fact that he'd got his feet wet pushing the boats into the water, arrived back at his chair. Something caught his eye, something moving, a dark figure, hiding, trying not to be seen. Too quick it had disappeared. He stood for a moment. Almost as an afterthought he undid the Judas door and looked inside.

"Alarm! Prisoners escaped!" His screaming voice pierced the silence of the night.

Ap Ewan led the trio out of the cloister and to the bottom of the steps to the Bishop's Apartments.

"Upstairs, through the door," he said. "I'll follow when Feliz arrives."

He'd expected him to arrive in seconds. After a minute he started to worry. When he heard the guard shouting the alarm a tremor of panic ran through his body. As he desperately needed to do something, he pulled the M16 up to the horizontal position. He had absolutely no idea what he would do if anybody approached. Then he heard running steps, coming towards him, not from the cloister but from the back of the building. Feliz appeared out of the darkness, panting for breath.

"They saw me," he gasped. "But I think I lost them. I ran all the way around. Hold this," he said passing his M16 to John.

He disappeared into the dark doorway at the back of the stairway, returning a few moments later with two more M16's slung over his shoulders. In his hands he dragged two hessian sacks. "Take these to the apartment. I'll follow you in a moment. Ap Ewan staggered up the stairs, each step an effort, under the weight of the two sacks and his own gun.

By the time he got to the Bishop's Apartment Jane had ushered James and Grace into Lubala's bedroom. Jane went from window to window, peeping through the shutters, trying to get

244

some kind of perspective on the place to which she had been led. James and Grace wandered over to the sick man in the bed who looked up at them vacantly. Ap Ewan watched panting as he recovered from his exertion. Grace turned around first. Ap Ewan did a double take, there was something familiar about the face he saw, but there was no time to ponder.

"Take these," he said. "I have to help my friend."

Feliz was coming up the steps backwards, dragging a wooden ammunition box. Over his shoulder was another hessian sack. It was an impossible load for such a small body.

"Let me take the box," said ap Ewan, pushing past and hooking his own hand into the carrying rope.

Relieved of that part of his burden, Feliz made the last few steps easily. Ap Ewan was close behind.

"Shut and lock the door. They're sure to realise we're here before too long," said Feliz, dragging the hessian sack behind him. "I'll take this through to the bedroom."

"You're the one who brought the notes," said Jane to Feliz as he came into the room. You know what is going on, tell us."

Feliz was not looking at Jane. He was suddenly frozen, fixed to the spot. His black skin had taken on a ghostly grey hue and his eyes almost appeared to be bulging. They were fixed and immovable, fixed not on a face but on the necklace that hung around Grace's neck. The sudden eerie silence had instantly created a chill in the room, unseen spirits were present. For Feliz it was as if a dam had broken in his mind and he experienced cerebral chaos. Doors, long shut doors were opening; doors that Feliz did not know existed. He couldn't process the flood of information. He turned and walked away.

After raising the alarm the SF Trooper who'd been guarding the cell had run after the shadow. He thought it must have been making for the main gate. He ran flat out, his gun at the ready. In seconds he was at the gate's guardhouse. The SF Trooper stationed there, alerted by the shouts, was standing in front of the closed gates.

"Did you see them?" shouted the guard.

"Nobody has come this way."

"They must have double backed. Stay here and watch out for intruders. If you see them shoot them. I'm going to the Operation's Room."

Gunter Siegburg's rage could not be controlled. "You fucking idiot. They're witnesses, they know what's going on. They have to be caught. How did they get away from you?"

"They must have had help; they couldn't have got out alone."

"If they didn't make the gate they must be around somewhere. Make a search – all the buildings." Siegburg thought for a moment. "Start with the Bishop's Apartment. I wouldn't be surprised to find out that the little African bastard had a part to play in this."

Chapter 46
Cabinda City Centre

Another rule of warfare is to sow confusion in the chain of command. Use surprise to knock the enemy off balance and it reduces their potential for resistance.

It was only a short drive from the telephone exchange to the police headquarters. It was a flat-roofed two-storey building. A single armed policeman was on guard outside the front, waiting impatiently for the end of his shift in an hour's time. Nobody was visible through the glass doors at the desk. The first floor was home to the commander's office and the communications' room. Three men were in the communications' room, sitting in a circle, talking and laughing in the quiet of the night. Nobody had noticed that the telephone lines were down. The power lights of the radio transmitters remained on green. They represented the only remaining contact with the city's outlying police posts.

The police force for Cabinda City numbered nearly five hundred men in total. Sixty men were on duty that night. Twenty-six of them were assigned to the thirteen outlying police posts. Six men were out in three cars. Taking away the one on guard outside and the three in the radio room that left twenty-four men. That was the exact amount of men in the 'staff room' at the back of the station. Some were sitting around a table playing cards, one who wanted to progress, was studying for his sergeant's exams with his head in a book, and the rest were either sleeping or dozing on the chairs and benches around the room.

They'd synchronised their watches before leaving their truck. They had plenty of time to position themselves. Both men carried heavy weapons as well as their assault rifles, both checked their watches and silently counted down the last ten seconds. The first rocket-propelled grenade, fitted with a high explosive fragmentation head, went through the window of the communications' room and exploded instantly. The men in the rest room barely had time to get to their feet before the second RPG round came through the open window. The carnage was devastating. About half the men died instantaneously, all the others received massive shrapnel wounds; many wished they'd died. Only the man on guard outside was uninjured by the initial explosions. For too long he stood there looking in disbelief. He made an easy target. The single shot rang out and he too crumpled to the floor, his spine shattered by a high velocity bullet.

Men at the nearer police outposts heard the explosions that had echoed through the silent city night. They tried to radio and phone the reports into the control room. As they struggled the two men got into their truck and set off for their last job of the night.

"It'll take them a couple of hours to sort that lot out," said the driver of the truck, "and by the time they do it will all be over."

Chapter 47
Road from Dinge to Cabinda City

The base commander at Dinge was emphatic.

"I have my orders, they are very clear. I am to do nothing that might be seen as provocative during the course of the referendum. I'm specifically forbidden to enter Cabinda City."

"But if your country is being attacked you have a duty to protect it," Duncan had argued.

"I have no reason to believe, other than your word, that any such attack is taking place. And to be honest I think your opinion is swayed by your personal circumstances. You are worried about your family. I will not mobilise my troops for a simple case of kidnapping just because the victims are foreigners."

"Capitan Marobi believes an attack is taking place."

"He is not part of the army; he is from the Presidential Guard. I do not take orders from him, besides he is of lower rank!"

In the end it was Duncan with Marobi and his twenty men that had set off from Dinge and that was only possible after winning the argument to get the Land Cruiser and lorry refuelled. "It was better than nothing," Duncan had thought. He would have gone on his own if he had to, walking if necessary.

As they set off Duncan tried to ignore the pain in the pit of his stomach. He felt sick with worry. He thought at first it was because his only son was in danger. However he quickly realised there was more than one person causing the pain in his heart and a wave of remorse swept over him, remorse for not having been more open to Jane, for not taking what she had offered. Now he knew he couldn't contemplate the thought of life without her and swore to himself that if he could sort this situation out he would put right what was wrong. He would never be such a fool again. He would tell her about his feelings when he saw her, if he saw her. It was a big 'if'. Duncan was rational enough to know the outcome depended on his actions now and there could be no room for emotions. The only way he would be able to resolve the situation was for him to keep his mind focused and clear.

"Is there an alternative way into Cabinda City?"

Marobi was driving. He looked at Duncan. "This is Africa. In this part of the world we are thankful if there is one way. Be happy it is such a good road."

"If there is some kind of take-over in progress the other side will know that the majority of Angolan troops are at Dinge and they will have done something to ensure they can't get into the town. We should expect some kind of roadblock, even an ambush. We need a *'point vehicle'*, something running ahead to make sure the road is safe."

"We're the point vehicle," replied Marobi. "All we can do is keep our eyes open and look."

"We have to think like them. Where would be the best place for them to stop us?"

The aluminium flat-bottomed boats were just over forty feet long and twelve feet wide with a square, sloping bow, not dissimilar in shape to military landing craft. But the similarity stopped there. They had been designed for the calm shallow waters of the mangrove swamps. They were unsuited for, and uncomfortable on, the open seas. Their stability had been further compromised by the necessity of putting a fifty gallon oil drum in the middle to act as a reserve fuel tank. The fuel tanks with the outboards motors had insufficient capacity for the magnitude of the task in hand.

The MV Brilliant Star had come inshore as far as possible but still it was more than a half mile run from the beach to the ship. As the first of the flat-bottomed boats approached, the light clusters hanging from the bow and stern were switched on bathing the area in light. A scramble net was let down over the side and men began to climb down, letting go and jumping the last couple of feet. The men had learnt well but even so it had taken an hour to get the first group off the ship and assembled on the fore shore. There the SF officer had struggled to get his CLF men into order in the darkness. He had no sooner achieved that objective when the silence of the night was broken by a burst of machine-gun fire. His men scattered and took cover, not knowing where the fire was coming from, or, more importantly at whom it was directed. It was clear though that it was coming from the general direction of Villa Santa Maria.

The SF officer ordered his men to stay behind as he went forward to investigate. Staying off the path he weaved his way through the scrubland. He made his way through the archway that led to the cloisters and courtyard. Crouched behind a pillar he found a man, one he already knew, one of the advance party that had been in Cabinda for the past few weeks.

"What's going on?"

"A couple of prisoners have escaped and locked themselves up in that building, the Bishop's apartment, up there, first floor, left. They've got guns and are resisting."

"Are they risking the operation?"

"No, but they're a fucking nuisance we could do without at the moment. Gunter is in the Operations' Room. You'll have to go right, around the outside of the building. The Ops Room is an old chapel, you can't miss it."

Gunter Siegburg's annoyance was tempered by the arrival of the first group from the Brilliant Star.

"Where are your men?"

"On the beach, ready to move out, a squad of twenty. Do you want me to clear that apartment for you? It'll only take me a few minutes?"

"No stick to the plan. It's only a couple of kids and a woman. We'll handle that when more men are ashore. I don't want delays." Gunter was resolute.

"A truck is waiting for you at the main gate. Go and set up your roadblock on the north road. Stop any attempt to bring reinforcements from the north. Stay there till relieved. Your radios are in the armoury," he added pointing to a room that had at one time been designated the chapel's vestry but now had a less ecclesiastical function.

"Fine. South covered?"

"There'll be nothing coming from that direction but I need to be ready to dispatch the next squad to the airport shortly."

The SF squad commander sat in the cab alongside his black driver. He gave the order to move out. With the aid of a pencil light he studied his map, marking off the landmarks as they were passed. After fifteen minutes of steady rolling they had left the urban areas behind them and continued the journey into open country. The tone of the lorry's engine deepened as it climbed away from the coastal plain. After the first big rise it entered the undulating land of the interior. As the truck reached the crest of a hill the driver eased his foot off the accelerator and let his vehicle coast down to the bottom of the dip.

"Stop, this is the place," ordered the squad commander. "This is where we will prepare our defensive position."

The two men parked their Nissan pick-up in the car park outside the terminal building. A half-dozen other vehicles were

251

scattered around, left their by the owners overnight. Six tall yellow sodium lights cast their shadows. Before they walked to the main terminal entrance with their cases, just like any other passengers arriving for their flight, they had one final check to make. One of them opened his case on the tailgate of the pick-up and switched on the battery powered VHF transceiver. He tuned to frequency 119.5.

"*Sporthalla*" was his simple message.

The response was immediate. "*Valkali 32 minutes*".

Cabinda City Airport was a small but relatively well organised place by African standards. It measured activity in flights per day, not flights per hour like big international airports. But it was governed by IAA rules. The runways had to be open to normal air traffic from 6am to 10pm and there had to be emergency cover for the night period, even though nobody who worked at the airport could ever remember a plane landing outside normal hours.

The doors to the combined arrivals and departure hall were never locked. The men walked across the empty space, going to the left and heading straight for the secure staff entrance that would take them '*airside*'. One of the men slid the plastic card that had been stolen from a member of staff three days previously, through the magnetic reader and the door mechanism clicked. They walked down the corridor and took the stairs on the right and continued climbing till they came to the top, by which time they had their weapons ready. The door to the control tower was open. The two African air-traffic controllers were both awake, drinking coffee, standing at the radio console. They turned to see the strangers entering the tower. One of the controllers, either through bravery or possibly just acting on instinct, moved to press the alarm button. Before he got anywhere near, two six millimetre bullets, fired from a silenced pistol, had stopped him in his tracks. He fell headlong, landing sprawled on the plastic tiled floor, his heart pumping its last few beats. The other controller raised his hands.

"Change your VHF frequency to 119.5," ordered the gunman.

"The airport frequency is 118.3," replied the frightened remaining controller.

"Change your frequency to 119.5. We don't need you for this. You can join your friend if you want to."

The controller turned and punched the numbers into the keypad of the main VHF radio.

252

One of the men put on a headset. He pressed the transmit button. "Sporthalla to Valkarie. Over"

"Go ahead Sporthalla. Valkari over."

"Sporthalla Open. Over", was his response. The airport tower was secure.

"Thank you Sportshalla. Illuminate as soon as possible. Over".

The man removed his headset and turned his attention back to the remaining air-traffic controller.

"Switch on the airport lights now," he said.

"Just the runway?"

"Everything: approach, main runway and apron. Light the place up."

The controller went to a second console and flicked a row of switches.

The gunman shut the door into the control tower and pushed a desk against it. All they had to do now was hold their position for a few minutes.

Cabinda Airport was not designated an international gateway, it was just a regional airport. No major airline had declared it as an alternative emergency destination, so it was not subjected to the extremities of international regulation or security. Unusually for that part of Africa it did not have a dual civil / military function. That's why security was left to a squad of ordinary infantry soldiers with no specialist training. The major in charge saw the main threat coming from the poverty stricken residents of the shanty towns that spread right up to the perimeter fence on three sides. He had no plan on how to react to an airborne assault; he had never considered that such a threat might exist.

An hour before dawn five soldiers were on duty. Two were supposed to be patrolling the airport buildings on foot. As there was virtually nobody about in the early hours their main focus had been to find an air-conditioned 'cubby hole' in which to make themselves comfortable. Two of the others had a busier time of it. They patrolled the perimeter in a jeep. Their job was to continuously check the fence, looking for breaks and chasing off intruders. It was a task not made any easier by the absence of a continuous internal roadway. The last of the five was tasked with manning the base VHF radio. He was supposed to rouse the Major and the rest of the sleeping squad in the event of an incident but actually saw his main function as being ready to warn the other four if the Major was on the prowl carrying out one of his infrequent night time inspections.

The pilot had aimed to hit the coastline a little north of Cabinda and follow its contours, guided by the moonlight glistening on the shimmering waters, until his dead reckoning had put him within fifty miles of his destination. He was relieved when radio communications had been established and even happier when he saw the lights of Cabinda Airport suddenly come to life in front of him.

"Six minutes," he said. "Get the men ready."

The airport had a single paved runway. The terminal buildings were all concentrated at the north end of that runway. Landings and take-off could be undertaken from the north or the south, depending on wind direction. Landing on southwards would mean touching down near the terminal buildings, stopping at the far end of the runway, turning and taxiing back the full length of the runway to the apron. A landing on southwards severely eroded the element of surprise for any airborne attacker. That's why, despite a light tail wind, the pilot of the DC3 was going to approach from the other direction, from the north.

There would be no extended approach following electronic beacons. The pilot needed all his concentration for the night time visual approach. Every nerve was tingling.

The touchdown was perfect; many people going on package holidays to Spain had experienced worse landings but the normal sharp application of the brakes didn't happen. The pilot continued rolling up the full length of the runway at an alarming speed till he was close to the terminal buildings. The turn to the right, as he left the runway for the apron, was sharp. The men in the back, who had already unbuckled from their bench seats, were thrown to the left. They had just about all regained their balance when the pilot applied the brakes sharply and the men were then all sent stumbling towards the front. The man designated as dispatcher clung tightly on to a handle near the rear door and was able to counter the sudden movements.

This version of the DC3 had originally been constructed for wartime cargo transportation. It had an extra wide rear door on the port side, designed to be big enough to allow a WW2 Willis Jeep to be driven on board. By pulling a couple of levers the whole door would drop off leaving an extra wide exit space. This facilitated the speedy disembarkation of the assault force. It took only twenty seconds for the thirty heavily armed troops to exit the plane and as the pilot had taxied to within fifteen feet of the army compound the place was overrun in less than sixty seconds. There was only one casualty. The radio operator was shot in the head without warning; this eliminated the chance of any *'request for assistance'* message being sent.

The two Angolan soldiers in the Jeep, returning from their perimeter patrol, were curious. They wanted to know why the unexpected DC3 had stopped so close to their base. As the driver slowed and rounded the tail of the plane he came face to face with three soldiers pointing assault rifles directly at his vehicle. Both occupants immediately surrendered and quickly found themselves sitting on the floor of their mess room, with the rest of the captured troop, hands fastened behind their backs with cable ties. The major was staring at them intensely, as if he blamed them for the debacle.

The remainder of the SF men had, according to plan, split up and scoured the rest of the buildings, gathering whoever they could find and assembling them behind the glass-fronted wall of the departure lounge, all of them bound with cable ties and made to sit cross legged on the floor. Once the sweep had been completed an SF sergeant arrived at the control tower and was greeted by the sight of his smiling colleagues.

"The airport is ours," he said. "Any sign of our support yet?"

One of the men that had taken the tower picked up a pair of field binoculars that had been resting on the sill of a window. He looked, not across the airfield, but along the approach road to the airport, down the Rue das Forcas Armadas.

The darkness of the night was only just beginning to be pushed back. One or two vehicles were using the road. In the distance he thought he saw the shadowy outline of a military truck approaching.

Chapter 48
Bishop's Apartment, Casa Santa Maria.

It had been a curious encounter.

Feliz had repeated the question. "Where did you get the necklace?"

Grace put a defensive hand over her neck.

"It was my mother's," she'd replied.

Feliz had shaken his head as if he did not believe her.

Grace repeated the words, "It was my mother's."

The two stood staring at each other for a while. It was Feliz who broke first. He turned and left the room, going to the rear of the apartment, squatting in the corner of the room that would have been the kitchen if it had ever been fitted out. Ap Ewan followed a few moments later and squatted next to his friend.

"Hey, fellow, what was that about?"

Feliz didn't respond, he just kept staring ahead. Ap Ewan repeated the question and put a soft hand on Feliz's shoulder.

"Don't go silent on me again. I was just getting used to you talking. I can't do this without you. I'm scared."

As if to order the momentary silence was broken by banging that echoed through the building. The banging was coming from the apartment's main entrance in the cloister yard. It deepened and intensified as the soldier reverted to trying to kick the heavy double-door open.

Feliz's spell was broken by the imperative of the moment. The glaze went from his eyes. He stood, picked up his weapon and ran to the bedroom door, calling on ap Ewan to follow.

There was a double window that opened on to a Juliet balcony, a place where the Bishop that had never arrived, had planned, in his own mind to stand and wave at adulating crowds. It was covered by decaying louvered shutters.

As the soldier continued to kick at the door below, Feliz pulled at one of the louver shutters and then at the full length window sash. Both gave way easily. Leaning over the balcony rail he fired a short burst, downwards into the darkness. The bullets embedded themselves harmlessly into the soft ground of the courtyard but still had the desired effect. The SF Trooper, aware of his exposure, dashed for cover making a half-turn on the run and firing a short return burst.

Ap Ewan was standing with his back hard pressed against the wall, heart pounding. He took a deep breath and saw the whites of Feliz's teeth. He was smiling.

"You get used to it," he said. "People firing at you."

"You've done this before?" asked ap Ewan.

"Not shooting. But they used to take me on attacks to reload their weapons. You just have to remember that most people that shoot at you miss. You begin to believe you will be alright."

"I'm not at that stage yet," admitted ap Ewan. "That thing with the necklace seemed to shock you more than this."

"Don't ask me about that now. I can't explain. Come on we have to prepare. We haven't got much time."

Jane came into the room. "What can I do to help?"

"What can we do you mean," said James standing behind her.

"Can you shoot a gun?" asked Feliz.

"I've used a pistol before," replied Jane.

"I haven't used an automatic weapon but I'm a pretty good shot with a hunting rifle," added James.

"Is there help coming? How long do we have to hold out?" asked Jane.

Feliz told them how he'd taken another note to the hotel where the UN HQ was now based, told them about the UN making plans to evacuate and most of all the plan of Gunter Siegburg to take over Cabinda, to carry out a coup. He finished by asking a question.

"How many armed men do the United Nations have available."

"None," replied Jane quietly. I don't see how they can mount a rescue. Should we be thinking of surrendering?"

"No. Their plan was always to kill you. That is why I came for you."

"So what do we need to do?"

For half an hour they ran around frantically.

"Leave the shutters closed, just break away some of the slats, enough to give you a field of view. It will be harder for them to see us. There are enough windows to cover all approaches."

"I'll make a fire position at the top of the stairs," said ap Ewan. "That way if they break in the main doors I can get at them. If they do manage to get past then we can fall back into the main reception room and close those doors. They're big heavy buggers. I'll make a barricade to fire at them there too if they come through."

"And if they get past that?" asked James.

"We'll fall back into Lubala's bedroom."

Nobody asked what would happen after that.

"I have a sack of empty magazine clips. We need to load them with bullets." Feliz pointed to the hessian sack and the wooden crate."

Grace stepped forward. "If you show me how I think I could do that."

"Good," said Jane. "That would really help."

"I have something to do alone," said Feliz, picking up the other, heavier hessian sack. Before he left he turned to Grace his expression softer.

"Can I touch it," he asked. "The necklace."

"Why?" asked Grace, her hand returning to cover the precious possession.

"Because it would be important to me."

She hesitated, only slowly lowering her hand. "All right if it's so important to you."

Feliz rested the flat of his hand on the jewellery, letting it linger for a while, almost as if he were receiving some secret telepathic message.

"It is the one," he whispered to himself as he turned to walk away, his eyes full of tears.

Bernd Groelsh came ashore on the second trip. He stepped off the boat into the gently lapping surf just as it ran up on to the sand. With wet feet he splashed the last few steps till he was out of the water. He watched as the other men disembarked from the front of the boats. When all were off he shouted to the boat's helmsman. "Be as quick as you can."

"I just need to connect up the reserve fuel drum. We'll run out before too long," he shouted back.

Groelsh waited till the job was done and watched as the powerful outboards pulled the vessels backwards off the sand and into open water. He made his way to the operation's room along the path, stopping briefly to look back out to sea. The first hue of daylight was appearing. Avoiding the Bishop's Apartments he finished his short pedestrian journey.

Gunter Siegburg looked up from the map table. The comradely hug was absent, his concentration elsewhere.

"Thank God you've arrived. Time is tight. I need to deploy your men quickly; our SF Troopers are on the move. They are already in the city and about to surround State House and the Governor's Residence. The attack will start soon. It won't be long before people realise what we are up to. We need to get the CLF men into position. Are you clear about your part of the plan?"

"Everything is according to plan. We will be at State House, giving support, within half an hour. But you have a problem here?"

"Nothing that can't be dealt with. I need to handle it myself. We caught some snoopers. They're contained in the Bishop's Apartment for now. They have some weapons."

"Why don't you just storm the place or just blow it up?"

"They have Lubala with them. We need him for the next part of the plan."

"Is he '*with*' them in that sense?"

"I don't think so. All he is thinking about is the next woman and bottle of scotch. The last I heard he was sick. It doesn't matter really. Once I get hold of him he'll be back on track."

Groelsh nodded. "Don't worry about my part. I will radio as soon as we hold State House and the Governor is neutralised. Half my men should be ashore by now."

"Good. As soon as I get your message that you have control I will send the press release. That will mean we have succeeded."

Groelsh left.

Gunter Siegburg gathered the men he had kept around him and explained the plan.

Fully loaded the flat-bottomed boats bobbed about less and were more comfortable, although the passengers might not have thought so. The lines attaching them to the '*MV Brilliant Star*' were cast off at the same time as the scramble nets hung over the side were raised a little. The helmsman of the first boat pushed open the throttle to get steerage. He brought the bow around till it was facing directly at the shore, only then did he push the throttle lever fully forward. With speed the aluminium bottom slapped on the water as it pushed forward into the small waves. The second boat followed a hundred yards behind.

The helmsman thought the first splutter was just a misfire. A few seconds later the engine did it again, this time for longer. Soon the engine was stuttering continuously and losing power rapidly. He pulled the gear lever into neutral, disengaging the propeller. The engine, instead of idling smoothly, spluttered for a few more seconds before finally dying completely. The vessel lay dead in the water.

The second boat, seeing the first one in difficulties slowed and came alongside.

"The engine's died," shouted the helmsman of the first boat. "Tow us to the shore; I'll take a look at the engine there."

Somebody threw the bow-line of the first boat. Quickly it was fastened to a cleat on the stern of the second boat. The second boat edged forward, taking up the slack in the line. Only when both boats were moving forward slowly did the second boat speed up. They were within two hundred yards of the shore when the engine of the second boat began to splutter.

Chapter 49
Road from Dinge to Cabinda City

The sky was changing from black to grey, soon it would be blue. The road ahead, bordered both sides by tall trees, was for now still dark, a fuzzy jagged line. The silhouettes of the tree tops, separated the black from the grey. Only their headlights lit the darkness of the road. They came over the brow of a hill and the road began to descend.

"Are we going down towards the sea now?" asked Duncan.

"No," replied Marobi. "We're crossing a valley. There is one more hill before the coastal plain is in sight."

Duncan strained his eyes looking into the darkness. He put out a hand and touched David Marobi on the arm. It was a warning.

David Marobi eased his foot off the accelerator. "What is it?"

"Look there, ahead."

"I can't see a thing."

"In the sky, just above the tree line. There's a big shadow, it's moving."

"It's most probably just a flock of birds," replied Marobi.

"Exactly," replied Duncan. "What's stirred them?"

Marobi slowed further, almost to a crawl. "What do you want to do?"

"Is there a river at the bottom of the valley?"

"Yes, it's just a dry riverbed most of the year. I suppose there will be a little water running just now; we're not quite out of the rainy season. But there's a high level concrete bridge; it never gets flooded.

"I think it's better to stop now. We need a plan. Are any of your men good with a rifle?"

"Water, give me some water."

It was a hoarse whisper, from a throat that rasped raw with dryness. Jane turned around to see Lubala struggling to raise his head from the pillow. Beads of sweat no longer trickled down his cheeks but his brow still glistened with moisture. On the floor beside the bed was a plastic cup filled with water. Jane offered it to the man. His hand clasped hers and drew the cup to his lips. He was no longer shaking uncontrollably but Jane could feel the tremor in his fingers. Lubala sipped several times before letting his head fall backwards.

"Where am I?" he asked through bloated and cracked lips.

John Rolands came back into the room. "Looks like he's making a recovery. Those are the first words he's said for ages. I thought he was a gonner to be honest."

Jane looked at Lubala. "He still doesn't look great," she said. "Seen anything?"

John shook his head.

"I thought they'd be coming for us by now," said Jane.

"That Siegburg is a rum bastard. He'll have something up his sleeve, you can be sure of it."

The Sergeant of the night watch had woken up the Major in charge of the State Building's defence troop when he heard the explosions at the police station. When there was no response on the phone he drove the quarter mile to police HQ. The street outside was littered with bodies, many dead and others being tended. Some civilians who had come to see and some policemen too dazed to act wandered around. Nobody had come forward to lead and organise. The Major pushed his way through the people and looked around the building, trying to determine what had happened.

He spotted a young policeman, sitting on the floor, leaning back against a wall, his hands covering what looked like a wound to his right thigh. There was a pool of blood surrounding him.

The Major squatted beside him. "What happened?"

"We were in the mess room. There was an explosion upstairs. We all jumped up and almost immediately there was a second explosion in our room."

"Was there any shooting? Did you see anybody? Did you see people attacking the building?"

The wounded man shook his head. "No, there was no shooting, no people."

The Major stood up. "Two separate explosions, that means most likely not an accident. But no shooting, nobody trying to take over," he thought. "Probably a terrorist hit and run attack. But what has happened to the telephone system. It's seems unlikely to be a coincidence."

He hurried back to his post at State House having made up his mind to contact Army HQ at Luanda on the Army radio network. The radio operator switched on the set and dialled in the correct frequency. He shouted in pain and ripped the headphones from his ears. The piercing screech that had been emitted was of a high frequency and intensity, designed to hurt.

"Somebody is jamming our communications," he said aloud. Now he was convinced. Something was happening. He shouted his orders.

"Get the whole guard up, issue ammunition, man the defensive positions, prepare a patrol to check the surrounding area and get the Governor out of his bed. Expect an attack imminently!"

The Major had done everything correctly and according to the book. But he was too late.

As the alarm claxon sounded, soldiers tumbled out of their cots, quickly pulling on bits of their uniform. With their weapons in hand they ran to the magazine where the Quartermaster was ready and waiting. Hurriedly he issued personal ammunition without any formality. The first eight of the soldiers were required to carry boxes, one box between two men, containing higher calibre ammunition for the four machine-gun dugouts that constituted the main defence position for State House.

The barrack building was of steel-framed construction, set back in the gardens of State House, hidden from sight by a combination of camouflage and natural vegetation. During drills the men had to stick to the paths when going to their posts, in an emergency they were allowed to run straight across the well-kept and manicured lawns. This was an emergency. The first eight men, slowed by the weight of the ammunition boxes began their run across the lawns.

They had not expected that two belt-fed, tripod-mounted general purpose machine-guns had been set up in diagonally opposed positions. Their locations had been carefully chosen on a previous reconnaissance trip. They gave a line of fire criss-crossing the lawn, providing a killing field that it was impossible to penetrate. Each gun was manned by two of the paratroopers that had been on the DC3 less than forty-five minutes earlier. As the first men approached the point where the two lines of fire intersected, triggers were pulled; the effect was devastating. The eight men carrying the ammunition ran straight into the trap and fell immediately, riddled at waist height by a stream of 7.62 millimetre bullets. Those following, realising their exposure, stopped in their tracks. Their choice was to continue their journey across the lawn or turn and run back to the barrack. It wasn't much of a choice.

The machine-guns chattered in the early morning light. After the first burst the machine-gun operators traversed the guns, effectively moving the point of intersection back toward the barrack and into the exposed troops, most of whom fell before they'd made up their mind. None managed to fire a single shot of return fire.

At the end of the traverse the machine-gunners moved their guns to the original position. Each machine-gun had discharged a two hundred round belt. Quickly the assistant gunner came forward and flicked a catch on the machine-gun and, with gloved hand removed the red hot barrel and slipped a new cold barrel into place. A second later the gunner fed the beginning of a fresh ammunition belt into the breach and the machine-guns were ready for another episode of their murderous work.

The result was that twenty-seven of the forty men in the barracks lay dying or dead on the by now blood-red grass while the remaining thirteen were trapped in their barracks. Only the ten men on the night watch remained ready to defend the State buildings and Governor but they were woefully short of ammunition.

Bernd Groelsh arrived in the a street close to State House, with the first batch of CLF soldiers, just as the echo of the machine-guns was resonating around the buildings. He ordered his men off the truck and organised them into a line, bayonets fixed. He knew that decisive action was necessary; he could not afford a siege situation to develop. They could not claim to have taken power whilst the Governor remained at large and in charge of the main Government buildings.

One of the SF Troopers from the airport came running up, a Dutch army deserter turned soldier of fortune. His speech was heavily accented.

"The ambush worked perfectly. The men out there," he nodded towards the sandbagged emplacements of the defenders, "they will not be receiving any reinforcements. Do you want to give them the opportunity to surrender?"

Groelsh didn't hesitate. "No, no negotiation. We'll have a sixty second mortar barrage. Last three rounds of smoke. Strafe the positions simultaneously with machine-gun fire. As soon as you're finished we'll charge." He looked at his watch. We'll go in five minutes. Check."

"Check," replied the Dutchman, looking at his own watch before running off to organise his men.

Exactly on time the pop and whistle of the first mortars were clearly audible to Groelsh and his crouching men. The explosions were loud and frequent, each explosion interspaced with bursts of machine-gun fire. The men in their dugouts kept down, shocked at the ferocity of the attack. The Major had intended to dash from emplacement to emplacement, preparing his remaining men for the inevitable charge that would follow the bombardment. He didn't get to the second emplacement; he was cut down by a burst of machine-gunfire and was dead before he hit the ground.

The last pops and whistles of the mortars were not followed by explosions, only the clearly audible hiss of the smoke canisters discharging their opaque shield. Groelsh readied his men.

"On my command charge," he shouted and counted the final rounds. The light breeze was too weak to quickly disperse the dark grey-black smoke that began to envelop the area. The emplacements could no longer be seen but the men knew where they were going. Groelsh shouted the word: "Attack," and they ran forward firing into the mist.

Of the remaining defenders two were shot in their positions, the others captured. Not a single shot had been returned by the defenders. The attackers didn't stop; they ran straight on. The doors to State House offered no resistance. Some civilians stood on the wide sweeping marble staircase that led up from the foyer, their hands held high in the air. The attackers ran past them, heading straight for the Governor's Suite. Groelsh was not far behind. At the top of the stairs a bodyguard in European style business suit and black sunglasses, was the only remaining obstacle. He stood defiantly, pistol drawn at the door. He took two shots to the chest, the event effectively ending organised resistance.

The Governor stood behind his desk as the men came in, pale and shaking but otherwise motionless facing the attackers. Groelsh arrived and pushed his way through. He motioned one of his men to pass over an automatic assault rifle. The man handed the weapon over. Groelsh checked the safety catch and pointed the weapon at the frozen Governor and pulled the trigger, emptying the balance of the magazine into him.

In the confines of the office the gun smoke lingered and the smell of cordite was pungent. Groelsh coughed to clear his dry throat. He returned the weapon to the soldier. "Go and tell the radio operator to send the message, 'Mission complete. Governor killed in heavy fighting'."

The message arrived in the Operation's Room at Villa Santa Maria. Gunter Siegburg smiled.

"Okay you can now send the prepared text. Let the world know what has happened," he said to the electronics' officer.

"Shall I also transmit the good news on the satellite phones?"

Siegburg shook his head. "No. Everybody that needs to know is here, if they don't already know they soon will."

"What about the Baron?" asked the naive electronics officer? "Shall I send him a message?"

"As I said," replied Siegburg, "Everybody that needs to know, knows."

"And what about the bit about Lubala? It's not quite correct. It says he's in full control."

Gunter thought for a while before taking the sheets of paper with the prepared text to the map table. He put a line through the last paragraphs and quickly wrote an amendment in longhand that gave him some leeway. He handed the papers back to the electronics' officer.

"Do you need me to bring it back to you after I type it up?"

"No just send it. And don't disturb me anymore there is something that I have to do, something that won't wait any longer" Gunter went over to the improvised rack, picked up his assault rifle and left the Operations' Room.

He looked back over his shoulder as he got to the door. "And get ready to leave; I want the Operations' Room moved to State House within the hour. We're the Government now. I'll be along with the new '*leader*' shortly."

Chapter 50
The Bishop's Apartment

The sun was rising but the shadows were still long. For seven out of eight days the morning breeze came from the sea, fresh and salty. But today it came from the East, no more than a gentle lazy waft, carrying with it the warm damp odours of the swamp and rainforest over which it had passed. Even before the sun's heat had had an opportunity to do its work, sweat was running down the brow of the apartment's occupants.

Lubala lay silently on his sick bed, conscious but weak, the soiled and crumpled bed sheet dark with dampness. Across the bedroom James sat cross-legged, face to face with Grace, an outstretched hand holding hers. All the magazines for the guns had been filled; the ammunition box was against the wall, still three-quarters full. Jane had been keeping a lookout at the back entrance. She came into the room and sat down with them, resting her pistol on the floor.

"Do you think they've forgotten about us?" asked Grace. "Perhaps we'll be able to just wait here quietly till somebody comes for us."

Jane tried to keep her tone calm and reassuring. "I doubt that they have forgotten us, but it may be that they are too busy with other things just now. But you can be sure that we have been missed by the UN by now. They will be doing what they can."

"We could be here for a couple of days," said James. "It'll take time for them to get help and find us won't it?"

Jane nodded although she knew that would not be possible. She'd just checked, there were only two full and one half-full litre bottles of drinking water. That wasn't enough for even a day. Just the thought made her throat dry.

Ap Ewan was going from room to room, window to window, peeping through the louvers. He wondered why he didn't feel as scared as he should have. He felt strangely calm. The main double doors to the reception room, the ones that led on to the mezzanine and staircases were open. Feliz was sitting on the mezzanine floor, watching the downstairs doors to the courtyard. Ap Ewan came alongside and crouched next to him.

"There's no sign of anybody outside."

Feliz nodded.

"You stopped talking again?"

"No," replied Feliz.

"That necklace is really bothering you. What's wrong with it?"

267

Feliz kept his eyes on the downstairs doors. "I know that necklace."

"It belonged to Grace's mother; it must be one like it that you know."

"It's just that a lot of things are coming back to me, things that I'd forgotten, bad things."

"This is bad enough. Our plan wasn't up to much was it? I've been looking; we're in a bit of a pickle here. There's been a lot of soldiers coming up that path from the beach. I don't think there's much chance of us talking our way out of this? That Siegburg fella is a nasty bastard, knew it from the day I met him. Kill you as soon as look at you."

"There's no doubt they will kill us. I have heard them talk. They don't want witnesses to what they have done."

"What have they done, you know more than me," said ap Ewan, "You've be wandering around that operations' room."

"They've taken over Cabinda. That was their plan from day one. They never intended to win the referendum. We are witnesses. They don't want witnesses."

"So why don't they do something? I suppose they could just lob a few grenades through the windows, and then we'd be buggered," replied ap Ewan.

"Because we have something they want."

"The people from the cell?"

"No...."

Feliz didn't have time to complete his sentence. From the courtyard a rough guttural voice broke the silence.

"You inside! Come and talk to me."

Feliz and John scrambled to the shuttered window, pressing their backs up against the wall, one either side, their hearts suddenly pounding. It was quiet for a moment.

"It's Siegburg," said Feliz sneaking a glance through the broken louver slats. "He's out of sight, behind one of the cloister pillars I expect."

"So what's next?"

"It's down to them," replied Feliz.

The two men inched their way along the outer wall of the building, till they were in position, directly under the window. The aluminium scaling ladder was already fully extended.

"You just make sure you hold the ladder steady," whispered the lead SF man, "I hate ladder entries. I don't know why we just don't go up the back stairs and blow the fucking door off."

"Because they're watching and it wouldn't be a surprise."

"The result would be the same though."

It was the end of their conversation. They checked their weapons and then stood motionless, ready for the signal, when it came.

The plan was improvised. Not what Siegburg had wanted. He'd hung on as long as he could for more of the African troops to arrive from the ship. But they hadn't come. That was another problem. He'd have to deal with that next. But first he'd have to get hold of Lubala. For now he had only three of his own men, plus four Africans he'd trained himself. He thought it would be enough; there was only the idiot Welshman, the dumb African and the three UN workers. They should be no match for his trained troops.

"I'm trying to give you a chance," Siegburg shouted, stepping out from behind the cloister pillar. "I have an offer, but you need to talk to me."

Feliz looked at John and shook his head. "You can't trust him," he whispered.

"It can't do any harm to find out what his offer is," replied ap Ewan in a hushed tone.

Feliz shrugged.

"What is your offer?" shouted ap Ewan turning to look through the louvers.

It was all that Siegburg wanted. Evidence that he'd got their attention and, with a bit of luck, drawn people from the rear of the apartment. In a well-practiced movement Siegburg raised his assault rifle and pulled the trigger, raking the front of the apartment and the window with automatic fire.

It was the signal the men had been waiting for. In a second the scaling ladder was up, it's top resting on the concrete sill of the bedroom window. The lead man scrambled to the top; a single blow with the butt of his assault rifle shattered the rotten shutters; from the ground they'd seen the wood was completely rotten and would offer no resistance. Light flooded the room and he saw the three people on the floor directly in front of him, literally sitting targets. He levelled his rifle and brought it to bear on the startled group. As his finger tightened on the trigger he felt an unexpected resistance. The gun barrel was going downwards and to the left, forced by the grip of a strong black hand.

Lumbala, whether lucid or delirious, nobody would ever know, had raised himself from his bed. It was only two steps to the window. He grabbed the burnished gun metal barrel of the assault rifle and pulled it forward and towards himself. The finger on the trigger had to do nothing, the sudden movement was enough. A short burst of bullets crossed Lubala's chest. He dropped, like a stone, releasing his grip on the barrel. The attacker wobbled, struggling to regain his balance on the ladder. He tried to bring the gun on to the original targets. He thought he'd done it, but he hadn't seen Jane's hand-gun, he hadn't expected such a quick reaction.

The .45 Colt had quite a kick in Jane's hand but not as much as the thumps that hit the attacker. The first bullet hit him in the abdomen. The second one, higher because of the recoil from the first shot, hit him in the forehead. He leaned backward, tottering for a second or two. The body that landed on the man below was dead before it impacted. Struggling free of the dead weight, the attack foiled, he scurried away, keeping close to the wall. He ran back to where Siegburg was standing.

"They were waiting for us," he gasped, trying to regain his breath.

Siegburg shook his head. "Go and see where the next bunch of Africans from the ship are.

Chapter 51
Maiombe Hotel, Cabinda

André Piet hadn't slept, nor had most of his staff. He stood alone on the back terrace of the hotel and sipped at a glass of re-constituted orange juice in the hope that the combination of a sugar rush and sunshine would freshen him up. He screwed his face at the sickly sweet taste and wondered why a hotel in this part of the world, where oranges grew in abundance, would be serving re-constituted Californian orange juice.

They'd got as many of the UN staff bedded down in hotel rooms as was possible but the foyer remained congested with baggage and the unlucky few who had not been allocated a bed. He was trying to work out a plan but in reality knew there was just nothing he could do at the moment. He tried to sum up the situation. He'd got everybody together in one place, apart from the three missing people, the ones that had precipitated this crisis. One of his field workers was still unaccounted for. The UN Secretariat's Office in New York had been informed. There was some kind of evacuation plan in progress, but he wasn't aware of the details because the phones, fax, telex and all radios had gone out of service. There had been a couple of explosions and some shooting in the city during the hours of darkness. That had put the '*kibosh*' on his intention to get everybody out to the airport during the night, in preparation for an airlift. He'd decided to wait till daylight, but with the sun had come the arrival of armed guards, black African soldiers, in uniforms he didn't recognise. He'd tried to parley, asking for an officer but his requests had just been met with shrugs and now in the last hour or so there had been sporadic bursts of machine-gun fire from different parts of town.

Just as he got all that straight in his mind one of the female UN workers came running out of the hotel.

"André, André, quick come. Listen to the radio."

André went to the dining room where a group of his staff were clustered around an ancient and oversized radiogram. The radio presenter spoke in the local Kikongo language, his deep voice sombre and authoritative. A member of the hotel staff was doing his best to give a simultaneous translation into English.

"*As a result of atrocities carried out against the ordinary people of Cabinda in the name of the Angolan Government, the Cabinda Liberation Front has been forced to take decisive action to secure the peoples safety and defend democracy. The situation has been further complicated by the kidnapping of United Nations Officials. This later action quite clearly demonstrates that the Angolan Government never intended a free and fair referendum.*

A state of emergency is declared. The so called Governor of Cabinda has been arrested and will face charges of crimes against humanity. State House, the airport, the harbour, the radio station and all the main Government buildings are in the hands of the Cabindan Liberation Front. General Moses Lubala is declared the first executive president of Cabinda. Cabinda is now free of the Angolan yolk.

A twenty-four hour curfew is declared for the general population. Until the situation is settled people must expect firm control from the new security forces. Off-duty police officers and members of the Angolan Army must give themselves up to patrols of the Cabinda Liberation Front or make their way immediately to Cabinda football stadium. Nobody surrendering will be harmed. Any member of the police or Angolan Army seen heading in any other direction or bearing arms will be considered as an enemy of the State and will be subject to immediate execution.

As soon as calm is established national celebrations will be organised. Long live General Lubala and long live Cabinda."

"A coup," said André Piet. "God knows who we're supposed to talk to now!"

In New York the offices of the United Nations Secretary General had been buzzing. It was not that they were overwhelmed by information, as was often the case in a crisis. It was the dearth of information that was making decisions difficult. The duty officers had gleaned what they could; now they needed a decision from their boss.

The Secretary General sat at his desk scanning the briefing papers in his hands with half an eye on the single sheet Executive Order that lay on his desk waiting for his signature. Five other people, all UN 'staffer's', sat silently in the room with the Secretary General, waiting for him to deliberate.

Briana Bondevik, broke the silence. The daughter of a former Norwegian Prime Minister she had devoted her life to the United Nations. Unusually she had risen through the administration ranks on the basis of her decisive nature, rather than by cronyism, which was the more normal route to the top. Of course such a strategy only worked as long as she made the right calls and she had an uncanny knack of doing that.

"All communications are cut with Cabinda," she began. "Most of our people are holed up in a hotel – that is the last information we have. At least three people under UN protection are missing. The airport is closed. We know that major atrocities have taken place and a Zairian radio station is now claiming that a state of emergency has been declared in Cabinda and that gunfire has been heard in the capital overnight. We have already authorised an evacuation operation for our staff, which has been delayed for technical reasons. The only decisive option open to you is the one that is lying on your desk, awaiting your signature."

"What do the Angolans say?" asked the Secretary General.

"The last we heard from the Angolan Ambassador to the United Nations was that he was awaiting instructions from his government. That was several hours ago. Since then he has been unavailable."

"So what is your advice?"

"Sign the Executive Order. It is the only offer we have at the present time. True it means that technically a UN mission will breach a member state's sovereignty but that member state is failing to protect our staff that are there to help them. Sign it." There was finality about Briana Bondevik's statement.

"Does anybody have an objection to me signing?" asked the Secretary General looking around the room.

His question was met with the silence and neutral faces associated with those who felt most comfortable when sitting on a fence.

The Secretary General huffed and signed the Executive Order.

Fifteen minutes later an electronic copy of that order arrived in the British Foreign Office. Another fifteen minutes and the order was with the adjoining Ministry of Defence Situation Room. Ten minutes after that a pre-prepared coded despatch with orders and rules of engagement was transmitted via the latest Royal Navy satellite communications system.

At last the plane had been repaired.

Dane Akai had filed his flight plan for his C130. He'd be taking off from runway 17/35 and heading just about due north. Flight time was just over five hours at the maximum cruise speed of 366

273

mph and, fortunately, as his was an extended range variant of the C130, Dane would not need an intermediate refuelling stop.

The four Allison Turboprop engines picked up speed and sent a little judder through the fuselage as they passed through the vibration barrier. The plane slowly crept forward from the apron towards the taxiway. Dane leaned forward and changed the frequency from 122.65, the apron, to 121.30, the tower. He received clearance for immediate take-off.

The plane was designed for short take-offs, added to that it was light. The trip down the runway was short, which was ironic as they were on the longest paved runway in the world. The co-pilot said, "V1," more as a courtesy than anything else. It was supposed to signify the point in the run when the plane had passed the point of no return. Truthfully the runway was so long they could easily have cruised to a halt at any time. A second or two later he said, "V2", which signified that the plane had achieved the speed at which it could fly. Dane pulled back on the yolk. The plane's nose lifted and the wings, now angled into the air, suddenly took on a massive amount of lift. The plane began its climb to cruising altitude at what any civilian air passenger would have considered an alarming rate.

Marie, the cargo master, had been sitting in the jump seat for the take-off, her favourite position. "What we going to do if they won't let us land?" she asked when the plane had levelled out into straight flight; the autopilot was set and Dane had taken off his earphones.

"Land in any case," was Dane's response. "You know those arseholes States-side really annoy me. They sit in some cosy office without any appreciation of what they are asking. They don't even know the size of Africa, they say *'just pop'* over there as if it were a five minute detour. So if they can be stupid so can I. I tried to contact Cabinda but they didn't respond, so I'm going in any case."

Chapter 52
Road from Dinge to Cabinda City

It had taken more than an hour to get into position, pushing through undergrowth where it couldn't be avoided, running across clearings where they could, but always keeping in the dips, never breaking the sky line and always staying parallel to the road but out of sight. Eventually they slithered down a steep slope and came to the riverbed. There was only a trickle of water and the obstacle was easily forded. The scramble up the far bank was more difficult though; slipping and sliding on loose scree-like pebbles was not easy. Duncan was panting loudly by the time they'd finally got out of the dip and swung right to get back on the road, this time behind the roadblock set up by the rebel forces.

They stopped to catch their breath. The two African marksmen of Marobi's Presidential Guard recovered first. They smiled at Duncan.

"I'm getting too old for this nonsense," he said. "How long have we got?"

One of the Africans looked at his watch. "Less than five minutes."

"Give me the field glasses."

Duncan slithered forward the last five yards on his belly through the tall grass that ran either side of the paved roadway. It was a cursory look; he didn't have time to take a detailed scan.

"Okay," he said when he got back to the two marksmen. "There's a vehicle, a lorry on the right-hand side. Nobody around it as far as I can see. There are three men on the bridge itself, AK assault rifles. They haven't had time to establish a proper roadblock but I'd guess they have the bridge covered with at least two machine-guns, most probably one either side of the road. I'm sure they'll be shielded by vegetation only. Not a chance of a sandbag emplacement. I'm going to the other side of the road, you two stay here. When the shooting starts you know what to do?"

Both men nodded.

Duncan checked his weapon.

Since the middle of the twentieth century the AK47 had been the standard issue weapon for Soviet infantry. The advantage of the AK is that it is a perfect assault and close-quarters weapon but its big disadvantage is that it is grossly inaccurate at any distance. To counter this all Soviet and Soviet trained infantry units had a complement of sharp-shooters attached to them equipped with sniper rifles. The standard Soviet sniper weapon, the Dragunov 7.62, was first issued in 1962 and had proved to be a rugged and reliable weapon, accurate up to 1200 metres without telescopic sites and at much longer distances when fitted with the standard PSO-1 optical sight with its 4 x's zoom and 6 degree field of vision. It was a Dragunov that Duncan dragged behind him as he made his way to the edge of the road, through the long grass again. He'd use it with the built in iron sights and not the removable optical sights that would have required him to take a ranging shot first. As he reckoned that the range he'd be shooting would be less than three hundred metres he didn't think it would be a detrimental decision. As he lay in the grass waiting for the opportunity to cross the road he remembered the time long ago when he'd been a prisoner at Colchester military prison with all the time in the world to study military weapons. He'd never in his wildest dreams expected to find himself with one of those weapons, preparing for action in the African bush.

As agreed, Marobi moved forward towards the bridge at a snail's pace. He led the way in the Land Cruiser, the lorry following a good distance behind. At two hundred and fifty metres he drew his vehicle to a halt and got his men to get out of the lorry and form two lines, one on either side of the road, ready to dart into the bush when they came under fire. The two lines began walking forward, weapons at the ready.

On the bridge, the men standing guard, CLF soldiers, saw the columns coming towards them. They readied their weapons and sought what shelter they could from the bridge's structure. They knew they were exposed but were sure of the covering fire that they would receive from the machine-guns.

Marobi led the line on the left. His eyes darted from the roadblock to the sides of the road; he was picking his place with care. At last he found it, a small stretch of road that had a sunken drainage ditch on either side, just deep enough to provide cover for his men. They were now less than a hundred and fifty metres away; they could see the faces of the rebels on the bridge. He took a deep breath and went down on one knee. His counterpart on the other side of the road did the same. Suddenly the silence was shattered by the stutter of automatic fire as the two men let off a full magazine in the direction of the bridge.

One of the rebels just hid behind a stanchion, frozen stiff at the fusillade of bullets that whistled above his head. The other two had the presence of mind to return fire.

It was what Duncan had been waiting for. He quickly jumped up, dashed across the road and disappeared into the vegetation on the other side whilst everybody was distracted. He didn't have much time to pick a vantage point; the best he could find was a defunct ant hill; well he sincerely hoped it was defunct. He didn't have long to wait.

Marobi looked back along his line of men. He raised his hand and brought it down with a sharp movement. Two men from the rear, one from either side jumped up and ran forward to the front. Even before they had jumped back into the ditch they had what they wanted. The two rebel machine-guns, hidden in bushes, opened up. Chips flew from the road next to Marobi as bullets struck the surface harmlessly.

The rattle of the machine-guns drew Duncan's watching eyes, as it did the two marksmen on the other side of the road. What had a moment ago been invisible was now apparent, now that their eyes could concentrate on a fixed area.

One of Marobi's African marksmen was the first to pick his target. He didn't need an order to pull the trigger. The machine-gunner, busy strafing the road ahead, didn't hear the shot from behind, all he saw was his belt feeder slump forward, a blood patch appearing and spreading on his green camouflage tunic, centre back, emanating from the tiny entry hole that the sniper bullet had made. The second Presidential Guard sniper was next to shoot at the other machine-gun position. His shot at the machine gunner himself was as accurate and crisp as his colleague's. Both machine-guns were suddenly silent.

Duncan watched and waited. His calm was rewarded. To the right, a man suddenly came to his feet, a white soldier this time, probably the leader, guessed Duncan, looking around to see what had happened. Duncan had plenty of time to take aim. His finger gently squeezed the trigger.

Chapter 53
Windhoek Airport, Namibia

"You look so wonderful my darling." Freifrau von Swartzstein could not hide her delight. "I am so proud of you, my man, ready and willing to enter the fray in a just cause. I am so sure that this day will add another page to the history of our dynasty. It will be remembered by all future generations."

Freiherr Artur von Swartzstein of Brandenburg stood correctly, erect and square shouldered. "My only regret is that I am dressed in this morning-suit. But I have to agree that a formal uniform might not be appropriate, particularly if a lot of photographs are going to be taken. I leave now my darling, to do my duty. Please do not worry about me."

Freifrau von Swartzstein was not worried, she never worried about anything but her duties to her husband and the household; those were the limits of her responsibilities.

Von Swartzstein entered the chartered Hawker 850XP using the planes integral steps. He wasn't overly impressed on entering. Despite his height of five feet seven inches, he still had to stoop to walk down the aisle. There were only six passenger seats, three either side. He had trouble deciding which of them enjoyed the most prestigious position. In the end he chose the one on the front port side, deciding it didn't really matter as he was going to be the only passenger. He had toyed with bringing the rest of the Board with him but had been swayed by his wife's argument that he needed to impress his leadership and arriving with 'a committee' might detract from his authority.

When he was finally seated and belted in, the pilot came to see him.

"Herr von Swartzstein," he began but was stopped abruptly.

"Freiherr von Swartzstein," said the Baron.

"Sorry, Freiherr von Swartzstein," the pilot corrected himself, not sure what he was apologising for. "I have filed a flight plan for Kinshasa as you requested. I understand that at some point you want me to *'divert'* to Cabinda. Is that correct?"

""That is correct."

"You do realise the irregularity of your request?"

"I do," replied von Swartzstein. "And I am sure you are aware of the special clauses in the charter agreement?" He was referring to the one thousand US dollar supplementary fee that would

278

become payable in the event of deviation from the original flight plan.

"I am," said the pilot. "I just wanted things to be clear. I hope you will excuse me."

Chapter 54
Cabinda City

"I don't care about radio or communications problems," said Bernd Groelsh to his communication's officer. "It's the soldiers I need from the *'Brilliant Star'*. I can't secure all the facilities; I don't even have enough manpower to guard the surrendering Angolan police and soldiers at the football stadium. Where are the CLF Troops?" he demanded. His frustration was growing with tiredness. "My thirty men are not enough on their own; we need the African CLF rebels."

The two SF men stood outside the main entrance to State House. Now it was Groelsh's men in the sandbag emplacements providing protection. The square was empty; people were taking notice of the curfew, but that situation wouldn't last for long without reinforcements.

"Siegburg has a problem at Villa Santa Maria," replied the electronics officer who was more concerned with completing the move of the Operations' Room to State House. "That's all I know; something to do with his UN prisoners. Now where can I set this lot up?" He pointed to the equipment in the back of the lorry he'd just arrived in.

"Set-up your stuff wherever you want. How long before you can establish contact with the *'Brilliant Star'*? Our hand held VHF sets are useless; some don't have the range and the others are only partially charged. We need to establish authority before the opposition have a chance to reorganise themselves. And when you get through, find out where Lubala is. He needs to make an appearance now!"

"I got my own problems," replied the Communication's Officer. "It'll take me more than an hour to get set up. You'll have to manage till then."

Gunter Siegburg's patience was running thin. He knew the making of irrational decisions was becoming a possibility. He took a few seconds to take stock of the situation. Already they were running late; the rebel soldiers were not disembarking the ship quickly enough. That was going to have knock-on effects. Lubala needed to be presented to the world quickly. He needed to be seen as the saviour of the Cabindan people. That would subdue local opposition and stop an international reaction. And the UN witnesses needed to be eliminated so that the truth would not get out, not too soon in any event. And now he only had four men remaining: three CLF Africans and the last of his SF mercenaries. To cap it all off the VHF handsets were not working properly. His train of thought was broken by a shouting voice.

One of the CLF men came running through the arch, into the cloister. "Men are coming from the beach, men from the ship, they....."

He didn't let the man finish. It was what he wanted to hear, "The circle is broken," he thought. "Soon they would be back on track." He didn't wait for the men to arrive from the beach. He called two of his remaining African rebels.

"We will make a frontal attack as soon as the men from the ship arrive but first I want you to blow the main doors of the apartment in preparation."

The Bishop in Rome, when he was planning the construction of Villa Santa Maria, had paid a lot of attention to cosmetic detail. He thought it was appropriate that the entrance to his apartments should be suitably imposing, to reflect his own stature. He insisted on Norman-style, pointed-arch, double-doors. They were to be made of tropical hardwood, intricately carved with depictions of the Stations of the Cross. He wanted to associate his own journey through life with that of the last journey of his saviour, Jesus Christ. Designs had been presented, passed backward and forward several times before the Bishop was satisfied. Perhaps predictably the emphasis on symbolism had resulted in a neglect of structural integrity. The wood of the door would undoubtedly last a thousand years; unfortunately the steel hinges chosen were somewhat less durable, particularly without regular maintenance in the salt air and tropical climate where they were situated.

Two CLF men zigzagged across the courtyard, as fast as they could, towards the doors. They carried no guns. Cover, if necessary, was going to be provided by Gunter Siegburg. It was not necessary. The two men slammed the prepared plastic charges on to the door hinges and quickly retreated. They'd hardly made cover when Gunter pressed the tiny remote electronic detonator switch. The four charges exploded simultaneously with a noise far in excess of their explosive power, the sound resonating around the ground floor reception area behind the doors. The half rotten hinges offered little resistance. They crumbled under the shock waves and the heavy doors dropped an inch to the ground and then began their journey from the vertical to the horizontal at an ever increasing speed until they met with the dry concrete floor of the reception area creating a dense dust cloud that billowed up the stairs to the first floor and into the apartment.

Even before the dust had settled the first of the CLF fighters from the ship came staggering through the cloister arch. Siegburg was shocked at the disarray of the men but he had no time to query the situation. Immediately he ordered them to attack what was now a gaping chasm that led to the Bishop's Apartment. He was unaware of the drama that had unfolded on the beach in the past hour.

The Captain of the *'Brilliant Star'* had been standing on the bridge watching the operation through binoculars. The two flat-bottomed boats looked like they were still tied together. There was no trailing wake; they were not making any headway in the water and they were now at the mercy of the tides and wind. The current was carrying them slowly northwards, in the direction of a small outcrop of jagged rocks that extended into the sea, the peaks of which were only intermittently visible above the water as the waves rose and fell. The catastrophe that was looming was obvious. He turned to the seaman who was on the bridge with him.

"Get the lifeboat launched. They are going to need our help."

The *'MV Brilliant Star'* boasted a single lifeboat powered by a small twin cylinder diesel engine. The lifeboat was to be launched from a dual point gravity roller davit. This system allows one person to lower the lifeboat, without the need for power. Those were the systems good points. The bad points being that the pivot points, rollers and steel ropes need to be kept well-greased to avoid seizing up, which they are prone to do in salty sea water conditions.

The boatswain of the *'Brilliant Star'* arrived at the boat deck. He removed the looped clip that held the retaining bolt in position and picked up a lump hammer. He stood back as he took a swing at the retaining bolt. It should have shot out of the hole but rust held it back. He took two more swings before it came loose. Free of restraint, gravity should have taken over and the lifeboat started its trip down to the water but nothing happened. The boatswain started hitting the steel work around the pivot points. After a few minutes of heavy slogging the davit arms began to groan their way forward not stopping till the lifeboat was hanging over the water.

Two steel cable drums should have started to unwind. Only one ran freely. The result was that the front of the lifeboat began to lower itself whilst the rear remained stubbornly at the level of the boat deck. There was nothing the boatswain could do, once in motion the davit mechanism could not be stopped. Within seconds the mechanism came to a rest, not how the design engineer had planned it but with the lifeboat dangling vertically from a single steel rope. That was the end of the *MV Brilliant Star's* rescue effort.

The captain on the bridge brought his binoculars to his eyes and watched as the two flat-bottomed boats drifted helplessly. On deck the remaining desperately needed CLF men, nearly half the force, waited patiently to be taken ashore, unaware that their journey was at an end.

For fifteen minutes the captain watched. In any circumstances flat-bottomed boats do not handle well but at least when there is power they can be kept bow facing into the seas. Without power they are just tossed about and roll dangerously, threatening to capsize. Some of those aboard realising what was about to happen searched vainly for lifejackets but there weren't any.

Because of the shallow draft they were in the breakers before the first impact took place. A wave lifted the first vessel and dropped it hard. There was a horrible screeching jarring sound as the jagged pointed bit of unyielding rock came into contact with the soft bottom of the aluminium boat. The metal surrendered without much fight, the tear more than six feet long. Water gushed in through the opening. There was still just enough buoyancy in the craft to allow the next wave to lift the boat clear. Men scrambled in panic, the boat listed heavily to port, water rushed over the gunwale and the craft began to sink beam end first, spilling the CLF troops into the surf.

The depth was not great, but the waves swirled around the rocks and the men were weighed down by uniforms and equipment. Only six men in any kind of fighting condition reached the shore from the first boat. Exhausted from their efforts they were unable to help the hapless victims in the second boat. It didn't fare so well.

It was the surviving CLF fighters from the flat-bottomed boats that had staggered through the cloister archway and been ordered to immediately attack the doorway, the ones that Siegburg was watching go forward now.

Gunter Siegburg turned to his one remaining SF Trooper, "Keep them pushing forward, don't let them fall back, I want the prisoners fully occupied. I have something to do."

Siegburg checked his assault rifle and spare magazines before disappearing through the archway.

Inside the apartment the sound of the explosions had been deafening. The shock wave had blown off most of the ramshackle shutters and the rooms were filled with a swirl of choking dust that settled slowly.

Feliz had been on the mezzanine and had been blown backwards. By the time ap Ewan had made his way there Feliz was sitting, coughing and wiping grit from his eyes.

Ap Ewan came forward on his knees. He smiled when he saw Feliz's face.

"What are you laughing at? he asked.

"You look like a white man, a very pale white man, with grey hair. You look about eighty years old."

Feliz returned the smile.

"That's worse, now you've got bright red lips."

The two got to their feet. It's hard to know who initiated the next move, perhaps it was a spontaneous response. The two of them hugged, the first physical contact they'd had in the years they'd known each other.

"I expect they're coming now," said ap Ewan. "Do you think this is going to be the end?"

"I don't know, it looks hopeless doesn't it?"

"It might be like Roark's Drift," replied ap Ewan.

"Roark's Drift?"

"A long time ago some of my fellow countrymen thought they were in an impossible position but they came through. They just didn't give up."

Feliz didn't reply. He scrimmaged around for his hessian sacks. On hands and knees he moved forward to the top of the landing and looked over the balustrade down into the reception hall. The dust was settling slowly. He heard the crunch of rubble underfoot before he saw the man coming forward. He only took his gaze off the broken door for a second to quickly distinguish what was what in the sacks. He held a grenade in each hand, carefully keeping them separate. Removing the pin from one of them with his teeth, he waited, holding the spring loaded clasp tightly.

Suddenly the hall was filled with the rattle of automatic fire. Bullets embedded themselves harmlessly into the mouldy plaster work of the ceiling, bits of which began to fall. Feliz kept his head down, out of sight of the attackers; he closed his eyes, waited a moment and then threw a grenade over the landing to the reception room below. The automatic fire stopped abruptly as the attackers took cover.

Three seconds passed, although it felt a lot longer, before the fragmentation grenade exploded; the bits of shrapnel flew about harmlessly. Feliz pulled the pin out of the second grenade and held it ready. A moment later the gunfire re-started. CLF men came forward. Feliz threw the second grenade. It landed on the reception hall floor. Men dived for cover again and counted. One, two, three. There was no explosion. Ap Ewan, lying on the floor slightly behind Feliz started to get to his feet, gun ready, "DUD!" he shouted.

Before he had a chance to fire, Feliz's hands pulled him firmly back on to the ground.

"They're coming," said ap Ewan.

"Stay down, watch the stairs."

As seconds passed the CLF regained courage, men re-emerged and came forward. The first of them reached the bottom of the stairs and started his assent, others followed, letting off short intermittent bursts. They too, like ap Ewan believed the second grenade was a dud. It was not. Feliz had carefully primed the grenades that morning. One batch he'd set to the minimum time, 3 seconds, the second batch he'd set to the maximum eighteen seconds. By the time the second one exploded five of the attackers were out of cover. The shards of metal, in a confined place, did the work they were designed for, tearing though material and skin and into flesh, ripping organs and blood vessels. The screams were piercing. Feliz pulled the pins from another short-fused grenade and sent it rolling down the staircase. Three seconds later eight of the remaining CLF attackers were dead or had crippling wounds; others came forward but now they were more cautious.

"I can hold them here on my own," said Feliz. "You need to check and see if they are trying to come in another way."

Ap Ewan wriggled himself backwards.

In the master bedroom Lubala's body had been dragged away from the window and placed on the bed where it now lay covered with the soiled bed sheet. The blood had soaked into the dry wooden floorboards, leaving a deep red stain. Grace sat on the floor, close to the internal wall. James went around the room from window to window, gun in hand, checking for signs of another ladder attack. Jane, with her Colt, came into the bedroom. She had no words of reassurance to offer. The dry dust that had incapacitated everybody's nasal receptors was clearing and now the sharp acetate smell of plastic explosive was being replaced with the more comforting and strangely attractive odour of cordite.

Seeing her charges were still safe Jane stepped backward out of the room, ready to continue her rounds, checking the other rooms. She came to the rear room and had only taken two steps in the direction of the window that was adjacent to the rear door when she was taken by surprise.

He'd been quick. Only seconds had passed since she'd last looked out of that window. Siegburg had been watching. He knew he had to take the opportunity. He ran up the steps two at a time. Facing the door he fired three single shots into the old mortice lock; the mechanism disintegrated. The flat of his boot ensured the door flew open. Suddenly he was face to face with Jane. He needed only a second or two to react. His gun was almost level before she'd even started to raise her Colt.

Jane had faced death before. In an instant the adrenalin induced feeling of helplessness and dread flooded her mind and events felt like they were occurring in slow motion.

She became aware of strange words from behind.

"No you don't you bastard!"

From somewhere ap Ewan stepped between Jane and Siegburg just in time to intercept the two 7.62 mm bullets from Siegburg's double tap. Ap Ewan didn't even have time to release the safety catch from his own weapon.

He dropped to the floor, exposing Jane once more but now her gun was horizontal and she pulled the trigger. A six inch wood shard flew from the door jam, the sharp end pierced the sleeve of Siegburg's tunic and sank into the soft flash of his upper arm. Jane pulled the trigger again. Nothing happened. The gun was jammed.

Siegburg's lips curled upwards at the edges as he allowed himself a brief victory smile. It was then that two clear shots in quick succession rang out to his right, quickly followed by another one that ricocheted off the outside wall. Now it was Siegburg's adrenalin that was pumping, suddenly aware that he was under attack from an unidentified direction. The only possible response was to take cover. It was an instinctive reaction. He vaulted over the balustrade and dropped twelve feet to the ground below. Siegburg had lost the element of surprise. He withdrew to the courtyard.

Jane was on her knees next to ap Ewan when he came in. She looked up, expecting another threat but she saw something else.

"Duncan! Thank God! Help me, he's been shot. He saved my life, our lives."

Feliz came running through and sank to the floor next to his friend. Ap Ewan opened his eyes and focused on Feliz. "You should be taking care of the front stairs."

"They've stopped attacking. I think they're waiting for more men to come from the ship."

Ap Ewan appeared relieved. A twinkle almost shone in his eyes despite the pain.

"In that case we'll be alright then!" were his last words before consciousness slipped away.

Chapter 55
State House, Cabinda City

Since the bridge, where they'd neutralised the machine-guns, they'd met no resistance: no ambushes, no roadblocks. Marobi was surprised. He'd expected them to have been better organised. The Land Cruiser had been abandoned, Marobi now sat in the cab of the truck, directing – directing the way to the centre of town, to State House. He knew that while State House held no strategic importance it had political and symbolic importance. Whoever held State House held Cabinda.

He directed the truck through the side streets stopping on a piece of waste land short of the main square, between two buildings.

"Stop here," ordered Marobi. "Line the men up. Get them ready for an assault."

The men piled out of the back of the truck and gathered around Marobi, whilst he spoke.

"My father has a dream of democracy for our country, Angola. I share that dream. I think my father would want Cabinda to remain a part of Angola but he would have respected the result of a free and fair referendum, whatever it was. But it appears *'the people'* are to be denied that referendum, that is unless we succeed. We are all that remains to stop a military coup. I do not know the strength of the opposition; I am not sure what we are facing. It may already be a hopeless cause but I am willing to try. Are you with me?"

Even Marobi was surprised at the spontaneous cheer of support.

"My plan is to cause as much disruption around State House as we can, possibly even take it but I do not want to sacrifice your lives needlessly. We will probe at first."

"You two," he pointed at the marksmen that had been with Duncan. "You get a chance to prove yourselves again. We need snipers to cover the building. Who do you want to take with you?"

The sharpshooters pointed out two others.

Marobi continued. "You four find places where you can get clear shots at the State House defences. I will take the rest of the men. We will advance towards different parts of the perimeter they have established. When they open fire we will retreat. For a time their men will be exposed. You must pick them off. Can you do it?"

The men nodded.

"We have only five hand-radios; I need them for the assault so you will be alone. If you see either a white flag or the Angolan flag flying you are to stop shooting. Are you clear?"

The men replied "Yes," in unison.

"Good, then go. You have half an hour to prepare. The rest of you distribute the radios one for each pair."

In the skies to the south the C130 had just reached its 'light' cruising altitude of thirty-three thousand feet, ten thousand feet higher than its 'laden' cruising altitude. Dane preferred to be higher; he avoided much more of the weather. The refuelling stop had gone smoothly. Now they could settle down for a couple of hours but first he wanted a coffee. He called Marie on the plane's intercom. She was settling down for a sleep in the canvas cot that was adjacent to the tiny crew's galley and was just getting comfortable. She pulled herself up without complaint. Fifteen minutes later she entered the cockpit with three cups of coffee on a tray. She took the jump seat for herself before passing the cups around. The co-pilot adjusted his headphones and held his hand up,

"Hold on a second Marie. Skip you might just want to hear this."

Dane pulled on his headphones. Both men listened for a while.

"What do you think Skip, do we abort?"

"I don't know, I don't think we have an option."

"What's happened?" asked Marie.

Dane turned and smiled. "Message from Intel at Langley. There's been a coup at our destination, the airport might be closed. I think we check out the alternates. Might not be a good place to go just now."

"Why is that?" she asked.

"Well we don't want to be in the middle of a coup do we, it could be dangerous."

"Suppose you're right Dane, nobody wants to be in the middle of a coup. But just refresh my memory, why were we going there in the first place. Some fool's errand I suppose?"

"We were going to pick up some UN officials," said the co-pilot.

"I thought it was to rescue some UN officials," replied Marie.

There was silence in the cockpit for some time. Eventually it was Dane that spoke.

"Do you think it could be a bit premature to divert?"

Marie smiled and went back to her cot.

Chapter 56
Casa Santa Maria

Not counting the wounded Siegburg had eight men left, one SF Trooper and seven CLF fighters. His attack had been a disaster and now it looked like somebody else had got inside the apartment, somebody who wasn't afraid to fight. He called his men together.

"Forget Lubala now. Get the RPG's, I want that apartment destroyed. Nobody should walk out of there. I want a high explosive head into every window." Siegburg looked at his watch. "Five minutes. Then we're heading for State House, our business will be finished here."

"What about our wounded?" asked a CLF fighter.

"Don't bother me with that kind of stuff. Leave them. They were stupid enough to get themselves wounded, they can sort themselves out."

Ap Ewan had been moved to a mattress. Jane had wrapped the wounds as best she could and managed to slow down the bleeding. Feliz kept coming to the door to check up on him once he came over to the mattress to look at the unconscious figure. Jane sensing his deep concern left them alone. She met with Duncan in the hallway.

"I suppose you have got a lot of questions that you want answered," she said.

"That's an understatement," he replied. "But they're going to have to wait till later, if there is a later."

"I've got a question. How did you find us?"

"We broke through a roadblock. Marobi needed to do what he could to stop the coup but he guessed, rightly, that you had been brought here. He couldn't spare any men but he gave me his Land Cruiser and a weapon. I'd just climbed over the fence and was doing a recce when the trouble started. I saw somebody coming in around the back. I tried to position myself but it was happening so fast that I had to fire on the run."

"That's why you missed him?"

Duncan shrugged.

Feliz came into the corridor. "There are men moving around, they have RPG's."

"We'll have to try and pick them off. Can you shoot straight," Duncan asked Feliz.

Before he had a chance to reply a voice came from behind. "I can, I've been hunting all my life and I had a good teacher."

James was standing there. "Give me a gun."

Duncan smiled, "Good man. Take ap Ewan's weapon. Don't expose yourself."

Siegburg wanted every window covered before he gave the order. He waited. The sound didn't register with him at first, not until it got closer, then he heard the tell-tale crack as the tips of the blades broke the sound barrier, something that only happened during dramatic manoeuvres.

The Lynx HMA8 variant helicopter was not designed for a ground attack. It was configured for anti-ship and anti-submarine warfare. However it did have a mount for a 0.5 inch heavy machine-gun on the starboard side door opening and the capacity to carry six fully armed marines, at a push. The Lynx, built by Westland in Yeovil, England had been adopted by many navies throughout the world because of its speed, manoeuvrability and versatility. However it was a bit of a handful for the pilots.

The aircraft came in low and fast from the sea, the pilot only pulling back on the stick as he crossed the shore line. The helicopter then reared upwards before pulling a tight circle around Villa Santa Maria. The machine-gunner, secured only by a thin inertia reel tether, trusted to gravity and the theories of Sir Isaac Newton to stop him falling out of the aircraft. He'd seen the men on the ground running, each with an RPG on their shoulder. He didn't know if they were good guys or bad ones but took the initiative to let off a couple of warning rounds, just so that they knew he meant business. A few seconds later the helicopter swooped down and skipped the ground, slowing. Five Marines dismounted before the rotor blades had stopped and ran towards Villa Santa Maria.

Siegburg saw them coming. He let off a short burst in their direction. The dramatic and sudden response of the return fire was enough for him; he turned tail and ran. The remaining men of the CLF dropped their weapons and waited, hands in the air, for their captors to arrive. The men of 40 Commando, Royal Marines had been well trained in the art of shock attack.

The last man off the helicopter had not run forward with the others but walked calmly towards the buildings.

The sound of the helicopter rotor blades and heavy thump of the 0.5 inch calibre machine-gun had brought Duncan Murdoch rushing to the rear of the building. He could not believe the sight before him. He opened the door and went down the steps, hardly daring to believe his eyes. He walked forward towards the man who wore a beaming smile. The two men stood face to face.

"Her Majesty's Forces at your service," said Colonel Stuart Cameron to his old friend.

Duncan took one further step and embraced the man. Within seconds Jane was following Duncan, running down the steps.

"Like old times," said Stuart.

"What, you getting us out of a mess again," replied Jane.

"Hold on a second," interjected Duncan, "Whose rescuing who here? It looks to me as if everybody is rescuing somebody. And what's the British Army doing here anyway?"

"Strictly speaking not the British Army, we're a UN rescue force, with a mandate signed by no less a person than the Secretary General himself."

"But how did you get here?"

"If you'd care to take a walk down to the shore you will get a nice view of HMS Liverpool. I think they're just in the process of putting a boarding party on to a freighter that's anchored nearby."

"Does the ship have facilities to handle casualties?"

"What have you got?"

"One badly wounded, a good guy," replied Jane.

"I'll radio ahead and we'll helicopter him out immediately but I can't hang about. Once that's done we have a number of UN personnel to secure. That was supposed to be our first priority."

"So how did you end up here?"

"Our scanner picked up a radio signal. A Captain David Marobi, Presidential Guard. Do you know him? He told us you were more in need of help than he was. Jolly nice of him as he was under fire at the time. I'd like to get back asap."

A marine sergeant came over. "All prisoners secured, except the one that ran. One of our men says he got away in a vehicle. We couldn't follow."

"Thank you sergeant." Cameron turned his attention back to Duncan. "I'll see you later no doubt. Heard anything about a chap called Lubala, he's supposed to be in charge of the coup."

"Don't think he's in charge," chipped in Jane. "He's upstairs in the apartment, dead."

"So who is responsible now?"

James stood with his arm around Grace's shoulder as they watched the marines carry ap Ewan out on a combat stretcher. Jane came into the room and saw Feliz standing, back against the wall, his eyes transfixed on Grace's face.

Chapter 57
The Skies above the Congo

Von Swartzstein was sitting upright in his seat contemplating his arrival at Cabinda. His face was serious, not betraying his feelings. The Baron dreamt of the glory that would be his, the gratitude that he would receive from his dependants, the restoration of the family honour and of how he would be able to justly stand alongside his heroic forefathers. His deeds too would be celebrated by future von Swartzsteins.

The captain came through from the cockpit.

"It is now almost too late for me to make the diversion to Cabinda. I have been trying to raise the airport on the radio for over an hour. They are not replying. I think we will have to continue to our original destination."

"That is not possible," von Swartzstein's response was immediate and uncompromising. "We must go to Cabinda, there is no choice."

"Without landing permission I am afraid that is not possible."

"The reason the airport is not responding is that it is now in the hands of my people and they are waiting for me. You must go there."

"I won't risk it, not for a thousand dollars."

"So what do you require to *'risk it'*?"

"You can stick a nought on the end and I might consider it," replied the pilot without batting an eyelid.

Von Swartzstein seethed at the mercenary attitude and the blackmail that was being applied, but he was realistic enough to know that he had no choice in the matter. "Very well you will have your ten thousand dollar bonus for taking me to Cabinda."

"When will you pay me?"

"You will get a bank draft when we land. I have some in my briefcase."

"I'll take a bank draft now."

"I am a man of my word. You don't trust me?"

The pilot didn't reply, his silence was enough.

Chapter 58
State House Cabinda City

The Milan anti-tank missile is a hand-held weapon for use by the infantry. As its name suggests it was designed for destroying tanks and armoured vehicles. In practice it had been found very useful for eliminating many other types of battlefield obstacles. It had become part of the standard issue equipment for the Royal Marines and the soldiers of 40 Commando took particular pride in the way they handled the weapon.

Bernd Groelsh had achieved all his objectives; it was others that had failed. That's what he thought but he couldn't be sure because he still hadn't established communications either with the Airport or Villa Santa Maria. He didn't even know where Gunter Siegburg was. What he did know was that a helicopter had just landed somewhere around the plaza in front of the Catholic Church. He also knew that he'd been subject to probing attacks for the last hour. They'd been easily repulsed by the machine-gun emplacements, but the damn snipers were becoming a nuisance.

Two teams of Royal Marines had disembarked from the helicopter in under an hour. Marobi had provided help for the Marines to carry their equipment into place and pointed out the targets. It took only a few minutes to arm the warheads and set up the wire-guided missiles. It only took a few seconds more to take out all four of the machine-gun emplacements. State House was now effectively defenceless. And Groelsh knew it. It didn't take long to sum the situation up; surrounded by opposition with superior firepower and without prospect of support, there was no option but to surrender. He came to the main door of State House. He ordered one of the CLF Troopers to get a white flag. The man looked blankly at him.

"A tablecloth from the restaurant," he'd shouted, the urgency of the command obvious. The danger of another incoming missile was clear. Groelsh, normally so cautious, couldn't resist the temptation to check. He moved towards the open doorway.

Snipers are chosen not only for their skills in shooting. The second requirement is an infinite amount of patience. A sniper has to be able to get himself into position and then wait, possibly for hours without moving, until a target opportunity presents itself. This sniper had his sights trained on the doorway for a long time.

Not quite a heroic soldier's death, going down fighting, but it was at least quick and painless. Groelsh knew nothing. It was a clear shot through the centre of his forehead.

The CLF man returned with a handful of tablecloths he had grabbed from the restaurant. The first one he draped over his dead commander.

Two streets away, tucked down a side alleyway in a Jeep was Gunter Siegburg. It was a debacle, it was over. His only thought now was escape. He backed his vehicle out of the alleyway.

Chapter 59
Cabinda Airport

The SF Trooper in the tower was the first to see Gunter Siegburg's vehicle racing up the airport's approach road. It was not what he'd been hoping for or expecting. By now the CLF troops should have been arriving in force. Not only had they not arrived but radio contact with the other units had been lost. It was clear that the plan was not working. He took the initiative and sent a message to the pilot of the DC3 to prepare for a hasty departure. Risking his life in battle was fine by him but he didn't want to spend years languishing in an African jail. Nobody had sympathy for mercenaries in those circumstances. As liberty stood in the balance, self-preservation became the imperative, over and above loyalty.

The Dakota's pilot had got his plane refuelled immediately on landing. To him a plane that wasn't ready to fly was nothing more than a sitting target. Even before the warning had come from the control tower he'd been going through his pre-flight checks. The news of Siegburg's impending arrival could mean only one thing. He put down his check-list and prepared to fire up the plane's engines. The unmistakable spluttering sounds of the Pratt and Whitney radial engines starting up was enough warning for the rest of the SF Troops. Without any orders being given they began to withdraw from their positions and converge on the plane. By the time Siegburg arrived they were only a few minutes from departure.

The pilot of the Lear Jet circled the airport once at low level with the co-pilot looking out of the window checking for other air traffic and obstructions on the runway. Then without even trying to make contact with the tower he banked the plane and came straight in on to the runway. The plane was still rolling, taxiing towards the apron, when von Swartzstein arrived on the flight deck.

"There, over there," said the Baron for once letting a little excitement creep into his voice. "There is my man, over there by the Dakota and Jeep."

The Lear pilot overshot the terminal buildings and swung his plane through one-eighty degrees, coming back to stop just twenty metres from the parked vehicle. He cut the main engines. The co-

298

pilot left his seat, opened the cabin door, and flipped the toggle switches to deploy the plane's internal steps.

Von Swartzstein still found time to check his appearance. He ran a comb through his hair and straightened his tie before putting on his jacket. "I only hope it is enough for the photographs," he thought as he made his way off the plane.

Siegburg had taken charge. He'd ordered an immediate evacuation. Only ten of the original SF Troopers were at the airport, together with twenty CLF fighters. At a push there was room for everybody on the DC3, but that thought never crossed his mind. The CLF fighters had been positioned on the perimeter and would be left behind to fend for themselves. By the time the Lear had landed embarkation on to the Dakota had started and only three men remained covering the withdrawal. Siegburg ordered them to point their weapons at the Lear.

Von Swartzstein stepped out of the plane and on to the tarmac. He took two steps forward and stood erect, at attention, as if expecting to see a guard of honour. It was an incongruous sight.

Gunter Siegburg moved forward, his assault rifle hanging from his shoulder by its canvas strap.

"You are not pleased to see me?" said von Swartzstein, who was willing to make an exception for the lack of a formal greeting.

"Pleased to see you? What are you doing here you idiot?" was the unexpected response.

Von Swartzstein controlled his anger. "I have come here to congratulate you on your achievement and take my prize."

"We have failed. It's all for nothing. We are leaving."

"That is not possible," replied von Swartzstein. "Prussians do not give up so easily. It appears that it is fortunate that I have arrived at this time. I will put some backbone into the operation."

"You put '*backbone*' in if you want. We are leaving," was Siegburg's flat response. "They are too strong; we do not have enough men. It's over, soon they will be here."

"I have thought of that," replied von Swartzstein. "This is Africa, do not tell me about Africa. What cannot be achieved by force can be achieved with money. I have brought money, blank bank drafts. You can parley with and bribe what is left of the resistance. Everybody is corrupt and dishonest here." Von Swartzstein smiled smugly, pleased at his own foresight.

Gunter Siegburg also smiled, "How much have you brought?"

"Nearly one-hundred thousand dollars. The drafts are in my briefcase on the plane. Is that not enough? All is not lost. Am I not right?"

Siegburg thought for a moment. "Yes what you say is correct. All are corrupt and dishonest in this part of the world and it appears that we may yet leave here with something."

In the distance half a dozen single shots rang out, followed by two short bursts of automatic fire.

"What is that?" demanded von Swartzstein.

"That is the approaching Angolan forces. There's no time for talk."

Also in the distance the engines of an approaching helicopter could be heard.

Siegburg levelled his weapon and pointed it at von Swartzstein.

"I do not have time to deal with an idiot. I can shoot you now or you can stand aside. Which would you prefer?"

Von Swartzstein got a shock. It was totally unexpected. Nobody had ever spoken to him like that before. He knew he was in a hopeless position. "People who abandon loyalty abandon life," were his only words of resistance.

Siegburg turned to the men who had been witnessing the encounter.

"I will leave in the Lear, there is room for two or three with me. The rest must go in the DC3. You will be paid from von Swartzstein's money later in South Africa. There is no time for discussion. Who will come with me?"

Nobody came forward but one spoke. "The rest of us will go together on the DC3. We will try and get back to South Africa. You go in the Lear if you want. You won't cheat us, you know what we are capable of."

"That's true," replied Siegburg, "There is no need for you to remind me."

The men ran towards the DC 3 just as the gunfire on the perimeter began to intensify. Even as the last men were clambering on board, the DC3 had begun to edge forward.

Siegburg brushed past von Swartzstein and took the few steps on to the Lear. The pilots had not moved from their seats.

He stuck his head into the cockpit. "How much persuading do you need?"

"None replied the pilot, but I have to warn you we have little fuel."

"Can you make it to Boma?"

"Most probably."

"Let's go."

The co-pilot went to withdraw the steps and close the door. He saw the forlorn figure of the Baron standing alone.

"What about my luggage?" he shouted. "It contains heirlooms; they are of no value to you."

"It's here in the rack," said the co-pilot. "It weighs a tonne, we'd be better off without it."

Gunter Siegburg nodded his head in agreement. "Throw it out. He'll be the best dressed prisoner they have!"

Three oversized suitcases were thrown out of the door. The jet engines wound up, the Lear moved forward, taxiing to the end of the runway at speed. Already the DC3 was making its take-off run.

The last of the CLF men offering resistance saw the planes depart and realised they had been deserted. Their will to resist the attack by the few men of David Marobi's Presidential Guard evaporated.

As soon as the backwash from the Lear's jet engines had subsided Von Swartzstein gathered his scattered baggage. Gently he ran his hands over the scuffs on the expensive monogramed calfskin suitcases. He hated mistreatment of his possessions and hoped the contents had not been damaged; he was unable to resist the temptation to check.

In the C130 Dane had told Marie to strap up, he was going to make a 'rapid descent' approach from over the airfield. It was a manoeuvre he'd practiced several times and felt happy with even though it was uncomfortable for the passengers because of the prolonged period of excessive '*G*' force they were going to be subjected to.

The manoeuvre had actually been developed in Rhodesia during the war of independence. On the 3rd September 1978 Air Rhodesia flight 828 was hit by a Soviet supplied Strela 2 surface-to-air missile fired by guerrillas. The plane crashed killing many of the passengers. There were however fourteen survivors. Ten of the survivors were found by the guerrillas and machine-gunned on the ground. A similar incident happened to another Vickers Viscount in February 1979. The two incidents threatened to stop civil aviation in Rhodesia altogether. The Rhodesians worked on the problem.

They concluded the most dangerous part of the flight was when the plane was coming into land and was travelling both low and slow. The solution was innovative. Rhodesian civilian pilots started arriving at their destination airports still at cruising altitude, out of range of the missiles. They would then circle directly over the airport whilst descending in a steep spiral only flaring out of the spiral at the last minute. The tighter the spiral the better. The manoeuvre did cause high 'G' forces that strained both passengers and plane. It was particularly frightening at night for the passengers when all the cabin lights were turned off and the window blinds closed. But Air Rhodesia never lost another plane. Since that time the method has been adopted throughout the world by pilots attempting to land at hazardous airports and it was this manoeuvre that Dane Akai was undertaking now.

It took all of his concentration. He eyes were fixed on two instrument readings; the compass, that was spinning at an alarming rate as the plane was in a tight circle and the altimeter which was displaying a rapid descent. When the plane reached fifteen hundred feet Dane pulled back on the stick gently, slowing the descent. He waited for the compass reading to come around to ten degrees north then quickly straightened the plane into level flight for a few seconds to give himself a little distance for final runway alignment. The last violent manoeuvre was to turn the plane through one-hundred and eighty degrees, to face the runway. All this was done whilst the plane was shuddering violently because of the strain on the airframe. By now the C130 was less than a kilometre from the runway threshold and at only eight hundred feet.

It was not as if the co-pilot was idle. He had to watch all the same instruments as the pilot, operate the flaps and undercarriage and keep an eye out of the windows for obstacles. This was important because there was a flaw in the manoeuvre. The C130 did have radar, but it was forward facing, as were the cockpit's windows. Neither pilot nor co-pilot had any idea if anything was below them.

The pilot of the Lear took his plane to the threshold of the runway and immediately started his roll. There was nobody in the control tower to ask for permission and he was as anxious as anybody to get out of the place. He opened the throttles to one-hundred and five percent power. The co-pilot watched the air speed indicator. When it was registering one-twenty-seven knots he declared 'V1'. They were now committed to take-off, past the point of no return. The pilot should have waited for the co-pilot to declare 'V2' at 134 knots and 'V3' at 137 knots, take-off speed. And he should have waited before attempting to get the plane off the ground. He didn't, he was in a hurry. He pulled back on the stick early, the nose lifted and the plane reluctantly took to the air travelling too slowly, too close to the stall speed. The pilot looked straight ahead. It never occurred to him to look upwards. The last thing he expected was a giant C130 coming down on him almost vertically. When he did see the plane it was too late. He tried to take evasive action by pulling back on the stick further and turning to the left. The plane did veer to the left a little but was otherwise unresponsive. At five-hundred feet it went into a deep stall and dropped to the ground, the tail hitting first and exploding into flames. There could be no survivors. Dane was blissfully unaware and landed normally, glad that his manoeuvre had been successfully completed.

Captain David Marobi, with his Presidential Guard, was moving forward on foot, the final couple of hundred yards towards the terminal buildings. Marobi saw the black mushroom cloud from the Lear Jet rise into the air and the C130 land and slow. But something else, something far more bizarre caught his attention.

Von Swartzstein, his mind apparently now totally disconnected from the reality of the situation, was worried about the contents of his suitcases, particularly the large one that contained his most prized possessions. He took the suitcase keys from his pocket and opened it. On top, lying diagonally was his ceremonial sword sheathed in its ornately decorated leather and silver scabbard. He withdrew the sword to check the blade. He was unaware of Marobi's men till they were upon him.

He stood, straightened his jacket and tie before placing the silk sash over his shoulder and fixing the scabbard to the hook. At attention, he raised the sword to the vertical position, as if in salute to the African troops with automatic weapons.

"I declare the creation of the Republic of Cabinda and claim the country for myself," he said.

Marobi was unsure how to react.

Beside Still Waters

Chapter 60
Casa Santa Maria

For a while they thought he'd disappeared, just gone. It took more than an hour to find him. He was on the beach, near to the water's edge sitting on a rock, staring blankly out to sea.

Jane came up from behind; she stopped a few steps short. Beside her were James and Grace.

"Feliz, we were worried about you. We thought you'd run away."

Feliz didn't move. Jane took the final steps alone and sat beside him. He lifted his head and she saw the tears streaming down his cheeks. From behind Grace quietly lifted the necklace over her head and also stepped forward, coming to face Feliz. Bending she reached for his hand and placed the precious necklace in it.

"This is the most important thing I have," said Grace. "I want you to have it. You risked your own life to save ours. I can never repay you for that but I think you like the necklace. I know it's not much but I promise you it is the best thing I have to give. It's yours now."

Feliz held the necklace. He caressed the individual beads, kissed them and rubbed them gently against his cheek. Then he began to talk, not to anybody in particular, just to the sea. Grace and James sat down. They listened in silence as the boy told his story and it was a boy that spoke, a little seven year old whose life had been destroyed one day, a day that had started out so happily. He spoke for more than an hour, always caressing the necklace. It was as if horrible secrets had been encased in his mind and now they had been released. The necklace was the key that had unlocked the truth that had been buried for so long.

He spoke of his life with his mother and baby sister in the jungle village. His mother, who herself had been an orphan had been looked after by the nuns. His mother who had been educated in the convent, who had learnt to speak many languages, who had learnt about the ways of the world and made a life for herself in the city. The mother who had come back to her village when her husband had died. His mother who had dedicated her life to teaching her own people. He spoke about the happy times, the loving times. And he spoke about that day; the day the soldiers had come. The fear on his mother's face, the way she'd pushed him out of the hut and told him to run, to go and get help. He spoke of how he had run and run through the jungle, of

304

how he'd come across the old man, Sithole. Of how they'd come back to the village together and listened, all through the night, from their hiding place. Of how in the morning the old man had tried to stop him looking into his own hut, tried to stop him seeing what they had done to his mother. He told of how he'd tried to find his baby sister but couldn't. He spoke of his despair as Sithole had lead him by the hand to the river's edge, taking him to the mission to tell his story, of how halfway across the river, bereft with despair, only wanting to be with his mother and sister, he had jumped into the waters hoping the Gods would take him. But they hadn't, they had thrown him on to the river bank where the men had found him.

He told of how his mind had closed, how memories of his old life had been shut off, of how he'd learnt that the only way to survive was to be dumb, to be silent, to be stupid and subservient. He told of how he had survived by the titbits of kindness that had occasionally been thrown to him – like the goodness ap Ewan had shown to him. Enough to keep him going but not enough to release him from his prison.

That release had only come when he'd seen the necklace, the necklace that his mother had always worn, the necklace whose smooth stones he'd rubbed against his own cheeks when he was a baby. Now that he'd seen and felt that necklace it was all coming back to him.

He took his eyes from the sea and looked at Grace. "I came down here to be alone," he said. "Thoughts have come into my mind that I am too scared to hold. I cannot dare to believe that I have found my sister, because if I am wrong it would be just too much for me to bear." He held his hand out with the necklace. "You take this back it is yours."

Grace reached forward, she didn't take the necklace; instead she held his hand. "It is not mine, it is ours."

Chapter 61
Cabinda Airport
Next Day

"Standard take off?" asked Marie.

"Think so," replied Dane.

"Good. But I've just had a little thought," she began.

Dane interrupted her. "Keep your thoughts to yourself," he said looking back at her with a smile. "Just go back there, strap yourself in for take-off and then you can keep yourself busy looking after your passengers and I'll concentrate on getting us all to South Africa."

André Piet was happy to be leaving despite not having achieved his objective. Somehow he believed that things had changed forever in Cabinda, changed for the better. Time would tell. For now it was enough to have got all his people out without detriment. As well as the flight crew and UN staff there were a couple of extra passengers on board, one of them a person who had never flown before, who had never dreamt of flying before. But Feliz was not nervous; he'd been in far more frightening situations. Sitting between James and Grace he felt very comfortable. The main problem was that everybody knew his story and wanted to shake his hand. For somebody who'd refused to talk for most of his life the deluge of words was daunting so he was thankful for the protection of James and Grace. It was not like that for others.

The sick bay on HMS Liverpool was quite an elaborate affair and the medical facilities were as good as anything the Royal Navy had to offer. The medical staff were trained and ready to deal with the kind of problems that Ap Ewan had presented to them. There had been surgery, of course, to remove the two bullets that had fortunately done less damage than they might have. Ap Ewan himself had been resilient and recovered quickly; he was not going to miss *'his moment'*.

When Stuart Cameron had finished his business ashore he made time to visit the patient. Unfortunately, when he arrived, there wasn't room for him to get close, so he stood at the door and listened.

Ap Ewan, propped up in his bed, was surrounded by a group of younger ratings, men who'd trained but never seen combat. To some the questions might have sounded silly but he took them in his stride.

"What's it like to get shot, were you scared?"

Ap Ewan contemplated the question for a moment before answering with authority. "You'll learn that in combat there is no room for fear! It's the time when the training kicks in. It's a matter of duty you see. I've never personally suffered from fear."

"You're army aren't you?" asked another. "What unit were you with?"

A recovery platoon of the Territorial Army would not normally be considered to be an *'elite'* unit. Ap Ewan was fully aware of this.

"I'd rather not say," was his non-committal reply.

"Were you in special forces?" was the enthusiastic follow-on question.

He put on his most enigmatic expression. "I can neither confirm nor deny anything like that. It's the rules."

Cameron stepped back into the companion-way. The ship's surgeon was standing there. The two men smiled at each other.

"There's a strong smell of bullshit in there," said Cameron.

"We call him *'the atom'*," replied the surgeon.

"'The *atom'* replied Cameron. "Why *'the atom'*?"

The surgeon raised his eyebrows. "Atoms make up everything – and so does he!"

Both men laughed.

"I am told he's quite a nice chap," said Cameron.

"Actually I would believe that," confirmed the surgeon. "I'll clear the men out so you can have a private word."

The men cleared from the sick-bay and Colonel Stuart Cameron stepped forward and introduced himself. Ap Ewan, realising his visitors rank was both awestruck and speechless for a moment.

"I believe we owe a formal debt of gratitude to you," began Cameron. "As I understand it you acted very bravely in the last twenty-four hours, even providing convincing evidence of your commitment by managing to get yourself wounded. I'm informed that you should make a full recovery thankfully. But I also want to add my personal thanks. I consider Jane Ashton to be a personal friend and I would have been deeply upset if something bad had happened to her. So thank you."

"No problem Sir," replied ap Ewan, finding his tongue. "What's happened to the Germans?"

"I think everything is under control now. We have a few prisoners to hand over to the Angolan authorities. They came close but in the end their reinforcements from the ship didn't arrive in sufficient numbers. I think that was the decisive thing; that and the failure of the radio sets."

"So it worked then," replied the patient.

"What worked?" asked a curious Cameron.

"Just before we rescued the people from the cell I slipped down to the beach and put sugar in the fuel tanks of the landing craft; thought it might slow them down a bit."

"What! You sabotaged their boats?"

"Well that was certainly the intention Sir. And on the way back from the beach I stuck my head through the window of the vestry that the Germans were using as an armoury and turned off the electricity. I think they were charging the batteries of their hand-held radios in there."

Cameron was astounded. "Are you serious? My God you most probably stopped this coup almost single-handed. You're even more of a hero than I appreciated. You deserve a medal."

Ap Ewan smiled. "Well actually Sir I have to say a medal would go down a real treat. I believe they give a '*Purple Heart*' for people injured in action don't they. The people back home in Wales would be impressed by that."

Cameron began to laugh. "Wrong Army I'm afraid, it's the Americans with the '*Purple Hearts*' and I don't think the British would be able to award you anything. This is not our show, but leave it with me. You know you are really turning out to be some kind of character. I've a feeling I haven't heard the last of you."

"Well thank you very much for that Sir."

The C130 was two hours into its flight. Marie came into the cockpit carrying coffee. Dane sniffed.

"Hey what's with the perfume?" he turned to look at her and noted the lipstick and make-up. "We never asked for the coffee. What do you want? Women are only nice when they want something."

"Aw come on, can't I just be nice?" protested Marie.

"Yeah right. Now what do you want?"

"Nothing, but don't you think we live in the greatest country in the world?"

"Actually I do," replied Dane. "But what's that got to do with anything?"

"And don't you agree that being a democracy is our greatest asset? I mean that's what we fight for isn't it?"

"What's the angle?"

"All the guys in the back believe in democracy."

"Good. Now what do you want?"

"We had a vote. Everybody is in agreement, we should stop off at Maun Airport in Botswana to drop off our special passengers."

"What! Don't be stupid, I've filed a flight plan."

"Plans change. Come on, it'll get them home two days early. It would be nice. It's on our way."

"This plane belongs to the United States Air Force and we are on duty. It's not a frigging bus service. What about the cost?"

"Uncle Sam can afford it."

"Do not smile at me like that," said Dane.

They'd only been back at Stirling farm for three hours and already it seemed like it had been a dream. Even Jane was questioning the reality of what had happened. Perhaps it was something to do with Mary Scobie. When they'd walked into the kitchen she hadn't batted an eyelid.

"Weren't you worried?" asked James disappointed at the apparent lack of concern.

Maggie, standing next to Mary in the kitchen had responded, "Not really, everybody was pretty good at keeping us informed. Somebody from South African Immigration phoned, a real nice lady and told us what happened. Then that French man from the UN was very good. After that the man from the British Foreign Office, Ralph something or other, he'd kept us informed. We knew that the Royal Navy was coming to rescue you. And after all we knew Dad was there, he wouldn't let anything happen."

"It was very hairy there for a while," protested James.

"Oh you're always exaggerating and being over dramatic," said Maggie turning away.

"What about my Mom and Dad?" asked Grace.

"Oh they don't know," said Mary. "For most of the time they were not contactable in the Ugandan jungle. When they did get back to civilisation you were on your way home so I thought there was no point in worrying them."

"So they don't know?"

"No. But they are on their way back. They'll be here this afternoon and that's why I can't keep chatting, I have a lot of food to prepare.

It was late afternoon when they saw the dust from an approaching vehicle. Before it arrived everybody had gathered outside. Even Tembo and Morgan had come up from the Kraal.

Melanie and Simon were delighted at the reception committee, they hadn't expected it. Melanie hugged Grace.

"Darling you don't know what you've missed; it was such an adventure in Uganda, we hope you didn't get too bored here."

Neither Melanie nor Simon could understand why everybody started laughing.

Grace stepped forward, holding the hand of Feliz, pulling him after her.

"Mom, Dad, I want to introduce you to somebody."

Simon automatically held his hand out to shake hands.

"Dad this is Feliz. He's my brother!"

Duncan looked at Jane. "I think we know the story, it's still fresh in our minds. Shall we go for a walk?"

"I'd like that," replied Jane.

The two of them walked, hand in hand, towards Gus's pool. The sun, a deep red, was setting for another day. The air was still, the surface of the water mirror-smooth. Duncan and Jane could see the sun and its reflection converging on the horizon.

"We shouldn't carry on like this," said Duncan.

"What?" replied Jane, "You always having to come and rescue me?"

"No not that. I'll always be there to rescue you, as long as I'm able. But something happened this time, somehow it was different. When I heard you'd gone missing I can't tell you how bad the pain in my heart was. I swore to myself that if I got you back I'd never let you go again. I want to keep that promise. I think you know I've had feelings for you for a long time and you also know how long it has taken for me to get over Elizabeth's death. It just wasn't fair on you I know that."

Jane squeezed his hand. "Your loyalty to Elizabeth is part of your character, a part I so admire – and love. I know how deep your feelings for her were. I was happy to wait. I thought you were ready a couple of years ago. I dared to have hope in my heart, but I think I was wrong now."

"No, that's just so untrue. I just couldn't bring myself to ask you to make the commitment. You know my place is in Africa, I have made promises to people here, I cannot desert them. How could I ask you to give up everything you have, your family, your career, your country, just to fit in with me? If I asked I was scared you might say no and then I'd never see you again. I couldn't take that risk. That would be just unbearable."

"Well if you don't ask you will never know."

They turned to face each other. Duncan looked into her eyes.

"Will you marry me; will you share the rest of your life with me?"

"I will, I love you so much. Nothing could make me happier."

They embraced and kissed. Only when they eventually loosened their embrace did Jane ask her question.

"Where will we marry?"

"Where do you want to be married?"

"Here, right here on this spot, beside still waters."

Chapter 62
Stirling Farm
Six Months Later

The wedding day started with a task. It wasn't a sad duty. It was something they all wanted to do. As the sun was rising Duncan led his children to the top of the Kopje. They stood together at the grave of Elizabeth. Nobody spoke, nobody had to, they were of a single mind. Duncan knew he was not abandoning his dead wife and the children would never let the memories of their beautiful mother escape from their minds. They also knew that Elizabeth would have given her blessing if she were able. They all believed that the Spirit of Elizabeth, wherever it was, would be sharing in the happiness of this day. Before they returned to the farmhouse they stopped at Gus's resting place to pay a silent tribute.

Duncan had looked up first and seen, in the distance, the dust cloud rising from the approaching vehicle.

"I think it's the bus. It looks like they're starting to arrive," he said. "We better get ready to make our way back to greet our guests."

When Duncan had arrived at Stirling Farm with his wife, children and one-hundred and twenty African refugees from Zimbabwe he'd never imagined that it would have developed to what it was today. They had come to a long abandoned strip of arid unproductive land. Now it was a thriving farm and commercial business. Gus's reservoir, that was the name that would always be attached to it, had transformed everybody's life. Crops grew, cattle thrived and thanks to the pest-control business, malaria had ceased to be a major threat in the surrounding area.

The few African huts in the Kraal had grown to a full African village with proper water and electrical supplies, albeit still temporary, ruled over by the joint gentle paternal hands of Tembo and Morgan. Duncan put an arm around each of his children and looked at what was once brown and dry but was now green and lush.

Duncan and Jane had been mistaken. They'd totally miscalculated. When they'd sent out the invitations they'd never believed that even a quarter of the guests would have accepted an invitation to a wedding in a remote part of Africa. But just about everybody had. The planned quiet union of Jane and Duncan had taken on almost epic proportions. So many people were coming that all the accommodation in a nearby safari lodge had been booked and a tourist coach been hired for shuttling guests back and forth. And now they were arriving. With villagers from the Kraal more than three hundred people would be in attendance.

Grass had been planted, irrigated and manicured, from the farmhouse right down to the lakeside. At the very water's edge a bower of vine and flowers had been constructed. Seats had been laid out, a few yards back from the bower, an aisle for the bride to walk down formed and awnings had been hung from poles to protect people from the heat of the sun. All night men from the Kraal had taken it in turn to wind the handle of the great spit and kindle the fire that was slowly roasting the whole ox that would provide the wedding feast.

Jane would be arriving from the Safari lodge leaving the farmhouse for Duncan to make his preparations. With him was his best man, Stuart Cameron. As the time approached Stuart came to Duncan.

"This is it my friend," he'd said. "You're just about at the point of no return. Are you nervous?"

"I haven't felt so scared since my Court Martial in Colchester more than twenty-five years ago."

Stuart laughed. "You got a life sentence there too."

"Well I managed to get out of that one."

"If I'm right I don't think you'll be trying to escape this one."

"Shall we go?"

The two men walked on to the stoop and paused a few moments to look at the assembled guests who'd taken their seats.

David Marobi stood out in his full formal Presidential Guard uniform. Duncan wondered if he was still entitled to wear it. He was no longer a Captain in the Angolan Presidential Guard; he was now the Governor of Cabinda. A referendum had taken place in Cabinda. David's father, the President of Angola, had promised that ten percent of all oil revenues would stay in Cabinda for the benefit of the people. That promise had been enough to secure the vote, Cabinda would remain part of Angola. David Marobi was considered by all to be the honest broker that would ensure the deal was fulfilled.

Duncan had managed to get some time to speak with him. David's main headache appeared to be not matters of State but one of the prisoners in his jail. A certain Freiherr Artur von Swartzstein of Brandenburg, supported by a band of lawyers and his wife, who had moved to Cabinda to help her husband, were managing to tie up much of State House's administration. No one would be more happy than David Marobi when *'The Baron's'* ten year sentence was completed. He was thankful that he didn't have to take care of the rest of the Baron's helpers. Of course his main lieutenants, Siegburg and Groelsh had been killed. The balance of the troops had tried to make their escape by plane. It was the Zimbabweans that had intercepted that plane and locked up what was left of the mercenaries. They'd be there for a long time.

To the left of Marobi stood a tall thin figure with square shoulders and head held high. You could almost say he had a proud bearing although there was something not quite right, perhaps it was his suit that appeared to be hanging a little too loosely. The last time Duncan had seen him he was being carried to a helicopter on a stretcher.

Ap Ewan had recovered well and had managed to wangle it so that he could attend the wedding whilst on his way to Angola to collect his medal; an award he'd been granted for his part in quelling the coup. He'd come all the way from his native Wales where he'd been basking in his newly found notoriety that had been considerably enhanced when it became known that he was to receive a special letter of commendation from the Secretary General of the United Nations. Ap Ewan wasn't sure what the future held in store for him. He was unaware he'd been seated next to David Marobi because Marobi wanted to get to know him before offering him the post of *'security advisor'* for the Cabindan oil industry. The two men appeared to be getting on well.

The next row was taken up by the newly expanded Shapiro family. Simon and Melanie sat either end with Grace and Feliz in between. They'd come over from the States a couple of weeks previously and had been travelling in the Congo River region. They would have come earlier but Feliz had needed quite a lot of counselling to help him understand what had happened to his mind over the years and restore it to where it should be. Despite having to relive some horrific incidents it had gone reasonably well and Feliz had handled the Congo visit in his stride. Grace and Feliz had held hands in mutual support when they were in front of Banda Sithole and he released the final demons for Feliz and enlightened Grace. After the wedding they were going back to the States; all together as a family and Feliz was going to start a college course. The Shapiro's were a happy and complete family unit at last, all members comfortable with their past.

Ralph Foulkes was in the next to front row. He was on an *'official'* visit to Africa on behalf of the British Foreign and Commonwealth Office. When the Treasury had been looking for somebody to go and negotiate the return of British assets he'd volunteered. He was proud of the deal he'd done. The physical equipment and oil extraction licences, which had been confiscated by the old Angolan Government, would be returned to the original British holding companies. The cash, bonds and interest had been a little more problematic to deal with. In the end it had been agreed that the Cabindian State Government would hand over all liquid assets due. This satisfied the Treasury. In return the Overseas Development Department would be donating a similar sum, as part of the Foreign Aid Programme, to Cabinda for investment in primary health care and the building of a new football stadium in Cabinda City. All but one of the loose ends had been tied up. Ralph was uncertain how he was going to explain to Jane that her claim for expenses covering her original trip to Angola had been rejected. But he wasn't going to mention that today.

James and Maggie were in the front row, an empty chair between them. They were enjoying the day although there was a little trepidation in the air. Things were going to change. Maggie was going to study nursing at a Cape Town medical college after she'd finished school. James wanted to study agriculture. He'd had a chat with ap Ewan the previous day. Ap Ewan had enthusiastically endorsed Llysfasi Agricultural College in North Wales. James had listened with mannerly interest but did not let Ap Ewan know that he really had a different study centre in mind, a small college in up-state New York, that was coincidentally less than an hour's commute from the Shapiro's house. In conversation it appeared that Grace thought that the New York College had the better academic merits. Neither James nor Maggie could forget that the study opportunities, and a lot of other things in their life, were due to Gus's generosity. That's why they were keeping a seat for their departed friend at the ceremony – between them. As far as they were concerned he was there.

On the other side of the front row sat Mary Scobie and Mafutzi. It was a funny sight from behind, the thinning wispy grey hair of a frail old woman with a scraggy neck next to the thick black curls and rolls of fat of her African friend. Duncan couldn't see the endearing way Mafutzi's plump hand enveloped Mary's wrinkled bony fingers.

"It's time," said Stuart, rousing Duncan from his thoughts. "We need to get down to the front. Your bride's on her way."

The two men walked to their places, passing through the seats occupied with an eclectic mix of blacks and whites, rich and poor. Hardly had they settled when the drums began to beat the traditional African wedding rhythm. In front the Baptist Preacher took his position. The ceremony, the whole day, would be a blending of two cultures and traditions. By the end of the day Duncan and Jane would be united in Christian marriage but more than that, the people of the Kraal would have acknowledged Jane's arrival and acceptance as the legitimate successor to their beloved but departed Elizabeth, daughter of King Dingiswayo.

The drums stopped, signifying the arrival of Jane. Duncan turned to see the beginning of the bridal procession.

Jane would walk down the aisle on the arm of her father but she would be led by Tembo and Morgan, clad as traditional Matabele warriors, each carrying a shield and asagi and crowned with a Chief's resplendent ostrich feather headgear, the visible symbol of their authority to sanction the solemn moment. The two men began their chant and dance, slowly leading the bride forward to the Christian order. The ceremony and celebrations had begun.

It was more than twelve hours later, the union was still being celebrated, women danced, men drank and the moon rose on the strange mix of guests that were proving that two diverse cultures could live together in harmony. Mary laid a hand on Mafutzi's arm. The women looked at each other. Mafutzi knew it was time. She helped the tired and stooped frame of Mary to the steps of the farmhouse. The two women turned and looked for a moment at the people still assembled around the fire whose flames were beginning to ebb. They saw Duncan and Jane happily surrounded by the family and friends that were important to them. Maftuzi and Mary hugged and said their farewells. Mary took the last few steps alone. She went to her bed, lay down and fell into a final happy sleep, one that she would not wake from. It was not a moment of sadness for her; she'd left a note with her papers asking that nobody mourn her passing. Her leaving was to be a celebration of a life well lived.

Beside Still Waters

HISTORICAL NOTES

Most of the background information and setting for the book is factually correct.

Cabinda continues to exist as a province of Angola. In African terms it is small, covering only three thousand square miles. The ambiguity of its status is as described in *'Beside Still Waters'*. In 2013 Angola was producing 1.85 million barrels of oil per day (as compared to the UK's 1 million). The vast majority came from Cabinda.

After a violent separatist war a deal was done between the separatists and the Angolan Government, (finally signed in 2006), giving Cabinda *'special status'* and ten percent of all oil revenues. In 2003 a United Nations report stated that many violent, abhorrent and unjustified crimes had been committed against civilians during the struggles mainly after the Cubans had left.

Military coups, as described in *'Beside Still Waters'* used to be fairly common in Africa. Rarely were they spontaneous and invariably they included the use of *'foreign mercenaries'*, which are surprisingly abundant. (They have gained a lot of *'respectability'* in recent years. The Americans have made wide use of them in Afghanistan but they refer to them as *'private security contractors'*).

'Free enterprise' coups still occasionally occur. For instance in 2004 an *'in transit'* Boeing 727 crammed with military equipment and sixty-seven men was intercepted at Harare airport. All the men were arrested. After spending an horrific time at Harare's infamous Chikurubi prison some of the captives were sent to Equatorial Guinea where they were convicted of attempting to carry out a coup in that country. Mark Thatcher, son of British former Prime Minister Margaret Thatcher, was arrested in Cape Town in connection with this attempted coup and after a plea bargain was fined three million Rand and given a four year suspended sentence by the South African courts.

The events written about in *'Beside Still Waters'* were taken from a real *'battle plan'* for a different (failed) coup that I had sight of some years ago.

ALSO BY THE AUTHOR

"The Valley of the Shadow." The author's best selling first book in the *'Murdoch's Africa'* series. A highly praised story exposing many truths about Rhodesia, the birth of Zimbabwe and the human consequences.

"Fear No Evil." A fast moving and dramatic novel based on the true events surrounding the South African nuclear arsenal and the release of Nelson Mandela from prison.
ALSO

"Three Pomegranates and a Half Bottle of Scotch". This novella is a total departure from the author's main genre. It was written in memory of a friend and to fulfil a promise. It has received critical acclaim.

SAMPLE CHAPTERS *'VALLEY OF THE SHADOW'*

Aden, July 1967

Duncan looked through the open window. The sky was cloudless and the sun at its zenith. Over the rooftops he watched an Arab dhow in the bay as it tacked towards the harbour, its lateen sail gasping for a whiff of hot desert air. Along the shore a string of pelicans effortlessly glided, skimming the water's surface. Four crisp shots somewhere in the distance broke the serenity of the scene.

"Move away from the window you dimshit," barked the Corporal.

Without a word Duncan dropped to the floor and leaned against a kitbag, cradling his FN rifle. Minutes passed. None of the eight-man squad said anything as tension built on the top floor of the commandeered building that served as Company HQ. In the next room a radio operator spoke unintelligible words into his mouthpiece.

Duncan closed his eyes, remembering seven days ago when they'd boarded the chartered Tri-Star planes at Gatwick. He was in the lead plane with 'B' Company. They'd joked about going on holiday, laughing about forgetting their buckets and spades. They'd been in the air for an hour when the CO came on the PA. Lt Col Mitchell's reputation for directness was well established in the regiment.

"Men," he started in an accent that had been part anglicised at Sandhurst but which retained its Scottish grittiness. "As you know our task was to take over from the Cheshire's for a spot of garrison duty. Unfortunately there has been a change of plan. It appears the native police have seen fit to exploit the confusion of regimental changeover and decided to create some mayhem. They have mutinied and taken over the Crater District. The result is the Cheshire's have lost our billets for us. This is of course unacceptable.

So on reaching Aden we will have a short rest before advancing from the airport to our accommodation in the Crater District on foot with fixed bayonets. We will start as we mean to go on."

The change in mood was instant. Duncan felt a shiver of nervousness deep inside but drew courage from Sergeant Scobie and the other seasoned soldiers, veterans of the Malaya campaign.

"Finally, men," continued Lt Col Mitchell, "remember if you're soft in the beginning they will sense weakness and you will lose the initiative. Hard and quick is the motto. It will make it easier in the long run. Let them know who's boss."

When Mitchell finished a buzz of anticipation grew within the cabin. Sergeant Jim Scobie, sitting next to Duncan, remained calm. He leaned towards Duncan.

"Looks like you'll see your first action a bit sooner than expected. Nervous?"

"A little, Sarge," was Duncan Murdoch's honest reply to his mentor and protector.

"I've always looked after you haven't I?" said Scobie.

"Yes Sergeant."

"Well nothing has changed. Don't worry. You'll be fine".

Duncan relaxed. He trusted Jim Scobie.

Lt Col Mitchell was true to his word. Within an hour of landing Duncan watched the first reconnaissance patrol leave the airport. Two hours later "A" Company began its probe in force. First reports were that the native police disappeared into the ether as soon as bullets started flying. Duncan heard that by dusk 'A' Company had penetrated the walled citadel and was bedding down for the night in the streets. Before dawn 'B' Company had received orders. Duncan advanced with his troop and passed through 'A' Company to take the lead.

Remnants of the native police barricaded themselves in the police compound. Duncan watched as two grenades were thrown over the wall. It was enough. A white flag appeared at the gate. Out came the renegades, two abreast, hands raised, hungry, having made the unfortunate mistake of locking themselves in the compound without supplies.

But the police mutiny had set off others. News of the first action came mid-morning. This time it was communist insurgents, embedded in the population, beginning to put up resistance, ambushing and sniping at isolated patrols. Word came through that Lt Col Mitchell was making 'routing them out' a priority. Nobody stood on etiquette. Duncan's squad didn't knock at doors or wait for an invitation before entering buildings. Duncan learnt firsthand about shock tactics and the effect that facing the wrong end of a British Army Service Revolver had on people's tongues. The Regiment ran riot. Everybody knew the press were around but nobody cared. Neither Duncan nor his unit were aware that by day three of the operation the Daily Mirror had coined the name the whole media was to adopt. Everybody in the UK soon knew that 'Mad Mitch' of the Argyle and Sutherland Highlanders had arrived in Aden.

The crackle of static from the radio room increased and urgent voices roused Duncan from his thoughts. Instinct made the rest of the men stir. They began pulling on their webbing and checking weapons. Suddenly the Lieutenant appeared in the doorway shouting.

"Move your arses. Western Patrol ambushed and split. Man down. Get over to the Mosque Square. Return fire. Extradite the patrol if possible. If not form a defensive position till relieved by Lieutenant Cameron from Battalion HQ. Go!"

Boots clattered on wooden stairs. Duncan pulled himself on to the back of the first open Land Rover in the courtyard. The engine barked into life. The vehicle jerked forward. He jarred his back on the metal seat. Duncan watched the others as they pulled back the bolts on their FN's and pushed a round into the chamber. He followed suit. The streets were quiet. They always were at the hottest part of the day. The hard suspension of the vehicle gave no comfort as the Land Rover wove through the narrow cobbled streets. It would be impossible to take an accurate shot on the move so Duncan flicked the lever on his rifle to automatic. If he saw anybody suspicious he would let the whole magazine go in the general direction. He knew the labyrinth of streets was a bad place to get ambushed. The terrain favoured the enemy.

The Land Rovers burst into the square. In front was the grandiose dome of the mosque, a building of opulence that was in stark contrast to the rest of the buildings in the Crater. To the right stood the pencil thin minaret, the tower from which the faithful were called to pray five times a day. Rumour had it that Mitchell had warned the Mullah. "One sniper uses the minaret and the minaret becomes horizontal". No sniper had used the minaret from then on, confirmation that the Mullah had lied when he said he had no influence over the insurgents.

In the middle of the square was the fountain, intricate and ornate. Water bubbled from the centrepiece and ran down channels to the circular trough where the faithful ceremonially washed in running water before praying.

The Corporal pointed at the fountain. Cowering under its protecting overhang were two khaki clad British soldiers.

Born in another place Ahmed Kahn might have been studying to be a doctor or lawyer. Unfortunately the harsh desert interior of Yemen offered limited opportunities for the intelligent and quick witted. He could have taken the way of Allah and would have made a good Mullah. But the relentless rote learning of the verses of the Koran was not stimulating enough for him. Instead his mind became fertile ground for those that preached that all ills were the fault of the colonial oppressors. But like most members of the Yemen Socialist Liberation Army he was attracted to communism not for the people but for himself. He wanted to be a leader in his country once the Colonialists had been expelled. Now they were on the cusp of success. The old guard was tottering and just needed a final push.

He peered over the low parapet on the roof. Across the square he could see the two soldiers still hiding behind the fountain. He worked his way across the roof looking into the side street below. He saw the upturned cart and behind it the tell-tale whip aerial of the soldier's radio.

Ahmed turned and sat with his back to the parapet. He spoke quietly.

"Mohamed, Yousif. You two stay here as long as you can. If the soldiers at the fountain move shoot at them. You must also watch the ones behind the cart. If they try to break out throw a grenade. I will go back for the one who is alone, the wounded one. When you hear my shots you can make your escape, God willing."

"Allah Akbar", both men replied in unison.

Ahmed moved off in search of his quarry.

A few moments later Mohamed looked over the square and saw the Land Rovers drive over to the fountain. He looked to Yousif. Without word they gathered their weapons and slipped away.

The two Land Rovers made an imperfect triangle with the fountain. The troop dismounted and took covering positions behind their vehicles. The Corporal shouted at the two cowering soldiers.

"You can come out now, the cavalry's here. Tell me what happened."

322

The younger one spoke. "We was in single file coming to the square from that tiny alley over there."

The soldier pointed to a narrow entry midway along the side of the square facing the mosque. "The Sarge was bringing up the rear. We was in front of him. The rest of the patrol was a few yards ahead again, just coming into the square. Then somebody lobbed a grenade at us, out of nowhere. It landed between us and the Sarge. We ran forward and ducked into a doorway before it went off. We didn't see much then. Somebody started shooting and the Sarge shouted for us to fuck off or something like that. We ran after the rest of the patrol but couldn't see them when we got to the square so we ran to this fountain. Then we heard shots from that big entry next to the alley." He pointed to another entry a few yards further along from the alley.

"We reckon the rest of the patrol went down there for cover."

"And what's happened to Sergeant Scobie?" asked the Corporal.

The soldier shrugged his shoulders. "He might be with the rest of the patrol. We was cut off and just waiting for you lot. Not much we could do."

"You're a pair of bloody heroes you two."

"Thanks Corp," they replied in unison, the sarcasm going over their heads.

The Corporal called his men together. "Right we'll go on foot to the big alley where we think the patrol is. If they're all together and it's clear of snipers we'll signal for the Land Rovers to collect us and we'll piss off out of here. If Sergeant Scobie is not with the rest of the patrol we'll have to form on the square and start a search. Okay?"

The Corporal turned to Murdoch. "You stay here with those," he said pointing at the two heroes. "Give us cover and watch out for my signal. If I call you come with one Land Rover and they can bring the other."

Jim Scobie was alone in a doorway in the narrow alleyway. He hadn't felt the shrapnel at first. He mistook the wetness for sweat. Then it started to ache, like he'd banged his thigh. He looked down and saw the pool of blood forming around his foot. The numbness began and his leg wouldn't support him anymore. He knew he'd have to stay put.

Ahmed worked his way into position below the parapet. Every second he was exposed Ahmed risked a premature meeting with his maker but he needed to look. He saw the soldier sitting in the doorway and the scorch marks from the grenade on the whitewashed wall. He saw the trickle of blood that ran towards the centre of the alley. Silently he worked his way from rooftop to rooftop to reduce the angle for his shot. He needed to look once more. He edged his head upwards and spotted his target, just as his target saw him. He ducked as the rifle cracked. A chip of mortar flew from the edge of the parapet. Ahmed thanked Allah for sparing him.

The single shot didn't echo. Duncan was sure of the direction.
"That came from the little alley," he said, "we should go over and take a look. Sergeant Scobie needs our help."
"Our orders were to stay here," said the little one.
Duncan was agitated.
"You go if you want," said the other soldier, "we'll cover you and keep an eye on the Land Rovers. Keep weaving. You should be all right."
"Arseholes," said Duncan. He knew it was pointless arguing with the heroes. He got up and ran, zigzagging across the square.

Scobie saw Duncan edging up the opposite side of the alley pressed tight against the wall. He motioned a warning, touching his eye and pointing to the rooftops. Duncan read the signal. They didn't need to speak. He crept forward, eyes scanning. He drew level with the Sergeant.
"You okay Jim," he whispered.
"Yeah, I'll do. But watch out there's one around here somewhere."

Ahmed knew the wounded soldier was looking at the roofline so he made his way to the back of the flat roof and dropped the six feet to an external half landing. The shutters on the first floor window were open. He climbed into the building and worked his way to the front room. It was in semi-darkness, the louvered shutters were closed. He peered downward through the slats at the wounded soldier. He could see the legs outstretched. The soldier was sitting, leaning against the door. Ahmed kissed his weapon and silently prayed. He would trust in Allah and surprise. He steadied himself in front of the window and raised his gun, pushing the louvers with the barrel of his gun, they swung open freely.

324

The shot was crisp. It was close, so close it rang in Duncan's ears. He saw Scobie's legs kick involuntarily, a reflex action. He saw the body stiffen for an instant before slumping forward.

Duncan was frozen still but his senses were razor sharp. For the first time in his life he felt the acute awareness produced by a real adrenaline rush. A few grains of sand fell past his face. He instantly knew and stepped out, raising his gun. Too late, he caught only a glimpse of the barrel as it disappeared back into the room. In two steps he was at the double front doors of the building. In a single movement he threw his weight against them. They gave easily and revealed the dusty wooden stairway. He took the treads two at a time. One of the doors on the landing was ajar. He pushed and entered with levelled gun. The pungent whiff of cordite lingered. A shell casing lay on the bare boards by the window. From the window opening he saw Jim Scobie's motionless body. There were shouts. Duncan saw Lt Cameron running up the alley at the head of the HQ support squad.

Somewhere behind a floorboard creaked. Duncan turned and went back to the landing. The second door on the landing was shut. He applied pressure. It was firm. From inside came muffled sounds. With the flat of his foot he kicked the door. It yielded. A window shutter swung. He stepped forward to the opening. Below, in the alley, a white robed figure raced, panic in his stride. He clung to an AK.

The Arab glanced back over his shoulder. For a second the eyes of both men locked together. There was no time to take proper aim. Duncan squeezed the trigger too soon. A puff of dirt erupted ahead of the Arab which gave him added impetus. Duncan squeezed again but didn't see where the second round struck. He cursed. There was no time for a third shot. The figure suddenly swerved and disappeared into an opening.

"Any luck Murdoch?" Lt. Cameron was at the doorway.

"No sir, missed. Can we go after him?"

"No point he will be in the Mosque in a few seconds and that's out of bounds," the Lieutenant said.

"Jim Scobie?" asked Duncan.

The Lieutenant shook his head. "Come on, you did well."

Daylight was fading as Ahmed made his way through the narrow passage ways of the bazaar that was coming to life as the sun's heat dissipated. He passed a hundred shops and stalls before coming to the coffee house. White robed Arabs in identical keffiyeh headdress and rope agal occupied the tables and chairs. His four Comrades were already huddled in conversation.

"Mohammed blessed our mission today", said Ahmed as he joined them.

"Allah Akbar," was the response.

Ahmed continued. "Allah blessed the mission but Comrade Khrushchev provided the weapons. Long live the USSR."

"Long live the Revolution," the others replied in quiet unison.

Ahmed spoke. "Today will soon be over. Now we look toward tomorrow. In the morning we strike another blow for our liberation. "Insha Allah, God willing."

"Insha Allah," they replied. "We are ready."

The night was long and restless for Duncan. His camp bed offered little comfort. He'd received more from Jim Scobie than he had from any other man in his life. Duncan knew he would not weep for his father but he wept for Jim Scobie. His confused mind compared the men.

He'd only ever made one trip with his father. From his home on the Isle of Lewis to the army recruitment centre in Glasgow. It was a frugal journey, like his life on the Croft. His father would not have gone had it not been necessary. Duncan believed the thought of one less mouth to feed was the only pleasure derived from the trip for his father. Throughout the long bus journey the two had only spoken through necessity. It was as if words needed to be conserved. He recalled the dingy bed and breakfast, the shared bed and the long walk into town the next morning.

Duncan remembered how he'd flown through the battery of physical and mental tests while his father sat waiting, impassively. When presented with the consent papers he signed away his son without thought or question. Six weeks later Duncan left the tiny crofter's cottage that had been his home since birth. He never looked back. Janet, his mother, stoically concealed her tears. Angus, as a concession, came down from the high field and shook his son's hand. It was the only time Duncan remembered touching his father's flesh.

Basic training was easy, an improvement on his past life. He'd expected hardship. Instead he found hot showers, three meals a day and central heating. He was sent to Sterling Barracks after basic training. The unit was working up for Borneo. Duncan, in his mind was ready. He shared in the excitement and anticipation of the battalion. When individuals were given embarkation leave to say goodbye to family Duncan didn't apply. He just wanted the posting to start. The last days dragged. The unit's main kit had gone off by sea, inoculations were complete. They were ready and waiting. Then the message came.

From diagnosis to burial was only five weeks. She never asked for Duncan, not because she didn't love him, but because she didn't want to disturb the happiness he had found. But the Pastor insisted. By the time Duncan arrived there was nothing to be done. He sat at her bedside for the last twenty-four hours. It was a morbid scene. The cancer had taken her will to live. She slipped away holding the hand of her only child but drawing little comfort.

Duncan remembered his father, as emotionless in death as he was in life. It was a wintry, cloudy day when they buried her, father and son not even united in grief. He'd been given two weeks compassionate leave but Duncan went back to Sterling the day after the funeral, vowing never to return to his home.

He'd wandered the deserted barracks. The battalion had left the previous day. His sense of loneliness was complete. Everything that mattered to him was now gone. But he was not alone. Sergeant Jim Scobie had the job of sorting out the barracks and tiding up the unit's administration. He'd been chosen by lottery to stay. Only married men with kids were entered into the lottery.

"What are you doing in my nice clean barracks?" was Duncan's greeting when Scobie found him.

"You ain't supposed to be here son. You're supposed to be on compassionate leave."

"I came back early Sergeant. Thought I could stay here till I get orders," said Duncan.

"You can't stay here son. There are others moving in."

"I'll find somewhere else then Sarge," said Duncan.

"Where will that be then?"

"Don't know Sarge," he replied.

"Well seeing as you're here you can most probably earn your keep for the next few days. You can get your head down in my place. My Missus will look after you. She likes waifs and strays. Get your kit."

"What you brought home this time?" said Mary Scobie. "Come in. Take your coat off."

He remembered her warm open face. Crows feet evidenced her almost permanent smile. But there was a no nonsense side to her. Managing three children made her quick and to the point, the practicalities of life dominated, by necessity. Duncan was immediately drawn into the family. That's the way it was in the Scobie home. For two weeks he worked with Jim during the day and returned to the family home in the evening. He recalled never knowing the meaning of family before.

Duncan was an attraction for the children. Their persistence eroded any reserve that might have lingered. He found himself rolling around on the floor, kicking footballs, playing games, wiping tears.

Oh God! His mind came back to reality, to Aden, as if somebody had stuck smelling salts under his nose. He could see the children. There would be rivers of tears to wipe away now. Dawn came slowly and, as the sun rose, so did his anger.

"Stand easy Private," Lt Cameron sat behind a trestle table that served as his desk.

"It's hard seeing your first casualty. Worse if you know the chap. I understand you were close to Sergeant Scobie?"

"Yes Sir," replied Duncan still at rigid attention.

"Duncan, isn't it? Listen relax, stand easy. You're a young lad. We can cut a bit of slack. I'll send you back to the airport for a few days and you can work with the Quartermaster. How would that suit?"

"No thank you Sir."

"No? Not many people get offered that," said the Lieutenant.

"I appreciate that Sir but I'd like to stay with the lads. I'm not a special case."

"All right, well done, I'll I see you get light duties for a couple of days, alright?"

"No Sir."

"I'm only trying to help you know." Exasperation tinged the Lieutenant's voice.

"I know sir. I just want to go out on patrol with the lads Sir. In the Crater," said Duncan.

"Not sure if that's a good thing just now. But tell you what; I'm taking a foot patrol to the harbour mid morning. You can go on that and we'll see how you get on."

"Thank you Sir." Duncan saluted and left the room.

"Mustafa, where did you learn to drive?" Ahmed was still in buoyant mood after yesterday's success.

"The British taught me. I worked in the Civil Administration Office," he replied.

"You should be good then. Their training is the best," said Ahmed.

All four men laughed.

Mustafa slapped his hand on the bonnet of the Austin Cambridge saloon. "Good British engineering too."

"Check your weapons," said Ahmed, "Remember we must be quick. When the call comes we move. We will have only minutes to complete our mission. Insha Allah." Ahmed looked towards the wall phone that hung on the garage wall and waited.

Lt Cameron organised the patrol. He took mid-point with the radio operator immediately behind him and Duncan immediately in front. They set off in line quietly working their way towards the southern gate and then on to Marine Drive, the road that led down from the Crater to the harbour. The patrol was safest once past the gate, away from the narrow streets where there were less ambush points or cover for snipers.

Motorised traffic was rare in the narrow streets of the Crater but Marine Drive was a thoroughfare. Most days overloaded trucks lumbered up the incline, hauling supplies from the docks, around the walls of the Crater and into the high interior. But today was Saturday and there were no trucks, only occasional cars going to the yacht club that was the centre of Aden's elite social life.

The Patrol was well spaced. European occupants of cars waved as they passed, coming down from their protected area, high in the hills. The patrol passed the half way point.

"Halt!" shouted Lt. Cameron. "Two minutes rest and a radio check."

The men dropped to a crouch. Every direction was covered. There was no chatter, only observation. The radio operator unslung his backpack and pulled back the stiff canvas cover that protected his equipment. He donned headphones over his berry. He fiddled with the tuner. "BRAVO, NOVEMBER this is CHARLIE ALPHA MIKE. Radio Check, over." He repeated the message.

Tail End Charlie, the rear guard, watched as the Morris Oxford came towards him. He raised his hand ready to return the wave. When the vehicle was close he realised the occupants were

Arabs. He turned to tell the Lieutenant but the officer was preoccupied with the radio operator. The car passed.

"Up, let's go!" Lt Cameron was on his feet.

The men rose. Tail End Charlie said nothing.

"Volunteer for the point?" asked Lt. Cameron.

"Me," Duncan put his hand in the air.

The Lieutenant hesitated for a second.

"You have to do it sometime I suppose. Okay. Take the point as far as the harbour."

Duncan moved up, twenty paces ahead of the next man. He raised his hand high and motioned the troop forward with an exaggerated wave to the front. Somebody at the back said, "He thinks he's on bloody Wagon Train". It was the first banter of the day.

Duncan concentrated; watching for mines, booby traps, shadows, anything. A couple of cars came up the hill. Duncan didn't return the waves, leaving it to those behind him.

Ahmed's heart was pounding. It happened fast and to plan. He climbed in beside the driver and slammed the door. He placed his pistol in the folds of his robe.

"Go Mustafa, quickly as Allah will allow."

Mustafa was sweating, gripping the steering wheel tightly. He over-revved the engine and the rear wheels spun on the dry gravel of the yacht club car park. A cloud of dust billowed from the rear of the vehicle. The tyres gained traction and the car moved forward.

Ahmed looked into the rear view mirror and saw three strained faces in the back.

"Relax. We've done it. Cover your guns and be calm, just look ahead."

Duncan saw the Morris Oxford exit the Marina gates too quickly. He watched the car's progress as it came towards him. His instinct told him something was wrong. He pulled the FN closer to his chest and let his thumb slide the safety to off. He stopped walking and gave the halt signal to the patrol. The car drew close. He turned with it, keeping eye contact with the occupants. The Arabs ignored his gaze and stared ahead. As the vehicle came level everything went into slow motion and Duncan felt that sharpness once more.

The face was indelibly etched on his mind. He levelled his gun and fired. The patrol dropped and brought their guns to bear. Lieutenant Cameron raised his hand in restraint.

"It's the bastard that shot Scobie," Duncan shouted.

The occupants of the car suddenly sprang to life. The driver dropped a gear and drove at the patrol. Ahmed withdrew his gun and fired out of the window.

The Lieutenant's arm fell and no further orders were necessary. The patrol split and fired on the move. The first shot hit the driver of the car, a clear shot straight through the windscreen. The toughened glass deformed the lead point of the bullet as it passed so that it acted like a dumb dumb. The round entered absolute centre, between nose and lip. It was no clean wound. The Arab's face exploded splattering the occupants with bits of blood and tissue. In the mess an artery had been severed and blood pumped wildly. In his last seconds of consciousness Mustafa tried to scream but his mouth was gone and the remnants of his jaw hung limply. His throat flooded with blood and he emitted only a low-pitched gurgle. The car veered wildly to the left, coming to an abrupt halt as it crashed into a low wall. Ahmed took several rounds any one of which could have been his ticket to paradise. Bullets peppered the car body with a hollow metallic thud. The frenzy of fire from the patrol began to abate. The rear car door opened. A passenger fell onto the road. Duncan ran towards the vehicle.

Lt Cameron barked the order, "Cease fire. Make safe."

Duncan reached the car. He looked with contempt at Scobie's killer. There was no doubt. It was him. From inside came a moan. A body moved. A head lifted. The face half smiled at Duncan and a hand moved toward the pocket of his jeans.

Duncan didn't hesitate; he emptied the remainder of his magazine into the body then turned away. He had avenged Scobie with his first blood.

The first indication that something was amiss came at the debriefing.

"Yes Lieutenant it was the same car that came down the hill," said Tail End Charlie, "The only thing is I was sure there was only four people inside when it passed me."

"Well there are five bodies now," said the Lieutenant. "How do you account for that?"

Charles Henderson followed silently. His escort stopped and reached for the handles of the ornate double doors and glanced over his shoulder to see if the diplomat was ready. Henderson nodded. The escort opened the doors and stepped aside to give Henderson free passage.

"His Excellency, the British Ambassador."

Henderson strode into the office of the Egyptian Foreign Minister. "Minister, it's so good to see you again." Henderson offered his hand. The Minister shook it without enthusiasm.

"I do not wish to beat about the bush; it is a matter of extreme concern. I hope that you have come prepared with a satisfactory explanation," said the Minister.

The two men remained standing, facing each other, an indication of the seriousness of the situation.

Henderson spoke without notes. "I have the preliminary response from my Government in London. Two days ago a British Army foot patrol became suspicious of a car observed leaving the marina at the port of Aden. When they attempted to stop this car the occupants drew weapons and fired on the patrol. The patrol returned fire causing the vehicle to come to a halt. The exchange of fire continued. Unfortunately there were no survivors from the vehicle. On searching the bodies one was found to be in possession of an Egyptian diplomatic passport. Enquiries identified the carrier of the passport as the eldest son of the Egyptian Ambassador to Aden. It is understood that the other occupants of the car had just kidnapped the Ambassador's son from the marina. The other occupants of the car are believed to have been communist inspired insurgents."

The Foreign Minister nodded. "How many of the British Army patrol were killed?"

"None Foreign Minister," said Henderson.

"Wounded?"

"Also none."

"Very lucky people," said the Minister. "Can you tell me what unit the patrol came from?"

"The Argyle and Sutherland Highlanders, an historic and highly disciplined unit Minister."

"Really, I believe this unit is commanded by, eh, a Mad Mitch?"

"Lieutenant Colonel Mitchell to be precise, a very experienced Officer."

The Foreign Minister picked up a newspaper from his desk. "Daily Mirror Mr Ambassador, it is British isn't it?"

"It is Minister."

"I have a little difficulty Mr Ambassador. You see I did not give this Lt. Col. his name. It's actually what YOUR NEWSPAPERS call him. You do read your own newspapers don't you? It would appear that even people in Britain think he is out of control."

"I think this is a little unfair Minister. This patrol almost rescued your poor chap from a kidnap situation. It is only accidental he did not survive. You might have ended up being very grateful had the rescue attempt been successful."

"It's not accidental Mr Ambassador." The Minister's voice rose in anger. "You insult my intelligence. It is typical of British arrogance and colonialism. Do you honestly think that boy would have been shot if he was white? Don't answer that. You will only make me angrier. NO. He was only shot because he was the same colour as his kidnappers. As far as the British are concerned we all look the same."

Henderson spoke calmly. "Minister I do think you might be over reacting to the situation."

"Tell that to the parents of the dead boy Mr Ambassador. But there is more. I have information the Officer leading the patrol gave the order to cease fire and it was after this order was given that our national was murdered."

"Murder is a very strong word Minister," Henderson protested.

"If a soldier disobeys a direct order from his commanding officer and shoots a man what do you call that in the British Army? In the Egyptian Army we call it murder."

"I give you my unequivocal assurance that Her Majesty's Government will uphold the rule of law. If an offence has taken place the individual responsible will be punished."

"We will see about that Mr Ambassador. I expect your Government to inform me of the consequences of this formal protest. When you have done that the Government of the Republic of Egypt will decide what further action is necessary."

"If any?" added Henderson.

"That is all for now. You may go. Thank you."

"Why do they call it the Glass House?" asked Duncan.

The Red Cap looked at his prisoner. It's to do with the old military prison in Aldershot. They pulled it down just after the war and built a spanking new one in Colchester, that's where you are going. But the old one used to have a big glass atrium in the middle. It was the only daylight anybody saw when they went inside. They called it a glass house. The name just stuck. Any army prison is called the glass house now."

"Why is the prison…?"

The Red Cap cut Duncan short. "Listen bud, I didn't ask to be handcuffed to you; I'm just taking you back to England. Just give me a break. It's a long time before we get you to your cell. Then you can speak all day long, in fact for the rest of your life, if they don't hang you that is."

Beside Still Waters

Salisbury, Rhodesia, May 1968

From the corner of her eye she saw the small hand shoot forward across the table. She moved quickly and grabbed the wrist before it had a chance to retreat. Clasped firmly between the child's fingers was the last piece of meat, snatched from her enamel plate.

"Joshua that is mine, it is bad to steal from your mother," she scolded.

"I want it," demanded the boy wriggling his hand to break free without lessening his grip on the prize. Her resistance melted and she allowed his hand to slip away. He pushed the chunk of meat into his mouth and chewed. Only when the last morsel had been swallowed and he'd sucked each finger clean did he look at his mother again.

"You can have my sadza. I don't want it," he said pushing his plate towards her across the boxwood table.

"You're a growing boy," she sighed, the excuse more for her own benefit rather than his. "You need food to study now you are going to secondary school. Soon enough you will be a man!"

The child drank from at a mug of sickly sweet tea whilst his mother silently cleared up around him.

"Mother," he spoke between gulps, "I was cold last night. I need another blanket."

"You already have the best blankets," she sighed. "Blankets are very expensive."

"I was cold," Joshua was persistent. "You must do it."

"I will do what I can."

Joshua smiled knowing his demands would be met. They always were because he was special. From the very beginning he'd felt different, better than others. At first he thought it was because he was an only child but later he knew it was something else, something about him that was unique.

Some things however were non-negotiable for the child. Bedtime was one of them. When darkness fell in the crowded African ghetto, the anonymous two-roomed cinderblock house took on a clandestine role. Each night Joshua would lie in his metal-framed bed, pushed tight up against the party wall and listen to the words of his father in the next room.

It always started in the same way. Quiet knocks on the door. His father would ask in a hushed voice, "Who comes?"

"Shamwari," was the invariable response, friend.

"Enter Shamwari." Joshua would hear the door open as someone entered. Then a few moments later would come another knock and the ritual would be repeated. Soon there would be seven or eight with his father, all speaking in hushed tones. But it was Silas, his father, who did most of the talking. Silas Sovimbo always spoke with excitement and enthusiasm, as if he had just discovered something fresh, something he wanted to share with his visitors. Each night Joshua listened till he fell asleep. He became familiar with the hallowed names; Karl Marx, Fredrick Engels, Trotsky, Lenin and most importantly of all, the great leader, Chairman Mao. Joshua knew Mao was the most important because his name was spoken with utmost reverence. He learnt unusual words too; colonialism, imperialism, the proletariat and the bourgeoisie. It was never said but Joshua knew the words he had learnt must never be repeated outside the house.

Joshua discovered the pattern too. After somebody had been coming to the house for some time his father would ask that person a series of questions to see if they had understood what had been taught. When his father was satisfied he would make the person swear an oath. Then they would be changed. No longer would they be a simple Shamwari or friend. After the oath was taken they would be called Comrade.

But this night was different, special. Only one man had come to speak with his father. The tone was urgent. It was a conversation not of teacher and student but of equals. The stranger was insistent.

"There is no choice. You must go before it is too late."

His father replied, "I should not desert my people. I should stay with them during difficult times."

"Whatever happens you will not be staying with your people. You go into exile or you go into prison. These are the options." The stranger was angry. "You can do good in exile. You are the ideological leader. You alone can convince the Chinese to help us. There is no point in arguing. The arrangements are made."

"The basic strength of communism is that all men stand together," said Silas. "In this way they become stronger than their oppressors. I should stay here," Silas persisted.

"Above all you should know that communism is the doctrine of pragmatism," responded the stranger. "Chairman Mao himself went on his long march into exile only to return when he was strong enough to overcome the agents of imperialism. Silas, you and your family must make your own long march. You must start in the morning." The stranger was unyielding.

Joshua slipped into an uneasy sleep with the unappealing prospect of a long march!

Silas Sovimbo was born on the citrus estates in the Mazowe valley, north of Salisbury, in 1922. His parents laboured in the orange groves and lived in the native compound. When Baptist missionaries taught Silas to read they unleashed an insatiable appetite for the written word. In the early years the written word was the Word of the Lord. The Baptist church became Silas's life. As a young man he stood outside beer halls extolling the virtues of abstinence. By the age of twenty he was a Baptist preacher. He attended any gathering in the hope of speaking. That is why he was at a meeting of the newly founded African Youth League in 1955.

The organisers would not let him speak. He had to listen, listen to another man of the Cloth, the Reverend Edson Sithole. Sithole was two years older than Silas and was concerned as much with the temporal as the pastoral. For him the present carried as much weight as the life hereafter. Sithole opened a door for Silas who willingly entered another domain. Silas met Joshua Nkomo and his side kick Robert Mugabe for the first time. The Communist manifesto became his bible of the present. Silas saw no contradiction with his faith, he saw Jesus as the first true socialist.

In the following years he dug deep into his intellect and grappled with concepts beyond the understanding of most of his peers. He became a purist and deplored the 'bastardisation' of communism that had occurred under Stalin. He stayed true to Marx and believed in the interpretation of socialism expounded by Mao. He became the intellectual and moral authority within the fledgling liberation movement.

In the 1960's he watched helplessly as fissures began to appear in the movement, cracks along tribal lines. Nkomo the authoritarian Matabele ran roughshod over his Shona deputies, including Mugabe. Eventually they split away. In his heart Silas had wanted to remain loyal to Nkomo but Nkomo's association with the Russians made Silas side with the breakaway Shona who leaned towards Mao.

As the fissures in the liberation movement grew, the Rhodesian whites moved to the right and elected Ian Smith as Prime Minister. Rhodesia unilaterally declared independence and there followed a crackdown on the liberation movement's leadership. Black political leaders were rounded up, Nkomo and Mugabe shared the same prison. Silas was missed in the first sweep.

Silas told his wife and child of his decision. "Today, in the next hours, we will leave our home. We are going away from this land now called Rhodesia. When we come back to this same place it will be called Zimbabwe and it will be a land liberated from oppression."

Silas's wife accepted without comment, only Joshua spoke.

"How far do we have to walk? Last night I heard you say we would go on a long march."

Silas laughed. "It is not that kind of march. We will actually travel mostly by bus, some by car and only a little walking. We will go to Zambia. Then later maybe we will move somewhere else."

"What are these places like?" Joshua asked.

"They are places that have already won their freedom. Places where black men are no longer dominated by white men. They are places where all men are equal. Even as guests we will enjoy freedom, equality and justice."

"Will I be the same as white boys? Will our families be equal?"

"Yes, you will be equal to the whites that still live in those places," said Silas.

"So we will have a car, servants and a swimming pool just like the white boys here?" asked Joshua with a glimmer of hope.

Silas shook his head. "Joshua, you do not understand. We will be rich in other ways. The things you talk about are unimportant. They are only the products of a material world. They will not make you happy."

The young mind of Joshua did not believe his father for half a moment.